Simone de Beauvoir was born in Paris in 1908. She was educated at Catholic schools and at the Sorbonne, where she read philosophy and qualified as a teacher of the subject. There she met Jean-Paul Sartre who was to be her lifelong companion. Together they developed the philosophical system of Existentialism, which informed all her fictional and philosophical writing. In 1949, *The Second Sex* was published in France and four years later in America, and was to become a landmark in the history of feminism. She devoted all her time to writing and lecturing, and as a novelist, dramatist and philosopher became, probably, the most distinguished woman writer in contemporary France.

She is author of several volumes of autobiography which include *Memoirs of a Dutiful Daughter*, *The Prime of Life* and *Adieux: A Farewell to Sartre*. She won France's highest honour, the prestigious Prix Goncourt, for her novel *The Mandarins* in 1954.

Simone de Beauvoir died on 15 April 1986.

D0877449

ALL MEN ARE MORTAL

Simone de Beauvoir

Translated by Euan Cameron
based on the original translation by
Leonard M. Friedman

Published by VIRAGO PRESS Limited 1995
20 Vauxhall Bridge Road, London SW1V 2SA

Translation © copyright
Euan Cameron and Leonard M. Friedman

*A CIP catalogue record for this title
is available from the British Library*

Typeset and designed by
Keystroke, Jacaranda Lodge, Wolverhampton

Printed in Great Britain by
Cox & Wyman Ltd, Reading, Berkshire

To Jean-Paul Sartre

PROLOGUE

CHAPTER ONE

❧

The curtain rose again. Regina took her bow and smiled. Beneath the glare of the brilliant lights pink spots flickered over the multicoloured dresses and dark suits. In every face there were eyes, and reflected in each pair of eyes was Regina, bowing and smiling. The roaring of cataracts and the rumbling of avalanches filled the old theatre, and then an impulsive force brought her back to earth and sent her soaring heavenwards. She bowed once more. The curtain fell and she could feel Florence's hand in hers; she dropped it sharply and walked towards the wings.

'Five curtain calls! Not bad!' said the stage manager.

'Not bad for the provinces.'

She walked down the stairs which led to the entrance hall. There they were, waiting for her with flowers. Suddenly she was brought back to reality. When they had been sitting in the darkness, invisible and anonymous, one did not know who they were; she could as well have been performing before a gathering of gods. But now, seeing them face to face, she found herself confronted by ordinary mortals of no special importance. They said the things that were expected of them: 'That was fantastic! An amazing performance!', and their eyes glowed with enthusiasm: a little flame that was lit at just the right time and which was snuffed out the moment it was no longer needed. They surrounded Florence, too. They had also brought her flowers, and when they spoke to her, that little flame shone in their eyes as well. As if they could like both of us, thought Regina angrily, a blonde as much as a brunette, and each completely different. Florence was smiling. Nothing would allow her to believe that she was not just as talented, and just as beautiful, as Regina.

Roger was waiting for Regina in her dressing room. He took her in his arms. 'You've never acted as well as you did tonight!' he said.

'Too good for an audience like that,' Regina replied.

'They certainly applauded enough,' said Annie.

'Oh! They applauded Florence just as much as me.'

She sat down at her dressing table and began combing her hair while Annie unbuttoned her dress. Florence doesn't give a damn about me, she thought, so why should I bother about her? But she did bother and it left a bitter taste at the back of her throat.

'Is Sanier really here?' she asked.

'Yes. He arrived from Paris on the eight o'clock train,' Roger answered. 'He's come to spend the weekend with Florence.'

'She has him pretty well hooked, hasn't she?'

'So it seems.'

She stood up and let her dress fall to her feet. Sanier did not interest her in the least, and she even thought him rather ridiculous, yet she felt upset by what Roger had told her.

'I wonder what Mauscot will have to say about it.'

'He lets Florence get away with a lot,' Roger said.

'But doesn't Sanier mind Mauscot?'

'I assume he doesn't know about him.'

'I suppose not,' Regina said.

'They're waiting for us at the Royal for a drink. Shall we go?'

'Sure. Let's go!'

A fresh breeze from the river was blowing in the direction of the cathedral, whose serrated towers were just visible. Regina shivered.

'If *As You Like It* is a success, I'll never go on tour again.'

'It will be,' Roger assured her. He squeezed Regina's arm. 'You'll be a great actress.'

'She is a great actress,' said Annie.

'It's very kind of you to think so.'

'Don't you think so?' asked Roger.

'What would that prove?' She tied her scarf tightly around her neck. 'There has to be some sort of sign. A halo suddenly appearing over your head, for example, and then you'd know you were a Duse or a Rachel . . . '

'There will be signs,' Roger said cheerfully.

'But none of them will really be certain. You're lucky not to be ambitious.'

He laughed. 'What's to stop you from imitating me?'

Regina laughed, too, but she did not feel as cheerful. 'Myself,' she replied.

A red cavern opened at the end of the dark street. It was the Royal. They went in and she noticed them immediately, seated at a table with the rest of the company. Sanier had his arm around Florence's shoulders. He held himself stiffly in his well-cut flannel suit and he was looking at her with that expression Regina knew well, for she had seen it so often in Roger's eyes. Florence was smiling, revealing her beautiful, childlike teeth. In her mind she was repeating the words he had just spoken, the words he would say again: 'You'll be a great actress. You're not like other women.' Regina sat down beside Roger. 'Sanier is wrong,' she thought, 'and so is Florence. She's nothing but a little girl without any real genius. No woman can compare herself to me. But how can I prove it? And she is not at all bothered about me, whereas for me she's like an acid wound in my heart. I will prove it,' she said fervently to herself.

She took a small mirror from her handbag and pretended to redraw the arc of her lips. She needed to look at herself. She loved her face; she liked the lively, subtle shade of her blonde hair, the haughty severity of her high forehead and her nose, her winsome mouth, the boldness of her blue eyes. She was beautiful, yet hers was a beauty that was so harsh and so unusual that at first it startled. 'Ah! if only there were two of me,' she thought, 'one who speaks and the other who listens, one who lives and the other who watches, then how I would love myself! I'd envy no one.' She closed her handbag. At that very moment, there were thousands of women who were smiling complacently at their reflections in mirrors.

'Shall we dance?' Roger asked.

'No, I don't feel like it.'

Florence and Sanier had stood up; they were dancing. They danced badly, but they were unaware of it, and they were happy. Love was in their eyes, love alone; the great human drama was unfolding between them as if no one on earth had ever loved before, as if Regina had never loved. For the first time, in all its anguish and its tenderness, a man desired a woman; for the first time a woman felt herself become an idol of flesh in the arms of a man. Spring blossomed once more, as unique as every spring, and Regina was already dead. She dug her pointed finger-nails into the palms of her hands. There was no getting away from it: no amount of success, no triumph could, in that instant, prevent Florence from shining in all her glory within Sanier's heart. 'I can't stand it, I won't stand it,' she thought.

'Do you want to leave?' Roger asked.

'No.'

She wanted to stay there; she wanted to watch them. She watched them and she thought, 'Florence is lying to Sanier; Sanier is deceiving himself about Florence; their love is nothing but a misunderstanding'. But when they were alone together, their love was indistinguishable from a true and great love, for Sanier was unaware of Florence's duplicity and Florence avoided thinking about it. 'Why am I like this?' thought Regina. 'When people seem so alive, when I see them in love and happy, I feel as if someone were twisting a knife in me.'

'You seem sad this evening,' Sanier remarked.

Regina winced. They had laughed, danced and emptied several bottles of wine. It was late now and the dance floor was almost empty; she had not noticed the time passing.

'I always feel subdued after giving a performance.'

She forced herself to smile. 'You're lucky to be a writer: books live on. The rest of us won't be around for long.'

'What does it matter?' Sanier asked. 'The important thing is to succeed in what you're doing.'

'What for?' she asked. 'For whom?'

He was slightly drunk; his face remained impassive and seemed to be carved in wood, but the veins of his temples jutted out.

'I'm sure that you will both have exceptional careers,' he said warmly.

'But there are so many exceptional careers!'

He laughed, 'You're very demanding.'

'Yes, it's one of my vices.'

'On the contrary, it's the chief virtue.'

He gave her a friendly look and it was worse than if he had scorned her completely. He saw her, he appreciated her, and yet it was Florence he loved. True, he was Roger's friend, and it was true that Regina had never tried to seduce him. Nevertheless, he knew her and he loved Florence.

'I'm tired,' Florence said.

The musicians were starting to put away their instruments. They were outside. Florence and Sanier had set off, arm in arm. Regina took Roger's arm. They walked down a little street with freshly plastered façades, decorated with signs painted in stained-glass colours: The Green Mill, The

Blue Monkey, The Black Cat. Old women seated in front of their doors greeted them as they passed. Then they turned off into streets with middle-class houses, their closed shutters decorated with heart-shaped vents. The sun had already risen, but the whole city was still asleep. The hotel was asleep. Roger stretched and yawned. 'I'm terribly tired!'

Regina walked over to a window that overlooked the little garden of the hotel. She drew open the blind. 'That man!' she exclaimed. 'He's already up! Why does he get up so early?'

The man was there, stretched out on a deckchair, as motionless as an Indian fakir. He was there every morning. He never read, he never slept, he spoke to no one; he did nothing but gaze at the sky with his wide-open eyes. From dawn to dusk he lay there in the middle of the lawn without moving.

'Aren't you coming to bed?' Roger asked.

She closed the window and lowered the blind. Roger was smiling at her. She would slip in between the sheets, lay her head on the plump pillow, and he would take her in his arms; no one else in the world would exist except the two of them. And in another bed, Florence was with Sanier . . . She walked towards the door.

'No, I'm going to get some air.'

She crossed the landing and walked down the silent staircase where shiny copper warming-pans gleamed on the wall. She hated falling asleep; while she slept there were always others who were awake, and one no longer had any hold over them. She pushed open the garden gate: a green lawn surrounded by gravel paths and enclosed by four walls on which thin virgin vines were climbing. The man did not blink an eyelid. He seemed to see nothing and hear nothing. 'I envy him. He doesn't realize that the earth is so vast and that life so short; he doesn't know that other people exist. He's perfectly content with that patch of sky above his head. Whereas I want every single thing to belong to me as if it were all that mattered in the world. I want everything, yet my hands are empty. I envy him. I'm sure he doesn't know what boredom is.'

She threw back her head and looked up at the sky. She tried to concentrate: 'I'm here and the sky's above me. That's all; that's enough.' But it was a ruse. She could not stop herself thinking of Florence lying in Sanier's arms and not thinking of her. She looked down at the lawn. It was an old, familiar pain. She would be lying on a similar lawn, her cheek pressed against the ground. Insects were scurrying about in the shade of the grass, and the lawn became an immense, monotonous forest in which thousands of little green shoots, all the same size, all alike, were concealing the world from one another. In anguish, she had thought, 'I don't want to be just another blade of grass.' She looked away. That man was not thinking of her either; he hardly distinguished her from the trees and chairs scattered about on the lawn: she was just another bit of decoration. He irritated her; she had a sudden desire to upset his tranquillity, to exist for him. All she had to do was speak; it was always so easy: they answered and the mystery vanished, they became transparent and hollow, and could then be cast aside with complete indifference. It was so easy, and even though the game hardly ever amused her any more, she always knew beforehand that she would win. And yet that imperturbable man intrigued her. She studied him. He was rather handsome, with his large, hooked nose, and he seemed very tall and athletic looking. He was young, or at least the colour of his skin was that of a young man. He seemed not to feel the presence of people or things about him. His face was calm as death, his eyes empty. As she watched him, a sort of fear came over her. She got up without saying a word.

He must have heard something. He looked at her. At least he looked in her direction and a trace of a smile crossed his face. The man's eyes fixed her with an insistence that must have seemed insolent. But he did not see her. She did not know what he saw, and for a moment she thought, 'Can it be that I don't exist? Is this not me?' Once before, she had seen eyes like those, when her father held her hand while he was lying in bed, the rattle of death in his throat. He held her hand and it was no longer hers. She remained rooted to the spot, without voice or face or life: a fraud. And then she came to her senses; she took a step forward. The man closed his eyes. Had she not moved, it seemed to her that they would have remained face to face for all eternity.

'What a strange man!' Annie said. 'He didn't even go in for lunch.'

'Yes, he's strange, all right,' Regina said.

She gave Sanier a cup of coffee. Through the window of the veranda she could see the garden, the stormy sky, the man lying on a deckchair, with his black hair, his white shirt, his flannel trousers. He was still staring at the same square of sky with those eyes that did not see. Regina had not forgotten that look; she would have liked to know how the world appeared when seen through such eyes.

'He's a neurasthenic,' Roger declared.

'That doesn't explain anything,' Regina said.

'To me he's a man who's been unhappy in love,' Annie said. 'Don't you agree, Princess?'

'Perhaps,' Regina answered.

Perhaps there was an image glued to those eyes which covered them like a film. But what kind of face did she have? Why was she so lucky? Regina ran her hand over her forehead. The weather was humid. She could feel the pressure against her temples.

'More coffee?'

'No, thanks,' Sanier replied. 'I promised to meet Florence at three o'clock.'

He stood up and Regina thought, 'It's now or never.'

'Try and persuade Florence that the role is not for her,' she said. 'It won't do her any good, you know.'

'I'll try, but she's stubborn.'

Regina coughed. There was a lump in her throat. 'Now or never,' she thought. 'I mustn't look at Roger. I mustn't think of the future. Just think of nothing and take the plunge.' She placed her cup on the saucer.

'You have to keep her away from Mauscot's influence. He gives her very bad advice. If she stays much longer with him, she'll ruin her career.'

'Mauscot?' asked Sanier. His upper lip revealed his teeth; it was his way of smiling. But his face had grown red and the veins in his forehead stood out.

'What? You mean you didn't know?' Regina exclaimed.

'No,' replied Sanier.

'Everyone knows,' said Regina. 'They've been together for two years now. He's been very useful to Florence, you know,' she added.

Sanier tugged at the lapels of his jacket. 'I didn't know,' he said absent-mindedly. He held out his hand to Regina. 'See you soon.'

His hand was warm. He walked slowly towards the door with his stiff, calm stride. He seemed embarrassed by his anger. There was a long silence. It was done; it could not be undone. Regina knew that she would never forget the tinkle of her cup against the saucer, the circle of black coffee on the yellow porcelain.

'Regina! How could you do that?' Roger asked.

His voice trembled; his tenderness, the familiar gaiety in his eyes had disappeared. He was a stranger, a judge, and Regina was alone in the world. She blushed and hated herself for having blushed.

'You know very well that I'm not good-natured,' she said slowly.

'But what you just did is really base.'

'Call it base if you like,' she retorted.

'What have you got against Florence? What happened between you two?'

'Nothing happened.'

Roger stared at her with a pained expression: 'I don't understand.'

'There's nothing to understand.'

'At least try to explain,' he said. 'Don't let me think that you acted out of pure malice.'

'Think whatever you like!' she said violently.

Annie was looking at her in dismay. Regina suddenly seized her by the wrists. 'And don't you criticize me, either!' she said.

She left the room. Outside, an opaque sky hung over the city; there was not a breath of air. Tears welled up in Regina's eyes. 'As if malice were ever pure! As if one was unkind just for fun! They would never understand, not even Roger could understand. They were easygoing and indifferent; there was none of this bitterness burning in their hearts. I'm not of their kind.' She walked faster, down a narrow street beside a small stream. Two small boys were laughing as they chased each other around a public urinal; a frizzy-haired little girl was bouncing a ball against a wall. No one took any notice of her: she was a mere passer-by. 'How can they all be so accepting? I refuse to accept.' The blood rushed to her face. 'Florence would know now, and this evening at the theatre, they would all know.' She would read their thoughts in their eyes: envious, treacherous, mean. 'I have given them a hold over me and now they'll be only too happy to hate me.' Even Roger offered no consolation. He stared at her with those sad eyes: envious, treacherous, mean.

She sat down on a stone parapet by the stream. A violin was scratching away in one of the more run-down houses. She wished she could have fallen asleep and woken up much later, far, far away from here; she sat for a long while without moving. Suddenly, she felt drops of water on her brow and the stream became ruffled. It was raining. She began walking again. She did not want to go into a café with her eyes all bloodshot, and neither did she want to return to the hotel.

The street led into a square overlooked by a forbidding gothic church. As a child, she had loved churches, and she had happy memories of her childhood. She went inside and knelt in front of the high altar, her head in her hands. 'My God, who sees into the depths of my heart . . . ' Often in the past, she had prayed like this when she felt distressed. And God understood her, he always agreed with her. At the time she had dreamed of becoming a saint. She would practice flagellation, and sleep on the floor at night. But there were too many of the chosen in Heaven, too many saints. God loved everyone; she could never be satisfied with such undiscriminating benevolence. She stopped believing in him. 'I don't need him,' she thought as she looked up. 'Condemned, despised, cast out, what does it matter, as long as I remain true to myself. I shall be true to myself; I shall never let myself down. I'll make them admire me so passionately that every move I make will be sacred to them. One day, I'll feel the halo above my head.'

She left the church and hailed a taxi. It was still raining and there was a great sense of peace and freshness within her. She had conquered shame! 'I'm alone, I'm strong, I've done what I wanted to do,' she thought to herself. 'I proved that their love was nothing but a lie; I proved to Florence that I exist. Let them hate me, let them scorn me: I've won!'

Darkness had almost fallen when she entered the lobby of the hotel. She wiped her feet on the door-mat and glanced through the window; slanting sheets of rain were lashing the lawn and the gravel paths. The man was still lying on his deck-chair; he had not stirred. Regina turned to the chambermaid, who was carrying a pile of plates into the dining-room.

'Have you seen Blanche?'

'What?' the maid asked.

'One of your guests is sleeping out in the rain. He'll catch pneumonia if you don't make him come inside.'

'Just you try talking to him!' said Blanche. 'You'd think he was deaf. I tried shaking him for the sake of the chair which will get ruined with all that water. But he didn't even look at me.' She shook her head and added, 'He's an odd one, he is . . .'

She wanted to continue talking, but Regina no longer felt like listening. She pushed open the gate to the garden and walked over to the man. 'You ought to go inside,' she said gently. 'Don't you feel the rain?'

He turned his head and looked at her, and this time she knew that he saw her.

'You should go in,' she repeated.

He looked at the sky and then at Regina. His eyes squinted as though dazzled by the light that still remained; he seemed to be in pain.

'Do go in. You'll get ill!' she said.

He did not move. She had stopped speaking, but he was still listening as if her words were coming from very far away and he had to make a great effort to decipher them. His lips moved.

'Oh, there's no danger,' he said.

Regina turned over on her right side. She was no longer sleepy, but she had no desire to get up. It was only eleven o'clock and she did not know how she would while away the long day until evening came. Through her window she could see a patch of sky that looked well scrubbed and gleaming: fine weather followed the storm. Florence had not reproached her, for she was not a woman who cared for scenes, and Roger had begun to smile again. It was as if nothing had happened, and in fact, nothing ever did happen. A sudden knocking on the door made her start.

'Who is it?'

'It's the chambermaid come to get the tray,' Annie replied.

The woman entered; she took the tray from the table and in her rough voice, said, 'Nice morning, isn't it?'

'It seems to be.'

'You know that crazy fellow in room fifty-two stayed outside all night,' said the woman. 'And this morning he turned up with his clothes drenched. He didn't even change.'

Annie went over to the window and looked outside.

'How long has he been in this hotel?'

'About a month now. Soon as the sun comes up, he goes down to the garden and stays there till night-time. Doesn't even get into bed when he goes to sleep.'

'How does he eat?' Annie asked. 'Are his meals brought to his room?'

'Never,' the chambermaid answered. 'He hasn't set foot outside the hotel since he's been here, and nobody's been to see him. Perhaps he just doesn't eat.'

'Maybe he's a fakir; you know, one of those Hindu ascetics,' Annie suggested.

'He must keep food in his room,' said Regina.

'I never saw any,' the woman replied.

'He hides it . . . '

'Maybe.'

The maid smiled and walked towards the door. Annie leaned out the window for a moment longer and then turned around.

'I really would like to know if he keeps food in his room.'

'Probably.'

'I'd like to know for sure,' Annie said.

She left the room abruptly and Regina stretched as she yawned. She looked in disgust at the rustic furniture and the light cretonne fabric that covered the walls. She hated these anonymous hotel rooms in which so many people had come and gone without leaving a trace of themselves, and where she herself would leave no trace. 'Everything will be exactly the same, except that I won't be here any more. That's what death must be like,' she thought. 'If only one could leave an impression of oneself in the air, where the wind howled as it rushed in. But no! Not a ripple, not a rift. Another woman will lie on this bed . . . ' She threw back the covers. Her days had been minutely planned, not a moment should have been lost; and yet there she was, cloistered in this dreary part of the country where she could only kill time, time which died so fast. 'One shouldn't count these days,' she thought, 'I ought to reckon that I haven't lived them. That would give me twenty-four times eight, a stock of one hundred and ninety-two hours to draw from at times when the days are too short.'

'Regina,' Annie called. She was standing in the doorway, an air of mystery about her.

'What is it?'

'I said that I'd left my key in my room, and I asked for a pass-key at reception,' Annie said. 'Come with me to the fakir's room and we'll see whether or not he has any food there.'

'You certainly are curious,' Regina declared.

'Aren't you any more?' asked Annie.

Regina went over to the window and glanced down at the motionless man. She was not concerned about whether he ate or did not eat. What she wanted to discover was the secret of his stare.

'Come on,' Annie said. 'Don't you remember the fun we had when we robbed Rosay's little house?'

'I'm coming,' Regina answered.

'It's room fifty-two.'

She followed Annie along the deserted corridor. Annie turned the key in the lock and the door opened. The room was furnished in the same rustic style; with the same materials on the walls and windows. The blinds were lowered, the shutters closed.

'Are you sure this is his room?' Regina asked. 'It doesn't appear to be occupied.'

'Room fifty-two, I'm sure,' said Annie.

Regina glanced slowly around. Not a single sign of human habitation was visible; not a book, not a paper, not a cigarette butt. Annie opened the wardrobe; it was empty.

'Well, where does he keep the food?' Annie asked.

'Perhaps in the bathroom,' said Regina.

There was no doubt it was his room. Above the wash-basin were a razor, a shaving brush, a toothbrush and a bar of soap; the razor looked like any other razor, the soap was real soap – these were solid, reassuring objects. Regina pulled open a cupboard door. She saw clean linen on one of the shelves and a flannel jacket on a hanger. She slipped her hand into one of the pockets.

'This is becoming interesting,' she said. She withdrew her hand; it was filled with gold coins.

'Good God!' Annie exclaimed.

In the other pocket there was a scrap of paper. It was a certificate issued by the Seine-Inférieure Asylum. The man had amnesia. He went by the name of Raymond Fosca. Neither his birthplace nor his age were known, and after a stay of unknown duration at the asylum, he had been released a month previously.

'Oh!' Annie said, disappointedly. 'Monsieur Roger was right after all. He's a lunatic.'

'Naturally, he's a lunatic,' Regina said. She put the paper back in the pocket. 'I'd like to know why they put him away, though.'

'Anyway, there's no food here,' Annie said. 'He doesn't eat.' She looked round the room with a perplexed look on her face. 'Perhaps he really is a fakir,' she said. 'A fakir can be mad, too.'

Regina sat down in a wicker chair next to the motionless man and she called, 'Raymond Fosca!'

He drew himself up and looked at Regina. 'How do you know my name?' he asked.

'Ah! I'm a bit of a witch,' said Regina. 'But that shouldn't surprise you. You're a sorcerer yourself. You survive without eating.'

'You know that too?' he asked.

'I know a lot of things.'

He fell back in the chair. 'Leave me alone,' he said. 'Go away. You haven't any right to follow me here.'

'No one is following you,' she said. 'I'm staying at this hotel and I've been watching you for the past few days. I'd like you to teach me your secret.'

'What secret? I haven't any secret.'

'I'd like you to teach me how you manage never to be bored.'

He did not answer. He had closed his eyes. She called him again, softly. 'Raymond Fosca! Do you hear me?'

'Yes,' he replied.

'I get so bored,' she said.

'How old are you?' Fosca asked.

'Twenty-eight.'

'You have, at most, fifty more years to live,' he said. 'They'll pass quickly.'

She grabbed him by the shoulders and shook him violently. 'What!' she cried. 'You're young, you're strong, and yet you choose to live like a dead man.'

'I haven't found anything better to do.'

'You must search,' she said. 'Would you like it if we searched together?'

'No.'

'You say no without even looking at me. Look at me.'

'It's not worth the trouble,' he said. 'I've seen you a hundred times.'

'But from far away . . . '

'From both far and near.'

'When?'

'Throughout every age,' he said. 'Everywhere.'

'But it wasn't me.' She bent over him. 'You must look at me. Now tell me, have you ever seen me before?'

'Perhaps not.'

'I knew it!'

'For the love of God, go away!' he pleaded. 'Go away, or else everything will begin again.'

'And supposing everything did begin again?'

❧

'Do you really want to take that lunatic back to Paris with you?' Roger asked.

'Yes, I want to cure him,' said Regina. She carefully packed her black velvet dress in her suitcase.

'Why?'

'It's amusing,' she said. 'You can't imagine the progress he's made in four days. Now when I speak to him, I know he hears me, even if he doesn't answer. And often he does.'

'And after you've cured him?'

'Then I'll lose interest in him,' she said gaily.

Roger put down his pen and looked at Regina. 'You frighten me,' he said. 'You're a real vampire.'

She leaned over him and put her arms around his neck. 'A vampire who's never done you much harm.'

'Oh! You haven't had your last word yet,' he replied warily.

She liked his thoughtful, tender ways, his intelligent devotion; he belonged to her body and soul, and she loved him as much as she could love anyone other than herself.

'How is your work going?'

'I think I have a good idea for the forest setting.'

'I'll leave you alone then. I'm going to see my patient.' She set off down the corridor and knocked at the door of room number fifty-two.

'Come in.'

She pushed open the door and he walked towards her from the back of the room.

'May I turn the light on?' she asked.

'Go ahead.'

She pushed the switch. On the bedside she noticed a pack of cigarettes and an ashtray full of butts. 'So you smoke?' she asked.

'I bought some cigarettes this morning.' He held out the pack to her. 'I guess you're satisfied.'

'Me? Why?'

'Time is beginning to flow again.'

She sat down in a chair and lit a cigarette. 'You know, we're leaving tomorrow morning.'

He was standing by the window looking at the starlit sky. 'Always the same stars,' he said.

'We're leaving tomorrow morning,' she repeated. 'Are you ready?'

He sat down opposite Regina. 'Why do you bother about me?'

'I've decided to cure you.'

'But I'm not ill.'

'You refuse to live.'

He observed her with a cold, anxious expression. 'Tell me, do you love me?'

She laughed. 'That's my business,' she said in an ambiguous tone of voice.

'Because you mustn't,' he said.

'I don't need any advice.'

'But this is a special case,' he said.

'I know,' she declared haughtily.

'What exactly do you know?' he said slowly.

She held his gaze. 'I know that you've just come out of an asylum and that you have amnesia.'

He smiled. 'Oh, dear' he sighed.

'What do you mean, "Oh, dear"?'

'If only I were lucky enough to have amnesia . . .'

'Lucky enough!' she said. 'You must never deny your past.'

'If I had amnesia, I'd be almost like other men. Perhaps I might even be able to love you.'

'You can spare me that,' she said. 'Don't worry, I don't love you.'

'You're beautiful,' he said. 'See what rapid progress I'm making. Now I know you're beautiful.'

She leaned toward him and placed her hand on his wrist. 'Come to Paris with me.'

He hesitated. 'Why not?' he said sadly. 'In any case, life's wheel is starting to turn again.'

'Do you really regret that?'

'Oh, I don't hold it against you. Even without you, it would have happened sooner or later. Once I was able to hold my breath for sixty years, but the moment someone tapped me on the shoulder . . . '

'Sixty years?'

He smiled. 'Sixty seconds, if you prefer,' he said. 'What's the difference? There are moments when time stands still.' He stared at his hands for a long while. 'Moments when you're beyond life and yet still see. And then time starts to flow again, your heart beats, you stretch out a hand, you take a step forward. You still know, but you no longer see.'

'Yes,' she said. 'You suddenly find yourself back in your room combing your hair.'

'You have to comb your hair, of course. Every day.' He lowered his head and all the features of his face seemed to slump.

She watched him for a long time in silence. 'Tell me, how long were you in the asylum?'

'Thirty years.'

'Thirty years! How old are you then?'

He did not answer.

CHAPTER TWO

'Well what's become of your fakir?' asked Laforêt. Regina smiled as she filled the port glasses. 'He goes to the restaurant twice a day, he wears off-the-peg suits and he's as boring as any office clerk. I think I cured him too well.'

Roger turned towards Dulac. We came across a wretched lunatic in Rouen who thought he was a fakir. Regina decided to bring him back to his senses.'

'Did you succeed?' asked Dulac.

'She succeeds in whatever she does,' Roger replied. 'She's a formidable woman!'

Regina smiled. 'Excuse me a moment. I'll go and see how dinner's coming along.'

She crossed the room, and she could sense Dulac's gaze. He was a connoisseur of the shapely leg, the well-rounded figure, the supple gait: he was a horse-trader. She opened the kitchen door.

'Everything all right?'

'Everything's fine,' Annie replied. 'But what shall I do with the soufflé?'

'Put it in the oven as soon as Madame Laforêt comes. She probably won't be long.' She dipped her finger in the sauce of the *canard à l'orange*. It had never turned out better.

'Do I look beautiful this evening?'

Annie examined her with a critical eye. 'I like your hair better in plaits.'

'I know,' Regina said. 'But Roger wants me to tone down all my distinctive features. They only appreciate obvious beauty.'

'It's a shame,' Annie said.

'Don't worry. As soon as I've made two or three films, I'll make them accept my real face.'

'Does Dulac seem interested in you?'

'It's never easy to attract that type.' Then, between her teeth, she muttered, 'I hate those horsetraders!'

'Be sure not to make a scene,' said Annie anxiously. 'Don't drink too much and don't get impatient.'

'I'll be as patient as an angel. I'll laugh at all of Dulac's little jokes. And if I have to sleep with him, I'll sleep with him.'

'He won't expect that much!' Annie laughed.

'What's the difference. I can just as well take my revenge wholesale as I can retail.' She glanced at herself in the mirror hanging above the sink. 'I can't wait much longer,' she said.

The door-bell rang. Annie rushed to the door while Regina continued to study her face: she hated the way her hair was done and the film-star make-up. She hated the false smile that she could feel forming on her lips and the social tone of her voice. 'It's degrading,' she thought angrily, and then, 'but I'll have my own back later.'

'It's not Madame Laforêt.' said Annie.

'Who is it?'

'It's the fakir.'

'Fosca? What's he doing here? You didn't let him in, I hope?'

'No. He's waiting in the hall.'

Regina closed the kitchen door behind her. 'My dear Fosca,' she said coldly, 'I'm very sorry, but I absolutely cannot ask you in this evening. I did ask you not to come to my home.'

'I just wanted to know whether you were ill. It's been three days since I last saw you.'

She looked at him irritably. He was wearing a gabardine overcoat and he held his hat in his hand. He looked as if he was wearing a disguise.

'You could at least have phoned me,' she said drily.

'I wanted to *know*.'

'Well, now you know. Forgive me, but I'm giving a dinner party this evening and it's very important. I'll drop by to see you as soon as I have a moment.'

He smiled. 'A dinner isn't very important.'

'My career is at stake. There's an opportunity of making a sensational film debut.'

'The cinema's not very important, either.'

'And I suppose what you have to tell me is of the greatest importance?' she retorted irritably.

'Ah! it's what you wanted. Before, nothing seemed important to me.'

The door-bell rang again.

'Go in there,' said Regina pushing him into the kitchen. 'Annie, tell them I'm just coming.'

Fosca smiled. 'Smells good!'

He took a mauve-coloured *petit four* from a bowl and put it in his mouth.

'If you have something to tell me, speak, but hurry up,' she said.

He looked at her amiably. 'You made me come to Paris. You pestered me to start living again. Well, now it's up to you to make my life bearable. You mustn't let three days go by without coming to see me.'

'Three days isn't very long,' she said.

'It's a long time for me. Remember, I have nothing else to do but wait for you.'

'That's really your fault,' she said. 'I've got a thousand things to do . . . I can't just look after you from morning till night.'

'You asked for it. You wanted me to take notice of you. Now nothing else matters to me. But you exist and I feel an emptiness without you.'

'Shall I start the soufflé?' Annie asked.

'Yes, we'll eat straightaway,' said Regina. 'Listen,' she said, 'we can discuss all this later. I'll come to see you soon.'

'Tomorrow?'

'All right, tomorrow.'

'What time?'

'About three o'clock.' She edged him gently towards the door.

'I'd have preferred to see you now.' He smiled. 'I'll go, but you must come tomorrow.'

'I will,' she promised.

She slammed the door behind him. 'What a nerve! He can go on waiting as far as I'm concerned! If he ever comes back, don't let him in.'

'Poor fellow, he's mad,' Annie said.

'He doesn't look it any more.'

'His eyes are so strange.'

'But, I'm not a sister of charity,' Regina declared.

She went into the drawing-room and, smiling, walked up to Madame Laforêt. 'Forgive me,' she said. 'Can you imagine! My fakir won't leave me alone.'

'You should have invited him to stay,' Dulac said.

Everyone burst out laughing.

'A little more brandy?' asked Annie.

'Yes, please.'

Regina gulped the alcohol and curled up in front of the log fire. She felt warm and cosy. A jazz tune was playing softly on the radio. Annie had lit a small lamp and was laying the cards, trying to read her fortune. Regina did nothing. She gazed into the flames, looked round at the walls on which shapeless shadows danced, and she felt happy. The rehearsal had gone very well. Laforêt, always so sparing with compliments, had praised her warmly. *As You Like It* would be a success, and after that anything was possible. 'I'm getting there,' she thought, and smiled. Lying in front of the fire in the house at Rosay, how often had she sworn to herself that one day she would be loved, she would be famous! She felt like taking that eager little girl by the hand, leading her into this room and saying to her, 'I've kept your promises. Look who you've become!'

'Someone's ringing,' Annie said.

'Go and see who it is.'

Annie ran off towards the kitchen. By climbing on a chair, one could see the whole hallway through a small pane of glass.

'It's the fakir.'

'I thought so. Don't open.'

The bell rang a second time.

'He's going to ring all night,' said Annie.

'He'll get tired soon.'

For a moment there was silence, then a series of prolonged, insistent rings, then silence again.

'You see, he's gone,' said Regina.

She pulled the skirts of her dressing-gown around her legs and rolled herself up again on the rug. But the door-bell ringing had been enough to cast a shadow over the perfection of the moment. On the other side of the door, the rest of the world existed again; Regina was no longer alone with herself. She looked at the parchment lampshades, the Japanese masks, all the trinkets she had carefully chosen one by one and which brought back memories of precious moments. But such things grew silent, the memories faded, and this moment, like the others, would fade, too. The eager little girl was dead, the ambitious young woman was going to die, and the great actress she hoped so passionately to become, would also die one day. Perhaps her name would be remembered for a while. But there would be no one to remember that special taste of life on her lips, that passion that burned in her heart, the beauty of the red flames and their phantasmagorial secrets.

'Listen!' said Annie, she had raised her head and there was a frightened look of fear on her face. 'I heard a noise in your room.'

Regina looked at the door. The knob was turning.

'Don't be frightened,' Fosca said. 'I'm sorry, but you didn't seem to hear the door-bell.'

'Ah! It's the devil!' exclaimed Annie.

'No,' said Fosca. 'I simply came in through the window.'

Regina stood up. 'I'm sorry the window wasn't locked.'

'I'd have broken the pane,' said Fosca. He smiled and so did Regina.

'Wouldn't you be frightened of doing a thing like that?' she asked.

'No. I'm never frightened. But it's nothing to be proud of.'

She pointed to a chair and filled two glasses. 'Do sit down.'

He sat down. He had climbed up three storeys and had risked breaking his neck, and he had caught her by surprise with her hair in disarray, her cheeks shiny and dressed in a pale pink, fluffy dressing-gown. He held a distinct advantage.

'You can go to bed, Annie,' she said.

Annie bent down to Regina and kissed her on the cheek. 'If you need me, just call.'

'Fine,' said Regina. 'Sweet dreams.'

The door closed and she glared at Fosca. 'Well?'

'You see,' he said, 'you won't get away from me so easily. If you stop coming to see me, I'll come to you. If you shut your door to me, I'll get in through the window.'

'You'll simply force me to barricade the windows,' she said coldly.

'I'll wait for you at the front door, I'll follow you in the street . . . '

'And what good will that do you?'

'I'll see you, I'll hear your voice.' He got up and went over to her chair. 'I'll hold you in my arms,' he said, seizing her by the shoulders.

'You don't have to squeeze so hard,' she said, wriggling herself free. Doesn't it matter to you that you're making yourself repulsive?'

'How could that affect me?' He looked at her compassionately. 'Soon you'll be dead and all your thoughts with you.'

She stood up and stepped backwards. 'Right now, I'm alive.'

'Yes,' he said, 'and I can see you.'

'Well then, don't you see that you're irritating me?'

'I do. But your eyes look beautiful when you're angry.'

'Then my feelings mean nothing to you?'

'You'll be the first to forget them,' he said.

'Ah!' she exclaimed in exasperation. 'You're forever talking about when I'll be dead! But even if you were to kill me in the next minute, nothing would change. I now find your presence disagreeable.'

He started to laugh. 'I certainly don't want to kill you.'

'I should hope not.'

She sat down again, not entirely reassured.

'Why are you leaving me?' he asked. 'Why do you concern yourself with those creatures and never with me?'

'What creatures?'

'Those here today and gone tomorrow little men who you're always laughing and joking with.'

'Can I ever laugh with you?' she said irritably. 'All you know how to do is look at me and not say anything. You refuse to live. But I love life. Can you understand that?'

'What a shame!'

'Why?'

'It will be over so soon.'

'Not again?'

'Again. Always.'

'Can't you talk about anything else?'

'But how can you think of anything else?' he asked. 'How can you manage to feel permanently installed in the world when you've only just arrived and when you'll be leaving it again in a few years' time?'

'At least when I die, I shall have lived,' she retorted. 'You, you're already a corpse.'

He lowered his head and looked at his hands. 'Beatrice used to say that, too,' he thought. 'A corpse.' He looked up again, saying, 'You're probably right, after all. Why should you think of death when you're going to die in any case? It will be so simple and it will come without you knowing. You won't have to bother about it at all.'

'And you?'

'Me?' He had such a desperate look in his eyes that she was afraid of what he was going to say. But he only said, 'It's different.'

'Why?'

'I can't explain.'

'You can if you want to.'

'I don't want to.'

'But I'd be interested.'

'No,' he said flatly. 'It would change everything between us.'

'Fine. Perhaps you'd seem less boring.'

He gazed into the fire. Above his large, hooked nose, his eyes gleamed, then his eyes grew dull. 'No.'

She got up. 'Very well. Go back to your room if you've nothing more interesting to say.'

He stood up, too. 'When will you come to see me?'

'When you decide to tell me your secret,' she replied.

Fosca's face hardened. 'All right. Come tomorrow,' he said.

She was lying stretched out on the iron-framed bed, the hideous, rust-flaked, iron bed. From where she lay, she could glimpse a patch of the yellow bedspread, the false marble top of the bedside table and the dusty tile floor. Nothing affected her any longer, neither the stench of ammonia, nor the screeching children on the other side of the wall. All of it, everything, was completely indifferent to her, whether it was nearby or far away, it was simply elsewhere. The chimes of a clock striking nine echoed into the night. She did not move. There were no longer any hours or days, no more time, no more place. Somewhere over there the gravy for the lamb had congealed. Somewhere, on some stage, *As You Like It* was being rehearsed and no one knew where Rosalind was. Somewhere over there, a man was standing on a wall and was stretching out his arms triumphantly towards a large, red sun.

'Do you really believe all that?' she asked.

'It's the truth,' he replied. He shrugged his shoulders. 'Years ago, it didn't seem so extraordinary.'

'There must be people who remember you.'

'There are places where people still speak of me, but as if I were some ancient legend.'

'What if you threw yourself out this window?'

He turned and looked at the window. 'I'd probably hurt myself very badly and be laid up for a long while. I'm not invulnerable, but no matter what may happen to me, my body always heals eventually.'

She stood up and looked at him fixedly. 'Do you really believe you'll never die?'

'Even when I want to die, I can't,' he answered.

'Ah!' she sighed. 'If only I were immortal!'

'What then?'

'The world would be mine.'

'That's what I thought, a very long time ago.'

'Why don't you think so now?'

'It's something you couldn't possibly imagine. I'll be here forever. I'll always be here.' He buried his head in his hands.

She stared at the ceiling and repeated to herself, 'I'll be here forever. I'll always be here.' There was a man who dared think that, a man sufficiently arrogant and solitary to believe himself immortal. 'I used to say I'm alone in the world,' she thought to herself. 'I used to say I'd never met a man or woman who could compare to me. But I'd never have the audacity to say, "I am immortal".'

'Oh, I'd love to believe that I'd never rot in a grave!'

'Immortality is a terrible curse.' He gazed at her. 'I'm alive and yet I'm lifeless. I shall never die and I have no future. I am no one. I've no past and no face.'

'No,' she said gently, 'I see you.'

'You see me' He passed his hand over his face. 'If only it were possible to be absolutely nothing. But there are always other people on earth and they see you. They speak and you can't not listen to them, and you reply to them, and you start to live again, knowing that you don't really exist. Endlessly.'

'But you do exist,' she protested.

'I exist for you, at this moment. But do you really exist?'

'Of course,' she answered. 'And so do you.' She took his arm. 'Don't you feel my hand on your arm?'

He looked at her hand. 'That hand, yes, but what does it mean?'

'It's my hand,' said Regina.

'Your hand . . . ' He hesitated for a moment. 'You will have to love me,' he said, 'and I have to love you. Then you'd be there and I would be where you are.'

'My poor Fosca,' she said, 'I don't love you.'

He looked at her and said in a studied tone, 'You don't love me.' He shook his head. 'No. That's no good. You've got to say: "I love you".'

'But you don't love me.'

'I don't know.' He bent over her. 'I know that your mouth exists,' he said abruptly.

His lips crushed against Regina's. She closed her eyes. The night exploded. It had begun centuries ago and would never end. From the depths of time, a wild, burning desire was pressing on her mouth, and she abandoned herself to the kiss – the kiss of a madman in a room rank with the smell of ammonia.

'Leave me alone,' she said, rising. 'I must go.'

He made no effort to stop her.

No sooner had she opened the door to her apartment than Roger and Annie rushed from the drawing-room.

'Where have you been?' Roger asked. 'Why weren't you back for supper? Why did you miss the rehearsal?'

'I forgot what time it was,' said Regina.

'Forgot what time it was? Who were you with?'

'You can't always have your eyes glued to a clock,' she said impatiently. 'As if every hour were exactly equal! As if it made any sense to want to measure time!'

'What's the matter with you?' Roger asked. 'Where were you?'

'I made such a wonderful dinner,' Annie said. 'There were cheese fritters . . . '

'Cheese fritters!' Regina laughed.

At seven o'clock, cheese fritters, and at eight o'clock Shakespeare. A time for everything and everything in its place. Not a minute must be wasted; soon they would all be used up. She sat down and slowly took off her gloves. Out there, in a room with a dusty tile floor, was a man who believed himself immortal.

'Who were you with?' Roger repeated.

'Fosca.'

'You missed the rehearsal for the sake of Fosca?' Roger asked incredulously.

'One rehearsal isn't so important.'

'Regina, tell me the truth.' He looked her in the eye and in his direct way asked again, 'What happened?'

'I was with Fosca and I didn't notice the time.'

'Then you too must be going crazy,' said Roger.

'I wouldn't mind that at all,' she answered.

She looked around her. 'My room,' she thought. 'My things. He's lying on the yellow bedspread, where I was just lying, and he believes he saw Dürer's smile, the eyes of Charles V. He has the audacity to believe it.'

'He's a very extraordinary man,' Regina said.

'He's a lunatic.'

'No. It's stranger than that. He just told me he's immortal.' She glanced at Roger and Annie disdainfully; they looked stupid.

'Immortal?' said Annie.

'He was born in the thirteenth century,' Regina stated casually. 'In 1848, he fell asleep in a wood and remained there for sixty years. Then he spent thirty years in an asylum.'

'Enough of this nonsense,' Roger said.

'Why shouldn't he be immortal?' she asked defiantly. 'It doesn't seem to be any greater miracle than being born or dying.'

'Oh, please!' Roger exclaimed.

'And even if he's not immortal, he believes he's immortal.'

'It's a classic case of delusions of grandeur. He's no more interesting than a man who thinks he's Charlemagne.'

'What makes you think that someone who believes he's Charlemagne isn't interesting?' Regina's face suddenly burned with anger. 'Do you think you're so interesting, you two?'

'That's not very nice of you,' said Annie, sounding rather hurt.

'You expect me to be like you,' Regina said. 'And to think I actually tried to be like you!'

She got up, walked towards her room, and slammed the door behind her. 'I'm like them!' she said furiously to herself. 'Little people with their little lives! Why didn't I stay there on his bed? Why was I afraid? Am I such a coward? He goes out in the street, dressed modestly in his felt hat and his gabardine coat, and all the while he's thinking, "I'm immortal". The world belongs to him, time belongs to him, and I'm nothing but some insect.' With the tips of her fingers, she stroked the narcissi in a vase on the table. 'And supposing I, too, believed I were immortal? The scent of the narcissi is immortal – and so is this fever that swells my lips. I am immortal.' She crushed the flowers in her hand. It was useless – death was within her. She knew it, and even now she welcomed it. To be beautiful for another ten years, to play Phèdre and Cleopatra, to leave a faint memory in the hearts of mortal men which would gradually crumble to dust – she had been satisfied with these modest ambitions. She took out the pins which held back her hair and the heavy tresses fell round her shoulders. 'One day I'll be old, dead, forgotten. And all the time I'm thinking like this, there's a man who is thinking, "I will always be here".'

'It was a triumph!' said Dulac.

'I like the way your Rosalind remains so coquettish, and has such ambiguous grace beneath her man's clothes,' Frénaud remarked.

'Let's not talk about Rosalind,' Regina said. 'She's dead.'

The curtain had fallen. Rosalind was dead, she died every evening, and there would come a day when she would not be born again. Regina took her glass of champagne and emptied it. Her hand was trembling. From the moment she left the stage, she had not stopped trembling.

'I'd like to have some fun,' she said plaintively.

'Let's dance,' Annie suggested.

'No. I want to dance with Sylvia.'

Sylvia cast a quick glance at the respectable people sitting at tables. 'Don't you think we'll draw too much attention to ourselves?'

'And when one's acting, don't you think one's drawing attention to one's self?' asked Regina.

She took hold of Sylvia. She was rather unsteady on her feet, but she was able to dance even when she could no longer walk straight. The orchestra was playing a rumba and

she began to wiggle obscenely, imitating a native dance.
Sylvia seemed very embarrassed. She moved about in front of
Regina, not knowing what to do with her body, and smiling
politely and good-naturedly. They all had the same smile on
their faces. That evening Regina could have done anything
she pleased and everyone would have applauded her. She
abruptly stopped dancing.

'You'll never be able to dance,' she said to Sylvia. 'You're
far too sensible.'

She fell back into her seat. 'Give me a cigar,' she said to
Roger.

'You'll be ill,' he warned.

'Very well! I'll vomit. It'll be some distraction.'

Roger handed her a cigar. She lit it carefully and drew
a long puff. A bitter taste filled her mouth. That, at least,
seemed real, thick, tangible. Everything else seemed so far
away – the music, the voices, the laughter, the strange and
familiar faces whose shimmering images were endlessly
reflected in the night-club's mirrors.

'You must be worn out,' Merlin said.

'I'm mostly thirsty.'

She emptied another glass of champagne. Drinking,
forever drinking. Yet despite the wine, there was a chill in
her heart. A moment beforehand, she had been burning
with emotion. People had been on their feet, shouting and
clapping their hands. Now they were sleeping or chatting,
and she felt cold. Was he sleeping, too? He had not
applauded; he had just sat and stared. 'Out of the depths
of eternity he looked at me and Rosalind became immortal.
If I could believe him,' she thought, 'supposing I could
believe him?' She hiccupped and her mouth felt pasty.

'Why isn't anyone singing? When you're happy, you sing.
You're happy, aren't you?'

'We're happy about your triumph,' Sanier said in his grave,
intimate manner.

'Well, sing then!'

Sanier smiled, and in a low voice he began to sing an American song.

'Louder,' she said.

He did not raise his voice. She clapped her hand over his mouth and said angrily, 'Shut up. I'm going to sing.'

'Don't make a scene,' said Roger.

'Singing isn't making a scene.'

She launched forth vigorously:

'The girls from Camaret say that they are virgins . . . '

But her voice did not obey her. She coughed and began again:

'The girls from Camaret say that they are virgins . . . But when they're in bed . . . '

She hiccupped again and felt the blood draining from her face. 'Excuse me,' she said in an upper-class tone of voice. 'I'm going to be sick.'

She walked to the back of the room, staggering a little. They were all looking at her – friends, strangers, waiters, the maître d'hôtel – but she slipped through their gazes as easily as a ghost moves through walls. She looked at herself in the mirror in the ladies. Her face was pale, her nose pinched and her cheeks were caked in powder.

'That's all that remains of Rosalind.' She leaned over the lavatory and threw up. 'Now what shall I do?' she asked herself.

She flushed the lavatory, wiped her mouth and sat down on the edge of a chair. The floor was tiled, the walls bare: it looked like an operating room or a cell belonging to a monk or a lunatic. She had no desire to rejoin them; they could do nothing for her, not even distract her for one evening. She would rather stay here all night, spend the rest of her life enclosed in whiteness and solitude, shut in, buried, forgotten. She stood up. She had not stopped thinking of him for a single moment all evening, this man who had not applauded, but who had devoured her with his ageless gaze. 'It's my last chance, my only chance!' she thought.

She collected her coat from the cloakroom and called to them as she passed, 'I'm going to get some air.'

She walked outside and hailed a taxi. 'Hôtel de la Havane, rue Saint-André-des-Arts.' She closed her eyes and for a few minutes she succeeded in calming herself. But then she thought wearily, 'It's all an act. I don't believe it.' She vacillated. She could have knocked at the window and had herself driven back to the 'Mille et une Nuits'. But then what? To believe or not believe? What did these words mean? She needed him.

She crossed the dingy courtyard and climbed the stairs. She knocked at his door. No one answered. She sat down on the cold stone steps. Where was he at this time of night? What visions – visions that would never die – passed through his mind? She buried her head in her hands. 'Believe in him. Believe that this Rosalind I have created is immortal, and to become immortal in his heart.'

'Regina!' Fosca exclaimed.

'I've been waiting for you,' she said. 'I've been waiting for you for ages.' She stood up. 'Take me with you.'

'Where?'

'Anywhere. I want to be with you tonight, that's all.'

He opened the door to his room. 'Come in.'

She entered the room. Yes. Why not here, between these cracked and peeling walls? Beneath his gaze, she was beyond space, beyond time; the setting was of no importance.

'Where have you been?' she asked.

'Just walking in the night.' He touched Regina's shoulder. 'And you've been waiting for me! You're here!'

'You didn't applaud me,' she said with a laugh.

'I wanted to cry. Perhaps I'll be able to cry another time.'

'Fosca, tell me the truth. You mustn't lie to me tonight. Is it really true?'

'I never lied to you,' he said.

'Are you sure it's not all just a dream?'

'Do I look like a madman?' He placed his hands on Regina's shoulders. 'Dare to believe me. Dare!'

'Can't you give me some proof?'

'I can.' He walked over to the wash-basin, and when he turned round he was holding a razor in his hand. 'Don't be frightened,' he said.

Before she could stop him, a stream of blood gushed from Fosca's throat.

'Fosca!' she cried out.

He staggered over to the bed and lay there with his eyes closed, pale as a corpse. The blood continued to flow from his slashed throat. His shirt and the sheets became sticky and the blood dripped onto the tiles. All the blood in his body, it seemed, was escaping through the gaping gash. Regina grabbed a towel, dipped it in some water and placed it against the wound. Her whole body was trembling. She stared in horror at this face that was unlined but looked as if it had never been young, a face that may have been that of a corpse. Froth was forming at the sides of his mouth and it seemed as if he was no longer breathing.

She called to him: 'Fosca! Fosca!'

He half opened his eyes and breathed deeply. 'Don't be afraid.' Gently, he removed her hand and pushed away the bloody towel. The blood had stopped flowing, the sides of the gash had drawn together. Above his crimson shirt, all that could be seen was a long pink scar on his neck.

'It's not possible!' she exclaimed. She hid her face in her hands and began to cry.

'Regina! Do you believe me now?' He got up and took her in his arms. She could feel the sticky moistness of his shirt against her breast.

'I believe you.'

For a long while, she stood there motionless, pressed closely against this mysterious body, this living body which time could not wither. And then she raised her eyes and looked at him in horror, in hope.

'Save me,' she said. 'Save me from death.'

'Ah!' he said fervently. 'It's you who must save me!' He took Regina's face in his hands. He looked at her so intently that it seemed as if he wanted to tear her soul from her body. 'Save me from the night and from apathy,' he said. 'Make me love you and know that you alone exist among all other women. Then the world will return to its original shape. There will be tears, smiles, expectations, fears. I'll be a living man again.'

'You *are a* living man,' she said, as she kissed him.

Fosca's hand was resting on the tiled table and Regina was looking at it. 'That hand . . . that hand which caressed me, how old is it?' she asked herself. 'Perhaps, at this very moment, the flesh will suddenly rot and leave nothing but a few white bones?' She raised her head. 'Is Roger right? Am I going mad?' The midday sun lit up the quiet bar where normal, unmysterious men were sunk into leather chairs, drinking their apéritifs. This was Paris, it was the twentieth century. Regina stared at the hand once more. The fingers were strong and elegant, with nails that were a bit too long. 'His nails grow, and so does his hair.' She looked up at his neck, his smooth neck, with no trace of a scar. 'There must be some explanation,' she thought. 'Perhaps he really is a fakir; he must know secrets . . . ' She sipped a glass of mineral water. She had a headache and her mouth felt furred. 'I need a cold shower and a rest. Then I'll be able to see things more clearly,' she told herself.

'I'm going home.'

'Ah!' he said, 'Of course.' Then he added angrily, 'Night follows day; day follows night. It never changes.'

They were silent. She took her handbag and he said nothing. She took her gloves and still he remained silent. Finally she asked, 'When shall we see each other again?'

'See each other again?' He looked absent-mindedly at the platinum blonde hair of a young woman nearby.

Suddenly the thought occurred to Regina that he might vanish into thin air from one moment to the next, and she felt as if she were falling dizzily down a deep chasm, through layer upon layer of dense fog; and when she reached the bottom of the abyss, she would turn into a blade of grass which would be withered away forever by the winter cold.

'You're not going to leave me, are you?' she asked in anguish.

'Me? But you're the one who's leaving.'

'I'll be back,' she said. 'Don't be angry. I must let Roger and Annie know that I'm all right – they must be worried.' She placed her hand on Fosca's. 'I'd much prefer to stay.'

'Then stay.'

She threw her gloves on the table and put down her handbag. She needed to feel his eyes upon her. 'Dare to believe me . . . Dare!' What was she to believe? He neither looked like a charlatan nor a madman.

'Why are you looking at me like that?' he asked. 'Do I frighten you?'

'No.'

'Do I look different to other people?'

She hesitated. 'No, not at this moment.'

'Regina!' he said. He sounded as if he were praying. 'Do you think you'll ever be able to love me?'

'Give me a little time,' she replied. She watched him in silence. 'I hardly know anything about you. You must talk about yourself.'

'It's not interesting.'

'But it is,' she protested. 'Have you loved many women?'

'A few.'

'What were they like?'

'Let's not talk about the past, Regina,' he said abruptly. 'If I'm to become a man amongst men again, I have to forget the past. My life begins here, today, beside you.'

'Yes,' she said. 'You're right.'

The young woman with the platinum blonde hair walked to the door of the bar, followed by a rather elderly gentleman. They were going to lunch. Life's daily routine continued in a world tamely submissive to all the natural laws. 'What am I doing here?' wondered Regina. She could find nothing more to say to Fosca.

He sat with his chin on his fist and a stubborn expression on his face: 'You'll have to think of something for me to do,' he announced.

'Something to do?'

'Yes. All normal men have things to do.'

'What would you be interested in?' she asked.

'You don't understand,' he said. 'You must tell me what interests you and in what way I can help you.'

'But you can't help me. You can't play my roles for me.'

'That's true.' He began to reflect again. 'Well, I'll have to find a job.'

'That's an idea. What can you do?'

'Very little that's useful,' he said with a smile.

'Do you have any money?'

'Not much.'

'And you never worked before?'

'I used to work as a colourist.'

'That won't get you far,' Regina said.

'Oh, I don't care about getting far.' He sounded disappointed as he added, 'I would have really liked to do something for you.'

She touched his hand. 'Stay near me, Fosca. Look at me and remember everything about me.'

He smiled. 'That's not difficult. I have a very good memory.' His face darkened again. 'Much too good.'

She squeezed his hand nervously. He spoke and she answered, as if everything they were saying were true. 'If it's true, he'll remember me forever. If it's true, then I'm loved by a man who is immortal,' she thought. Her eyes surveyed the room. It was an ordinary enough crowd; men who lacked any mystery. But hadn't she always known she was different? Hadn't she always felt herself a stranger among them, that she was meant for a destiny that was not theirs? Ever since childhood, there had been something special, something different about her. She looked at Fosca. 'It's him. He's my destiny. From beyond the centuries he has come to me and he'll guard me in his memory until the end of time.' Her heart thumped loudly. 'And if it's all a lie?' She studied Fosca's hand, his neck, his face, and she thought angrily, 'Am I like them? Must I have absolute proof?' He had said, 'Dare! Dare!' and she wanted to be daring. If it were an illusion, delirium, then there was more grandeur in it than in all their collective wisdom.

She smiled at Fosca. 'Do you know what you ought to do?' she said. 'You should write your memoirs. It would be an extraordinary book.'

'There are quite enough books as it is,' he replied.

'But this would be different to all the others.' She leaned toward him. 'Have you never been tempted to write?'

He smiled. 'I did write in the asylum. I spent twenty years writing.

'You must show me.'

'I tore it all up.'

'Why? It may have been excellent.'

He laughed. 'I wrote for twenty years. And then one day I realized that it was always the same book.'

'But now you're a different man,' she said with conviction. 'You must try again.'

'A different man?'

'Someone who loves me and who's living in this century. Try to start writing again.'

He looked at her and his face brightened. 'If that's what you want, I'll do it,' he said fervently.

He looked at her and she thought, 'He loves me. I'm loved by a man who is immortal.' She smiled, but she did

not want to smile. She felt frightened. She looked around at
the room. She would no longer be able to expect any help
from the world around her; she was entering a strange
universe where she would be entirely on her own with
this unknown man. 'What will happen to me now?' she
wondered.

'It's time now,' Regina said.
'Time for what?'
'Time to leave.'
Through the window of her dressing room one could see
snowflakes falling steadily under the light of a street-lamp. The
pavements were covered in white and there was a stillness
everywhere. Rosalind's dress was lying on a chair.
'Let's imagine that time has stopped,' said Fosca.
'It certainly hasn't stopped where I'm supposed to be
tonight.'
He stood up. She was always astonished at how tall he was:
a man from another age.
'Why do you have to go there?' he asked.
'Because it could be useful.'
'Useful for what? Who to?'
'Useful for my career. An actress has to meet a lot of
people and be seen everywhere, otherwise she's soon forgotten.' She smiled. 'I want to be famous. Won't you be proud
of me when I'm famous?'
'I like you just as you are,' he said in his low voice. He
drew her to him and kissed her long and passionately on the
mouth. 'How beautiful you look this evening.'
He looked at her and she melted under his gaze. She
could not bear to think that there would be a time when his
eyes would no longer look at her, when her life would sink
into indifference and oblivion. She thought for a moment
and then said, 'You can come with me if you like.'
'You know very well I'd like to,' he said.

Florence's drawing-room was filled with people. Regina hesitated as she entered: every time she felt this sharp pang in her heart. Each of these women in the room preferred herself to all the others, and for each woman there was at least one man who preferred *her* above the rest. 'How can anyone have the audacity to believe: "I alone have the right to prefer myself"?' Regina wondered.

She turned to Fosca. 'There are lots of attractive women here.'

'Yes,' he said.

'Ah! So you've noticed.'

'From looking at you, I've learned how to see.'

'Tell me, who do you think is the most beautiful?'

'From what point of view?'

'Now that's a strange question.'

'To have a preference, one must have a point of view.'

'And don't you have one?'

He hesitated, then a smile lit up his face. 'Yes, I do. I'm a man who loves you.'

'Well?'

'Well, you're the most beautiful. Who could look more like you than yourself?'

She looked at him slightly mistrustfully. 'Do you really think I'm the most beautiful?'

'Only you exist,' he whispered fervently.

She walked over to Florence. Normally, she disliked being welcomed as a guest in someone else's home, in someone else's life, but she could sense Fosca following behind her, looking awkward and timid, and she felt consoled in the knowledge that she alone existed in his immortal heart. She smiled at Florence.

'I hope you won't mind that I've brought a friend.'

'He's very welcome.'

She walked around the room, shaking hands. Florence's friends disliked her; she could sense the ill will concealed behind their smiles. But this evening, their opinions did not bother her. 'Soon they'll all be dead and their thoughts with them. They're just insects'. She felt invulnerable.

'Are you going to drag that man around with you everywhere?' asked Roger. He seemed annoyed.

'He didn't want to leave me,' she replied indifferently. She took a glass of fruit juice that Sanier had offered her. 'Florence looks ravishing this evening.'

'Yes, she does,' he said.

He and Florence had eventually gone back to each other and now Sanier appeared more taken with her than ever. Regina had watched them as they danced cheek to cheek. There was such love in their smiles, but it was only an ordinary, mortal love.

'We must talk seriously together,' said Roger.

'Whenever you like.'

She felt light-headed, she was free; there was no longer that bitter taste in her mouth. She was like a great oak whose branches touched the sky and beneath which the grass in the fields was ruffled in the breeze.

'I'm going to ask you a favour,' said Sanier.

'Ask it.'

'Would you recite a few poems for us?'

'You know very well that she never likes to,' said Florence.

Regina looked around the room. Fosca was leaning against a wall with his arms hanging loosely at his sides, and his eyes never left her. She stood up.

'All right. I'll recite *Les Regrets de la Belle Heaulmière*.' As she walked to the middle of the room, everyone fell silent. 'Fosca,' she murmured to herself, 'listen carefully. I'm reciting these lines for you.'

He bowed his head. He was studying her avidly with those eyes that had gazed upon so many women celebrated for their beauty, for their talents. For him, all those diverse destinies comprised one single story, and Regina was now a part of that story. Now she could compete for his affection with her dead rivals and with those who were not yet born. 'I'll triumph over all of them and I shall have won the contest both in the past and in the future.' Her lips moved and every inflection in her voice reverberated through eternity.

'Regina, I'd like to take you home now,' Roger said when she had returned to her seat amidst the applause.

'I'm not tired,' she protested.

'But I am. Please . . .' His half-pleading, half-imperious tone irritated her.

'Very well,' she said tartly. 'Let's go.'

They walked in silence through the streets. She was thinking of Fosca, whom she had left standing in the middle of the room and who was looking at other women. She no longer existed either for him or in eternity. The world around her was as hollow as a tinkling bell. 'He must always be with me, always,' she thought.

'I'm sorry,' Roger said as they entered the apartment, 'but I needed to talk to you.'

Burning embers glowed in the fireplace. The curtains had been drawn and the lights, beneath the parchment lampshades, cast an amber glow on the trinkets and the Japanese masks. And all these curios seemed only to be waiting for someone to look at them to make them spring to life.

'Well, speak,' she said.

'When is this going to end?'

'What?'

'This business with the lunatic.'

'It's not going to end,' she answered.

'What do you mean?'

She looked at him and she reminded herself: 'This is Roger. We love each other. I don't want to make him suffer.' But these thoughts seemed like memories from another world.

'I need him,' she said.

Roger sat down beside her. He said persuasively, 'You're just acting. You know very well he's a sick man.'

'You didn't see that gash in his throat,' said Regina.

Roger shrugged his shoulders. 'And suppose he is immortal?'

'Ten thousand years from now, someone will still remember me.'

'He'll forget you.'

'He says that he never forgets anything,' replied Regina.

'Then you'll be there, pinned in his memory like a butterfly in a collection.'

'I want him to love me as he has never loved before, as he never will again.'

'Believe me,' Roger said, 'it's better to be loved by someone who's mortal, but who loves only you.' His voice quavered. 'There's only you in my heart, Regina. Why isn't my love enough for you?'

She could see her tiny reflection in the depths of Roger's eyes, and her fur hat perched on her blonde hair. 'It's nothing but my reflection in a mirror,' she thought.

'Nothing's enough for me.'

'Then you don't really love this man?' Roger asked.

He looked at her anxiously. His mouth was quivering and he found it difficult to speak. He was suffering; a small, sad suffering which was throbbing very far away, in the midst of a dense fog. 'He'll have loved me,' she thought, 'he'll have suffered, and he will die – one life among many.' She knew from the moment she had left her dressing room what her decision would be.

'I want to live with him,' she said.

CHAPTER THREE

❧

For a moment Regina stood motionless at the entrance to the room. In a glance, her eyes embraced the red curtains, the beams in the ceiling, the narrow bed, the dark furniture, the books ranged on shelves. Then she closed the door and went back to the drawing-room.

'I wonder whether Fosca will like this room,' she said.

Annie shrugged her shoulders. 'What's the use of going to so much trouble for a man who looks at people like they were clouds! He won't notice a thing.'

'Exactly. He has to be taught to notice things.'

With the corner of her apron, Annie was polishing a port glass which she placed on the coffee table. 'Would he be more observant if you'd bought him lighter-coloured furniture?'

'You don't understand anything,' said Regina.

'I understand very well,' Annie replied. 'When you've finished paying the carpenters and the painters, you won't have a sou left. And he's not going to be able to live on those four old pieces of gold he keeps in his pocket.'

'Oh! Don't start that again.'

'You don't imagine he'll be capable of earning money, do you?'

'If you're frightened you'll starve to death, you can leave and look for another job,' said Regina.

'How mean you are!' Annie exclaimed.

Regina shrugged her shoulders without answering. She had done her sums; by cutting back a little it would be possible for the three of them to live on what she was earning. But she did feel rather anxious: he would be there night and day.

'Pour the port into a decanter,' Regina said, 'the vintage port.'

'There's only one bottle left.'

'Well?'

'Well, what will you offer Monsieur Dulac and Monsieur Laforêt?'

'Pour the vintage port into a decanter,' said Regina impatiently.

She gave a sudden start. Even before he had rung the bell, she had recognized his footstep on the stairs. She walked to the door. There he was with his felt hat and gabardine coat, holding a small suitcase in his hand, and, as she did every time their eyes met, she wondered: 'What does he see?'

'Come in,' she said. She took him by the hand and led him into the room. 'Do you think you'll like living here?'

'With you, I'd be happy anywhere.' When he smiled there was a vacuous, slightly stupid expression on his face. She took his suitcase.

'But this isn't just anywhere,' she said. There was a brief silence and then she added, 'Take off your coat and sit down. You're not a visitor.'

He took off his coat, but he remained standing. He looked around him, doing his best to look pleased. 'Did you furnish this room yourself?'

'Certainly.'

'You chose those chairs, those decorations?'

'Yes. Of course.'

He turned around slowly. 'Each of these things speaks for you, and you've assembled them so that they can tell your life's story.'

'And I also bought olives and shrimps,' said Regina rather impatiently. 'And I made these potato chips with my own hands. Come and try them.'

'Do you get hungry sometimes?' Annie asked.

'Yes, indeed! Ever since I began eating again, I get hungry.' He smiled. 'I'm hungry three times a day.'

He sat down and took an olive from a dish. Regina poured some port into a glass.

'It's not the vintage port,' she said angrily.

'No, it's not,' said Annie.

Regina grabbed the glass and emptied it into the fireplace. Then she walked over to the cupboard and took out a dusty bottle.

'Can you tell vintage port from ordinary port?' Annie asked.

'I don't know,' replied Fosca apologetically.

'There! You see!' exclaimed Annie.

Regina slowly tilted the old bottle and filled Fosca's glass. 'Drink it,' she said. Then, looking disdainfully at Annie, 'How stingy you are! I detest stinginess!'

'Do you?' said Fosca. 'Why?'

'Why?' Regina laughed. 'Are you stingy?'

'I used to be.'

'I'm not stingy,' said Annie, looking rather hurt. 'But I think it's awful to waste things.'

Fosca smiled at Annie 'I remember the pleasure of feeling that everything was in its correct place,' he said, 'every second, every movement. Sacks of wheat were piled up in the hayloft. Even the smallest grain felt heavy.'

Annie listened to him with a stupid, flattered expression, and the blood rushed to Regina's cheeks.

'I can understand bitterness,' he said, 'but not avarice. One can desire things passionately, but as soon as one has them, one should try to be indifferent to them.'

'Oh! But you're not indifferent at all,' said Annie.

'Me? Well, just look.' Regina took hold of the old bottle of port and emptied it in the fireplace.

Annie sniggered. 'Port! That's fine! But the time I broke one of your ghastly masks, you were furious!'

Fosca looked intently at both of them.

'Because you were the one who broke it!' Regina's voice shook with anger. 'But I can smash them to pieces at any time.' She seized one of the masks that was hanging on the wall. Fosca had got to his feet; he walked over to her and gently took hold of her wrist.

'What's the point?' He smiled. 'I've known that, too – the will to destroy.'

Regina breathed deeply and composed herself. 'So, according to you, whether one's like this or like that, it's neither good nor bad? Would it be all the same to you whether I was stingy or cowardly?'

'I like you just as you are.' He smiled at her tenderly, but there was a tight feeling in Regina's throat. Did he not place any value on those virtues in which she took so much pride?

She stood up suddenly. 'Come and see your room.'

Fosca followed her. He scrutinized the room in silence; his face was expressionless. Regina pointed to the table on which a ream of white paper had been stacked. 'That's where you'll work,' she said.

'What will I work at?'

'Didn't we agree that you'd start writing again?'

'Did we agree to that?' he asked cheerfully. He stroked the red blotter, the virgin-white paper. 'I used to like to write. It'll help me pass the time while I'm waiting for you.'

'You mustn't write just to make the time pass.'

'No?'

'You once asked me to give you something to do, something you could do for me.' She looked at him attentively. 'Try to write a good play for me to act in.'

He looked perplexed as he fingered the paper. 'A play that you could act in?'

'Who knows? Maybe you'll write a masterpiece. And then we'll both be famous.'

'Is fame so important to you?'

'Nothing else matters.' she replied.

He looked at her and suddenly took her in his arms. 'Why shouldn't I be able to do what mortal men do?' he said, half angrily. 'I'll help you. I want to help you.'

He pressed her to him in a frenzy. In his eyes there was love as well as something akin to pity.

Regina wove her way through the chattering throng that had gathered in the vestibule of the theatre. 'We've been invited to go and drink champagne with Florence, but I don't suppose you're very keen, are you?'

'Not very,' Fosca said.

'Neither am I.' She was wearing a new suit and she knew she was looking attractive, but she had no desire to parade in front of these ephemeral men. 'What did you think of Florence?' she asked anxiously.

'She didn't affect me at all,' replied Fosca.

Regina smiled. 'I agree. She seems unable to put any feeling into the part.'

As she left the stuffy theatre, she felt happy to breath in the warm street air. It was a fine February day and there was already a hint of spring.

'I'm thirsty.'

'So am I,' Fosca said. 'Where shall we go?'

She thought for a moment. She had taken him to the little bar in Montmartre where she had first met Annie, and the café near the Place de l'Opéra where she used to gulp down a sandwich before going to Berthier's courses, and that place in Montparnasse where she lived when she was playing her first role. She thought of a restaurant along the Seine which she had discovered a few days after arriving in Paris.

'I know a charming spot out towards Bercy.'

'Let's go there,' he said.

He was always easy going. She hailed a taxi, they got in and he put his arm around her shoulders. He looked youthful in the well-cut suit she had chosen for him; he no longer looked as if he was wearing disguise: he looked just like any other man. Now he ate, drank, slept and made love; he looked and listened like a normal human being. Only occasionally was there a faint, disquieting glimmer in the depths of his eyes. The taxi stopped.

'Have you ever been here before?' she asked.

'Perhaps,' he replied. 'Everything has changed so much. In times gone by, this wasn't even Paris.'

They went inside a sort of chalet and sat down at a table on a narrow wooden terrace overlooking the river. A barge was moored beside the shore and, on board, a woman was doing her laundry and a dog was barking. On the far bank were low houses painted in green, yellow and red. In the distance there was a view of bridges and tall chimneys.

'It's nice here, isn't it?' Regina said.

'Yes, I like rivers.'

'I often used to come here, she said. 'I would sit at this table and I would study parts and dream of playing them one day. I drank lemonade – wine was too expensive and I was poor then.' She broke off. 'Fosca, are you listening to me?' she asked. One could never be quite sure he was really listening.

'Of course,' he said. 'You were poor and so you used to drink lemonade.' He stopped suddenly, his mouth half-open, as if an important idea had just occurred to him. 'Are you rich now?' he asked.

'I'll become rich.'

'You're not rich and I'm costing you money. You must find me a job quickly.'

'There's no hurry.' She smiled at him. She had no wish to have him spend his days in an office or a factory; she needed to have him near her and share every moment of his life with him. He was sitting there, contemplating the water, the barge, the low houses, and all these things which Regina had loved so much were now passing into eternity with her.

'But I'd like to have a job,' he insisted.

'First you must try to write that play you promised me. Have you thought about it at all?'

'Of course.'

'Do you have an idea?'

'I've got lots.'

'I knew you would!' she said cheerfully. She summoned the proprietor who was standing by the entrance. 'A bottle of champagne.' She turned back towards Fosca, 'You'll see,' she said, 'we'll do great things together.'

Fosca's face darkened; an unpleasant memory seemed to be passing through his mind. 'A lot of people have told me that.'

'But I'm not like the others,' she said fiercely.

'That's true,' he agreed quickly. 'You're not like the others.'

Regina filled the glasses. 'To our plans!'

'To our plans!'

As she drank, she studied him somewhat anxiously. She could never tell exactly what he was thinking.

'Fosca, if you hadn't met me, what would you have done?'

'I might have succeeded in falling asleep again. But that's not very likely. It would have needed an exceptional stroke of luck.'

'A stroke of luck?' she asked reproachfully. 'Are you sorry that you've come back to life again?'

'No,' he said.

'It's wonderful to be alive!'

'It is wonderful.'

They smiled at each other. Children could be heard shouting on the barge, and on another barge, or in one of the small, colourful houses, someone was playing a guitar. Dusk was falling, but a ray of sunlight still shone on the glasses of pale, clear wine. Fosca took Regina's hand, which she had placed on the table.

'Regina,' he said, 'I feel happy this evening.'

'Only this evening?'

'Ah! You can't imagine how new this is for me. There were times when I rediscovered hope, boredom, desire, but never this illusion of plenitude.'

'Is it only an illusion?' she asked.

'What does it matter? The point is, I want to believe in it.'

He leaned towards her and she could feel her lips respond to his immortal kiss. Her lips were those of a spoilt child, of a lonely girl, of a fulfilled woman. And that kiss, along with the image of all these things she loved, was engraving itself indelibly in Fosca's heart. 'A man with hands and with eyes, my companion, my lover,' she thought. 'And yet he's immortal, like a god.' The sun was now sinking rapidly in the sky. 'It's the same sun for him as it is for me.' The smell of water rose from the river, the guitar was playing in the distance, and all of a sudden, neither glory nor death, nothing except the violent impact of that moment, had any importance for her.

'Fosca,' she said, 'do you love me?'

'I love you.'

'Will you remember this moment?'

"Yes, Regina, I'll remember it.'

'Always?'

He gripped her hand more tightly.

'Say it: always.'

'This moment exists, it is ours. Let's not think of anything else.'

Regina turned off to the right. It was not her most direct route, but she was fond of this narrow little street with its dark gutters and its wooden beams which shored up the walls of ancient houses. She loved the warm, damp, spring night air and the big yellow moon laughing in the sky. Annie would be in bed, waiting for Regina's kiss before going to sleep; Fosca would be writing. From time to time, they would look at the clock. Regina should have been back from the theatre by now, they would think, but she wanted to prolong her walk through these streets that she loved, and where one day she would walk no longer.

She turned to the right again. There were so many men, so many women, who had breathed the sweetness of spring nights just as fervently and for whom the world no longer existed. Was there really no recourse against death? Could they not be brought to life again, just for an hour? She had forgotten her name, her past, her face. There was only the sky, the humid breeze and that indefinable bitterness in the tender evening air. 'I am neither myself, nor am I like them; yet they exist as much as I do.'

Regina turned to the left. 'But I am me. The moon shines in the same sky, but in every heart it's unique, unshared . . . Fosca will walk the streets thinking of me, but it won't be me. . . . Oh! Why can't we break this hard, transparent shell inside which each of us is enclosed? . . . Only one moon in only one heart. But which one? Fosca's or mine? . . . I wish I could stop being myself . . . To win everything, one must lose everything. Who made that law?'

She pushed open the street door and crossed the courtyard of the old building. There was a light in Annie's window; all the others were dark. Was Fosca already asleep? She climbed the stairs quickly and quietly turned her key in the lock. She heard laughter coming from behind Annie's door: both Annie's laugh and Fosca's. The blood rose to Regina's cheeks and she felt as though claws were clutching at her throat. She had not experienced such a wrench for a long time. She tiptoed over to the door.

'And every evening,' Annie was saying, 'I would take my

seat in the gods. I couldn't stand the thought of her acting for others and not seeing her myself.'

Regina shrugged her shoulders. 'Why is she always making a fuss,' she thought irritably. She knocked and pushed opened the door. Annie and Fosca were sitting in front of a plate full of pancakes and two glasses of white wine. Annie was wearing her purple dressing-gown and a pair of ear-rings; her cheeks were flushed with animation. 'It's a parody!' thought Regina in a flash of anger.

'You're both very jolly,' she said icily.

'Look at the beautiful pancakes we made, Princess,' said Annie. 'He's clever, you know. He tossed them without dropping a single one.' With a smile, she held out the plate to Regina. 'They're still hot.'

'No, thanks. I'm not hungry.' She looked at both of them with hate in her eyes. 'Is there no way of preventing them from existing without me? How can they dare? It's pure insolence!' she thought. There were times when one stood proudly on the summit of a solitary mountain and, in a single sweep, one looked down on a uniform world in which the lines and colours blended into a single, unbroken landscape. And at other times, one was down below, where it seemed that every patch of ground existed on its own account, separately, with its hills and valleys and its sloping terraces. To think that Annie was pouring out her memories to Fosca, and that he was listening!

'What were you talking about?'

'I was telling Fosca how I met you.'

'Again?' Regina sipped the wine. The pancakes looked warm and appetizing and she felt like eating one, which only increased her anger. 'That's her usual prattle. She has to reel it off to all my friends. Anyhow, it's not a particularly remarkable story. Annie is a romantic; you shouldn't believe everything she says.'

Tears welled up in Annie's eyes, but Regina pretended not to notice.

'I'm going to make you really cry,' she thought with satisfaction.

'I walked home,' said Regina nonchalantly. 'It was so nice out! Do you know what I've decided we'll do, Fosca? We'll go for a little trip into the country between performances.'

'That's a good idea,' said Fosca. He was calmly eating one pancake after another.

'You'll take me with you?' asked Annie.

It was the question Regina was waiting for. 'No,' she said, 'I want to spend a few days alone with Fosca. I've got a few stories to tell him too.'

'Why?' asked Annie. 'I won't be in your way. I used to go everywhere with you and you never thought I was any trouble.'

'In the past, perhaps,' said Regina.

'But what did I do?' Annie asked, bursting into tears. 'Why are you so hard on me? Why are you punishing me?'

'Don't talk like a child,' said Regina. 'You're too old and it no longer becomes you. I'm not punishing you. I just don't feel like taking you with us, that's all.'

'You're mean!' Annie cried. 'Mean!'

'You certainly won't make me change my mind by crying. And you look horribly ugly when you cry.' Regina glanced regretfully at the pancakes and yawned. 'I'm going to bed.'

'You're mean! Mean!' Annie was slumped down on the table, weeping.

Regina went to her room, took off her coat and began to let down her hair. 'He's there with her! He's consoling her!' she thought. She felt like crushing Annie under her heels.

She was already in bed when he knocked. 'Come in,' she called. He was smiling as he walked towards her.

'You didn't have to hurry,' she said sarcastically. 'Have you at least had time to finish the pancakes?'

'I'm sorry, but I couldn't leave Annie alone. She was so upset.'

'She cries easily,' Regina said with a laugh. 'Of course, she told you everything, I suppose. How she kept the till at the little theatre bar, and how I suddenly appeared, dressed as a gypsy with a patch over my eye.'

Fosca sat down at the foot of the bed. 'You shouldn't be angry with her. She's trying to exist, too.'

'She, too?'

'We're all trying,' he said.

And for a brief moment she saw that look in his eyes again, that had so frightened her in the garden of the hotel.

'Do you hold that against me?' she asked.

'I never hold anything against you.'

'You must think I'm mean.' She looked defiantly at Fosca. 'It's true. I don't like seeing other people happy and I enjoy making them bow to my will. Annie wouldn't be in the way. I'm not taking her purely out of meanness.'

'I understand,' he said gently.

She would have preferred him to look at her in horror, like Roger. 'But you're kind,' she said.

He shrugged his shoulders nonchalantly and she threw him a quick glance. What could one say of him? He was neither miserly nor generous, neither courageous nor fearful, neither bad nor good. Where he was concerned, these words lost all meaning. It even seemed extraordinary that his hair and his eyes had any colour.

'It's undignified spending an evening tossing pancakes with Annie,' she said.

He smiled. 'But the pancakes were good.'

'You've got better things to do.'

'What, for instance?'

'You haven't yet written the first scene of my play.'

'Oh, I didn't feel inspired this evening,' he said.

'You could always read. All those books I chose for you . . .'

'But they always tell the same story.'

She looked at him anxiously. 'Fosca! You're not going to go back to sleep, I hope!'

'No,' he replied. 'No.'

'You promised to help me. You said to me, "Whatever a mortal man can do, I can do."'

'Ah! That's the crux of the matter!' he replied.

❧

Regina jumped out of the taxi and rushed up the stairs; it was the first time Fosca had missed an appointment. She opened the door to her apartment and stood there, glued to the floor. Perched on top of a ladder, Fosca was cleaning the windows and singing.

'Fosca!'

He smiled. 'I washed all the windows.'

'What's got into you?'

'You told Annie this morning that the windows had to be washed.' With a rag in his hand, he climbed down the ladder. 'Look, aren't they well done?'

'You were supposed to meet me at four o'clock in the vestibule of the Pleyel. Did you forget?'

'Yes, I did forget,' he said in a confused voice. He wrung out the rag over a bucket. 'I got so involved in my work that I forgot all about it.'

'Well, now we've missed the concert,' Regina said irritably.

'There'll be others.'

She shrugged her shoulders. 'But I wanted to hear that one.'

'That one especially?'

'Especially. Go and get dressed,' she added. 'You can't stay in those clothes.'

'I wanted to dust the ceiling too. It's not very clean.'

'What is this obsession anyway?'

'I felt like helping you.'

'I don't need that sort of help.'

Fosca walked meekly to his room and Regina lit a cigarette. 'He's forgotten about me,' she thought. 'I alone existed for him and now he's forgetting me. Has he changed so quickly? What goes on in his head?' She felt worried as she paced back and forth across the room.

When Fosca reappeared in the drawing-room, she laughed as she asked: 'Do you enjoy doing the housework?'

'Yes, I do. When they made me sweep out the dormitories at the asylum, I felt very happy.'

'But why?'

'It keeps one busy.'

'There are other things to occupy your time with,' she said.

He looked up at the ceiling; there was a look of regret on his face. 'What I really need is for you to find me a job.'

Regina winced. 'Are you that bored?'

'I need to be given something to do.'

'Didn't I suggest . . . '

'I want to a job which doesn't require me to think.' He gazed round at the clean, transparent windows.

'Well, I hope you don't intend becoming a window cleaner.'

'Why not?'

In silence, she took a few steps across the room. 'Why not, after all?' she thought. 'What else did he have to do with himself?'

'If you have a job, we'll be separated all day long,'

'That's how people live,' he said, 'They're apart and then they see each other again.'

'But we're not like other people.'

Fosca's face darkened. 'You're right,' he said. 'Whatever I did, I could never be like everyone else.'

Regina looked at him uneasily. She loved him because he was immortal. And he loved her in the hope that he could become like a mortal once more. 'We'll never make a couple,' she thought.

'The trouble is, you don't try to take an interest in things that are going on now,' she said. 'You could read, go and look at paintings, come to concerts with me.'

'That's pointless.'

She put her hands on his shoulders. 'I'm not enough for you. Is that it?'

'I can't make your life mine.'

'You used to look at me, you used to say that I was all . . . '

'When you're alive, you're not satisfied with just looking.'

She thought a moment. 'Well, why don't you study,' she said. 'You could do something interesting. You could become an engineer or a doctor.'

'No, it takes too long.'

'Too long? Surely you have enough time?'

'I need something to do right now,' he said. 'I don't want to do anything that makes me question myself.' He looked entreatingly at Regina. 'Tell me to peel potatoes or to wash the sheets . . . '

'No,' she said.

'Why not?'

'It would only be a way of making you go back to sleep again and I want you to stay awake.' She took him by the hand. 'Come for a walk with me.'

He followed her obediently, but he stopped a moment at the door. 'Yet the ceiling did need cleaning,' he said regretfully.

'We've arrived,' said Regina.

'Already?'

'Of course. Trains are fast; much faster than carriages.

'I'd love to know what people do with all the time they now save,' said Fosca.

'You have to admit that a lot has been invented in the last hundred years.'

'Yes, but they're always inventing the same things.'

He looked gloomy. For some time now, he often looked gloomy. They walked along the platform in silence, past the entrance to the little station, and set off down the road. Fosca walked with his head down, kicking a stone as he went. Regina took his arm.

'Do look,' she said. 'I spent my childhood here; I love this place. Take a good look.'

Irises were blooming in the gardens of the thatched cottages and roses were climbing the walls of the low houses. In orchards, closed in by wooden fences, there were hens pecking away under the apple trees in blossom. Memories of her past rose up in Regina's heart like a bouquet of faded flowers returning to life. She remembered the climbing wisteria, the peacock's feathers, the scent of the phlox in the moonlit garden and all those impassioned tears: 'I shall be beautiful, I shall be famous.' At the foot of the hill, beyond the fields of golden wheat, there was a village, and around the small church were slate roofs gleaming in the sun. The bells were ringing. A horse was climbing the hill, pulling a cart, and a peasant, walking alongside, was holding a whip in his hand.

'Nothing has changed,' Regina said. 'What peace! You see, Fosca, for me, this is eternity. These quiet houses, the bells that will go on ringing till the end of the world, that old horse climbing the hill just as his ancestor did when I was a child.'

Fosca shook his head. 'No, that's not eternity.'

'Why not?'

'There won't always be villages, or carts, or old horses.'

'That's true,' she said, struck by the thought. She gazed round at the serene landscape lying motionless beneath the blue sky, still as a painting, as a poem. 'What will there be instead?' Regina asked.

'Large-scale cultivation, perhaps, with tractors and geo-metrical fields. Perhaps a new city, building sites, factories.'

'Factories . . .'

It was impossible to imagine. Only one thing was certain: that this countryside, which was older than any living memory, would one day disappear. Regina felt a wrench in her heart. She might have played her part in an eternity that was unchanging, but suddenly the world was nothing more than a parade of fleeting visions, and her hands were empty. She looked at Fosca. Could anyone's hands be emptier than his?

'I think I'm beginning to understand,' she said.

'Understand what?'

'The curse.'

They were walking side by side, but each in a world of their own. 'What can I do to teach him to see the world through my eyes?' she wondered. She had not imagined that it would be so difficult; instead of growing closer to her, it seemed that from day to day he drew further away. She pointed to a road on their right, shaded by tall oak trees. 'It's there,' she said.

With a surge of emotion she recognized the fields in flower, the barbed wire fence beneath which she used to crawl on her stomach, the fishing pond with its mossy water. It was all there, so close; her childhood, her departure for Paris, that dazzling feeling when she came home again. Slowly, she walked round the outside of the garden with its white fence. The gate was closed and the little front door locked. She jumped over the fence thinking 'Only one childhood, only one life – my life.' For her, time would stop one day, it had already stopped, shattering itself against the impenetrable wall of death. Her life was a large lake in which the world was reflected in pure, still images. The copper beech trees would forever sway in the wind, the phlox would exhale their sweet scents, the waters of the river would always murmur; and in the rustling of the leaves, in the blue of the tall cedars, in the perfumes of the flowers, the whole universe was held captive.

There was still time. She had to cry out to Fosca, 'Leave me alone! Alone with my memories, with my brief destiny, and resigned to being myself and to dying one day.' For a moment she stood still, facing the house with its closed shutters – alone, mortal and eternal. And then she turned her eyes to him. He was leaning against the white fence, looking at the beech trees and the cedars with that look which would never die, and once again time flew away into infinity, the pure images clouded over. Regina was carried away by the torrent; it was impossible to stop it. All one could hope to do was to stay afloat a little longer before being transformed into foam.

'Come,' she said.

He leaped over the wooden railings. She put her hand on his arm. 'This is where I was born,' she said. 'My room was the one above the laurel bushes. In my sleep, I could hear the water running in the fountain, and the smell of the magnolias used to seep in through the window.'

They sat down on the front steps. The stone was warm, and insects were buzzing around their heads. And as Regina spoke, the garden filled with ghosts. A little girl in a long, flowing dress was walking along the gravel paths; an older, much thinner girl was declaiming the imprecations of Camilla beneath the shade of the weeping willow. The sun was sinking in the sky and Regina continued to talk, eager to resuscitate, however briefly, those little, transparent creatures in whose bodies her own heart had once beaten.

Night had already fallen by the time she had stopped speaking. She turned to Fosca. 'Fosca, were you listening to me?'

'Of course.'

'Do you remember everything I said?'

He shrugged his shoulders. 'It's a story I've heard so many times.' She jumped up. 'No! It's not the same!'

'The same one, the only one.'

'It's not true!'

'Always the same efforts, the same failures,' he said wearily. 'They always begin all over again, one after the other. And I begin all over again, like the others. It will never end.'

'But I'm different," she said. 'If I weren't different, why would you love me? You do love me, don't you?'

'Yes,' he replied.

'And for you I'm unique?'

'Yes,' he said again. 'A woman who is unique like all women.'

'But this is me, Fosca! Can't you see me any more?'

'I see you. You're blonde, generous and ambitious. You have a horror of death.' He shook his head. 'Poor Regina!'

'Don't feel sorry for me!' she said. 'I forbid you to feel sorry for me.'

She turned and ran away.

'I must be going,' said Regina.

She looked wearily over to the door of the bar. On the other side of that door was a street which led down to the Seine and, across the river, her apartment, and Fosca sitting at his table and not writing. He would ask, 'Did the rehearsal go well?' and she would answer, 'Yes.' Then there would be silence again.

She held out her hand to Florence. 'Good-bye.'

'Have another glass of port,' Sanier said. 'You have plenty of time.'

'Time? Yes, I've got all the time in the world,' she murmured. Fosca did not watch clocks.

'I'm sorry the rehearsal went so badly,' she said.

'On the contrary, it's wonderful to watch you work,' said Florence.

'You've got some amazing ideas,' said Sanier.

They spoke to her gently, they proffered the plate of sandwiches, unostentatiously offered her cigarettes, and their eyes were full of caring. 'They don't bear any grudges,' she thought. And for once, she did not feel the pleasant ripple of contempt in her heart; she could no longer feel contempt for anyone.

'Have you really decided? You're actually leaving on Friday?' Regina asked.

'Yes, thank goodness,' said Florence. 'I can't take any more.'

'It's your own fault,' Sanier said reproachfully. He turned to Regina. 'She doesn't spare herself in everyday life any more than she does on the stage.'

Regina smiled understandingly. 'He looks at her in the same way Roger used to look at me,' she thought. He measured Florence's weariness, he shared her joys, her worries, he advised her; there was a warm place for her in his heart. They were a couple.

Regina stood up. 'I must go now.'

She was not made for these ready smiles, the tender chit-chat and that simple, mutual human understanding. She pushed open the door and was plunged into solitude. Alone, she crossed the Seine and walked towards the red building where Fosca was waiting. But it was no longer the proud solitude of former days; now she was just another woman lost beneath the sky.

Annie had gone out and Fosca's door was closed. Regina took off her gloves and stood where she was. The big table, the curtains, the knick-knacks on their shelves, they all seemed asleep. It was as though there had been a death in the house and as though all these objects had been so fearful that they had withdrawn from existence. Hesitantly, she took a step or two; the slightest movement seemed out of place. She took out a pack of cigarettes and put it back in her handbag. She had no desire to smoke, no desire to do anything. In the mirror, even her face appeared to be asleep. She pinned back a lock of hair and then walked over to Fosca's room and knocked on the door.

'Come in.'

He was sitting on the edge of his bed and, with a determined expression on his face, was knitting a long length of green wool.

'Did it go well?' he asked.

'Very badly,' she said curtly.

'It'll be better tomorrow,' he said in a comforting voice.

'No, it won't.'

'Eventually I'm sure it will get better.'

She shrugged her shoulders. 'Can't you stop what you're doing for a moment?'

'If you wish.' With a look of regret, he put the scarf down beside him.

'What have you been doing?' she asked.

'Just what you saw me doing.'

'And that play you promised me?'

'Ah! that play . . . ' he said, and in an apologetic tone added, 'I was hoping that things would turn out differently.'

'What things? What prevents you from working on it?'

'I can't.'

'You mean you don't want to.'

'I can't. I wanted to help you but I can't. What have I got to say to people?'

'Writing a play isn't so complicated,' she said impatiently.

'It seems easy to you because you're used to that world.'

'Try! You haven't even put pen to paper.'

'I'm trying,' he said. 'For a brief moment one of my characters begins to breathe, but he fades away immediately. They're born, they live, they die. That's all I can say about them.'

'Yet you've loved women. You've had friends.'

'Yes, I have recollections. But that's not enough.' He closed his eyes. He seemed to be desperately trying to remember something. 'It takes a lot of strength, a lot of pride or a lot of love to believe that what one man does has any importance, or that life can conquer death.'

She drew close to him. 'Fosca, is my fate really of no importance to you?' There was a lump in her throat; she was afraid of what he might say.

'You shouldn't ask me that question.'

'Why not?'

'You shouldn't worry about what I think. That's a weakness.'

'A weakness?' she said. 'Would it be braver to run away?'

'I once knew a man,' Fosca said. 'He didn't run away. He looked me in the eye, he listened to what I had to say. But he made up his own mind.'

'You speak of him with a great deal of respect,' she said. She felt jealous of this stranger. 'Wasn't he also a poor man trying in vain to exist?' she asked.

'He did what he wanted to do and he expected nothing.'

'Is that what's important, then – to do what you want to do?'

'It was important for him.'

'And for you?'

'He didn't worry about me.'

'But was he right or wrong?'

'I can't answer for him.'

'It sounds as though you admire him.'

He shook his head. 'I'm incapable of feeling admiration.' Regina took a few steps across the room. She felt abandoned. 'And me?' she asked.

'You?'

'Am I just another wretched woman to you?'

'You think too much about yourself. It's not good.'

'What should I think about?'

'Ah! that I don't know,' he said.

Regina stepped down from the stage. Fosca was sitting in the shadows at the very back of the empty theatre, and as she walked over to meet him, a familiar voice stopped her: 'Regina!' She turned round: it was Roger.

'I hope you don't mind my coming,' he said. 'Laforêt invited me and I was so keen to see your Bérénice . . .'

'Why should I mind?' She looked at him in astonishment. She had imagined that she would be upset at seeing him again – lately, everything to do with her past seemed to unsettle her – but Roger looked both familiar and indifferent.

'Regina,' he said, 'you're a splendid Bérénice. You can play tragedy just as well as you do comedy. I'm quite sure now that you'll soon be the leading actress in Paris.'

His voice quavered slightly and a corner of his mouth twitched nervously. He was deeply moved. She looked towards the rear of the theatre, at the seat which Fosca had just left. With all his power of memory, what had he seen? Had he understood at last that she was unlike any other woman?

'It's very kind of you to think so,' she said. She realized that they had been looking at each other for a long time without speaking.

Roger studied her with a careful, anxious expression. 'Are you happy?' he asked quietly.

'Yes, of course,' she replied.

'You look tired . . . '

'It's all these rehearsals,' she said. She felt embarrassed by the way he stared; she was no longer accustomed to being scrutinized so minutely.

'Have I become ugly?'

'No. But you've changed.'

'Perhaps.'

'In the past you'd have been furious if I'd said that you had changed. You longed to remain just as you were.'

'Well, that's because I've changed.' She forced herself to smile. 'I have to say good-bye now. Someone's waiting for me.'

He held her hand for an instant. 'Will we see each other again? When?'

'Whenever you want. Just give me a ring,' she said indifferently.

Fosca was waiting for her at the theatre door.

'Forgive me,' she said. 'I was held up.'

'You don't have to apologize. I like waiting.' He smiled. 'What a lovely evening! Shall we walk home?'

'No, I'm tired.'

They got into a taxi. She was silent. She wanted him to speak spontaneously, but he said nothing the whole journey. When they arrived at the apartment, they went straight to her bedroom and she began to undress. Still he said nothing.

'Well, Fosca,' she said, 'did you enjoy this evening?'

'I always like to watch you act.'

'But did I act well?'

'I suppose so,' he answered.

'You suppose so, but you're not sure?'

He did not answer.

'Fosca, did you see Elisa Rachel act in the old days?'

'Yes.'

'Was she a better actress? Was she much better than me?'

He shrugged his shoulders. 'I don't know.'

'But you *must* know,' she said.

'Acting well, acting badly – I don't know what those words mean,' he said impatiently.

There was an empty feeling in Regina's heart. 'Wake up, Fosca! Don't you remember? You used to come to watch me every evening. You seemed fascinated. Once you told me you felt like crying.'

'Yes,' Fosca said. He smiled cheerfully. 'I do like to see you act.'

'But why? Isn't it because I'm a good actress?'

Fosca looked at her tenderly. 'When you act, you seem to have such faith in your own existence! I saw the same thing in two or three women at the asylum. But they believed only in themselves. For you, other people exist too, and there were times when you even succeeded in making me exist.'

'What!' Regina exclaimed. 'That's all you saw in Rosalind, in Bérénice? Is that all the talent you see in me?' She bit her lip; she felt like bursting into tears.

'That's not so bad,' said Fosca. Not everyone can be successful at pretending to exist.'

'But its not pretence,' she said disconsolately. 'It's true. I do exist!'

'Oh! you're not so sure of it as you'd like to believe,' he said. 'If you were, you wouldn't have insisted so much on taking me to the theatre with you.'

'I *am* sure!' she said furiously. 'I exist, I have talent and I shall be a great actress. You're blind!'

He smiled and said nothing.

'How does it look?' asked Annie. She was carefully laying pieces of scaly pineapple in bowls filled with crushed ice. Regina glanced at the table. Everything was in place: the flowers, the crystal glasses, the *hors d'oeuvres*, the sandwiches.

'It looks very nice to me,' she replied.

With a fork, Regina began to whisk a mixture of raw egg yolks and melted chocolate. Florence's parties were always carefully planned, but it was easy to estimate the cost of the vintage wines and top quality *petit fours* which she invariably served – expensive, impersonal, assembly-line items. Regina wanted this party to be a masterpiece, one that could not be matched. She liked to entertain. Throughout the entire evening, the furnishings among which she spent so much of her life would be reflected in their eyes; they would eat the delicacies that she had so painstakingly prepared; they would listen to the records she had chosen for them. Throughout the evening, she would reign over their pleasures. She beat the eggs energetically and the cream began to thicken in the bottom of the bowl.

From the front room came the sound of a monotonous, relentless pacing. 'Oh! How he irritates me!' she exclaimed.

'Do you want me to say something to him?'

'No . . . It's not worth it.'

For over an hour he had been pacing the floor like a bear in a cage, in a cage in eternity. She was beating eggs while he paced to and fro. Drop by drop, second by second, the black, rich, tasty mixture accumulated in the bottom of the bowl, while every one of his footsteps vanished into thin air without leaving a trace. *As You Like It, Bérénice*, the contract for *The Tempest* . . . Day after day, she patiently built up her future. And he came and went, cancelling out each of the steps he had just taken. For her, everything would be cancelled out at a single stroke.

'Finished,' she said. 'I'm going to get dressed.'

She slipped into her long, black taffeta dress and chose a necklace from her jewel box. 'Tonight I'll wear my hair in plaits,' she said aloud. For some time lately, she had adopted the habit of speaking aloud to herself. The doorbell rang; the guests were beginning to arrive. She slowly plaited her hair. 'Tonight, I want to show them my real face.' She looked in the mirror and smiled at herself; the smile froze. This face which she had so loved now seemed like a mask; it no longer belonged to her. Her body, too, had become a stranger to her – a mannequin in a shop-window. She smiled again, and again it was the mannequin who smiled back from the mirror. She turned around; in a minute she would have to start putting on faces.

She opened the door. In the room, the table lights were lit, and sitting around in armchairs and on the sofa were Sanier, Florence, Dulac and Laforêt. Fosca was sitting among them and was talking in a cheerful voice, while Annie served cocktails. Everything seemed real. With a smile, she offered them her hand and they smiled back.

'How beautiful you look in that dress!' said Florence.

'You're the one who's looking ravishing tonight.'

'These cocktails are wonderful.'

'They're a concoction of my own.'

They drank their cocktails and looked at Regina. The doorbell rang again, and again she smiled, and they smiled, and looked, and listened. In their benevolent, malevolent, captivated eyes, her dress, her face, the furnishings in the room, all glowed like a thousand little flames. And everything still seemed real. A brilliant party! If only she had been able to avoid looking at Fosca . . .

She turned her head away. She was sure of it: his eyes, those eyes full of pity which stripped her bare, were staring at her. He could see the mannequin, he could see the comedy.

She took a plate of cakes from the table and passed it around. 'Help yourself.'

Dulac bit into a cream puff and his mouth filled up with the thick, dark cream. 'A moment of my life,' Regina thought, 'a precious moment of my life is in Dulac's mouth. They're devouring my life with their mouths, with their eyes. Well, who cares?'

'What's wrong?' said an affectionate voice. It was Sanier.

'Everything,' replied Regina.

'Tomorrow you're signing the contract to do *The Tempest;* the opening nights of *Bérénice* have been a triumph; and you say that everything is wrong.'

'I have a perverse character.'

Sanier's expression became serious. 'On the contrary.'

'On the contrary?'

'I don't like contented people.'

He looked at her so tenderly that a little hope was rekindled in her heart. She felt suffocated by the desire to use words that were sincere and to make this moment, at least, true.

'I thought you despised me,' she said.

'Me?'

'Yes. When I told you about Mauscot and Florence. That was cheap . . . '

'I don't believe anything you do could be cheap.'

She smiled and a new flame rose up in her. 'If I wanted to . . . ' She had a sudden desire to feel herself burning in that scrupulous, passionate heart.

'I've always thought that you judged me harshly.'

'You were wrong.'

She looked him straight in the face. 'What do you really think of me?'

He reflected a moment. 'There's something tragic about you.'

'What?'

'Your feeling for the absolute. You were made to believe in God and to spend your life in a convent.'

'There are too many with that vocation,' she replied, 'too many saints. God would have had to love only me.'

All at once the flame died out. He was just a few feet away from her, watching her. He watched Sanier looking at her, saw her looking at Sanier, trying to set his heart afire. He saw the interplay of words and glances, the play of mirrors, empty mirrors, reflecting only each other's emptiness. Abruptly, she reached for a glass of champagne.

'I'm thirsty,' she said.

She emptied the glass, then filled it again. Roger would have said, 'Don't drink so much,' and she would have drunk and smoked, and her head would have grown heavy with feelings of revulsion and rebellion, and all the noise. But he said nothing, only watched and thought: 'She's trying, she's trying.' And it was true; she was trying. She was playing the game of being mistress of the house, the game of glory, the game of seduction – they were all one single game: the game of existence.

'I see you're enjoying yourself,' she said to Fosca.

'The time is passing.'

'I know you're making fun of me, but you don't intimidate me.'

She looked at him defiantly. In spite of him, in spite of his sympathetic smile, she wanted to feel the burning heat of her life once more. She felt like tearing off her clothes and dancing naked; she felt like murdering Florence. What happened afterwards was unimportant. Even if it were only for a minute, only for a second, she wanted to be a flame that would rip through the night. She began to laugh. If, in a single moment, she were able to destroy both the past and the future, she would know for certain that that moment existed. She jumped up onto the sofa, raised her glass and said in a loud voice, 'My dear friends . . . '

The faces all turned towards her.

' . . . the moment has come for me to tell you why I've asked you all here this evening. It's not to celebrate signing the contract for *The Tempest* . . . ' She smiled at Dulac. 'I'm sorry, Monsieur Dulac, but I'm not going to sign the contract.'

Dulac's face hardened and Regina smiled triumphantly. There was an expression of amazement in everyone's eyes.

'I'm not going to make this film, nor any other film. And I'm dropping out of *Bérénice*. I'm retiring from the theatre. I drink to the end of my career!'

One minute, no more than a minute, but during that minute she existed. They stared at her in astonishment and they looked rather frightened. She was the lightning, the torrent, the avalanche, the chasm which suddenly opened under their feet and from which rose a great feeling of panic and anxiety. She existed.

'Regina! Have you gone crazy?' said Annie.

Everyone was speaking, speaking at her: 'Why? . . . Is it possible? . . . It's not true! . . . ' And Annie, deeply upset, clung to her arm.

'Drink with me!' Regina cried. 'Drink to the end of my career!' She drank and began to laugh loudly. 'A beautiful ending!'

She looked at Fosca, she defied him. She was burning, she existed. She threw down the glass and it shattered on the floor. He was smiling and she was naked to her very bones. He tore away all her masks, saw through all her gestures, her words, her smiles. She was nothing but the beating of wings in the middle of a void. 'She's trying, she's trying.' And he knew, too, who she was trying for. Behind all the words, the gestures, the smiles, lay the same deceit, the same void.

'What a comedy!' she laughed.

'Regina, you've had too much to drink,' Sanier said gently. 'Why don't you rest for a while?'

'I'm not drunk,' she said cheerfully. 'Everything is as clear as day.' Still laughing, she pointed to Fosca. 'I see everything through his eyes.'

She stopped laughing. With his eyes, she could see through this new comedy, this comedy of self-conscious laughter and hopeless words. The words caught in her throat. Everything was fading away. The room grew silent.

'Come and lie down,' said Annie.

'Come,' said Sanier.

She followed them. 'Make them leave,' she said to Annie. 'Make them all leave!' And angrily, she added, 'And you two, leave me alone!'

She stood motionless in the centre of the room and then, distraught, she spun round. She looked at the black masks on the walls, the statuettes on the shelf, the old marionettes in their tiny theatre. And in those precious objects, she saw her whole past, the years of self-love. Now they seemed to her nothing but cheap trash.

She threw the masks to the floor. 'Cheap trash!' she repeated aloud as she trampled on them. She threw down the statuettes and the marionettes and stamped on them, crushing all the old lies.

Someone touched her shoulder. 'Regina,' said Fosca, 'what's the point?'

'I don't want any more lies.' She fell into a chair and buried her head in her hands. She was completely exhausted. 'I am a lie,' she muttered.

There was a long silence and then he said, 'I'm going.'

'Going? Where?'

'Far away from you. You'll forget me and you'll be able to start to live again.'

She looked at him in terror. She was nothing now. He had to stay near her. 'No' she said. 'It's too late. I won't forget. I'll never forget anything.'

'Poor Regina! What are we to do?'

'There's nothing to do. Just don't go away.'

'All right, I won't go.'

'Never,' she said. 'You must never leave me.'

She threw her arms around his neck, pressed her lips against his and her tongue slipped into his mouth. Fosca's hands pulled her to him and she shuddered. With other men, she felt only their caresses, never their hands, whereas Fosca's hands truly existed, and in them she became easy prey. Feverishly, he threw off his clothes, as if time, even for him, were slipping by too rapidly, as if every second were a treasure which must not be wasted. He clasped her in his arms and a furnace glowed inside her, sweeping away words, images. There was nothing except a great, dark shudder which shook the bed. He was inside her and she was the prey of that desire which is as old as the world; a wild, new desire that she alone could satisfy, and which was not a desire for her own satisfaction, but for everything. She was this desire, this burning void, this deep yearning; she was everything. The moment blazed; eternity was conquered. Feeling tense, and tingling with an expectant, anguished passion, she breathed to the same panting rhythm as Fosca. He groaned and she dug her nails into his flesh, ripped apart by the triumphant, hopeless spasm in which everything found completion and fell apart; she felt she had been torn from the burning peace of silence, and thrown back into herself once more: the same futile and betrayed Regina. She wiped the perspiration from her forehead; her teeth were chattering.

'Regina,' he said gently. He kissed her hair, stroked her cheeks. 'Sleep, Regina. We're allowed sleep.'

His voice was so full of sadness that she was on the point of opening her eyes, of speaking to him: was there no way out? But she knew that he had already read her thoughts; she knew that he had experienced too many other nights, too many other women. She turned over and pressed her cheek against the pillow.

Regina awoke to the dawn light. She stretched out an arm. There was no one lying next to her.

'Annie!' she called out.

'Yes, Regina.'

'Where's Fosca?'

'He went out,' Annie replied.

'Went out? At this time of day? Where did he go?'

Annie avoided her eyes. 'He left a note for you.'

She took the note, a scrap of paper folded in half:

'Good-bye dear Regina. Forget I ever lived. After all, it is you who are alive and I count for nothing.'

'Where is he?' She jumped out of bed and hurriedly began to dress. 'It can't be! I told him not to leave.'

'He left during the night,' said Annie.

'Why did you let him go? Why didn't you wake me up?' Regina said, seizing Annie by the arm. 'Are you a complete idiot? Why?'

'I didn't know.'

'What didn't you know? He gave you this note. You read it, didn't you?' She looked angrily at Annie. 'You let him leave on purpose. You knew and you let him go. You bitch! Bitch!'

'Yes,' Annie said. 'It's true. But he had to leave: it was for your own good.'

'For my own good! So the two of you plotted together for my good!' She shook Annie violently. 'Where is he?'

'I don't know.'

'You don't know!' Regina stared intensely at Annie and thought, 'If she really doesn't know, there's nothing left for me but to die.' In a flash, she sprang over to the window.

'Tell me where he is or I'll jump.'

'Regina!'

'Don't move or I'll jump. Where is Fosca?'

'At Lyons, in the hotel where you spent a few days together.'

'Are you telling me the truth?' asked Regina distrustfully. 'Why should he have told you?'

'I wanted to know. I . . . I was frightened of you.'

'So he asked your advice!' Regina put on her coat. 'I'm going to look for him.'

'I'll go and look for him for you. You have to be at the theatre this evening.'

'I told you yesterday that I was giving up the theatre.'

'But you had been drinking. Let me go. I promise I'll bring him back.'

'I'll bring him back myself,' said Regina. She opened the door. 'And if I don't find him, you'll never see me again.'

❧

Fosca was sitting at a little table on the terrace of the hotel. There was a bottle of white wine in front of him and he was smoking. When he saw Regina, he smiled. There was no trace of astonishment on his face.

'Ah! Here already!' he said. 'Poor Annie! She didn't hold out for long.'

'Fosca, why did you leave?' she asked.

'Annie asked me to.'

'She asked you!' Regina sat down opposite him and said angrily, 'But I asked you to stay.'

He smiled. 'Why should I obey you rather than her?'

Regina poured herself a glass of wine and gulped it down. Her hands were trembling. 'Don't you love me any more?' she asked.

'I love her, too,' he said softly.

'But not in the same way.'

'How can I make a distinction? Poor Annie!'

Regina felt a horrible nausea in the pit of her stomach. 'In the fields, there are millions of blades of grass, all equal, all identical . . . '

'There was a time when only I existed for you . . . '

'Yes, and then you opened my eyes . . . '

She hid her face in her hands. A blade of grass, nothing but a blade of grass. Everybody believed they were unique, preferred themselves above others. And they were all wrong, she as much as anyone else.

'Come back,' she pleaded.

'No. It's no good. I thought I could become a man again – it happened to me before, after other long periods of sleep – but I couldn't. I can't any more.'

'Try! Just once more.'

'I'm too tired.'

'Then I'm ruined,' she said dejectedly.

'Yes, I realize that. It's wretched for you.' He leaned towards her. 'I'm sorry. I made a mistake. I shouldn't make mistakes any more,' he said with a little laugh. 'I'm old enough to know better. But I don't think they can be avoided. When I'm ten thousand years older, I'll still make mistakes. You never really learn.'

She grabbed Fosca's hands. 'All I ask is twenty years of your life. Twenty years! What's twenty years to you?'

'You don't understand,' he said.

'No, I don't understand! If I were in your position, I'd try to help people; in your position . . . '

He cut her short. 'But you're not in my position.' He shrugged his shoulders. 'No one can imagine what it's like. As I told you, immortality is a curse.'

'You've made it a curse.'

'No. I fought. You don't know how I fought!'

'But why? Explain it to me.'

'It's impossible. I'd have to tell you everything.'

'Very well' she said. 'We've got time, haven't we? We've got all the time in the world.'

'What's the point?' he asked.

'Do it for me, Fosca. Perhaps it will seem less terrible when I understand.'

'It's always the same story. It will never change. I'll have to drag it around with me forever.' He looked around. 'All right, I'll tell it to you,' he said.

BOOK I

I was born in Italy on the 17th of May 1279 in a palazzo in the city of Carmona. My mother died shortly after my birth and I was brought up by my father who taught me to ride a horse and shoot with a bow and arrow. A monk was put in charge of my education and he tried to instill a fear of God in me. But from the earliest age, I've thought only of earthly matters and I've never been frightened of anything.

My father was handsome and strong, and I admired him. When I saw Francesco Rienzi, with his knock-kneed legs, ride by on his black horse, I would ask in astonishment, 'Why is he the ruler of Carmona?'

My father would look at me gravely. 'Never wish to be in his place,' he replied.

The people hated Francesco Rienzi. It was said that he wore a thick coat of mail beneath his clothes, and there were always ten guards protecting him. In his room, at the foot of his bed, lay a large chest secured by three padlocks, and this chest was filled with gold. One after the other, he accused the noblemen of the city of treason and confiscated their goods. A scaffold was erected in the main square and several times each month a head would roll to the ground. He took money from the poor as well as from the rich. Whenever I strolled in the city with my old nurse, she would point out the hovels in the district where the weavers lived, the children with their scabby buttocks, the beggars sitting on the cathedral steps, and she would say to me, 'The duke is responsible for all this misery.'

Carmona was built high on an arid rock; there were no fountains in the squares. Men would go by foot to the surrounding plains to fill their goatskin bags, and water cost as much as bread.

One morning the bells of the cathedral sounded the death-knell and the façades of all the houses were draped in black. Sitting astride a horse, alongside my father, I rode in the procession which was accompanying the remains of Francesco Rienzi to his final resting place. Bertrando Rienzi, dressed entirely in black, led the funeral cortege of his brother. The rumour spread that he had poisoned him.

The streets of Carmona were filled with the clamour of festivity. The scaffold opposite the palace was dismantled; the lords, dressed in silks and brocades, rode in cavalcade with their retinues; tournaments took place in the main square. The sound of hunting horns and the joyous barking of dogs echoed across the plains, and in the evening, the ducal palace glowed with a thousand lights.

But Bertrando soon began confiscating the wealth of the rich merchants and noblemen, and threw them into dungeons where they slowly rotted away. The chest with the three padlocks was always empty; new taxes were constantly being levied against the miserable artisans, and in alleys rank with the stench of plague, children fought over scraps of black bread. The people grew to hate Bertrando Rienzi.

Friends of Pietro d'Abruzzi often gathered at night in my father's house and whispered amongst each other by torchlight. Scuffles broke out daily between his supporters and those of Rienzi's. Even the children of Carmona were divided into two camps, and beneath the ramparts, among the brushwood and rocks, we used to fight with stones, some shouting, 'Long live the duke!' and others, 'Down with the tyrant!' We fought long and hard, but I was never satisfied with these games; the vanquished enemy rose again, the dead would come to life. The day after a battle, the victors and the vanquished found themselves unharmed. It was no more than a game, and I kept asking myself impatiently, 'How much longer am I going to be a child?'

I was fifteen years old when fires of celebration were lit at every crossroad. Pietro d'Abruzzi had stabbed Bertrando Rienzi on the steps of the ducal palace. The crowd carried him aloft in triumph. He spoke to the people from a balcony, promising them relief from their sufferings. The doors of the prisons were opened, the old magistrates were dismissed, the Rienzi faction driven from the city. For several weeks there was dancing in the squares, people began to laugh again, and in my father's house we began to speak in normal tones again. I looked in wonder at Pietro d'Abruzzi who had plunged a real dagger into a man's heart and delivered his city.

One year later, the noblemen of Carmona donned their heavy armour and set off across the plains at a gallop. The Genoese, spurred on by the exile faction, had invaded our lands. They tore our army to shreds and Pietro d'Abruzzi was killed by a lance. Under Orlando Rienzi's rule, Carmona became Genoa's vassal. At the beginning of every season, wagons laden with gold passed through the main square and, our hearts seething with rage, we watched as they disappeared on the road to the sea. In sombre workshops, the weavers' looms hummed day and night, and yet the townspeople walked about barefoot, dressed in tattered clothing.

'Can nothing be done?' I asked.

My father and Gaetano d'Agnolo would shake their heads in silence. For three years, day after day, I asked the same question, and they only shook their heads. One day, Gaetano d'Agnolo smiled at last.

'Perhaps,' he said, 'perhaps something can be done.'

Orlando Rienzi wore a coat of mail under his doublet and he spent almost every day behind a barred window in his palace. Whenever he set foot outside, there were twenty guards to protect him. Servants tasted the wine in his glass, the meats on his plate. However, one Sunday morning while he was in the cathedral attending mass, the soldiers of his escort having been bribed, four young men sprang upon him and slit his throat. They were Giacomo d'Agnolo, Lorenzo Vezzani, Ludovico Pallaïo and myself. His body was dragged to the portico of the cathedral and thrown to the crowd, who tore it to pieces while the tocsin rang. Suddenly, all of Carmona's townsmen appeared in the streets carrying arms. The Genoese and their followers were massacred.

My father declined the opportunity to rule the city and we appointed Gaetano d'Agnolo our leader. He was an upright and prudent man. He had negotiated secretly with the condottiere, Pietro Faenza, whose armies had immediately stationed themselves at the foot of our walls. Supported by these mercenary troops, we resolutely awaited the Genoese. For the first time in my life, I took part in a real battle between men. The dead did not come to life again, the vanquished fled in disorder; every thrust of my lance helped save Carmona. That day, I would have died with a smile on my lips, certain of having contributed to the triumphant future of my city.

For days, fires of celebration blazed at every crossroad, there was dancing in the squares and processions circled the ramparts chanting *Te Deums*. And then the weavers began to weave again, the beggars to beg, and the water bearers to trudge through the streets, bent under the weight of their loads. The wheat grew poorly in the devastated plains and the bread that was eaten was black. The townspeople now wore shoes and their clothing was made of new material; the old magistrates were removed from office; but otherwise, Carmona remained unchanged.

'Gaetano d'Agnolo is too old,' Lorenzo Vezzani often told me impatiently.

Lorenzo was my friend; he excelled in all physical activities and I sensed in him something of that same fire which devoured me. One night, in the course of a banquet to which we had been invited, we seized old Gaetano and forced him to abdicate. He and his son were both exiled and Leonardo took up the reins.

The people had no longer expected anything from Gaetano and they joyfully greeted the birth of a new hope. The old magistrates were replaced by new men and there was feasting in the squares. It was springtime. The almond trees were in blossom on the plains and the sky had never seemed more blue. I would often ride my horse up to the hills which blocked out the horizon, and I gazed over the vast stretch of green and pink which extended to the foot of another line of blue hills. 'Beyond those hills, there are other plains and other hills,' I thought. And then I looked back at Carmona perched upon its rock, bristling with its eight proud towers. This was where the heart of this vast world beats, and one day soon my city would fulfill its destiny.

The seasons passed and the almond trees blossomed anew. Festivals continued to take place beneath the blue sky, but not a single fountain spouted in the squares; the old hovels remained, and the wide, smooth streets and white palaces existed only in my dreams. I questioned Vezzani.

'What are you waiting for?'

He looked at me in astonishment. 'I'm not waiting for anything.'

'Why don't you act?'

'Haven't I acted?' he asked.

'Why did you take power if you weren't going to do anything with it?'

'I took it; I have it. That's enough for me.'

'Ah,' I said fervently, 'if only I were in your place!'

'Well?'

'I would form powerful alliances for Carmona, I would undertake wars, I would enlarge our territory, I would build palaces . . .'

'All that would require a great deal of time,' said Vezzani.

'You have the time.'

His expression suddenly grew solemn. 'You know very well I don't.'

'The people love you.'

'They won't love me for long.' He put his hand on my shoulder. 'These great enterprises of which you speak, how many years it would take to bring them to fruition! And how many sacrifices they would require! It would not be long before I was hated and destroyed.'

'You can defend yourself.'

'I don't want to be like Francesco Rienzi,' he said. 'Besides, you know very well that all precautions are useless.' He smiled with that smile I liked so well. 'I'm not afraid of death. But at least I shall have lived for a few years.'

He was right; he was a man condemned. Two years later, Geoffredo Massigli had him strangled by his henchmen. He was a crafty man who appeased Carmona's noblemen by according them great privileges; he ruled no better nor worse than anyone else. In any case, how could one expect a single man to control the city long enough to bring about prosperity and glory?

My father was growing old. He asked me to find a wife so that he might smile upon his grandchildren while still in this world. I married Caterina d'Alonzo, a girl of noble birth, who was both beautiful and pious, and whose hair gleamed like pure gold. She bore me a son whom we called Tancredi. Not long afterwards, my father died. He was buried in the cemetery overlooking Carmona and I watched as the coffin was lowered into the grave. It was as if I were watching the coffin that contained my own desiccated body, the grave where my useless past was buried, and I felt as if my heart were caught in a vice. 'Will I die like him, without having accomplished anything?' I wondered. During the days that followed, whenever I saw Geoffredo Massigli ride past, my hand tightened on the hilt of my sword; but what good would it do, I thought, since they would only kill me, too.

At the beginning of the year 1311, the Genoese set out to attack Florence. They were rich, powerful and devoured by ambition. They had conquered Pisa, they wanted to become masters of all northern Italy, and perhaps their arrogant plans went even further than that. They sought an alliance with us in order to crush Florence more easily and then subdue us in turn; they asked for men, horses, provisions, fodder and free passage through our territory. With great pomp, Geoffredo Massigli received their ambassador. It was said that the Genoese were prepared to buy his support with gold, and he was a greedy man.

On the 12th of February at two o'clock in the afternoon, while a magnificent procession escorted the Genoese emissary towards the plains, Geoffredo Massigli, who was riding past my window, was struck in the heart by an arrow. I was the best archer in Carmona. At the same moment, my men raced through the city, shouting 'Death to the Genoese!' and the townsmen, whom I had secretly alerted, invaded the ducal palace. That evening I was prince of Carmona.

I had every man armed; the peasants left the plains and entrenched themselves behind the ramparts, bringing their wheat and livestock with them; I sent messengers to Carlo Malatesta, the condottiere, asking him to come to our aid. And I shut the gates of Carmona.

'Send them back home,' Caterina pleaded. 'For the love of God, for the sake of your love for me and for our child, send them back home.'

She fell to her knees before me and tears streamed down her cheeks which were marbled with red blotches. I put my hand on her head. Her hair was dull and brittle, her eyes colourless, her body thin and grey beneath the coarse fabric of her dress.

'Caterina, you know very well that the granaries are empty.'

'You can't do it! It's inhuman!' she said in a distraught voice.

I turned my head away. Through the half-opened window, the cold air from the streets blew into the palace – and the silence. In silence, the black procession advanced along the main street, and men standing in the doorways of their houses and leaning out of windows, silently watched it pass. All that could be heard was the soft shuffling of the crowd and the metallic click of horses' hoofs.

'Send them back home,' she said.

I looked at Giovanni, then Ruggiero. 'Is there any other solution?'

'No,' said Giovanni.

Ruggiero shook his head. 'No.'

'Then why don't you get rid of me, too?' asked Caterina.

'You're my wife,' I replied.

'I'm another useless mouth. My place is with them. Ah, what a coward I am!' She buried her face in her hands. 'Dear God, forgive us! Forgive us!'

They came down from the market place, they came up from the lower part of town.

A cold sun glazed the red-tiled roofs which were separated at intervals by dark crevices. Along each crevice, they advanced in little groups, surrounded by mounted guards.

'Dear God, forgive us! Dear God, forgive us!'

'Stop these litanies,' I said. 'I know that God is protecting us.'

Caterina rose and went to the window. 'All these men!' she said. 'They just watch and say nothing!'

'They want to save Carmona,' I said. 'They love their city.'

'Don't they know what the Genoese will do to their wives?'

The procession emerged in the square: women, children, old men, the infirm. They came from the highways and the byways, carrying small bundles in their hands – they had not yet lost all hope. Some of the women were bent beneath heavy loads, as if blankets, pots and happy memories would still be of use on the other side of the ramparts. The guards had pulled up their horses, and behind the barrier they formed, the great pink enclave slowly filled up with a black and silent crowd.

'Raimondo, send them back home,' Caterina pleaded again. 'The Genoese won't let them pass. They'll all die of cold and hunger in ditches.'

'What did the soldiers get to eat this morning?' I asked.

'Boiled bran and grass soup,' Ruggiero answered.

'And this is the first day of winter! How can I worry about women and old men?'

I looked out the window. A cry broke the silence. 'Maria! Maria!' A young man was shouting. He crossed the square, dashed under the horses' bellies and forced his way through the crowd. 'Maria!' Two soldiers seized him and threw him back to the other side of the barrier. He struggled.

'Raimondo!' Caterina cried. 'Raimondo, it would be better to surrender the city.' With both hands, she gripped the bars of the windows. She looked as if she were about to fall, crushed beneath a heavy weight.

'Do you know what they did to Pisa?' I asked. 'The walls razed to the ground, all the men in slavery. Better to cut off one's arm than to perish.' I looked up at the high, white stone towers which rose proudly above the red roofs. 'If we refuse to surrender Carmona, they'll never be able to take her.'

The soldiers had released the young man and he stood motionless beneath the windows of the palace. He raised his head and shouted, 'Death to the tyrant!' No one moved. The cathedral bells began to ring; they tolled the death-knell.

Caterina turned to me. 'One of them will kill you,' she said vehemently.

'I know.'

I pressed my forehead against the window-pane. 'They will kill me.' I felt the chill of the coat of mail against my chest. They had all worn a coat of mail and none of them ruled more than five years. Upstairs, in the icy attic, shut up among their flasks and philters, the doctors had been searching for months for an antidote to poisons but they had found nothing. I knew they would never find anything. I was a condemned man.

'Caterina,' I said, 'swear to me that if I die you'll never surrender the city.'

'No,' she retorted, 'I will not swear to it!'

I walked over to the fireplace. Tancredi was lying on a rug in front of the sparse fire of vine branches. He was playing with his dog; I picked him up in my arms. He was pink and blonde; he looked like his mother. He was a very small child. I lay him back on the floor without saying anything. I was alone.

'Father,' Tancredi said, 'I'm worried that Kounak may be ill. He seems sad.'

'Poor Kounak, he's very old.'

'If Kounak dies, will you give me another dog?'

'There's not a single dog left in Carmona,' I answered.

I went back to the window. The bells were still tolling and the black mob began to move forward. Without a word, without a gesture, men watched as their fathers and mothers, their wives and children, shuffled past. With resigned expressions on their faces, the herd of people slowly descended towards the ramparts. 'As long as I'm here, they won't weaken,' I thought. An icy coldness crept into my heart. Will I be here long enough?

'The service is about to begin,' I announced.

'Ah, now you're going to pray for them,' Caterina said. 'The men will pray while the Genoese rape their wives!'

'What I've done had to be done.' I drew near to her. 'Caterina . . .'

'Don't touch me,' she said.

I beckoned to Giovanni and Ruggiero. 'Let's go.'

At the top of the main street, the cathedral gleamed – white, red, green, golden – as joyfully as it did on a morning in peacetime. The bells continued to toll the death-knell and the sombrely dressed men walked in silence up towards the church. Even their faces were mute; they looked at me with eyes in which there was neither hate nor hope. Above the closed shops the rusty signs jangled in the wind. Not a blade of grass was left in the cracks of the pavements, nor a single nettle at the foot of the walls. I climbed the marble steps and turned around.

Beneath the scrub-covered rock on which Carmona stood, the red tents of the Genoese could be seen among the grey olive trees. A black column flowed out of the city, descended the hill and straggled towards the camp.

'Do you think the Genoese will take them in?'

'No,' I replied.

I entered the cathedral and the clicking of arms mingled with the funeral hymn that reverberated under the vaulted stone ceiling. When Lorenzo Vezzani walked past these flowers and the scarlet wall-hangings, there were no guards surrounding him and he was smiling. He was not thinking of death. Yet here he was, dead, strangled. I kneeled down. They were all stretched out under the flagstones of the choir: Francesco Rienzi, poisoned; Bertrando Rienzi, stabbed; Pietro d'Abruzzi, killed by a lance; and Orlando Rienzi, Lorenzo Vezzani, Geoffredo Massigli, and old Gaetano d'Agnolo who died of old age in exile ... There was an empty space next to them. I bowed my head. 'How much longer will it be?' I wondered.

Kneeling at the foot of the altar, the priest prayed softly and solemn voices rose up to the vaulted ceiling. I pressed my gloved hands to my forehead. 'A year? A month?' My guards were standing behind me, but behind them was a void. Only men – feeble, treacherous creatures – between me and that void. 'It will happen from behind . . . ' My hands pressed harder. 'I must not turn my head; the people must not know.' *Miserere nobis . . . Miserere nobis . . .* 'There will be the same monotonous mumbling of prayers, and the black catafalque, studded in silver, will stand on this exact spot. And this three-year struggle will have been to no avail . . . If I turn my head, they'll think me a coward . . . But I don't want to die without accomplishing anything.'

'Dear God!' I muttered. 'Let me live!'

The murmur of the prayers rose and fell like the sound of the tide. Did it reach as high as God? Was it true that the dead found a new life in heaven? 'Up there I will have neither hands nor voice,' I thought, 'I will see the gates of Carmona open, I will see the Genoese raze our towers, and I will be helpless. Ah! I hope that the priests lie and that I die completely.'

The voices were stilled. A halberd pounded the flagstones and I left the church; the light dazzled me. For a moment I stood motionless at the top of the main stairway. There were no invalids begging, no children playing on the steps. The polished marble gleamed in the sunlight. Down below, the slopes of the hill were deserted. There among the red tents, people were swarming in confusion. I turned my eyes away. What went on in the plains, what went on in the heavens, did not concern me. It was for women and children to question themselves – 'What are they doing? Will they hold out much longer? Will Carlo Malatesta arrive in the spring? Will God save us?' As for me, I did not expect anything. I kept Carmona's gates closed and I expected nothing.

Slowly I walked back towards the palace. A heavy silence hung over the city like a malediction, and I thought, 'I'm here now, but one day I'll no longer be here. I won't be anywhere . . . It will happen from behind and I won't even know it happened.' Then I said to myself fervently. 'No, it's impossible. It can't happen to me, not to me!'

I turned toward Ruggiero. 'I'm going up to the attic.'

I climbed up the winding staircase, took a key from my belt and opened the door. A rancid, bitter smell gripped my throat. The floor was strewn with rotten herbs; pots and retorts were heating on a stove in an atmosphere of thick steam. Bent over a table covered with phials and beakers, Petrucchio was grinding a yellow paste in a mortar.

'Where are the others?'

Petrucchio raised his head. 'They're sleeping.'

'At this time of day?'

The door to the living quarters was slightly ajar; I pushed it open with my foot. The eight doctors were lying on beds which had been put up for them against the walls. Some were sleeping and the others were staring absent-mindedly at the great beams of the ceiling. I closed the door.

'They're working too hard! The task will kill them!' he said.

I leaned over Petrucchio's shoulder. 'Is that an antidote?'

'No. Its a balsam for chilblain.'

I took the mortar in my hand and threw it violently to the floor.

Petrucchio looked at me coldly. 'I'm trying to do useful work.' He bent down and picked up the heavy marble mortar.

I walked towards the stove. 'I'm certain it can be found,' I said. 'Everything has its opposite. If there are poisons, there must be antidotes.'

'Perhaps, in a thousand years time, one will be discovered.'

'Then it exists! Why can't it be discovered now?'

Petrucchio shrugged his shoulders.

'I need it immediately,' I said.

I looked around me. The remedy was there, hidden among those herbs, in those red and blue powders, and I was unable to see it. I stood in front of those beakers and phials like a blind man before a rainbow, and Petrucchio was blind, too. The antidote was there and no one in the world was capable of seeing it.

'Oh, God!' I exclaimed.

I slammed the door behind me.

The wind was whistling around the covered way. I leaned against the stone parapet and I watched the crackling flames which rose from the bottoms of the ditches surrounding the ramparts. In the distance, fires were glowing in the Genoese camp, and behind them, in the shadows, was the plain with its deserted roads and abandoned houses, immense and useless like the sea. Alone on her rock, Carmona was an isle lost in the middle of that sea. Gusts of wind brought the smell of burning brambles and red sparks flew into the cold night air. 'They're burning the scrub from the hill, but it won't last more than two days,' I thought.

The sound of steps, a click of steel, made me raise my head. They were moving along one by one behind a guard who was carrying a torch; their hands were tied behind their backs. The guard passed in front of me, followed by a woman with big red cheeks, then an old woman, and a young one who looked at the ground and whose face I could not make out, then another who looked as if she were pretty. Behind them came an old bearded man and another old man. They had hidden themselves to save their lives, and now they were going to die.

'Where are you taking them?' I asked.

'To the west rampart. It's the steepest side.'

'There aren't very many.'

'They're the only ones we found,' the guard said. He turned towards the prisoners. 'Let's go. Move on.'

'Fosca!' cried one of the men in a piercing voice. 'Let me talk to you. Don't let me die!'

I recognized him. It was Bartolomeo, the oldest and most miserable of all the beggars who held out their hands beneath the porch of the cathedral. The guard struck him lightly. 'Move along.'

'I know the cure,' cried the old man. 'Let me talk to you.'

'The cure?' I walked over to him. The others had already disappeared into the night. 'What cure?'

'The cure. It's hidden in my house.'

I stared at the beggar; he must be lying. His lips were trembling and despite the icy wind there were beads of sweat on his yellow brow. He had lived for more than eighty years and he was still struggling to preserve his life.

'You lie,' I said.

'I swear on the Gospel that I'm not lying. My father's father brought it with him from Egypt. If I lie, you can kill me tomorrow.'

I turned towards Ruggiero. 'Have this man brought to the palace with his cure.'

I leaned over the battlements and cast one last glance at the forlorn fires which were twisting into the night. A great cry ripped through the silence; it came from the west rampart.

'Let's go back,' I said.

Caterina was sitting by the fireplace, wrapped in a blanket; she was sewing by the light of a torch. When I entered the room, she did not look up.

'Father,' Tancredi said, 'Kounak doesn't move anymore.'

'He's sleeping,' I said. 'Let him sleep.'

'But he doesn't move at all.'

I leaned over and touched the old dog's faded coat. 'He's dead.'

'He's dead!' Tancredi exclaimed. His pink face creased up, and tears welled from his eyes.

'Come on, don't cry,' I said. 'Be a man.'

'He's dead forever,' he said.

He sobbed bitterly as I thought 'Thirty years of caution, thirty years of fear, and yet one day I'll be stretched out, stiff, and nothing will depend upon me anymore. Carmona will be left to these feeble hands. Ah, how short is the longest life! What's the point of antidotes? What's the point of all these murders?'

I sat down beside Caterina. She was darning a piece of

cloth and her fingers were covered with chilblains. I called to her softly. 'Caterina . . . ' She turned to me; there was a deathly expression on her face. 'Caterina, it's easy to blame me, but try to put yourself in my place for a moment.'

'May God forbid that I should ever have to be there.' She leaned over her work again and said, 'It's going to freeze tonight.'

'Yes.' I watched the pale, shifting shadows as they trembled on the tapestry on the wall and suddenly I felt very tired.

'Children,' she said, 'with their whole lives before them.'

'Ah! be quiet!'

'They will all die, but Carmona will be saved,' I thought. 'And then I will die and the city I saved will fall into the hands of Florence or Milan. I shall have saved Carmona and I shall have done nothing.'

'Raimondo, let them come back to Carmona.'

'Then we shall all die,' I replied.

She lowered her head and pushed the needle with her red, swollen fingers. I felt like laying my head in her lap, caressing her legs, smiling at her. But I no longer knew how to smile.

'The siege has lasted a long time,' she continued. 'The Genoese are tired. Why not try to negotiate with them?'

I felt as if I had been struck a dull blow in the hollow of my chest. 'Is that really the way you think?' I asked.

'Yes.'

'You want me to open the gates to the Genoese?'

'Yes.'

I passed my hand across my face. They all thought the same way, I knew. For whom was I fighting, then? What was Carmona? A mass of unfeeling stones and men who had a horror of death. In all of us, the same horror. If I deliver Carmona to the Genoese, perhaps they will spare us; we might live a few more years. A year of life; just one night, the old beggar had pleaded. 'One night, a whole life . . . Children with their whole lives before them . . . ' Suddenly, I felt like giving it all up.

'My Lord,' Ruggiero said, 'here is your man and his cure.'

He was clutching Bartolomeo by the shoulder and handing me a dusty bottle filled with a greenish liquid. I looked at the beggar, with his wrinkled face, his dirty beard, his blinking eyes, and thought 'If I escape sickness, poison or the swords, I'll be like him one day.'

'What is this cure?' I asked.

'I'd like to speak to you alone,' replied Bartolomeo.

I gestured to Ruggiero. 'Leave us alone.'

Caterina got to her feet, but I put my hand on her wrist. 'I've no secrets from you.' And turning to the beggar, I said, 'Well, speak.'

He looked at me with a strange smile on his face. 'In this bottle,' he began, 'is the elixir of immortality.'

'Is that all!'

'You don't believe me?'

The crudeness of his ruse made me smile in turn. 'But if you're immortal, why are you so afraid of being thrown off the ramparts?'

'But I'm not immortal,' replied the old man. 'The bottle is full.'

'And why haven't you drunk it?'

'Would you dare to drink it?'

I took the bottle in my hand; the liquid was cloudy. 'You drink first.'

He shook his head. 'Is there a living animal in this place? Some small animal?'

'Tancredi has a white mouse.'

'Ask her to get it,' said the old man.

'Raimondo, he's fond of that mouse,' Caterina said.

'Go and get it, Caterina,' I ordered.

She got up.

'The elixir of immortality!' I said in a mocking tone of voice. 'Why didn't you think of selling it to me sooner. You would never have needed to beg again.'

Bartolomeo brushed his finger across the dusty neck of the bottle. 'It's this cursed bottle that made me a beggar.'

'How did that come about?'

'My father was a wise man. He hid the bottle in his attic and forgot about it. When he was dying, he told me of its secret, but he advised me to forget it, too. I was twenty years old and I was being given a present of eternal youth. What did I have to worry about? I sold my father's shop and squandered his fortune. Each day I said to myself, "I'll drink it tomorrow."'

'And you never drank?'

'I grew poor and I didn't dare drink it. Old age came, and so did infirmities. I would say to myself, "I'll drink the moment I'm about to die." A little while ago, when the guards discovered me inside the hut where I was hiding, I didn't drink.'

'There is still time,' I said.

He shook his head. 'I'm frightened of dying, but a life of eternity — how long that must be!'

Caterina placed a little wooden cage on the table and sat down again in silence.

'Watch carefully,' the old man said. He uncorked the bottle, poured a few drops in the palm of his hand and grabbed the mouse. It let out a squeal and plunged its nose into the green liquid.

'It's poison,' I said.

The mouse lay inert in the old man's hand and looked as if it had been struck by lightening.

'Wait.'

We waited. Suddenly the motionless little body twitched.

'It was sleeping,' I said.

'Now,' Bartolomeo instructed, 'twist its' neck.'

'No!' Caterina cried.

He put the mouse in my hand. It was alive and warm. 'Twist its' neck.'

I tightened my grip suddenly; the little bones cracked. I threw the lifeless body on the table. 'There.'

'Watch, watch!' said Bartolomeo.

For a moment the mouse lay on its side and did not move. Then it recovered and began to scamper over the table.

'It was dead,' I said.

'It will never die again.'

'Raimondo, send him away. He's a sorcerer,' Caterina said.

I seized the old man by the shoulder. 'Must I drink the whole bottle?'

'Yes.'

'Will I ever grow old?'

'No.'

'Send him away,' Caterina repeated.

I looked distrustfully at the old man. 'If you've lied to me, you know what will happen to you?'

He lowered his head. 'But if I haven't lied, will you let me live?'

'Ah, your fortune is made,' I replied. I called for Ruggiero.

'My Lord?'

'Keep a close watch on this man.'

I closed the door and went towards the table. I reached for the bottle.

'Raimondo, you're not going to drink it?' Caterina said.

'He's not lying,' I reassured her. 'Why would he lie?'

'Ah! that's just it,' she said.

I looked at her and my hand withdrew.

'When Christ wanted to punish the Jew who laughed in his face, he condemned him to live forever.'

I did not answer. 'What things I'll be able to do!' I thought, and I seized the bottle. Caterina hid her face in her hands.

'Caterina . . . ' I looked around me. Never again would I see this room with the same eyes. 'Caterina, if I die, open the gates of the city.'

'Don't drink,' she pleaded.

'If I die, you can do whatever you like.'

I raised the bottle to my lips.

❧

When I opened my eyes, it was broad daylight and the room was filled with people. 'What's the matter?' I asked. I raised myself on one elbow; my head felt heavy. Caterina, standing by my bedside, was looking at me with a petrified expression. 'What's the matter?' I repeated.

'You've been lying on that bed for four days now, cold as a corpse,' Ruggiero answered. He, too, seemed frightened.

'Four days!' I leaped up. 'Where's Bartolomeo?'

'Here I am.' The old man drew near and looked at me grudgingly. 'You gave me a bad fright!'

I took him by the arm and led him to an alcove near the door. 'Has it happened?'

'Of course.'

'I'll never die?'

'No. Not even if you want to.' He began to laugh and wave his hands wildly. 'So much time!' he said. 'So much time!'

I raised my hand to my throat; I was suffocating. 'My coat, quickly.'

'Are you going out?' asked Giovanni. 'I'll alert the guards.'

'No. No guards.'

'It's unwise,' Ruggiero warned. 'The city's not calm.' He looked away. 'It's not easy to get used to hearing that wailing coming from the ditches day and night.'

I stopped at the door. 'Were there any disturbances?'

'Not exactly. But every night someone or other tries to throw down provisions over the ramparts. Sacks of wheat have been stolen from the warehouse. And the people are grumbling.'

'Anyone who complains will be given twenty lashes' I ordered. 'And any man found at night on the ramparts will be hanged.'

The expression on Caterina's face suddenly changed; she took a step towards me. 'Don't you want to let them return?'

'Ah! don't start that again,' I said impatiently.

'You said to me, "If I die, open the gates."'

'But I'm not dead.'

I looked at her swollen eyes, her sunken cheeks. 'Why is she so sad? Why do they all seem so sad?' I wondered. As for myself, I was bursting with joy.

I crossed the pink square. Nothing had changed – there was the same silence, the same shops behind their heavy wooden shutters. And yet everything was as new as the dawn, the grey, silent dawn of a sparkling day. I looked at the red sun suspended in the cottony sky and I smiled; I felt as if I could have plucked that great joyful ball right out of the clouds. The sky was within my hands' grasp, and I could feel the entire future within my heart.

'Is everything all right? Nothing to report?'

'Nothing to report,' replied the sentry.

I made a tour of the sentry posts. The rocky hill was bare; there was not a single fire left in the ditches, not a blade of grass. 'They will all die' I thought as I pressed my hand against the stone battlement; I felt harder than the stone. What had I deprived them of? Ten years? Half a century? What was a year? A century? 'They were born to die.' I leaned over. The Genoese, those little black ants that were scurrying about their tents, would also die. But Carmona would not die. She would stand beneath the sun forever, flanked by her eight tall towers, and every day she would grow bigger and more beautiful; she would govern the plain, she would dominate the whole of Tuscany. I gazed at the undulating hills which stood on the horizon. 'Beyond those hills, lies the world,' I thought, and something exploded in my heart.

The winter passed. In the ditches, the fires had been extinguished and the groaning had ceased. The first warm spring days brought gusts of a dull stench of decaying flesh into Carmona. I inhaled it quite nonchalantly. I knew that

these mortal miasmas which drifted from the ditches were
infecting the Genoese camp. They were losing their hair,
their limbs became swollen, their blood turned purple, and
they were dying. When Carlo Malatesta and his army
appeared on the crest of the hills, the Genoese hastily broke
camp and fled without joining battle.

Wagons laden with sacks of flour, sides of meat and casks
filled with wine followed the condottiere's troops into the
city. Great fires were lit in the squares and songs of triumph
broke out everywhere. Men embraced each other at street
corners. Caterina hugged Tancredi tightly in her arms and,
for the first time in four years, she smiled. In the evening, a
huge feast was held. Malatesta, sitting on Caterina's right,
laughed and drank like a man who had achieved his heart's
desire. I, too, felt the warmth of the wine coursing through
my veins, and I was filled with joy. But it was unlike anyone
else's joy; it was hard and dark, it crushed my heart like
a stone. 'This is only the beginning,' I thought.

When dinner was over, I took Malatesta to the Treasury
and paid him the sum of money that had been agreed upon.

'And now,' I said, 'would you be willing to pursue the
Genoese and lay hold of the castles and cities that border my
lands?'

He smiled. 'Your coffers are empty.'

'They will be full tomorrow.'

At dawn, I sent heralds through the city. Under pain
of death, every citizen had to surrender, before nightfall, all
the gold, all the silver, all the precious stones he possessed.
I was told that several men had grumbled but none had dared
disobey. When the sun had set, heaps of jewels were piled high
in the chests. I divided these riches into three parts. One was
entrusted to the provost in charge of provisions so that he
could purchase wheat; another was given to the weavers to
procure wool. The third chest, I showed to Malatesta.

'How many months will this keep your troops in my
service?'

He plunged his hand into the sparkling jewels. 'Several months.'

'How many?'

'That will depend upon the spoils of war,' he said. Then he smiled. 'And also on my own good pleasure.'

He let the precious stones slip casually through his fingers while I watched him impatiently. Every pearl, every diamond represented seed for future harvests, a fortress to defend our frontiers, a piece of land wrested from the Genoese. I summoned experts who spent the night evaluating the precise value of my treasure, and I reached an agreement with Malatesta for a fixed daily wage to be paid to each man. Then I had all of Carmona's men assemble in the square in front of the palazzo and I addressed them.

'There are no women in your homes,' I said, 'nor wheat in your granaries. Let us go and harvest the wheat of the Genoese and bring back their daughters to our homes.'

I added that the Holy Virgin had appeared to me in a dream and had promised that not a single hair of my head would fall until Carmona became the equal of Genoa and Florence.

The young people put on their armour. They all had hollow cheeks, sallow complexions and dark circles under their eyes, but the hunger which had sapped their bodies had also stiffened their spirits, and they followed me without protest. So as to arouse their courage, I pointed out the purple bodies of the Genoese sprawled out all along the ditches. Malatesta's soldiers with their florid complexions, their full cheeks and robust shoulders, seemed to us as though they belonged to some superhuman race. The condottiere led them as his fancy took him, sometimes prolonging a halt more than was necessary to give them a rest, occasionally galloping on a stage further simply because he felt like riding by moonlight.

Instead of pressing on the heels of the fleeing Genoese, he wanted to take the castle of Monteferti by storm, explaining that he was bored with encountering only enemies who were dead or dying. This cost us a full day and several of his captains. When I reproached him for this waste, he answered haughtily, 'I make war for my own pleasure.'

Thanks to the respite we had given them, the Genoese were able to avoid combat by taking refuge in Villana, a fortified city protected by impregnable ramparts. In view of this, Malatesta declared that we would have to give up our venture. I asked him to be patient for just one night. On the westerly approach to Villana, an aqueduct led into the city, bringing the waters from the stream which met beneath the ramparts along a subterranean canal. No man could have passed through that conduit without drowning. I told no one of my plan; I simply ordered my lieutenants to lie in wait by the west postern and, after stripping off my armour, I disappeared down the dark tunnel. At first, I was able to breath the stagnant air under the vaults, then the ceiling became lower and I could see that there was no space between the stones and the water. I hesitated; the current was very strong. If I had gone in any further, I would not have had the strength to turn back towards the light. 'And supposing the old man had lied?' I thought. A dense blackness closed in on me from all sides, and the only sound I could hear was the gushing of water. But if the old man had lied, if I were mortal, what difference would it make if my life ended that day or the next? 'Now I'll know,' I thought, and I plunged in.

He had lied. My head was buzzing, a vice was compressing my chest. I was going to die and the Genoese would throw my bloated body to the dogs. How could I have believed that insane fairy tale? I was suffocating from rage as much as from the icy water; my only wish was that the agony would be over quickly. There seemed no end to my dying. And suddenly it dawned on me that I had been swimming for a very long time and that I was not going to die. I swam to the opening at the end of the tunnel. There was no longer any possible doubt – I really was immortal. I wanted to fall to my knees and thank the devil or God, but there was no sign of their presence anywhere near me. All I could see was a crescent moon in the icy silence of the sky.

The town was deserted. I reached the west postern where I slipped behind the sentry and felled him with a single thrust of my sword. In the sentry post, two soldiers were sleeping; I killed the first while he was still asleep, and the second after a brief fight. I opened the gate. My men silently entered the city, took the garrison by surprise and massacred every soldier. At dawn, the terrified inhabitants discovered that they had changed masters.

Half of the men were sent to Carmona as prisoners to work on our lands, and a large number of young, nubile girls, who would assure our posterity, were taken away with them. From Villana, our troops gained control of the plains and seized several small towns without difficulty. I led the assaults through hails of arrows and my men called me the Invincible.

I wanted to press home my advantage and lay siege to the port of Rivella, which was subject to Genoa, and would have given Carmona an outlet to the sea. But Malatesta suddenly decided that he was tired of fighting and that he and his troops were going to withdraw. I had no alternative but to turn back to Carmona and I rode alongside Malatesta. We parted at a crossroads; he set off in the direction of Rome in search of new adventures and for a long while my eyes followed this man who had no objective in his life and who disposed of himself with all the insouciance of mortals. Then I dug my heels into the flanks of my horse and galloped on towards Carmona.

I did not want the fate of my city ever again to depend on mercenaries, and I resolved to equip her with an army. I needed a great deal of money. I levied heavy taxes; I decreed a law against luxury, prohibiting all men and women from wearing jewellery and from owning more than two suits of coarse cloth. Even noblemen were obliged to eat only from earthenware or wooden dishes. Those who rebelled were thrown into dungeons or whipped in public, and I confiscated their wealth. I forced all the men to marry before the age of twenty-five, and the women to bear numerous children for their city. Labourers, weavers, merchants and noblemen – I made soldiers of them all. I, myself, kept an eye on the training of recruits. Soon, I had built up a company, then two, then ten. At the same time, in order to increase our wealth, I encouraged the growth of agriculture and commerce, and every year a great fair drew hundreds of foreign merchants to Carmona who came to buy our wheat and our cloth.

'How much longer must we go on living like this?' asked Tancredi. He had his mother's fair hair and an eager mouth. He hated me. He did not know I was immortal, but believed I was protected against illness and old age by some mysterious drug.

'As long as it serves a purpose,' I answered.

'Serves a purpose!' he exclaimed. 'What purpose? For whom?' His eyes hardened in hopeless rage. 'We're as rich as Siena and Pisa and yet the only time we ever celebrate is at weddings or christenings. We dress like monks and live in convents. I'm your son and yet morning and night I have to drill under the orders of a boor of a captain. My friends and I will grow old without ever having been young.'

'The future will reward us for our pains,' I said.

'And who'll give us back the years you've robbed us of?' he asked. He looked me straight in the face. 'I've only got one life.'

I shrugged my shoulders. What was one life?

At the end of thirty years, I had the largest and best-equipped army in all of Italy. I had begun preparations for an expedition against Genoa when a great storm broke out over the plain. For a whole day and night, the rain fell in torrents. The rivers rose, the streets of the lower town were transformed into streams of mud which seeped into the houses. In the morning, while the women were sweeping their ruined floors, the men looked in dismay at the squares invaded by a yellowish silt, the fissured roads, and the new crops flattened by the violence of the downpour. The sky remained a leaden grey. In the evening, the rain started to fall again and I began to realize the peril that threatened us. Without further ado, I sent merchants to Genoa in order to buy up wheat in Sicily, Sardinia and all the barbarian lands to the north.

The rains fell throughout the spring and summer. All over Italy, the harvests were ruined, the fruit trees were destroyed and the fodder was lost. But before the end of autumn, Carmona's granaries were filled with sacks of grain which ships, equipped at our expense, had brought from overseas. Avariciously, I inhaled the dusty odour; the tiniest grain mattered. I had public ovens constructed and each morning I doled out in person the hundred measures of wheat which were distributed to the bakers to make loaves of bran and flour, the weights of which I controlled. Those in need were fed free of charge. Throughout Italy there was a shortage of wheat; the price rose to thirty-six pounds per hundred-weight, and bran cost almost as much. During the course of the winter, four thousand men died in Florence. In Carmona, however, not a single poor or sick person, nor a single foreigner was sent away from the city, and there was enough grain left over for sowing. During the first days of spring in the year 1348, when all the fields in Italy were barren, the crops thrived on our plain and a fair took place in Carmona's main square. Leaning over the ramparts, I watched the caravans climbing the hill and I thought, 'I have conquered famine'.

The blue sky and the sounds of feasting drifted in through the open window. Caterina was sitting next to Louisa, Tancredi's wife; they were both embroidering. I had perched my little grandson, Sigismondo, on my shoulders and I was galloping around the room which was strewn with branches of almond blossom.

'Giddy-up, giddy-up!' cried the child.

I loved him; he was closer to me than any other being. He was unaware that his days were numbered; he knew nothing of years, months or weeks. He was lost in this one, long resplendent day that had no tomorrow and no end, an eternal beginning, an eternal presence. His joy was as infinite as the sky. 'Giddy-up, giddy-up!' he shouted. And as I ran, I thought, 'The blue of the sky will never fade away, and there will be more springtimes for me than almond flowers. My happiness will last forever.'

'But why do you want to leave so soon?' Caterina asked. 'Wait until Pentecost. It's still cold up there.'

'I want to leave,' Louisa replied. 'I want to leave tomorrow.'

'Tomorrow? How can you think of it? It will take at least a week to get the house ready.'

'I want to leave,' Louisa repeated with finality.

I came up to her and looked with curiosity at her stubborn little face. 'Would you mind telling me why?'

Louisa threaded her needle into the canvas of her tapestry. 'The children need fresh air.'

'But they seem to me to be in wonderful health!' I said. I pinched Sigismondo's calf and smiled at the two little girls sitting on a rug in the sun. 'Springtime is so beautiful in Carmona!'

'I still want to leave,' Louisa insisted.

Tancredi smiled coldly. 'She's afraid.'

'Afraid?' I said. 'Of what?'

'She's afraid of the plague,' Tancredi replied. 'And she's right. You should never have let those foreign merchants inside the city.'

'But this is foolish!' I exclaimed. 'Rome and Naples are far away.'

'At Assisi, apparently, it rained big, black, eight-footed insects with claws,' said Louisa.

'And near Siena, the ground opened up and began to spit fire!' I said mockingly. I shrugged my shoulders. 'If you start believing all the rumours around . . .'

Caterina turned toward Ruggiero who was dozing in a chair with both hands on his belly; lately he slept almost constantly. He was growing heavy.

'Ruggiero!' Caterina called to him. 'What do you think?'

'A Genoese merchant told me that the plague had already reached Assisi,' he replied nonchalantly.

'Even if what you say is true, it could never reach us here,' I assured them. 'The air is as pure as in the mountains.'

'Of course, you have nothing to worry about,' said Louisa.

'Did your doctors forecast the plague, too?' Tancredi asked.

'Alas! my dear son, they forecasted everything,' I answered. I looked at him maliciously. 'I promise you that in twenty years it will be Sigismondo who'll rule alongside me.'

He got up and slammed the door violently behind him.

'You shouldn't provoke him so far,' Caterina said.

I did not answer.

She looked at me hesitantly. 'Aren't you going to receive those monks who asked to speak to you?'

'I refuse to allow their hordes to enter Carmona,' I replied.

'But you can't very well refuse to hear what they have to say,' said Caterina.

'Perhaps they can tell us something about the plague,' suggested Louisa.

I beckoned to Ruggiero. 'Very well. Tell them to come in.'

Throughout Italy's famine-ravaged cities, there were now fanatics fervently preaching penitence. At the sound of their voices, merchants abandoned their businesses, artisans their workshops, labourers their fields. They wore white habits and hid their faces beneath hoods; the poorest among them wrapped themselves in sheets. Barefooted, they wandered from city to city, singing hymns and exhorting the inhabitants to join them. That morning they had arrived at the walls of Carmona and I had forbidden them to pass through our gates. The monks who led them were, however, allowed to come up to the palace. They followed Ruggiero into the room; they were dressed in white habits.

'Sit down, brothers,' I said.

The smaller of the two monks took a step towards a damask-covered chair, but the other stopped him with a sharp gesture. 'There's no point,' he said.

I looked coldly at the taller monk with the weather-beaten face who stood in front of me with his hands hidden in his sleeves. 'This man is passing judgment on me,' I thought.

'Where have you come from?'

'From Florence,' replied the little monk. 'We've been travelling for twenty days.'

'Have you heard people say that the plague has reached as far as Tuscany?'

'Good God! No!' exclaimed the little monk.

I turned towards Louisa. 'You see!'

'Is it true, Father, that the famine caused more than four thousand deaths in Florence?' asked Caterina.

The little monk nodded his head. 'More than four thousand,' he affirmed. 'We ate bread made of frozen grass.'

'We once lived through that,' I said. 'Have you ever been to Carmona before?'

'Once. Almost ten years ago.'

'Isn't it a beautiful city?'

'It's a city that needs to hear the word of God,' said the tall monk enthusiastically.

Everyone turned towards him. I frowned.

'We have priests here who deliver excellent sermons every Sunday,' I said curtly. 'Besides, the people of Carmona are pious and their life is austere; there are neither heretics nor libertines among them.'

'But pride is corrupting their hearts,' the monk said passionately. 'They no longer care about their eternal salvation. You think only of dispensing worldly blessings, and these blessings are mere vanity. You have protected them from famine, but man does not live by bread alone. You believe you have accomplished great things, but what you have done is nothing.'

'Nothing?' I said. I began to laugh. 'Thirty years ago there were twenty thousand men in Carmona. Now there are fifty thousand.'

'And how many will die saved?' the monk asked.

'We are at peace with God,' I replied angrily. 'We have no need of sermons, nor processions.' Turning to Ruggiero, I said, 'Have these monks led outside of our walls and have the penitents sent into the plain.'

The monks left in silence; Louisa and Caterina said nothing. At that time, I was not sure whether heaven was empty or not, but I did not worry about heaven. And the earth in any case did not belong to God; the earth was my domain.

'Grandfather, take me to see the monkeys,' Sigismondo said, pulling me by the arm.

'Me too! I want to see the monkeys,' said one of the little girls.

'No,' said Louisa. 'I forbid you to go outside. If you go out, you'll catch the plague, you'll turn black and you'll die.'

'Don't tell them such balderdash,' I said impatiently. I put my hand on Caterina's shoulder. 'Come down with us to the fairground.'

'If I go down, I'll have to climb back up again.'

'Well?'

'You forget that I'm an old woman.'

'Don't be silly,' I said, 'you're not old.'

Her face was still the same: the same timid eyes, the same smile; but for some time now she had seemed tired; her cheeks were puffed and yellow, there were lines around her mouth.

'We'll walk slowly,' I said. 'Come.'

We went down the old Via dei Tintori. The children walked in front of us. On both sides of the street, workers with blue fingernails plunged skeins of wool into vats filled with azure and blood-coloured dyes. A violet liquid seeped between the cobblestones.

'Ah!' I sighed. 'When will I ever be able to pull down these old hovels.'

'What will you do with all these poor people?'

'Yes, I know,' I answered. 'They'll have to die first.'

The street led directly to the fairground. The air smelled of cloves and honey. The drumming of tambours and the tinny sound of a brass-band could be heard above the cries and shouts of the merchants. Crowds of people pressed against the stands which were full of woollen goods, rolls of linen, fruits, spices and cakes. The women lovingly fingered the heavy yarns and delicate laces, children were biting into honey-covered waffles, and wine flowed from the heavy jugs that stood on wooden counters. Both their stomachs and their hearts were warm. As I walked across the square, there was a great cheer: 'Long live Count Fosca! Long live Countess Fosca!' A bouquet of roses fell at my feet; a man took off his coat and laid it on the ground. I had vanquished famine and all this happiness was my doing.

The children shrieked with joy. I stopped obediently in front of the trained monkeys, I applauded the dancing bear and the acrobats in their striped costumes walking on their hands. Sigismondo excitedly pulled me to the right, then the left.

'This way, grandfather! This way!' he cried out, pointing to a group of onlookers who were watching with rapt attention a performance we were unable to see. I moved nearer and tried to make my way through the crowd.

'Don't go any closer, my lord,' yelled a man who was looking at me with a terrified expression on his face.

'What's going on?'

I forced my way through the crowd. A man, no doubt

a foreign merchant, was stretched out on the ground, his eyes closed.

'Well, what are you waiting for? Why don't you get him to the hospital?' I said impatiently.

They gazed at me in silence and no one moved.

'What are you waiting for?' I asked. 'Take this man away.'

'We're afraid,' one of the men answered. He stretched out his arm in front of me to bar the way. 'Don't go any nearer.'

I pushed him aside and knelt down beside the inert body. I took hold of the foreigner's wrist and rolled up his wide sleeve. His pale arm was covered with black spots.

❧

'The priests are downstairs,' said Ruggiero.

'Already?' I passed my hand across my face. 'Is Tancredi here?'

'No,' Ruggiero replied

'Is anyone here?'

'No. I had to hire four men and even then I had to promise them a fortune.'

'No one!' I exclaimed.

I looked all about me. The candles were almost burned out; a grey light penetrated the room. I would have said, 'Caterina, no one is here.' And she would have replied, 'They're afraid. It's only natural.' Or perhaps she would have blushed and said, 'They're too cowardly.' I couldn't think of how she would have said it. I reached out my hand and touched the wooden coffin.

'There are only two priests,' Ruggiero said. 'And they say the cathedral is too far away. They want to hold the service in the chapel.'

'As they wish.'

I let my arm fall back to my side. The four men, big, red-faced peasants, tramped into the room. They walked over to the coffin without looking at me and heaved it roughly onto their shoulders. They hated the frail body that lay inside, the white corpse speckled with black. They hated me. Ever since the plague had broken out, a rumour circulated that I owed my youth to a pact with the devil.

The two priests were standing at the foot of the altar; a few servants and several guards were lined up against the walls. The pall-bearers set the coffin down in the middle of the empty nave and the priests hurriedly muttered some prayers. One of them traced a large sign of the cross in the air and then they both walked rapidly to the door. The pall-bearers followed. Behind me were Ruggiero and several soldiers. Dawn was breaking, the air was warm and pink. In their homes, people were waking up and discovering with horror that their arms were covered with black spots. Those who had died during the night were taken from their rooms; corpses, still warm, lined the streets. The stench of pestilence that hung over the city was so thick that I was astonished the sky remained visible.

Two men carrying a plank on which a corpse was lying stepped out of a doorway. They fell in behind the soldiers in order to take advantage of the prayers the priests were mumbling.

'My lord,' Ruggiero said.

'Let them be.'

A mule laden with bundles emerged from a side street. A man and a woman were trudging along behind it; they were fleeing. Many people had fled during the first days, but the plague followed them wherever they went. It spread in every direction like wildfire; they came upon it in the plains and in the mountains. There was nowhere left in which to take refuge. Nevertheless, these two were attempting to escape. As she passed by me, the woman spat on the ground. Further on, a band of young men and dishevelled women were coming down the street, singing and reeling drunkenly. They had spent the night dancing in one of the large abandoned palaces. They laughed as they crossed in front of us and a voice cried out, 'Son of the devil!'

Ruggiero started toward them.

'Never mind, let them be,' I said.

I looked at the pall-bearers' thick necks, at their large hands gripping the wooden coffin. 'Son of the devil!' they repeated and spat on the ground. But their words and acts were unimportant: they were all condemned to death. Some fled, some prayed, others danced; and they would all die.

We arrived at the cemetery. There were four coffins behind Caterina's. From every street, funeral processions climbed toward the sacred burial grounds. A canvas-covered cart passed through the gate and drew up before a pit in which bodies were piled high. Priests and gravediggers pushed and shoved their way along weed-infested paths. All one could hear were the sounds of picks and shovels. The whole of Carmona had taken refuge in this place of death. Caterina's grave was dug at the foot of a cypress tree. The bearers lowered the coffin into the hole and threw a few shovels of earth over it. The priest made a sign of the cross and set off towards another grave.

I looked up and breathed the fetid air of the cemetery, I put my hand to my mouth and walked towards the gate. A cart was slowly making its way up the street and men were heaving corpses into it which had been lying against the walls. I stopped. What was the point of going back to the palace? There was nobody there. Where was she? Beneath a cypress tree lay an old, mean-looking woman, while in heaven there drifted a featureless soul, unhearing and silent, like God.

'Come, my lord,' said Ruggiero.

I followed him. In front of the palace, standing on one of the stalls abandoned by the merchants, the dark-faced monk was preaching and flapping his arms about wildly. When the plague had broken out, he had returned to the city and I did not dare send him away. The people listened to him devotedly; too few guards were left in my entourage for me to challenge him with sacrilege. He saw me and called out in a strident voice, 'Count Fosca! Now do you understand?'

I did not answer

'You built new houses for the people of Carmona, and now they are buried in the earth. You dressed them in fine clothes, and now they lie naked in shrouds. You filled their stomachs, and now they are food for worms. In the plain, untended flocks are trampling down the useless crops. You vanquished famine. But God has sent the plague and the plague has vanquished you!'

'That proves that we must learn to vanquish the plague, too,' I replied angrily.

I entered the palace and stopped at the door in surprise. Tancredi was standing by a window; he seemed to be waiting for me. I walked over to him.

'How could anyone be such a wretched coward?' I said. 'A son who hasn't the courage to accompany his mother to her last resting place!'

'I'll prove my courage in other ways,' he replied disdainfully. He blocked my way. 'Wait,' he said.

'What do you want?'

'As long as my mother was alive, I restrained myself. But now I've had enough.' He stared at me with menacing eyes. 'You've ruled long enough. It's my turn now.'

'No,' I said. 'It will never be your turn.'

'It's my turn!' he said violently.

He drew his sword and struck me full in the chest. A dozen fellow conspirators sprung suddenly from an adjoining room shouting, 'Death to the tyrant!' Ruggiero threw himself in front of me. He fell. I thrust my sword and Tancredi fell. I felt a sharp pain between my shoulder blades. I spun around and struck out. Seeing Tancredi on the floor, several of the plotters fled, and soon my guards rushed into the room. Three men lay sprawled on the floor. The others were subdued after a short fight.

I knelt down beside Ruggiero. He was gazing at the

ceiling; there was a look of terror frozen on his face. His heart had stopped beating. Tancredi's eyes were shut. He was dead.

'You're wounded, my lord,' a guard said.

'It's nothing.'

I got up, slipped my hand beneath my shirt and drew it out wet with blood. I looked at the blood and began to laugh. I went over to the window and breathed in deeply. The air filled my lungs and swelled my chest. The monk was still preaching and the crowd listened to him in silence. My wife was dead, so was my son and my grandchildren; all my friends were dead. I lived on, and I was alone of my kind. My past was buried; there was nothing now to hold me back, neither memories, nor love, nor duty. I was without the law, I was my own master, and I could dispose as I pleased of poor human lives that were doomed to die. Under the featureless sky, I drew myself up erect, feeling alive and free, and knowing that I would forever be alone.

I leaned out the window and smiled. A strange army! There were at least three thousand men in the square, wrapped in long, sheet-like cloaks which hid even their faces. Each of them was holding a horse by the reins. Beneath their outer garments, they had donned their armour and belted on their swords. I went over to the Venetian mirror. Beneath my white, woollen hood, my face seemed as dark as a Moor's; my eyes were not those of a pious man. I pulled my hood over my face and went down to the square. Towards the end of the epidemic, the population of the city, distraught at the horror of the catastrophe from which they had just escaped and bewildered by the preaching of the monks, had abandoned itself to the extremes of exalted piety. Pretending to have been won over to their fanatical beliefs, I exhorted all able-bodied men to accompany me on a long pilgrimage; we were only armed in order to defend ourselves against the brigands who infested the countryside. Most of my companions believed in the sincerity of my aims, but some only followed me because they were not entirely sure.

We left the city by way of the old Via dei Tintori; the houses were nothing but heaps of rubble. The devil had no doubt heard my prayers: all the inhabitants of this district had died of the plague and workers had just finished knocking down their hovels. They were dead; other men would be born. Through it all, Carmona lived on, set proudly on top of her rock, protected by her tall towers, devastated but intact.

The first city we came to was Villana, which we traversed, singing canticles as we went. The townspeople joined us in great numbers. Then we passed into Genoese territory. At each city along the route I would seek out the governor and ask him to welcome us, and we would move forward in a procession along the streets, preaching penitence and collecting alms. Once we were deep into the heart of the country, I pretended that the Genoese officials had refused to receive us. The surrounding countryside, devastated by famine and pestilence, provided almost no food. Soon, we began to suffer from hunger. A few penitents suggested returning to Carmona, but I objected that it was too far and that we would die of starvation before reaching our homes. It would be best to journey on to Rivella, a large, prosperous port where we would certainly be well provided for.

The governor of Rivella did, in fact, agree to open his gates to us. But the news I carried back to my companions was of impious men who had once again rejected our prayers. The pilgrims then began to mutter among themselves, saying they could take by force what was refused them out of charity. I pretended to recoil from such proposals, but in preaching resignation I insinuated that the only alternative left us was to die where we stood. Angry indignation soon seethed in all their hearts, and I was obliged to yield to the will of that famished horde.

The procession passed through the gates of Rivella without arousing suspicion. When we reached the main square, I suddenly threw off my white robe and galloped towards the governor's palace shouting, 'Come on lads! Long live Carmona!' The penitents hastily tore off the garments which enveloped them and beneath which they were fully armed. The surprise was so great that no resistance was offered. Drunk with victory, their passions inflamed by the smell of blood, the pious pilgrims were soon transformed into soldiers. A night of orgy completed the metamorphosis. The Genoese magistrates were massacred, their houses looted, their wives raped. For a whole week, wine flowed freely in the taverns and obscene songs echoed through the streets.

I left a small army of soldiers in Rivella; with the rest of my troops I set out to conquer the castles and fortresses which commanded the route leading from Carmona to the sea. The garrisons, decimated by the plague and half-starving, were unable to defend themselves against our assaults. I was not unaware that my perfidy had aroused indignation throughout Italy. But the Genoese were still too weak to undertake a war and they were obliged to accept my conquests.

Master of Rivella, I immediately ordered high taxes to be paid on all merchandise entering the port. The Florentine traders insisted in vain on being exempted from these taxes, but I did not want to accord them any special privileges. I knew that I was rousing the ire of Florence, but I did not shrink at the prospect of war with the powerful republic.

I began preparations for battle. I was rich enough to enlist the services of most of the captains who had joined mercenary armies all over Italy. I paid them regular partial wages and in return they agreed to place their men at my command whenever I had need of them. In the mean-time, I invited them to wage war on their own account and to live on the spoils of pillaging the neighbouring lands, thus weakening the cities that I planned to attack while everything was still peaceful. When I wanted to take a fortified town by surprise, I ostensibly gave leave of absence to one of my captains whom I secretly entrusted with the task of carrying out my project. If he failed, I disclaimed him. Without having declared war, I was soon in possession of all the castles and fortresses along my frontiers. By the time the Genoese decided to invade the plain of Carmona, I had built up a formidable army, and the best of Italy's condottieri were in my pay.

At first, I let the Genoese and their army of Catalan mercenaries spread out over the countryside. Warned of their approach, the peasants, bringing their crops and livestock with them, took refuge in villages that I had had fortified. The soldiers of the enemy could find scarcely enough to live on in these plundered plains. They attempted to take a few of the villages, but, situated as they were on isolated hill-tops and fiercely defended, our castles defied all assaults. The troops commanded by Angelo de Tagliana were split up and grew exhausted under these attacks. It was easy to ambush isolated groups of soldiers and to make prisoners of the marauders searching for food in the abandoned farms. When Tagliana had advanced as far as the river Mincia, I decided to join battle.

On a fine June morning our armies stood face to face. A slight mist rose from the river and the blue sky was tinged with grey. Steel armour sparkled in the early light, the glistening horses neighed, and the joy in my heart was as fresh as the dew-covered grass. Tagliana, using conventional tactics, divided his army into three corps; I divided mine into small groups. Judging by the delicate grey of the sky, I forecast a stifling, sun-baked afternoon, and I had pitchers and barrels prepared in advance for watering the horses and refreshing my soldiers after each skirmish. When the signal for combat was given, the two armies charged at each other with a roar. The advantage of my tactics was soon evident. The Genoese troops were unable to shift positions except in large numbers, while my soldiers attacked in small, independent groups, and then fell back into line before attacking again. Nevertheless, the Catalans grouped around their general and stoutly repulsed our assaults. The sun climbed high in the sky, the heat became intense, and we had not yet gained an inch of ground. By the middle of the afternoon our horses were treading over seared, yellow grass, and the air was thick with dust. My men hastily quenched their thirst between attacks, but not a drop of water had wet the lips of our enemies. Through the clanging of steel and the heavy beat of horses' hoofs could be heard the sound of water flowing less than five hundred yards to the south. Finally, Tagliana's soldiers could no longer resist the temptation; they broke ranks and went down to the river. Then, with a sudden charge, we drove a large number of them into the water where they were drowned. The rest fled in disorder, leaving some five hundred prisoners in our hands.

I wanted to celebrate this victory with festivities worthy of a race of warriors. Upon our return to Carmona, I arranged for a huge tournament to be held between the upper and lower cities. In the morning, children, then, later, young people engaged for three hours in various types of combat. During the afternoon, it was the men's turn to face each other. Lightly protected, they threw stones at one another which they tried to parry with their left arms which were wrapped in heavy cloaks. The men from the upper city wore green and those from the lower city, red. Next, two groups of more heavily armoured men entered the square. The combatants were clad in coats of iron beneath which they wore small cushions stuffed with coarse hemp and cotton to soften the blows. In his right hand each man held a lance from which the steel tip had been removed, and in his left hand, a shield. Victory consisted in occupying the centre of the square. A great crowd gathered at the lists; at every window there were women smiling. Spectators urged on their relatives, their friends, their neighbours with gestures and shouts, crying out, 'Hurrah for the Greens!' or 'Hurrah for the Reds!' I had neither friend, nor relative, nor neighbour. Seated on a velvet canopy, I watched the tournaments indifferently as I drained several small jugs of wine.

'I drink to the prosperity of Rivella and to the ruin of Genoa!' I said, raising my goblet.

They raised their goblets and docile voices echoed, 'To the prosperity of Rivella!' But Palombo, who was head of the weaver's guild, did not join in the toast; he was contemplating his goblet attentively.

'Why aren't you drinking?' I asked.

He raised his eyes. 'I've heard from an unimpeachable source that the Florentine merchants in Rivella have received orders to cease all trading by the first of November.'

'Well?'

'On that date, they'll leave the city and transfer their businesses to Sismone in the Maremma d'Evisa.'

There was a long silence around the table.

'To hell with the Florentine merchants!' I exclaimed.

'All the other merchants will follow them,' said Palombo.

'That will be unfortunate for Evisa and Sismone, then.'

'Florence will back them,' he argued.

They all looked at me; in their eyes I read: 'The Florentines must be exempted from tax.' But had I conquered just to follow the advice of these old men? To submit to Florence?

'It's Florence's misfortune!' I said. I turned to my captains and raised my goblet. 'I drink to our victory over Florence!'

'To our victory over Florence!' they shouted in chorus.

There was a cold note to Bentivoglio's and Puzzini's voices and a shifty smile twisted Orsini's lips. I grabbed hold of a wine jug and threw it to the ground. 'That's how I'll destroy Florence.'

They looked at me placidly. The war was over and we were celebrating our victory; they asked for nothing more. As for me, I wanted to hold onto my victory, to keep it alive in my mind. But where was it? I searched their faces in vain for the fervour of that afternoon's battle, for the smell of dust and sweat, for the crushing weight of sun on the steel armour. They laughed and voiced their petty concerns but I no longer wanted to listen to them. My shirt was choking me; I stood up and tore it open. The blood rushed to my head, air filled my chest; I felt as though my life were about to burst open like a flame. The cloth tore in my fingers and I let my empty hands fall back to my sides. In the centre of the square, a herald was lowering a barrier and proclaiming the victory of the Reds, and the delirious spectators threw flowers and handkerchiefs and shawls at the feet of the contestants. Five of them had been killed, nine others wounded. But all these men, capable of coveting ephemeral, insignificant victories were mere, puerile creatures. I could not be bothered with their games. The sky was as blue as it had been on the banks of the Mincia, but now it seemed faded. It was beneath the walls of Florence, with the future within our grasp, that it flamed red and golden, like the sky that burned in my memory.

Palombo was right. In the course of the winter all of Rivella's merchants took their businesses to Sismone, a port situated in the Maremma d'Evisa. The artisans of Rivella found themselves without resources. Taking advantage of the widespread discontent, the Alboni faction aroused the people and proclaimed Rivella's independence. To try to have retaken her would have required a naval fleet. I had to content myself with ravaging the surrounding countryside, with burning crops and farms. But I decided to take my revenge on Evisa in exemplary fashion.

This city, which was allied with Florence, was situated at the mouth of the Mincia, the river whose upper reaches flowed through my lands. On either side of Evisa's ramparts, it split into two branches, each about a mile wide, which served as natural defences in place of the usual moats. Too deep to be forded, their banks were too muddy to permit the use of boats. I ordered one of my engineers to divert the Mincia. For six months they worked to construct a dyke of extraordinary strength in order to change the course of the river. At the same time, to give the river an outlet into the plain of Carmona, I had a tunnel dug through a mountain. Evisa's inhabitants imagined their lakes already being transformed into pestilential swamps, their healthy air contaminated, and their defences destroyed. They sent emissaries who pleaded with me to give up my plans, but I replied that every city had the right to carry out whatever works were deemed necessary on its own territory. But one day, just as I was reckoning that Evisa, deprived of her natural defences, would fall into my hands, a great storm burst. The Mincia, swollen by the rain, swept away the dykes and in one night destroyed the fruits of months of labour.

So I sent my captains, Bentivoglio, Orsini and Puzzini, to lay waste to Evisa's outlying lands. Knowing that Florence was raising an army to come to her ally's aid, I formed an alliance with Siena. We put together an army of ten thousand men. My troops and the condottieri's joined forces in Siena and I attempted to break through into Florentine territory. While we skirted the outer perimeter of her borders, the Republic's army followed us from inside to prevent our entering. I pretended to threaten the state of Arezzo, and when the Florentines sent troops to defend that province, we gained entry by way of Chianti in the valley of the Greva. Following the course of the Arno, we marched as far as Florence itself. During the campaign, an immense amount of booty was taken; since war had not been declared, the peasants had not taken the precaution of hiding their belongings and livestock.

For ten days we advanced without encountering any obstacles. The soldiers sang and stuck flowers in their horses' manes, and our cavalcade gave the appearance of a peaceful, triumphal procession. And when we caught sight of Florence from the top of the hill, with her vermilion domes bathed in sunlight, a great cry of joy burst from every throat. We set up camp, and for four days the soldiers lolled about in the fresh grass and passed around heavy goatskins of wine. Oxen and cows with full udders wandered freely among the carts laden with rugs, mirrors and laces.

'And now?' Orsini asked. 'What are we going to do?'

'What do you want us to do?'

I could not even dream of attacking Florence. She was stretched out at my feet, radiant and calm, a ribbon of green water running through her centre. The idea of wiping her out was inconceivable.

'We've taken a fairly rich booty,' I said. 'We'll bring it back to Carmona.'

He smiled without answering and I walked away feeling irritated. I was well aware that the campaign had cost a great deal of money and had resulted in nothing. Florence was at my feet and yet I was powerless to do anything about it. Of what use then were my victories?

I announced to my troops that we would turn back to Carmona. Throughout the camp there were mutterings. We were masters of Tuscany, were we now going to abandon it? Slowly, we packed our belongings. When the time came to set off, I noticed that Paolo d'Orsini was no longer with us. During the night he had passed over into the service of Florence, taking a part of my cavalry with him.

Weakened by this defection, we began to return speedily along the valley of the Arno. The soldiers were no longer singing. Orsini's men were soon harassing our rearguard, and my troops, dulled by their meaningless triumphs, were longing to join battle. But he knew the country better than I did and I was fearful of his cunning. He followed us all the way to the frontiers of Siena and, in full view, began attacking Mascola, a village surrounded by swamps. My men considered themselves insulted and clamoured loudly for a fight. But a battle seemed to me a dangerous under-taking: the crusty earth covering the silted swamp could support foot-soldiers but would sink beneath the weight of a horse.

'I fear a trap,' I said.

'We have more men; we're stronger than they are,' said Puzzini zealously.

I opted for battle. I, too, was anxious to taste the blood of victory against enemies made of flesh and bones. A narrow road, which Orsini appeared to have left unguarded, crossed through the swamp. I ordered my troops to follow it. Suddenly, when it was too late to retreat, they were assailed by a shower of arrows from every direction; Orsini had prepared an ambush. Then his light cavalry and his infantry struck at our flanks, and as soon as my soldiers left the road to repulse the enemy, they sank into the muddy swamp and were unable to move. No sooner had our columns been thrown into confusion than Orsini's foot soldiers ventured onto the road and, thrusting their swords into our horses' bellies, knocked off the riders who were so weighed down by their heavy armour that they could not get up again. Pietro Bentivoglio discovered an escape by way of a footpath cutting across the swamp; as for me, I galloped the entire length of the road, straight through the enemy's midst, and left them behind me. But Ludovico Puzzini was taken prisoner along with eight thousand men. Not a single soldier had been slain. All our belongings, as well as all the booty we had taken in Tuscany, fell into the victors' hands.

'Honour demands that we avenge ourselves for this defeat,' my lieutenants declared. Their eyes sparkled in their humiliated faces.

'What's one defeat?' I said.

Orsini's soldiers, who had served under me at the beginning of the campaign, considered their prisoners as brothers in arms, less fortunate than themselves, and had set them free on the first night. In Villana two armourers sold me five thousand suits of armour, and I returned to Carmona with my troops practically intact. I had gained nothing by my victories, and in losing a battle, I had lost nothing.

My lieutenants frowned and looked at me uncompre-hendingly. I shut myself in my study and there I remained for three days and three nights. Tancredi's face, hardened by despair, flashed before my eyes. 'What purpose? For whom?' And I heard the voice of the dark-faced monk: 'What you have done is nothing.'

I decided to change my methods. Renouncing military parades, pitched battles and useless cavalry thrusts, I would henceforth do my best to weaken the hostile republics with cunning policies.

The cities of Orci, Circio and Montechiaro had broken away from the Florentine alliance by signing commercial treaties; agents posing as merchants in cities that were subject to Genoa fomented conspiracies, and in Genoa itself, they fostered rivalry between the factions. I was careful to respect the institutions of cities which were ruled by me, and therefore many small republics, weary of maintaining freedom that was too difficult to defend, and preferring security to independence, accepted my protection.

Life was harsh in Carmona. The men slept for less than five hours, working from dawn well into the night, endlessly weaving wool in their sombre workshops and obliged to take part in tough military exercises even in the most torrid heat. The women spent their youths expecting and bringing up children who, from the youngest age, were given training. Yet within thirty years, our territory had become as vast as Florence's. Genoa, on the other hand, as a result of my scheming, had fallen into complete decadence. My captains had devastated her countryside and destroyed her fortresses; her commerce was in decline, her navigation abandoned, and the city was prey to all the disruptions of anarchy. She was dealt a final blow when the Duke of Milan attacked her by surprise. General Carmagnola had no difficulty making his way through the mountains with his three thousand horses and eight thousand foot soldiers, and he was soon ravaging the valleys. I immediately set out for the port of Livorno which controlled the mouth of the Arno. I did not even have to lay siege, for the Genoese, unable to defend the city, ceded her to me for the sum of one hundred thousand florins. Proudly, I raised the standard of Carmona over Livorno's castle, while my army loudly acclaimed the triumph of my patient manoeuvres. With Genoa destroyed, Livorno became the principal port of all Italy.

All our hopes seemed about to be realized when a messenger arrived announcing that the King of Aragon, joining forces with the Duke of Milan, was preparing to attack Genoa from the sea. Suddenly, I became aware of the Duke's ulterior aims. Genoa was incapable of protecting herself against both of these powerful adversaries. Once he had become master of Liguria, the Duke would invade Tuscany and reduce Carmona, and then Florence, to slavery. I had only ever seen Genoa as a strong rival and I had done everything in my power to weaken her, without imagining that her ruin could one day bring about my own.

I was forced to offer my aid to Genoa. Torn apart by the quarrels I had obligingly helped fuel, the Genoese were in two minds as to whether to offer resistance; they were hesitant about whether or not they should surrender to the Duke. I tried to lift their spirits, but they had long neglected to maintain an army, and their mercenaries were always liable to leave at a moment's notice. Following the valley of the Arno, so often ravaged by my captains' incursions, I set out to cut off Carmagnola's advance. Everywhere, fortresses had been demolished and abandoned, castles destroyed. Instead of entrenching ourselves behind solid walls, we were forced to fight in open countryside, but there was scarcely enough food to live on in this land which had too often been devastated. All our past successes now turned against us. After six months of campaigning, my army, hungry, worn out and weakened by fever, was now only a shadow of its former self. It was then that Carmagnola decided to attack.

Carmagnola's forces consisted of ten thousand cavalry and

eighteen thousand foot soldiers. Compared to his, my cavalry was so inferior in numbers that I decided to risk a new tactic. Against Carmagnola's mounted soldiers, I sent my infantry, which firmly withstood the first assault. Armed with halberds, they hacked at the legs of the charging horses or grabbed hold of them by the feet and pulled both horses and riders to the ground. Four hundred horses had already been slain when Carmagnola gave orders to his cavalrymen to dismount. The battle was fought tooth and nail, and a great number of soldiers were killed on both sides. In the evening, the youngest and bravest of my lieutenants secretly led six hundred cavalry through the mountains to the Miossena Valley and, with horrifying cries, they burst down upon Carmagnola's rearguard. The Milanese, terrified by this surprise attack, fled in disorder. We had lost three hundred and ninety-six men, but the number of soldiers dead on Carmagnola's side was three times as great.

'Now,' I said to Doge Fregoso, 'you mustn't lose a minute. Arm all the men of Liguria, rebuild your fortresses, and send emissaries to Florence and Venice to ask their help.'

He seemed not to hear me. Beneath his long white hair, his face was noble and serene; his clear eyes gazed into the distance.

'What a beautiful day,' he remarked.

From the terrace, shaded by oleanders and orange trees, I looked down upon Genoa's main street. Women dressed in velvets and silks walked languidly in the shade of the fine buildings; cavaliers wearing embroidered doublets sauntered proudly through the crowds. Four of Carmona's soldiers were sitting in a doorway looking emaciated, dirty and tired; they were watching a group of girls chatting with some young men by the fountain.

'If you don't try to defend yourself,' I said angrily, 'Carmagnola will be outside Genoa's walls by spring.'

'I know,' Fregoso replied. 'But we're unable to defend ourselves,' he added indifferently.

'You can,' I said. 'Carmagnola isn't invincible, for we've beaten him. My soldiers are tired; now it's your turn.'

'There is no dishonour in admitting one's weakness,' he said softly with a smile. 'We are too civilized not to love peace.'

'Peace? What peace?'

'The Duke of Milan has promised to guarantee us our constitution and our internal liberty,' he answered. 'I would not renounce the dignities of office my city has bestowed upon me without a wrench, but I will not shrink from that sacrifice.'

'What are you going to do?'

'I shall abdicate,' he said with dignity.

I stood up and clenched my fists. 'That's a betrayal.'

'I must only consider the interests of my country.'

'And this is the sort of prison we've been fighting for these past six months,' I said.

I leaned over the balustrade. Three young girls with flowers in their hair were passing by; I heard them laughing. My soldiers watched them gloomily, and I knew the images that were flashing through their minds: the parched pink streets of Carmona where even noblemen travelled on foot; unsmiling women dressed in black who suckled their children as they walked; little girls who climbed the hill carrying buckets of water too heavy for them; men with exhausted expressions on their faces eating watery soup in their doorways. The centre of the city, where the old hovels had once stood, was now a weed-infested wasteland. We had had no time to build fire houses, or to plant lemon trees, or to sing, or to laugh.

I turned around. 'It's not fair!'

'The Duke of Milan would like to come to terms with you, too,' Fregoso said.

'I refuse to bargain with him.'

That very evening, I set out with my men on the road back to Carmona. More than one was missing. Looking at their dejected faces, I could almost hear them thinking: 'Who, then, are the victors?' And I was unable to answer.

We were approaching Pergola, a city I had always coveted, but which fiercely refused to accept my domination. To make up for my soldiers' disappointment, I decided to make them a present of a tangible victory. I led them beneath the walls of the proud city and promised them that all the spoils they carried off would be shared between them. Pergola was rich and they were excited at the prospect of looting her. The city was strongly fortified, and on the east, she over-looked the Mincia. We had tried several times to lay siege to her, but she had withstood all our assaults. Now, however, I had new weapons: heavy mortars which were powerless against moving objects, but extremely effective when used against stone walls. I began by calling upon Pergola to surrender. My soldiers fired arrows over the ramparts which carried messages threatening to destroy the city if they refused to open her gates to us. But the inhabitants, massed behind the battlements, answered only with cries of hate and defiance. I then positioned a corps of soldiers at each of the city's gates and had the ground levelled between them to facilitate communication. Next, I ordered the mortars to be brought up; my soldiers looked incredulously at these engines of war. The first cannonballs that were fired crashed against the walls without shaking them. From the tops of the city's towers, the people of Pergola sang and hurled insults at us. But I was not discouraged. These marvellous contraptions, perfected by my engineers, could each fire sixty shots in a single night. For thirty days we battered the walls and little by little the towers and ramparts fell to pieces. The debris began to pile up in the moat surrounding the city and it was not long before there were penetrable breaches. The besieged inhabitants withdrew from the ramparts; their songs and insults were no longer heard. On the final night of the bombardment, as the cannonballs struck against the tottering stones, a leaden silence hung over the city. When dawn came, I saw that we had created a wide breach in the wall and I ordered my men to attack. They rushed off with cries of joy; Genoa had been forgotten along with all the enticements of peacetime. We accomplished a unique feat: for the first time, mortars had battered down powerful ramparts; for the first time, an army had entered a large, fortified city by force.

I was the first to pass through the breach. To our astonishment, we discovered that there was no one lying in wait for us behind the walls, and the streets were deserted. I stopped, fearing an ambush. Alarmed by the silence, my soldiers did not speak. We looked up at the roofs and towers. We saw no one. The windows of the houses were closed, the doors open. We advanced cautiously; there was not a sound. At every street corner my men aimed their crossbows at the roofs, looking anxiously to right and left, but not a single stone or an arrow disturbed the air. We reached the main square. It was empty.

'Search the houses,' I ordered.

The soldiers went off in small groups. Followed by several guards, I entered the governor's palace. The marble floor of the hall was bare, the walls were bare. In the drawing-rooms, all the furniture was still in its place, but there were neither rugs, nor tapestries, nor paintings anywhere in the palace. The linen and silver coffers and the jewel boxes were all empty. When I left the palace, I learned that mattresses and copper pots had been found on the banks of the Mincia. Under cover of night, the entire population had crossed the river, and while we believed that they were lying in wait for us behind the ramparts, they had fled, taking all their treasures with them.

Surrounded by my silent, motionless soldiers, I stood in the middle of the square. They had found nothing to pillage in the abandoned houses apart from some old wrought-iron ornaments. The tavern floors were wet with wine; all the casks had been emptied. In the huge fireplaces, sacks of flour, loaves of bread and sides of meat, had been burned to cinders. We had believed that we were conquering a city, and all we possessed was a shell of stone.

Towards noon, one of my lieutenants brought a woman to me whom the soldiers had discovered in a house on the outskirts of the city. She was small, with heavy plaits of hair wound about her head. There was neither fear nor defiance in her eyes.

'Why didn't you leave with the others?' I asked her.

'My husband is ill. They couldn't take him.'

'And why did the others leave?' I said angrily. 'Do you think that when I conquer a city I have the eyes of babies gouged out?'

'No,' she replied. 'We don't believe that.'

'Then why?'

She did not answer.

'More than twenty cities prosper under my domination. Never have the people of Montechiaro, Orci and Paleva been more happy.'

'The people of Pergola are different,' she said simply.

I looked at her fixedly and she held my gaze. The people of Pergola. The people of Carmona. Once, long before, I too had used these words. I had driven the women and children from the city. Why? . . . I turned my eyes away.

'Let her go,' I said to the guards.

She left without hurrying.

'Let's get out of here.'

My captains assembled their soldiers who obeyed without protest. No one would have wanted to spend the night in that accursed city. I was the last to leave the deserted square; the silence of the stone walls troubled my heart. A dead woman lay at my feet. It was I who had killed her, and I no longer knew why.

Eight days later, I signed a treaty with the Duke of Milan.

Peace reigned. I disbanded my army, lowered the rates of tax, abolished the anti-luxury laws. I loaned money to Carmona's traders and became their banker. With my encouragement, industry and agriculture developed strongly. My wealth, which I consecrated to the city, became as legendary as my eternal youth. On the ground where the old hovels once stood, I erected palaces more beautiful than Genoa's. Architects, sculptors and painters were summoned to my court. I had an aqueduct built and fountains spouted in every square. The hill was soon dotted with new houses and vast suburbs spread out over the plain. Attracted by our prosperity, many foreigners came to live within our walls. I had doctors come from Bologna and I built hospitals. The number of births increased; the population grew rapidly. Soon Carmona had two hundred thousand inhabitants. Proudly, I thought, 'They owe their lives to me. They owe everything to me.' It lasted thirty years.

The people, however, were no happier than before. They had better lodgings and were somewhat better dressed, but they worked without respite, and never before had the noblemen and the rich displayed their wealth with such insolence. The ambitions of both the poor and the rich grew ever greater, and from year to year the workers found their conditions less and less tolerable. I wanted to improve their lot, but the master weavers explained to me that if the work hours were reduced, or if wages were raised, the price of goods would have to increase. Then, unable to compete with foreign producers, we would all be ruined, workers and merchants alike. They were right. Unless I could rule the whole world, no serious reforms were possible. In the summer of 1449 the harvest was poor. Throughout Italy the price of wheat rose steeply and our greedy peasants sold most of their crops to Pisa and Florence. When winter came, bread was so expensive in Carmona that many workers, unable to provide food for their families, had to ask for public charity. I bought up wheat wherever I could and distributed it to the people, but it was not only bread they wanted. They also wanted not to have to beg. One morning, the members of the various guilds gathered in arms around their banners. Their plans had been kept a closely guarded secret. They spread out over the city and pillaged several palaces. The noblemen and the wealthy, caught unaware, could do nothing but barricade themselves in their houses. The weavers, fullers and dyers, by now effectively in control of Carmona, appointed a council of sixty-four knights who were anxious to take advantage of the revolt to oust me from power. They promised bread to the people and the cancelling of their debts, and having proclaimed that I had made a pact with the devil and that I should be burned at the stake like a sorcerer, they launched an attack on my palace. 'Down with the son of the devil!' they shouted. 'Death to the tyrant!' From the palace windows, my guards let loose a hail of arrows. The attackers hastily retreated, leaving the square deserted, but a few moments later, they charged at the door again, attempting to break it down. That evening, just as the door was about to give way, the noblemen from the surrounding villages and castles, who had been told of the attack by messengers, came galloping through the city.

'The revolt has been quelled, my lord! The rabble are on the run!' cried the captain of my guards, bursting into my room. Behind him, I could hear shouts of joy and the loud clanking of metal. Albozzi, Ferracci and Vincenzo-the-Black, my rescuers, were climbing the stone staircase, laughing. Outside, horses were prancing beneath my windows, and I knew there was blood on their hoofs.

'Stop the massacre!' I shouted violently. 'Put out the fires and leave me alone!'

I shut the door, went over to the window and pressed my forehead against the iron grillwork. Against the sky, lit up like a bright dawn, there rose an enormous mushroom of black smoke. The weavers' houses were on fire and the weavers' wives and children were being burned alive in their homes.

It was late into the night when I moved away from the window and left the palace. The sky was dark now and neither the sounds of galloping horses, nor the savage shouts of soldiers, could be heard in the streets.

At the entrance to the district in which the weavers lived, soldiers were standing guard. The ruins were still smouldering. Dead bodies were scattered about the deserted streets – women with their chests staved in, children whose faces had been crushed by horses' hoofs. Charred corpses lay among the ashes. At the corner of a street I heard a long wail. The moon was almost full and in the distance a dog was howling. 'Serves what purpose? For whom?' From the depths of the past, Tancredi was sneering at me.

The dead were buried, the houses rebuilt. I decreed that the artisans should be released from their debts. In the spring, the almond trees blossomed as they did every spring and the weavers' looms hummed in quiet streets. But my heart was still full of ashes.

'Why are you so sad?' Laura asked me. 'Don't you have everything in the world a man could possibly desire?'

I had slept all night in her arms. The days now seemed too long and I welcomed the nights. With my head resting on her breast, I felt I wanted to dissolve once more into the milky languor of her body, but the light of day was already beating against my eyelids and I could hear the sounds of life stirring in the city. I was awake and I was bored. I jumped out of bed.

'What else is there to want in this world?'

'Many things.'

I laughed. I could easily have given her everything she wanted, but I did not love her. I loved no one. While I was dressing, I felt my legs grow weak, as on the day I buried Caterina when there seemed nothing left for me anywhere. 'Day after day, the same thing,' I thought. 'Endlessly! Will

I never awake in another world, where even the air will taste different?'

I left the bedroom and went outside. It was still the same world; it was still Carmona with her pink streets and her funnel-shaped chimneys. New statues stood in her squares and I was aware of their beauty. But I was also aware that they would stand motionless for centuries on the sites where they had been erected, and they seemed to me as old and as distant as the statues of Venus buried in the earth. The people of Carmona walked past them without a glance, they took no notice of either the monuments or the fountains. What purpose did these chiselled stones serve? I climbed up to the ramparts. What purpose did Carmona serve? High upon her rock, she stood unchanging through war, peace, plague, rebellion. And there were a hundred other cities in Italy standing upon their rocks, equally proud, equally useless. What purpose did the sky serve, and the flowers in the meadows? It was a fine morning, but the peasants, bent over the land, did not look at the sky. And as for me, I was weary of seeing it day in and day out for two hundred years, always the same.

I walked aimlessly for several hours. 'Everything a man could possibly desire.' I kept repeating these words to myself, but I was unable to awaken in myself the least desire. How long ago it seemed when every precious grain of wheat weighed so heavily in the palm of my hand!

Suddenly I stopped. In a small yard where chickens were busily nibbling, a woman was bent over a tub doing her laundry, and beneath an almond tree there was a little girl laughing. The ground was strewn with white petals and the child was squeezing them in her hands and eagerly cramming them into her mouth. She was very brown and had large, dark eyes. 'This is the first time those eyes have ever seen almond blossom,' I thought.

'The pretty little girl,' I said, 'is she yours?'

The woman looked up. 'Yes. She's rather thin,'

'You should feed her better,' I said as I threw a purse in the child's lap.

The woman looked at me mistrustfully and I left without so much as a smile from her. The little girl was smiling, but not at me. She had no need of me to smile. I looked up. The sky was a pale, fresh blue, and the blossoming trees sparkled as they did on the day I carried Sigismondo upon my shoulders. In the eyes of a child, the whole world was being born anew. 'I shall have a child, a child of my own,' I thought suddenly.

Ten months later, Laura brought a strong, healthy boy into the world. I sent him immediately to a castle on the outskirts of Villana. I did not intend to share my son with anyone.

While he was being cared for by his nursemaids, I eagerly made preparations for Antonio's future. First, I consolidated the peace. I did not want him ever to know the bloody vanity of war. For a long time, Florence had been demanding that I relinquish the port of Livorno and so I agreed to return it to them. A revolution had broken out in Rivella and the prince had implored my help, offering to place the city under my protection. I refused.

On a hilltop facing Carmona, I had a marble villa constructed and formal gardens laid out. I drew scientists and artists to my court; I collected paintings and statues and assembled an enormous library. The most distinguished men of the age were put in charge of Antonio's education. I attended their lessons with him and I, myself, took charge of my son's physical training. He was a handsome child, a bit slender for my taste, but robust. At seven, he knew how to read and write Italian, Latin and French. He could swim, and could shoot with a bow and arrow, and he was able to control a small horse.

In between his work and his games, he needed companions of his own age to play with. I gathered around him the best looking and most gifted children of Carmona. Among others, I had the little girl with the almond blossom brought up at the palace. Her name was Beatrice. As she grew up, she retained her thin, dark face and her enchanting smile. She played with Antonio like a boy, and of all his comrades, it was she he preferred.

One night while I was lying in bed, feeling bored (at that time I often became bored, even in my dreams), I decided to take a walk in the garden. It was a hot, fragrant, moonless night, streaked with shooting stars. I had taken only a few steps along the sandy paths when I noticed the two of them, strolling on the lawn, holding hands. Over their long night-dresses they had hung garlands of flowers. Beatrice had put strands of convulvulus in her hair and against her heart she held a full magnolia flower. They caught sight of me and stood frozen to the spot.

'What are you doing out here?' I asked.

'We're going for a walk,' Beatrice answered in a small, clear voice.

'Do you often go for walks at this hour of the night?'

'For him, it's the first time.'

'And you?'

'Me?' She looked at me boldly. 'I climb out of my window almost every night.'

They both stood there before me, looking guilty and tiny in their flower-bedecked robes which hid their bare feet. I felt a sudden pang in my heart. I had given them days of sunshine, of feasting, of laughter, as well as toys, sweets, and picture-books, and yet they conspired to taste in secret the sweetness of the night, which I had not given them.

'How would you like to go for a ride with me on my horse?'

Their eyes lit up. I saddled my horse and tossed Antonio in front and Beatrice behind. Her two little arms circled my waist. We galloped down the hillside and across the plain as shooting stars blazed in the sky above. The children let out shrieks of joy. I held Antonio tightly to me.

'You mustn't go out secretly any more,' I said. 'You mustn't do anything secretly. If there's anything you want, just ask me. You shall have it.'

'Yes, father,' he said docilely.

The next day I made them each a present of a horse, and often, when the nights were mild, I took them galloping with me. I had a boat built, with orange sails, so I could take them sailing on the Lake of Villamosa, where we often spent the sultry summer months. I did my best to anticipate their every wish. When they were tired of playing, swimming, galloping and running, I would sit down beside them in the pleasant shade of the pine tree and tell them stories. Antonio never tired of asking me questions about Carmona's history. He looked at me in wonder.

'And me, when I grow up, what will I do?' he sometimes asked me.

I would laugh. 'You'll do whatever you want.'

Beatrice said nothing. She listened with an inscrutable expression on her face. She was a wild little girl with long, spindly legs. She was only happy doing things that were forbidden. She would disappear for hours and would be found clambering on a roof, or swimming in a lake that was too deep, or traipsing around in the dung in a farmyard, or sprawled out across a path because she had chosen a horse that was too lively.

'Funny little creature!' I would say, stroking her hair. She would shake her head rebelliously; she did not like me to fondle her. Whenever I leaned over to kiss her, she would draw back and, with dignity, hold out her hand.

'Don't you like it here? Aren't you happy?'

'Yes, of course.'

She never imagined that she might have been living somewhere else, washing clothes and weeding the earth. But whenever I saw her intently reading a heavy tome or climbing a tree, I would say to myself proudly, 'I have shaped her destiny.' And my heart would leap even more joyfully when I heard Antonio laugh, and I would think, 'He owes his life to me, he owes me the world.'

Antonio loved life and he loved the world. He loved

the gardens, the lakes, the spring mornings and summer evenings, as well as paintings, books, music. At sixteen, he was almost as learned as his teachers. He wrote poems which he sang while accompanying himself on the viol. And he took no less pleasure in such violent activities as hunting, jousting, tournaments. I did not dare forbid him going in for them, but my mouth grew dry whenever I saw him diving into the lake from the top of a rock or jumping on an untamed horse.

One evening, I was sitting in the library at Villamosa reading a book, when Beatrice burst in and rushed up to me. I was surprised, for she never came to speak to me unless I called her. She was very pale.

'What happened?'

Her hands were clenching the material of her dress. She looked as though she were struggling against something that was suffocating her. Finally, she said, 'Antonio is drowning.'

I ran to the door.

'He wanted to swim across the lake, but he can't get back. I can't save him,' she murmured.

I was at the lake shore in less than a minute. I tore off my clothes and plunged into the water. It was still light and soon I caught sight of a black shape in the middle of the lake. Antonio was floating on his back. When he saw me he moaned and closed his eyes.

He was unconscious when I brought him back to the shore. I stretched him out on my coat and rubbed him vigorously. I could feel the heat of my hands penetrating his body. In the palms of my hands, I could feel his young muscles, his tender skin, his fragile bones, and it seemed as if I were moulding a completely new body for him. 'I'll always be here to save you from all harm,' I thought fervently. Gently, I carried in my arms my son to whom I had twice given life.

Beatrice was standing by the door of the house. She held herself erect and stiff; tears were streaming down her cheeks.

'He's safe,' I said. 'Don't cry.'

'I can see that he's safe.' She looked at me and there was hatred in her eyes.

I put Antonio to bed. Beatrice had followed me, and when he opened his eyes, his gaze fell upon her.

'I didn't cross the lake.'

She bent over him. 'You'll cross it tomorrow,' she said fervently.

'No! Are you mad?' I leaned over Antonio. 'Swear to me that you'll never try it again.'

'Oh, father!'

'Swear to it. For the sake of all I've done for you, for the sake of your love for me, swear to it.'

'All right. I swear.'

He closed his eyes again. Beatrice turned around and slowly left the room. I stayed beside him and for a long while I studied his smooth cheeks, his fresh eyelids, the face of my beloved son. I had saved him, but I had not been able to make him succeed in crossing the lake. Perhaps Beatrice was right to cry. With a sudden feeling of anguish I thought, 'How much longer will he obey me?'

Beneath the cypresses and yew trees, low above the pink terraces, the summer hovered. It glistened in the hollows of marble fountains, rustled in the folds of silk dresses, and its fragrance rose from Eliana's golden breasts. Suddenly, the sound of a viol hidden among the bowers, pierced the silence; at the same moment, a spray of sparkling water gushed forth from every fountain.

Ripples of surprise echoed along the length of the balustrade, and the women clapped their hands. From the heart of the burning earth, thin crystal shafts shot up towards the sky. The still pools of unruffled waters suddenly came to life.

'Oh!' Eliana exclaimed. The perfumed scent of her breath drifted across my face. 'What a magician you are!'

'What's so magical about it?' I said. 'They're just streams of water.'

The water cascaded down over rocks, gurgling and laughing, but in my heart, its laughter echoed in hard, sharp jolts. 'Mere streams of water,' I thought contemptuously.

'The waterfall, Bianca! Look at the waterfall!' Antonio had put his hand on the young woman's plump shoulder. I looked at his beaming, happy face and my scornful smile disappeared. These ridiculous fountains counted for nothing: it was this life, this happiness that I had created. Antonio was handsome. He had his mother's glittering eyes and the haughty profile of the Foscas. He was less robust than men had been in former centuries, but he had an agile, wiry body. He was caressing a willing shoulder, he was smiling at the joyous sound of the water. It was a beautiful day.

'Father,' he said, 'have I time to play a game of tennis?'

I smiled 'Who's counting the time?'

'But aren't the messengers from Rivella waiting to see us?'

I looked over at the horizon where the deep blue of the sky was beginning to fade. Soon it would merge into the pink earth. 'He has so few summers to live,' I thought. 'Should I let him miss this beautiful evening?

'Do you really want to see them with me?'

'Of course!' His young face hardened. 'May I even beg a favour of you?'

'It's granted.'

'Let me receive them on my own.'

I picked up a cypress twig and snapped it with my fingers. 'Alone? Why?'

Antonio blushed. 'You always say you'll let me share your power, but you never let me make any decisions of my own. Is it all just a game?'

I pursed my lips. Suddenly the cloudless sky had grown heavy as if a storm was imminent.

'You haven't enough experience yet,' I explained.

'Do I have to wait until I've lived two centuries?'

In his eyes I saw the same fire that I had once seen burning in Tancredi's eyes. I put my hand on his shoulder.

'I would willingly hand over my power to you; it weighs heavily upon me. But believe me, it will only bring you worries.'

'That's exactly what I want,' said Antonio bitterly.

'All I want is for you to be happy. Don't you have everything a man could possibly desire?'

'What's the good of giving me everything if you forbid me to do anything with it? Father,' he continued insistently, 'you, would never have been satisfied with this kind of existence. I was taught to reason, to think. But what is the point, if I have to go on blindly following your advice. Did I spend all those years developing my body just so that I could go hunting?'

'I know. You want it all to serve a purpose.'

'Yes.'

How could I have explained to him that nothing ever serves a purpose; that the palaces, the aqueducts, the new houses, the castles, the conquered cities, were all nothing. He would open wide his sparkling eyes and he would have said, 'But I can see these things, they exist.' Perhaps for him they existed. I threw the broken twig to the ground. All my love for him served no purpose.

'It will be as you wish.'

His face brightened. 'Thank you, father.'

He went off running. His white doublet stood out sharply against the dark leaves of the yews. So he wanted to shape his life with his own hands, his own clumsy, unsullied hands. Could one, after all, shut that life away in a greenhouse and cultivate it free from all danger? Stifled and tied, it would soon lose its brightness, its fragrance. He leapt up the staircase in three bounds and disappeared into the house. He was crossing the marble halls, but I could no longer see him. 'Someday,' I thought, 'everything will be exactly the same as it is now, except that he'll no longer be here.' There would be the same dark trees beneath the same sky, the same shallow murmur of laughter and water, and Antonio would not have left the slightest trace of himself, either on the earth, the sky or the water.

Eliana came up to me and took me by the arm. 'Let's go down to the waterfall.'

'No.'

I turned my back to her and walked towards the villa. I had to see Beatrice. She was the only person I could speak to and smile at without the thought crossing my mind that one day she would die.

I pushed open the door of the library. She was seated at the far end of the oak table, reading. Silently, I watched her attentive face. With her smooth skin, her black hair and her plain dress she seemed as hard and cold as a suit of armour. Absorbed in her reading, she was unaware of my presence. I went over to her.

'Still reading?'

She looked up without showing any sign of surprise; it was difficult to catch her off her guard.

'There are so many books to read,' she replied.

'Too many and too few.'

There were thousands of manuscripts piled on the shelves. They raised questions and problems, and it would be centuries before the answers could be known. Why did she persist in this hopeless quest?

'Your eyes look tired. You would have done better to watch the fountains playing.'

'I'll go tonight when there's no one in the garden.'

With the palm of her hand, she smoothed the page of the manuscript. I could find nothing further to say to her; and she was waiting for me to leave. Yet she needed help, and I could have helped her more than any of those unfinished books. But how could I give her what she persisted in not asking for.

'Won't you leave your books for a while? There's something I want to show you.' In the end, it was always I who asked.

She stood up without answering and smiled faintly, but there was no light in her eyes. Her features were so hard, her face so thin, that everyone found her ugly. Antonio found her ugly. We walked along the long corridors in silence and I opened a door.

'Look!'

The room smelled of a mixture of dust and ginger – a smell of the past that seemed strange in this new villa. The blinds were lowered, and bathed in the yellowish half-light were studded chests, rugs rolled into cylinders, heaps of silks and brocades.

'It's a cargo that arrived from Cyprus this morning.' I opened one of the chests and there was a glitter of precious metals and stones. 'Choose.'

'What?' she asked.

'Anything you like. Look there, at these belts, those necklaces. Wouldn't you like a dress made of that red silk?'

She dipped her hand in the chest and the stones clattered against the jewel-encrusted daggers and swords.

'No, I don't want anything.'

'You'd look beautiful wearing these jewels.'

Disdainfully, she threw back the necklace she was holding in her hand.

'Don't you want people to admire you?' I asked.

'I want them to admire me the way I am.' There was a glint in her eyes.

I closed the chest. She was right. What difference would jewels have made? It was just as she was then, with her simple dress, her unpainted face, her hair squeezed into a net, that I loved her.

'Then choose one of those rugs for your room.'

'I don't need one.'

'What do you need?' I said impatiently.

'I don't care for luxury.'

I grabbed her arm. I felt like digging my nails into her flesh. Twenty-two years old! And she had opinions, made

decisions, felt at home in the world, as if she had lived in it
for centuries. She was judging me.

'Come,' I said. I led her onto the terrace. The heat of the
afternoon had cooled. The fountains were playing.

'I don't care for luxury either,' I said. 'I had this villa built
for Antonio.'

Beatrice's hands were leaning against the warm stone of
the balustrade. 'It's too big.'

'Why too big? There are no limits.'

'It's money wasted.'

'And why not waste money? What else do you think there
is to do with it?'

'You didn't always think like that,' she said.

'That's true.'

I had lent money to the weavers, and Carmona's merchants
had amassed fortunes. Some worked as hard as ever, hoping
to grow even richer, and others squandered away their lives
in foolish debauchery. Once upon a time, the way of life in
Carmona had been pure and austere, but now brawls broke
out every night; husbands with daggers avenged wives who
had been raped, fathers their ravished daughters. And people
had so many children that these offspring grew up in poverty
too. I had had hospitals built and people lived longer than
before, but in the end, they always died. There were now two
hundred thousand inhabitants of Carmona and they were
neither happier nor better than in former times. There were
more of them, but each one of them still lived alone with his
joys and his sorrows. Carmona had been no less full when her
ancient ramparts had enclosed only twenty thousand people.

'Tell me,' I said suddenly, 'two hundred thousand men,
is that any better than twenty thousand? Who profits by it?'

She thought for a moment. 'What a peculiar question.'

'To me, it's the question that matters.'

'Ah! to you perhaps.'

She looked towards the horizon. She was very distant from
me, and in my mouth I could sense a bitter taste that I only

experienced when I was with her. A swarm of gnats hovered in the air. I wanted to believe that she was no different from these ephemeral insects, but she was just as alive, just as real as I was. Her fleeting existence weighed more heavily upon her than my own destiny upon me. For a long while we silently watched the waterfall, that insubstantial yet constant curtain which tumbled over the rocks, scattering its frothy white foam. Always the same foam and always different.

Suddenly, Antonio appeared at the top of the stairs. A flame lit up in Beatrice's eyes. Why was it he she looked at with such warmth? He didn't love her.

'What did those messengers want?' I asked.

Antonio looked at me gravely. Something quivered in his throat. 'They want us to help them capture Rivella.'

'What did you tell them?'

'I swore that Rivella would be ours within a month.'

There was a long silence.

'No' I said finally. 'We will not start those wars again.'

'Then you're making the decision after all,' Antonio said violently. 'Tell me the truth. I'll never rule Carmona, will I?'

I looked at the motionless sky. Time stood still. He had drawn his sword and I had killed him. And now Antonio, too, was hoping for my death.

'Do you want the first act of your reign to be a declaration of war?' I asked.

'How much longer do you want us to stagnate in your peace?' Antonio retorted.

'It took me a long time and great pains to achieve this peace.'

'And what good is it?'

The spouting water sang its foolish song. If it no longer made Antonio's heart rejoice, then what, indeed, was the point of it?

'We're living in peace,' Antonio continued. 'Our whole history is summed up in that word. The revolution in Milan, the wars of Naples, the rebellions of the Tuscan cities, and we played no part in any of them. Everything happens in Italy as if Carmona doesn't exist. What good is all our wealth, our culture, our wisdom, if we just remain here planted on our rock like a giant mushroom?'

'I know,' I replied. It was something I had known for a long time. 'But what can be gained by war?'

'How can you even ask?' said Antonio. 'We would have a port, an outlet to the sea. Carmona would be the equal of Florence.'

'Rivella belonged to us once, you know.'

'But this time we'll keep her.'

'The Manzonis are powerful,' I warned. 'The messengers won't get any help from within Rivella.'

'They're counting on the Duke of Anjou to help them.'

The blood rushed to my head. 'We're not going to bring the French here!'

'Why not? Others have called upon them before and they'll be called upon again – perhaps against us.'

'And that's precisely why there will soon be no more Italy.' I put my hand on Antonio's shoulder. 'We're not as strong as we were years ago. Those countries we used to call barbarian are growing and becoming powerful. France and Germany covet our wealth. Believe me, our only salvation is in union, in peace. If we want Italy to be able to ward off the invasions that threaten her, we must consolidate our alliance with Florence, forge stronger links with Venice and Milan and obtain the help of the Swiss mercenaries. If each city clings to its selfish ambitions, Italy is lost.'

'You've already explained that a hundred times,' Antonio said stubbornly. Angrily, he added, 'But we can't be Florence's ally except if we agree to vegetate in her shadow.'

'What difference does it make?'

'You'd resign yourself to that! You who have done so much for the glory of Carmona!'

'The glory of Carmona counts little in comparison to the salvation of Italy.'

'What do I care about Italy?' Antonio said. 'Carmona is my country.'

'Carmona is one city among others, and there are so many cities.'

'Do you really mean what you're saying?'

'Yes, I mean it.'

'Then how dare you continue to rule over us?' asked Antonio fiercely. 'What do you have in common with us? You're a foreigner in your own city.'

I looked at him in silence. A foreigner. He spoke the truth. I no longer belonged there. For him, Carmona was everything; he loved her with all his mortal heart. I had no right to prevent him fulfilling his destiny as a man, a destiny over which I had no control.

'You're right,' I said. 'From this day on, it shall be you who rule Carmona.'

I took Beatrice's arm and led her to the waterfall. Behind me, Antonio called in a faltering voice: 'Father!' But I did not turn round. I sat down beside Beatrice on a stone bench.

'I suppose it had to happen sooner or later,' I said.

'I can understand Antonio,' she replied with a note of defiance.

'Do you love him?' I asked suddenly.

Her eyelashes fluttered. 'You know I do.'

'Beatrice . . . He'll never love you.'

'But I love him nevertheless.'

'Forget him. You weren't made to suffer.'

'I'm not afraid of suffering.'

'What idiotic pride!' I said angrily.

He courted anxiety; she took pleasure in suffering. What demons possessed them?

'Will you always be the little girl who only enjoys playing forbidden games? Why do you have to ask for the only thing in the world I can't give you?'

'I ask for nothing.'

'You can have everything,' I said. 'This world is so vast, yet it can be yours if you wish it.'

'There's nothing I need.'

She sat erect on the bench, holding herself rather stiffly, her hands flat on her knees, and it occurred to me that she really did not need anything. Whether she was content or disappointed, she would always remain the same.

I seized her wrist and she looked at me in astonishment. 'Forget Antonio. Become my wife. Don't you realize that I love you?'

'You?'

'Do you think I'm incapable of loving?'

She withdrew her hand. 'I don't know.'

'Why do you loathe me?' I asked.

'I don't loathe you.'

'Do I frighten you? You think I'm the devil.'

'No, you're not the devil. I don't believe in the devil, but . . . ' She hesitated.

'What is it?' I asked.

'You're not a man,' she replied with sudden violence. She looked at me steadily. 'You're a corpse.'

I seized her by the shoulders. I felt like crushing her in my hands. And suddenly, I saw myself in the depths of her eyes – dead. Dead as the cypresses that never blossom and never know winter. I let her go and walked away in silence. She sat motionless on the stone bench. She was dreaming of Antonio who was dreaming of his war. And I was alone once more.

A few weeks later, Antonio, with the aid of the Duke of Anjou's troops, captured Rivella. He was wounded as he led the assault. While festivities were being organized in Carmona to celebrate the victory, I set out for Villana where they had taken him. I found him lying in bed, very pale, his skin stretched taut over his bones. He had a hole in his stomach.

'Father,' he said with a smile, 'are you proud of me?'

'Yes,' I answered.

I smiled too, but a volcano was erupting in my breast. Just

a hole in the stomach, and twenty years of care, twenty years of hope and love were wiped out.

'Are they proud of me in Carmona?'

'Never, in all of Italy, will there have been more magnificent festivities than those that will celebrate your victory.'

'If I die,' he said, 'please don't tell anyone until the celebrations are over. Festivals are so wonderful!'

'I promise.'

He closed his eyes with a look of happiness on his face. He died, glorious and gratified, as if his victory had been a real victory, as if the word 'victory' meant something. For him the future held no threat; there was no longer any future. He died, having done what he wanted to do. He would forever be a triumphant hero. 'But, for me there will never be an end to it,' I thought, looking up at the incandescent sky.

I had kept my promise. Beatrice alone knew that Antonio was dead. Happy and unaware, the people cried out, 'Long live Antonio Fosca! Long live Carmona!' For three days the streets of the city echoed to the sounds of parades; tournaments took place in the main square and mystery plays were performed in three of the town's churches. In the church of San Felice, during the performance of the Pentecost plays, sparks symbolizing the fiery tongues of the Holy Ghost fell on the tapestry and set the church ablaze. But the people looked on indifferently at the mounting flames. They were too busy singing and dancing. Flares lit up the square where the façades of the houses were draped with golden banners; fireworks cast a blood-red glow over the marble statues.

'Aren't they going to put out the fire?' Eliana asked. She was standing next to me on the balcony. The necklace of gold and rubies I had given her adorned her amber throat.

'It's a holiday. And besides, there are more than enough churches in Carmona.' It had taken thirty years to build it and now, in a single night, it was being destroyed. Who cared?

I went back into the huge, brightly lit hall. Men and

women, dressed in brocade and glittering with jewels, were dancing. Emissaries from Rivella and other cities under my domination were seated under a canopy with the Duke of Anjou's ambassadors. The Frenchmen spoke with gruff, coarse voices, and the others laughed obsequiously. Among the dancing couples, I caught sight of Beatrice. She was wearing a red silk dress and was dancing with a French nobleman. When the music stopped, I went over to her.

'Beatrice!' She smiled at me defiantly. 'I thought you were in your room.'

'As you see, I came down.'

'You were dancing!'

'Shouldn't I celebrate Antonio's triumph too?'

'What a triumph!' I exclaimed. 'Worms are devouring his body.'

'Be quiet,' she said in a low voice. Her face glowed like a burning ember.

'You're feverish. I can see it in your eyes. Why do you torture yourself? Why not let yourself give in to tears?'

'He died victorious.'

'You're as blind as he was. Look at them!' I pointed towards the Frenchmen with their insolent faces and their coarse hands, filling the room with raucous laughter. 'There are the real victors.'

'Well? They're our allies.'

'Much too powerful allies. They'll use the port of Rivella as a base for a campaign against Naples. And once they've taken Naples . . . '

'We can defeat the French, too,' Beatrice said.

'No, you're wrong.'

There was a long silence and then she said, 'I'd like to ask you a favour.'

I looked at her small, bruised face. 'That's the first time . . . '

'Let me go away.'

'Where will you go?'

'I'll go back to live with my mother.'

'To wash laundry everyday and take care of the cows?'

'Why not? I don't want to stay here.'

'Is my presence so unbearable to you?'

'I loved Antonio.'

'He died without a thought for you,' I said harshly. 'Forget him.'

'No,' she said.

'Remember when you were a child,' I said. 'How you loved life.'

'Precisely.'

'Stay here. I'll give you anything you want.'

'I want to leave. That's all.'

'Oh, you're as stubborn as a mule!' I said. 'What kind of a life will you have back there?'

'A life,' she answered. 'Don't you understand that no one can breathe near you? You kill all desires. You give and give, but you never give anything but trinkets. Perhaps that's the reason why Antonio chose to die – because you hadn't allowed him any other way of living.'

'Go back to your mother!' I said angrily. 'And die a living death there.'

I spun around and walked over to the ambassadors. The Duke of Anjou's emissary came to meet me.

'What a magnificent feast!'

'A feast like any other,' I said.

I recalled the palace's old walls when they were covered from end to end with faded tapestries. Caterina, wearing a woollen dress, was embroidering. Now those stones were hidden beneath mirrors and silk curtains. The men and women were dressed in silks and gold, but their hearts were unappeased. Eliana looked at Beatrice with hate in her eyes, and the other women envied Eliana for her necklace. Husbands watched jealously as their wives danced in the arms of strangers. All of them were eaten up by ambition, world-weariness, rancour, indifferent to their good fortune.

'I don't see the ambassador from Florence,' I remarked.

'A messenger came and delivered a note,' said Jacques d'Attigny. 'He read it and immediately left the room.'

'Ah!' I sighed. 'That means war.'

I went out on the balcony. Rockets were bursting in the sky and San Felice was still burning. The people were still dancing. They were dancing because Carmona had won a great victory and because the war was over. Now war was beginning again.

The Florentines demanded that I return Rivella to the Manzonis, but the French forbade me to do so. To conquer Florence with the help of the French would have meant giving them the whole of Tuscany. And to fight against the French would have meant the ruin of Carmona and made her an easy prey for Florence. Which yoke was I to choose? Antonio had died for nothing.

Faces were raised up to me. The discordant clamour of the crowd resounded with one voice: 'Long live Count Fosca!' They were acclaiming me and Carmona was lost.

My hands tightened around the iron railing. How many times had I stood up on that balcony, in pride, in joy, in horror? What good had come of so much passion, so much fear, and so much hope? Suddenly nothing seemed important any more; neither peace nor war were of any importance. Peace: Carmona would continue to vegetate under the sky like a giant mushroom. War: all that had been built would be destroyed only to be rebuilt the next day. In any case, all these people who were dancing in the square would soon die, and their deaths would be as pointless as their lives. San Felice was still blazing.

I had brought Antonio into the world and he had left the world. If I had never existed, nothing on earth would have been any different. 'Was the monk right?' I thought. 'Can nothing be done about it?' My hands gripped the railing. And yet I existed. I had a head, two arms and eternity before me. 'Oh, God!' I exclaimed.

I struck my forehead with my fist. 'There must be a way.

There must be something I can do. But where? What?'
I now understood those tyrants who burn entire cities to the
ground or decapitate a whole population to prove their
power to themselves. But the only men they ever killed were
those who were already condemned to death, and they only
destroyed future ruins.

I turned around. Beatrice was standing against the wall,
staring emptily into space. I walked over to her.

'Beatrice, I've just sworn to myself that you'll be my wife.'

'No,' she said.

'Then I'll throw you into a dungeon and there you'll
remain until you consent!'

'You wouldn't do that.'

'You don't know me very well,' I said. 'I would do it.'

She stepped back and said in a trembling voice, 'You told
me that all you wished for was my happiness.'

'I do want it and I'm determined to make you happy in
spite of yourself. I let Antonio lead his own life and he lost it.
He died for nothing. I don't intend to make a similar mistake
again.'

War broke out again. Too weak to take up arms against
my powerful ally, I had to refuse to give up Rivella. The
Florentines immediately laid siege to several castles situated
on the frontiers of my territory. They took a few fortresses
by surprise, and we tricked their captains into a few
ambushes. There were French soldiers serving in my army,
and Florence had hired eight hundred Albanian Stradiotes.
The battles were bloodier than ever before, for these foreign
soldiers neither asked nor gave any quarter. But the results
were as unresolved as ever. After five years of fighting, it
seemed as if Florence had no chance of ever subduing us, nor
Carmona of ever defeating Florence.

'It can last another twenty years,' I said. 'And there will be
neither victor nor vanquished.'

'Twenty years!' Beatrice repeated.

She was sitting beside me in my study, looking through the window at the evening light. The palms of her hands were resting on her knees. There was a wedding ring on her finger, but my lips had never touched hers. Twenty years . . . She wasn't thinking of the war. She was thinking that in twenty years' time she would be almost fifty. I stood up and turned away from the window. I could no longer bear the dusk light.

'Do you hear?' she asked.

'Yes.' I could hear the woman singing in the street and I could also hear the dull, rhythmic beating of Beatrice's heart that was breaking my own.

'Beatrice!' I said suddenly. 'Is it really impossible for you to love me?'

'Let's not speak about that.'

'Everything would be different if you loved me.'

'Well, at least I haven't hated you for a long time now.'

'But you don't love me.'

I stood in front of the big, tarnished mirror. A man in the prime of life, with a hard, unwrinkled face; that muscular body did not know what exhaustion was. I was both taller and stronger than other men of that era.

'Am I such a monster?'

She did not answer.

I sat down at her feet. 'Anyhow, we appear to have reached a certain harmony. I seem to understand you and I think you understand me.'

'Yes, I think so.' She ruffled my hair with the tips of her fingers.

'Well, what do I lack then? Whatever it was that you loved in Antonio, don't you find it in me?'

She drew back her hand. 'No.'

'He was handsome, generous, courageous and proud. Don't I have any of those virtues?'

'You seem to have them . . . '

'Seem? Am I an impostor?'

'It's not your fault,' she said. 'Now I understand that it's not your fault and I don't hate you any more.'

'Can you explain yourself?'

'What's the use?'

'I want to know,' I insisted.

'When Antonio plunged into a lake, when he led an attack, I admired him because he was risking his life. But where is your courage? I loved his generosity; you give freely of yourself, your wealth and your time, but you have so many millions of lives to live that you never really sacrifice anything. And I loved his pride. He was a man like any other, but he chose to be himself. It was wonderful. You, you're an exceptional person, and you know it, yet that doesn't move me.'

She spoke in a clear voice, without hatred and without pity, and through her words I suddenly heard a voice from the past, a voice long forgotten, which was saying in anguish, 'Don't drink!'

'Then no matter what I do, no matter what I am, I'm worth nothing in your eyes because I'm immortal?'

'Yes, that's right.' She put her hand on my arm. 'Listen to that woman singing. Would her song be so moving if she didn't have to die?'

'So it's a curse, then?' I asked.

She did not reply; there was nothing to reply to: it was a curse.

I got up suddenly and took Beatrice in my arms. 'But I'm here, I'm alive! I love you and I'm suffering. Throughout the rest of eternity, I'll never meet you again; I'll meet others, but none of them will be you.'

'Raimondo.' There was pity now in her voice and even tenderness.

'Try to love me,' I pleaded. 'Try.'

I held her tightly against me and felt her body grow limp in my arms. I crushed my mouth against her lips, her breasts quivered against my chest, her hands fell loosely to her sides.

'No,' she said. 'No.'

'I love you. I love you as any man loves a woman.'

'No!' She was trembling. She broke away and murmured, 'Please, forgive me.'

'Forgive you? Why?' I asked.

'Your body frightens me. It's of another species.'

'It's made of flesh like your own.'

Tears welled in her eyes. 'Don't you understand? I can't bear being caressed by hands that will never decay. It makes me ashamed.'

'You mean, rather, that it horrifies you.'

'It's the same thing,' she said.

I looked at my hands, my accursed hands. I understood.

'It's you who must forgive me,' I said. 'I've lived two hundred years and I never really understood. I do now. Beatrice, you're free. If you want to leave here, leave. And if ever you love someone again, love him without remorse.'

There was a long silence. 'You're free,' I repeated.

'Free?' she said.

❧

For ten more years our frontiers were ravaged by fire, looting and massacre. After that, Charles VIII, the King of France, marched into Italy to claim the throne of the Kingdom of Naples. Since Florence had agreed to be his ally, he decided to act as a mediator between us: we would keep Rivella on condition that we pay a heavy tribute to our enemy in exchange.

For years I had been forced to submit to the protection of the French. I watched in despair as Italy was subjugated to their tyranny and sank into the disruptions of civil war and anarchy. 'It's all my fault,' I said bitterly to myself. If long ago I had surrendered Carmona to the Genoese, Genoa would no doubt have succeeded in controlling all of Tuscany, and any foreign invasion would have been smashed against that solid barrier. It was my own stubborn ambition and the

ambitions of each small, independent city that had prevented
Italy from becoming a single nation as France and England
had done, as Spain had just recently done.

'There is still time,' Varenzi would say enthusiastically to
me. He was a celebrated scholar, author of a *History of Italian
Cities*, who had come to Carmona to plead with me to save
our unhappy country. He implored me to work for the
unification of the Italian states into one vast confederation
which I would administer. At first he had put his hopes in
Florence, but the powerful Penitents party, filled with
Savonarola's fanaticism, put their sole trust in prayer, and
they prayed only for the glory of their own city. Varenzi then
turned to me. As weak as Carmona was, impoverished by
fifteen years of war, his plans did not lack substance. In the
state of anarchy and instability into which Italy was plunged,
one resolute man would have sufficed to change her destiny.
When Charles VIII reluctantly decided to abandon Naples
and recross the Alps, I made up my mind to act. Having
secured my alliance with Florence by the scrupulousness
with which I paid her the promised subsidies, I began
negotiations with Venice. But the Duke of Milan had wind
of my plans and, alarmed at the prospective power of a
league he would not head, he sent emissaries to his nephew,
Maximilian, the German emperor who had been elected the
King of the Romans, inviting him to accept the crown of
Lombardy in Milan and that of the Holy Empire in Rome.
He thus hoped to re-establish the former authority of the
Emperors throughout Italy. He put pressure on Venice,
threatening to leave her at the mercy of the King of France
who, it was rumoured, was again preparing to cross the Alps
into Italy. And the Venetians, for their part, eventually sent
ambassadors to Maximilian promising him a subsidy.

Maximilian arrived in Italy and all the small territories of
Tuscany declared themselves his allies, hoping he would put
an end to the hegemony of Florence and Carmona. He laid
siege to Livorno, which he attacked by both land and sea.

Upon hearing of this, Carmona was plunged into a state of desperate anxiety. The hatred of our envious neighbours and the Duke of Milan's distrust, left us no hope of maintaining our independence in the event that Maximilian succeeded in becoming master of Italy. And if Livorno were taken, all of Tuscany would be in his power. The Florentines had sent a great number of cannon to the port and had established a large garrison there. They had only recently strengthened the city with new fortifications. But Maximilian was backed by the Venetian fleet and the Milanese army. When we learned that four hundred German cavalry and as many foot soldiers had advanced beyond Cicina in Maremma, and that they had captured the large market town of Balghein, his victory seemed assured. Our only hope was that the six thousand sacks of wheat and the army which Charles VIII had promised the Florentine rulers would arrive without delay. But we had long ago learned not to place much trust in a Frenchman's word.

'To think that our whole future is at stake and there's nothing we can do about it!' I said. With my head glued to the window, I anxiously watched the bend in the road for the arrival of a messenger.

'Don't think about it any more,' Beatrice said. 'Thinking is pointless.'

'I know. But one can't help thinking.'

'Oh, yes you can. It is possible, thank heavens!'

I looked at her bent neck, her plump neck. She was sitting at a table covered with paint brushes, powders and sheets of parchment. She still had her fine black hair, but her features had thickened and she had put on weight. The fire that used to burn in her eyes had gone. Everything a man could give a woman, I had given her, and yet she spent her time illuminating manuscripts.

'Put away those brushes,' I said sharply. She looked up at me in surprise. 'Ride out with me to meet the messengers. It will do you good to get some air.'

'But I haven't ridden a horse for so long . . . '

'Exactly. You never go out any more.'

'I'm quite happy staying here.'

I took a few steps across the room. 'Why have you chosen to live like this?'

'Did I make the choice?' she said softly.

'I gave you your complete freedom,' I retorted angrily.

'But I'm not blaming you for anything.' She bent over her manuscripts again.

'Beatrice,' I asked, 'since Antonio died, haven't you ever fallen in love again?'

'No.'

'Because of Antonio?'

She hesitated a moment. 'I don't think so.'

'Why not, then?'

'I suppose I'm not capable of loving.'

'Is that my fault?'

'Why do you torment yourself? You think too much. You think much too much.' She suddenly smiled at me. 'I'm not unhappy, you know,' she said lightheartedly.

Once again, I pressed my forehead against the window-pane, trying not to think – Beatrice's fate had been decided without her, and mine was now being decided without me. But I could not stop myself thinking. Had Maximilian already taken Livorno? I left the palace abruptly, mounted my horse and galloped to the crossroads. A large crowd had gathered there; some had come by foot, others on horseback. Sitting on the edge of the trenches, they were anxiously watching the road that led to the coast. Without stopping, I spurred my horse and sped off along the road. When I met the messenger, he informed me that the town of Castagneto had surrendered and that Billona was about to surrender.

No one ate that evening. Beatrice, Varenzi and I shut ourselves in my study, waiting to hear the hoof-beats of another messenger's horse. It was as if there were nothing left on earth for me to do but to stand there motionless with my forehead glued to a window-pane, watching an empty road.

'Livorno will be taken tonight,' I said.

'What a wind!' Varenzi remarked in a sombre voice.

The tops of the trees were swaying wildly. The wind was whipping up clouds of dust on the road. The sky was a leaden grey.

'The sea must be rough,' Varenzi said.

'Yes. We can't expect any help to arrive tonight.'

The road was empty. But further off, there were roads swarming with German soldiers, the feathers in their helmets blowing in the wind. They were advancing towards Livorno, massacring the entire population of villages through which they passed. German cannon were bombarding the port. And the stormy sea was as empty as the road.

'He'll give Carmona to the Duke of Milan,' I said.

'A city like this can never die,' Beatrice said proudly.

'It's already dead.'

I was the ruler of the city and yet my hands hung helplessly at my sides. Out there, foreign cannon were bombarding a foreign city: every volley struck at Carmona's heart just as surely as if she were under attack. And she could do nothing to defend herself.

Night fell. We could no longer make out the road, nor hear any sound at all through the howling wind. I moved from the window and began to watch the door through which the messenger would enter. I listened attentively for his step. But the night passed and the door did not open. Beatrice had folded her arms on her breast and, her head held straight, she had fallen asleep. There was a look of nobility about her. Varenzi was meditating. It was a long night. Time stood still in the bottom of the blue hour-glass which no one had bothered to turn over.

I remembered all those years, those two long centuries, when I had fought for Carmona. I used to believe I held her destiny in my hands: I defended her against Florence, against Genoa, and I worried constantly about the schemes of their rulers; I kept a close watch on every move made by Siena and Pisa; I sent spies to Milan. I did not concern myself with the wars that took place between France and England, nor what went on in the court of Burgundy, nor the struggles for power between the German electors. I never suspected that those distant battles, those disputes and treaties would culminate in this night of impotence and ignorance, or that Carmona's fate would be decided not just in Italy, but throughout the whole world. It was being decided at this very hour on the turbulent sea, in the German camp, in the Florentine garrison and, on the other side of the Alps, in the shallow, treacherous heart of the King of France. And no matter what happened now in Carmona, it could no longer have any effect upon Carmona. By the time dawn finally broke, all hope and all fear had died within me. No miracle could now bring us victory. Carmona no longer belonged to me. And in the shame of that wasted night watch, I had stopped belonging to myself.

It was not until noon that a rider appeared at the bend in the road. Livorno had been saved. In spite of the appalling weather, a French fleet consisting of six ships and two large galleons, laden with wheat and crowded with soldiers, had made its way into the port. The Genoese and Venetian fleets had sought protection from the strong winds in the port of Melina, and the French, not having to fight their way through, had entered Livorno under full sail.

A few days later we learned that a storm had wreaked havoc on the Emperor's fleet and that he had withdrawn his army to Pisa, declaring that he could not wage war both on God and on man at the same time. I listened indifferently to this news – it seemed as if it no longer concerned me.

'We must resume our negotiations with Venice,' Varenzi said. 'Maximilian is short of money and if Venice refuses him further subsidies, he'll have to leave Italy.'

The other counsellors approved of this suggestion. Years ago they used to talk about, 'The good of Carmona. The salvation of Carmona'. But now all I heard was 'The good of Italy. The salvation of Italy.' How long had they been discussing this? For hours or for years? Their faces and their manner of dress had changed in the meantime, but there were still the same measured voices, the same solemn eyes contemplating a narrow future; the same words, virtually. The autumn sun cast golden rays over the table and reflected on the chain I was dangling in my hands. It seemed as if I had lived through that precise moment in the past. A hundred years before? An hour before? Or perhaps in a dream? 'Will the quality of my life ever change?' I wondered.

'We'll continue with this discussion tomorrow,' I said abruptly. 'The meeting's adjourned.'

I closed the door of the council room behind me and went down to the stables to have my horse saddled. It was suffocating in the palace. I set off along the new road bordered by high white walls which were already turning yellow. 'Will I still see them a hundred years from now?' I spurred on my horse with both heels. It was suffocating in Carmona.

For a long while, I galloped across the plain. The sky flew past above my head, and beneath me the earth seemed to leap up and down. I wished that ride could last forever, with the wind on my face and that silence in my heart. But by the time my horse's flanks were dripping with sweat, there were still those words on my lips: 'Carmona has been saved again. And now what will I do?'

I followed the road which led up the hill. It twisted and turned and gradually I could see over the entire plain. Over there to the right, was the sea and there Italy stopped. She stretched out before me as far as the eye could reach, but at the foot of the Alps, on the coast, she stopped. With much care and patience, I could be her ruler in ten or twenty years time. And then one night with my hands hanging helplessly at my sides and my eyes fixed on the far horizon, I would anxiously await the echo of events taking place on the other side of the mountains and across the seas.

'Italy is too small,' I thought to myself.

I drew up my horse and dismounted. I had often stood on this summit, contemplating the unchanging landscape. But suddenly it seemed that what I had been dreaming about a few hours earlier – that Maximilian had conquered Livorno, that Carmona was lost – had actually come to pass. There was a strange taste in my mouth. The air seemed to quiver and all around me everything looked new. Perched on her rock, flanked by her eight sun-scorched towers, Carmona was nothing but a huge mushroom, and Italy herself, a prison whose walls had crumbled.

Out there was the sea, but the world did not end at our shores. Ships with white sails were making their way towards Spain, and far beyond Spain, towards new continents. On those unexplored lands, men with red skins were worshipping the sun and fighting with axes. And beyond those lands, lay other oceans and other lands. The world ended nowhere and nothing existed outside of it; it bore its destiny in its own heart. And I was no longer on a hill overlooking Carmona, I was no longer in Italy; I was in the middle of a vast world, unique and limitless.

I galloped down the hill.

Beatrice was in her room, sketching red and gold patterns on a piece of parchment. A vase filled with roses stood beside her.

'Well,' she asked, 'what did your counsellors have to say?'

'Inanities!' I answered sharply. She looked at me in surprise. 'I've come to say good-bye, Beatrice.'

'Where are you going?'

'To Pisa. I'm going to see Maximilian.'

'What do you hope from him?'

I took a rose from the vase and crushed it in my hand. 'I'll tell him that Carmona is too small for me; Italy is too small. Nothing can really be accomplished unless the whole world is ruled by one man. Take me into your service', I shall tell him, 'and I will give you the whole world.'

Beatrice stood up suddenly. She had grown very pale. 'I don't understand,' she said.

'It does not matter to me if I govern in my name or someone else's. Since that's the opportunity given to me, that's the one I'll take. I'll make use of the Hapsburg wealth and perhaps I'll finally be able to do something.'

'Are you going to forsake Carmona?' A flame was suddenly rekindled in her eyes. 'Is that what you mean?'

'Do you think I'm going to stagnate here in Carmona forever?' I said. 'What does Carmona mean to me, after all? I've felt I no longer belong here for a long time now.'

'You can't!' she protested.

'I know, I know. It's the city Antonio died for.'

'It's *your* city. The city you saved so many times, the city you've ruled over for two centuries. You're not going to betray your own people.'

'My people,' I said. 'They've died over and over again! How can I ever feel close to them? They're never the same.' I walked towards her and took her hands. 'Good-bye, Beatrice. When I'm gone, perhaps you'll be able to start to live again.'

The light in her eyes suddenly went out. 'It's too late,' she said.

I looked guiltily at her thickset features. Had I been less imperious in demanding her happiness, she might have loved, suffered, lived. I had lost her more surely than I had lost Antonio.

'Forgive me,' I said.

My lips brushed her hair, but already she was just another woman among millions, and my affection and guilt smacked of things long past.

Dusk had fallen. A chilly breeze was blowing up from the river. From the adjacent dining-room came the sounds of dishes and voices, and Regina remembered that a moment ago the clock had struck seven. She looked at Fosca.

'And you had the strength to begin all over again?'

'Can one stop life from beginning again every morning?' Fosca replied. 'You remember what we were saying one evening – whether one wants to or not, one's heart beats, the hand stretches out . . . '

'And you suddenly discover yourself combing your hair.' She looked around her. 'Do you think I'll be combing my hair tomorrow?'

'I suppose so.'

She stood up. 'Let's get out of here.'

They left the inn and Fosca asked, 'Where shall we go?'

'Anywhere.' She pointed to a road. 'There's nothing to stop us taking this road, is there?' She laughed. 'Your heart beats, and one foot follows the other. Roads go on forever.'

They began walking step by step down the road. 'I really would like to know what became of Beatrice,' said Regina.

'What do you imagine became of her? One day she died. That's all.'

'That's all?'

'Yes. That's all I ever knew. She had left Carmona by the time I returned and I didn't try to discover what happened to her. In any case, there was nothing to discover. She's dead.'

'Basically, all stories have a happy ending.' said Regina.

BOOK II

A long the dusty streets bordering the Arno, heavy-footed German soldiers were mingling among the crowds of Pisans whom they dwarfed by a good head. The ancient Medici palace was filled with the noise of their boots and spurs. I was kept waiting for a long while: I was unaccustomed to waiting. Finally a guard showed me to a study where I found the Emperor seated at a desk. He had straight, blonde hair which fell stiffly over his ears and a large, flat nose. He looked about forty. With a courteous gesture, he indicated that I should sit down. He had dismissed his guards and we were alone in the room.

'Count Fosca,' he began, 'I've always wanted to meet you.' He studied me with curiosity. 'What they say about you . . . is it true?'

'It is true that, until now, God has permitted me to conquer old age and death.'

'The Hapsburgs are immortal, too,' he said proudly.

'Yes,' I said. 'And that's precisely why they should rule the world. Nothing less than the whole world is worthy of eternity.'

'The world is vast,' he smiled.

'Eternity is long.'

He examined me silently, with a look of sly distrust. 'Why have you come?' he asked.

'To give you Carmona'

He laughed, revealing his white teeth. 'I'm afraid that such a gift would cost me very dearly.'

'It would not cost you anything. I've reigned over the city for two long centuries now and I'm tired of it. I ask only that you allow me to join you in your ventures.'

'And you demand nothing in return?'

'What can any man, even an emperor, give me?' I asked. He seemed so perplexed that I felt sorry for him. 'Italy will become prey to the King of France – or to you. I'm not concerned with Italy any more; it's the whole world that interests me now. I would like to see it unified under a single ruler, for only then will it be possible to make it function.'

'But why should you want to help me unify it under my power?'

'What difference does it make?' I said. 'Aren't you fighting for your son? For your grandson who hasn't yet been born, and for his children whom you'll never see?'

'But they're my descendants.'

'That doesn't make much difference.'

With a pained, childish expression, Maximilian reflected a moment and said nothing.

'After I've handed over my castles and fortresses to you,' I continued, 'nothing would stop you from conquering Florence. And once Florence is conquered, all Italy will be yours.'

'Italy will be mine,' he said dreamily. His furrowed, anxious brow relaxed. He smiled to himself for a moment and then said, 'I haven't paid my men in more than a month.'

'How much do you need?'

'Twenty thousand florins.'

'Carmona is rich.'

'Twenty thousand florins a month.'

'Carmona is very rich,' I said with a smile.

Three days later, Maximilian entered Carmona. The marble escutcheon, adorned with gilded fleur-de-lis, which had been erected in the centre of the city in honour of Charles VIII, was torn down to make room for the Emperor's coat of arms. And the people, who had acclaimed the King of France four years earlier, now cheered the Emperor and his retinue with equal fervour. The women threw them flowers.

An entire week was given over to tournaments and festivities, during which Maximilian devoured enormous quantities of highly spiced meats and consumed large jugs of wine. One evening, as we were leaving the table after a meal that had lasted three hours, I asked, 'And when are we going to march against Florence?'

'Ah! Florence,' he said. His eyes were pink and unfocused. Seeing that I was watching him, he declared majestically, 'Matters of state oblige me to return to Germany.'

I leaned forward, 'When are you leaving?'

'Tomorrow morning,' he said in a flash.

'I'm going with you.'

I watched as he strode off; his walk was dignified and yet uncertain. Very little could be expected from such an emperor; in one week I had formed an opinion of him: ignorant, whimsical, greedy, he lacked both ambition and perseverance. Nevertheless, it looked as if it might be possible to influence him; and he had a son whose temperament was perhaps better suited to my purposes. I had decided to follow him.

I left the palace. It was a clear, moonlit night; the raucous sound of singing drifted up from the plain where Maximilian's hordes were encamped. Two hundred years before, it had been the red Genoese tents that could be seen among the grey olive trees, and I had kept our gates closed. I passed through the cemetery where Caterina and Antonio were buried, sat down for a while on the steps of the cathedral, and then made a tour of the ramparts. The miracle had been achieved: my life had changed and I saw Carmona through new eyes. It was a foreign city.

In the morning, after I had passed through the postern, I looked back at the rock bristling with its high towers, the rock that had for so long been the heart of the earth for me. Now, it was only a minuscule particle in that vast conglomeration, the Holy Roman Empire. The earth had no other heart but my own. I was cast naked into the world – a man from nowhere. The sky above me was now no longer a roof, but an endless road.

For days and nights we continued riding north. The sky gradually paled, the air grew cooler, the trees less dark, the earth less red. Mountains appeared on the horizon and the wooden-roofed houses in the villages through which we passed were covered with paintings of flowers and birds. Strange odours drifted through the air.

Maximilian conversed freely with me. He told me that the Catholic monarchs had proposed a double marriage between his son Philip with their daughter Joanna and his daughter Margarel with the child Don Juan. He was reluctant to agree to this proposal, but I pressed him to accept. It was Spain with her powerful fleet of swift ships that held the key to the world.

'But Philip will never reign over Spain,' Maximilian said to me regretfully. 'Don Juan is young and strong.'

'Strong, young men have been known to die.'

We were slowly making our way down a steep road which smelled of fresh grass and pine trees.

'But the Queen of Portugal is Joanna's older sister,' Maximilian said. 'And she has a son.'

'They can always die, too . . . if God continues to protect the Hapsburgs.'

Maximilian's eyes shone. 'May God protect the Hapsburgs!'

Don Juan died six months after his youthful marriage and,

shortly afterwards, a mysterious illness resulted in the death of
the Queen of Portugal and her son Don Miguel. When
Princess Joanna gave birth to a son, there was no longer any
obstacle standing between him and the throne of Spain. I
leaned over the cradle in which the sickly infant lay crying,
this child who one day would rule over Spain, Holland,
Austria, Burgundy and several of the rich Italian provinces. In
his lace dress, he smelled of sour milk, like any other baby.
The pressure of my hands would have been enough to shatter
his tiny skull.

'We'll make an emperor of this child,' I said.

A cloud passed over Maximilian's nonchalant features.
'How?' he asked. 'I don't have any money.'

'When the time comes, there'll be money enough.'

'Can't we get hold of any now?'

'It's too soon.'

He looked at me with a perplexed, disappointed
expression. 'Are you coming with me to Italy?'

'No.'

'Why not? Don't you believe in my star any more?'

'The glory of your house means even more to me than to
yourself,' I answered. 'With your permission, I prefer to stay
here and watch over the child.'

'Stay here, then.' He looked at the infant and smiled.
'Teach him not to take after his grandfather.'

So I remained in the palace of Malines while Maximilian
campaigned unsuccessfully in Italy and fought in vain against
the Swiss. I had gained his confidence and he attached great
value to my advice, not that that was of much use to me, for
he seldom followed it. I had given up expecting anything of
him. His son Philip did not like me, but he was of delicate
health and there was little chance that he would ever reign. As
for Princess Joanna, she had become eccentric to the point
that those around her grew deeply concerned. All my hopes
rested in this child whose first steps and first words I awaited
anxiously. He, too, was fragile and would often throw himself

to the ground in a fit of hysterics. I alone managed to soothe him. I was with him constantly and the only rule he responded to was the knitting of my brow. But I anxiously asked myself: 'Will he live long enough? What kind of man will he be?' Supposing he were to die, supposing he grew to hate me, I may have to renounce my great dreams for several centuries.

The years went by. Philip died. Joanna, who was apparently completely insane, was confined to the castle of Tordesillas. And Charles lived, grew steadily to manhood. From day to day my plans became less fanciful; from day to day, strolling through the foggy streets of Malines, I anticipated the future with ever greater hope.

I liked that sad, quiet city. Whenever I walked through her streets, the lace-makers, bent over their spindles behind windows with small glass panes, followed me for a moment with their eyes. But no one knew me, no one knew my secret. I had let my beard grow and even I was sometimes slow to recognize myself when I looked into a mirror. Often I went up on the ramparts, or I would sit by the edge of the canal and day-dream as I watched the reflections frozen in the moving water. The sages of the day were saying that the time had come when man would be able to unravel the secrets of nature and control her. Then he would begin to conquer happiness. 'That shall be my task,' I thought. 'But first I will have to hold the whole universe in my hands. Then, no energy will be dissipated, no wealth wasted. I will put an end to the division which set nations, races and religions apart. I will put an end to all injustice. I will manage the world as carefully as I did Carmona's granaries. Nothing will be left to men's caprice or the hazards of fate. Reason will govern the earth. My reason. As dusk began to fall, I slowly made my way back to the palace. At the street corners, the first lamplights were already lit. Voices, laughter and the sound of mugs of beer being banged together echoed from the taverns. Alone and unknown under this grey sky, among people who spoke a foreign language, and already forgotten by Maximilian, it sometimes seemed as if I had just been born.

I leaned over the couch where Charles was resting. His paternal grandfather, Ferdinand, had recently died and, a few months earlier, Charles had been crowned King of Spain. But his subjects did not attempt to disguise their preference for his younger brother who had been born and had lived among them.

'My Lord, you can't delay your journey any longer,' I said. 'It would mean losing the crown.'

He did not answer. He was seriously ill and doctors claimed that his life was in danger.

'Your brother's supporters are powerful. We must act quickly.' I looked impatiently at this tall, pallid adolescent who listened to me with his mouth agape and a vacant expression on his face. Under his drooping eyelids, his eyes seemed lifeless, and his lower lip hung loosely. 'Are you afraid?' I asked.

His lips finally moved. 'Yes,' he admitted. 'I'm afraid.' His voice was grave and sincere, which I found disconcerting. 'My father died in Spain,' he continued, 'and the doctors have said the climate there would be dangerous for me.'

'A king must never shrink from danger.'

In his slow, slightly stuttering voice, he said, 'My brother would make a very good king.'

I reflected in silence for a moment. If Charles died, nothing was lost: his brother was young enough to become a willing instrument in my hands. But if Charles, who was now an archduke, continued to live and lost Spain, then the world would be split in two and all my plans would fail.

'But it's you whom God has designated,' I said forcefully. 'I've often told you what he expects of you – to take this world, this world that's carved up into fragments, and make it a single, unified world again, like the day it left his hands. If you give up Spain to Ferdinand, you'll only perpetuate the endless divisions that are tearing the land apart.'

He pursed his lips. Beads of sweat gathered on his brow. 'I could hand over everything to him,' he ventured.

I looked at him. He was slow-witted and sickly, but even his timidity served my purposes. I did not know Ferdinand.

'No,' I said. 'Your brother is Spanish. He'll be concerned only with the interests of Spain. Only you can fulfill the mission with which God has entrusted you. It's upon you that the task of ensuring the world's salvation has fallen. Your health, your happiness are as nothing compared to that.'

What I said had struck home. He grew even paler.

'The world's salvation,' he said. 'It's too much. I would never be capable . . . '

'You will with God's help.'

He sunk his head in his hands and I left him to pray in silence. He was still a child; he loved long walks in the fresh air, tournaments and music and he could sense the monstrous burden I wanted him to bear upon his shoulders. He continued to pray for a long while and then he looked up and said, 'May God's will be done.'

A few days later, Charles and his court set up quarters on the sand dunes of the beach at Flessingues. For several weeks, a fleet of forty ships lay at anchor off the port awaiting a favourable wind. When it finally came, we set sail for Spain. Leaning against the bulwarks, I watched the sun rise and set day after day. It was not only towards Spain that I was sailing; out there, beyond the horizon, were forests teeming with multicoloured parrots and doves that fed on exotic flowers. There were volcanoes which spewed forth streams of molten, bubbling gold, and over the flatlands, men dressed in feathers galloped freely. The King of Spain was the ruler of this wild paradise. 'One day I'll sail to those distant shores,' I thought, 'and I'll see them with my own eyes. And I'll fashion them to my own design.'

On the 19th of September, the fleet arrived within sight of the coast of Asturias in northern Spain. The shore was deserted, but on the side of a mountain I could see a long procession – women, children and old men walking behind mules weighed down with heavy packs. They seemed to be fleeing. Then suddenly, from behind a thicket, a salvo of gunfire was fired. The women of the court began shrieking and the sailors grabbed their muskets. Charles's expression remained impassive. Silently, he looked upon the land that was his kingdom; he was not disconcerted by this rude welcome: he had not come here to seek happiness. There was another burst of musket fire, then, with all my might, I cried out, 'Spain! This is your king!'

The whole crew took up the cry, and a moment later I noticed a stirring among the thickets which extended down to the sea. A man crawled out on all fours. He must have recognized the arms of Castile on the King's large standards, for he stood up and waved his musket, shouting, 'Spain! Long live the King!' Soon, from behind the bushes and rocks, the mountain people were running towards us with shouts of 'Long live Don Carlos!' Later, they told us that when they had seen such a great number of ships, they had feared a barbarian attack.

We arrived at Villaviciosa. No preparations had been made to receive us and most of the lords and even the ladies had to sleep on beds of straw. At the break of day, we set forth again. The King sat astride a small horse that the English ambassador had obtained for him. Eleonore, his sister, rode at his side. The ladies of the retinue travelled in ox carts and many of the lords were on foot. The road was rocky and we made our way with difficulty under the blue, obdurate sky.

The crossroads, the fields and the roads were deserted. An epidemic had ravaged the province and the inhabitants were forbidden to leave their homes. Charles, for his part, seemed impervious to the sun's cruelty, to the harshness of the landscape, and he never showed any sign of impatience or melancholy. It seemed that, contrary to the doctors' predictions, the climate of Spain had actually fortified his health. Perhaps it was his astonishment at still being alive that brought a faint glimmer to his eyes, such as I had never before seen. On the day he made his solemn entry into Valladolid, he smiled. 'I feel I'm going to like this country,' he announced.

As the weeks went by he seemed to blossom. He took part gaily in festivals and tournaments, and he was often seen laughing with young people of his own age. Joyfully, I thought, 'He's alive, he's King! The first round is won!' As soon as I learned of Maximilian's death, I hastened back to Germany. The moment had come to think of the Empire.

During the last years of his reign, Maximilian had lavished money and promises upon the imperial electors, and he believed he was assured of the votes of five of them on behalf of Charles. But the day after his death, despite the six hundred thousand florins he had paid them, the electors considered the field to be open again. François I, King of France, immediately entered the lists, vowing that if it were necessary, he would spend three million to obtain the Empire. Charles was poor. But across the oceans, he possessed gold and silver mines and fertile lands. I sought out the bankers in Antwerp and prevailed upon them to sign bills of exchange which were guaranteed by our colonial riches. Then I went to Augsburg where I obtained further bills of exchange from the Fugger family which were to be repayable after the election. I immediately sent messengers to convey my proposals to the electors, while I personally called on each of them in turn, visiting Cologne, Trier, and then Mainz. At every point, a stream of messengers sent by François and Henry of England arrived with new offers which the impassive electors inscribed in their notebooks. François was proportioning payment in hard, ringing, gold crowns, and the electors of Brandenburg and Trier, as well as the Archbishop of Cologne, began to snap at the bait. One day, I learned that François had offered the Archbishop of Mainz one hundred and twenty thousand florins and the legateship of Germany. That same evening I set out to seek the aid of Franz von Sickingen who commanded the army of the powerful Swabian League. I galloped through the night without stopping, and time, which until recently had lain motionless in the bottom of a blue hourglass, was now swallowed up beneath the hoofs of my horse.

Franz von Sickingen hated France. At the head of an army of twenty thousand foot soldiers and four thousand cavalry, we marched on Hochst, a few leagues from Frankfurt, while other troops threatened the Palatinate. The electors, frightened, preached the customary sermons, declared that their votes were pure and their hands clean, and they elected Charles emperor for the total sum of eight hundred and fifty-two thousand florins.

It was a beautiful autumn day when Charles made his entry into Aix-la-Chapelle. The electors had come to meet him and, with bared head, he silently accepted their homage. The procession then passed through the gates of the ancient city. First came the standard bearers, the counts, the lords, the councillors of Aix carrying white batons, the royal court with its pages and heralds, all of them throwing money to the crowd. Next, flanked by halberdiers, came the high dignitaries, the Spanish grandees, the knights of the Golden Fleece, the princes and the prince-electors. Marshal von Pappenheim, bearing the sword of the Empire, preceded the King who was clad in armour and brocade.

On 23rd October, 1519, the coronation took place in Charlemagne's ancient cathedral. The Archbishop of Cologne solemnly asked all present: 'Do you wish, in the words of the Apostle, to submit yourselves to the rule of this prince and lord?' And the people cried out joyously: 'Fiat! Fiat!' The Archbishop then placed the crown upon Charles's head, and as the Emperor ascended Charlemagne's throne to receive the knights' sworn allegiance, a *Te Deum* burst out beneath the vaulted arches.

'I owe the Empire to you,' Charles said to me in a deeply moved voice when we were finally alone in his study.

'You owe it to God,' I replied. 'He created me only to serve you.'

I had revealed my secret to him and he seemed scarcely surprised: he was too good a Christian to be astonished by any miracle. Yet while he no longer treated me with the timid docility of his childhood, he now respected me as a being marked by God.

'God bestowed a great blessing upon me when he gave you to me,' he said. 'You'll help me to prove myself worthy of it, won't you?'

'Yes, I'll help you.'

His eyes gleamed. From the moment the Archbishop placed the sacred crown on his head, his face had grown firmer, his expression more alert. 'I have great things to accomplish,' he said fervently.

'You shall accomplish them.'

I knew that he dreamt of resurrecting the Holy Empire, but it was the entire universe that I wanted him to re-unite. Cortés was conquering the Americas for us and soon gold would begin flowing into Spain. Then we would be able to form powerful armies and, once the federation of the German states had been achieved, Italy and France could be brought beneath our sway.

'One day, the whole universe will belong to you,' I said.

He looked at me with an expression of awe. 'No man has ever possessed the universe.'

'Until now, the time hasn't been ripe.'

He remained silent for a moment and then suddenly he smiled. Through the walls of the study, the sound of a viol could be heard. 'Aren't you coming to hear the music?' he asked.

'In a moment,' I replied.

He rose. 'It's going to be a beautiful concert. You should come.'

He opened the door. He was young, he was emperor. God had cast his protective shadow over him and in his heart the happiness of the world was fused with his own; he could relax peacefully to the tender song of the viols. But as for me, the swell in my breast was too powerful. A triumphant voice drowned all other sounds, a voice that would never echo in the ears of mortal men; it was my own voice and it said: 'Now the universe is mine forever, mine alone. It is my domain and no one can share it with me. Charles will govern for a few years, whereas I have eternity before me.' I went over to the window and looked up at the starry sky which was crossed by a milky white belt – millions upon millions of stars. And beneath my feet, there was only one earth: my earth. Its round mass floated peacefully in the ether, marbled with blue, yellow, and green; I could see it. There were ships sailing the seas, roads streaked across continents, and I, with a single sweep of my hand, could rip up deep-rooted forests, drain swamps, change the course of rivers. Farms, orchards, and pastures covered the earth, cities sprouted up at crossroads; the most humble weavers lived in large, bright houses; granaries were filled with pure wheat. Everyone was rich, strong and handsome; everyone was happy. 'I shall recreate a paradise on earth,' I thought to myself.

Charles was stroking the rainbow-coloured feather coat. He loved fine materials and precious metals. His eyes lit up when the sailors opened the chests and set down before him large alabaster vases full of turquoise and amethysts.

'What riches!' he exclaimed.

He looked at the gold coins and ingots heaped high in one of the chests, but I knew it was not of these riches that he spoke. Beyond the grey walls of the Brussels palace, he saw a fiery jet of gold soaring upwards into the blue sky, he saw rivers of vermilion lava bubbling down the sides of a volcano, he saw great avenues paved with glittering metals, and gardens planted with trees of solid gold. I smiled. Through the sparkle of a thousand little suns, I too saw galleons laden with gold entering the port of Sanlucar; we were showering the old continent with a stream of brilliant jewels . . .

'How can you even hesitate?' I asked.

Charles's hand released the soft, smooth coat. 'Those men have souls, too,' he said.

With slow, measured steps, he began to pace up and down the long gallery. He had slipped the letter from Cortés inside his doublet, the letter that the captain with the cracked lips had given him. On Good Friday of the preceding year, Cortés had landed on a desolate shore and there founded a city to which he gave the name of Vera Cruz. In order to prevent his men from returning to Spain, he had all of his ships scuttled with the exception of one, which he sent back to Charles laden with the treasures of the Aztec emperor, Montezuma. He was asking for help to counter the intrigues of the governor, Velasquez, who was trying to prevent him from continuing his expedition. And Charles hesitated.

I looked at him impatiently. The letters from the Dominicans of Hispandia and Father Las Casas's report had deeply disturbed him. We learned that, despite laws to the contrary, the Indians were still being branded like slaves, beaten, and massacred. Too weak for the work forced upon them, they were dying in their thousands. I refused to concern myself with these savages and their absurd superstitions.

'Send over some reliable men who'll make sure the laws are maintained,' I suggested.

'At such great distances, who is reliable?' He began to pace back and forth again beside a table covered with crystal bowls, jade necklaces and figurines of hammered gold.

'The good fathers exaggerate,' I said. 'They always exaggerate.'

'If just one of the things they report were true, it would be enough . . .'

'The black people of Africa don't have souls. And neither do these savages in America.'

'But the cure seems to me just as horrible as the sickness,' the Emperor said thoughtfully. His face had taken on that vacant, sleepy expression of his adolescence.

'Well, what do you propose doing?' I asked.

'I don't know.'

'Are you going to turn down an empire paved with gold?' I plunged my hand into the chest and let the coins slip through my fingers.

'I don't know,' he repeated. He looked very young and very unhappy.

'You haven't the right to throw it all away,' I said forcefully. 'God created all these riches to serve mankind. There's fertile land over there that will never be cultivated if we don't seize it from the Indians. Think of the misery of your subjects: they'll all be prosperous when the gold from the Americas flows through your ports. Are you going to condemn the German peasants to death from starvation out of pity for those savages?'

He did not answer. Never before had he been forced to make so grave a decision. He could not know how brief and unimportant a thing a human life was. In any case, in a hundred years' time not one of those wretched creatures who were causing Charles so much anguish would be alive to remember his suffering. As far as I was concerned, they were dead already. He, however, could not agree to deprive them of their lives so easily; he measured their joys and their hardships as he measured his own. Abruptly, I walked over to him.

'Do you imagine that you can ever do good in this world without doing evil? It's impossible to be just to everyone, to make everyone happy. If your heart is too tender to consent to necessary sacrifices, you ought to shut yourself away in a monastery.'

He pursed his lips. Something hard and cold shone beneath his half-closed eyes. He loved the age in which he was living; he loved luxury and power.

'I want to rule without doing anyone an injustice,' he said.

'Can you rule without wars, without the scaffold? You must see things as they are for once!' I said sharply. 'It will save you wasting precious time. The best of princes always have hundreds of deaths on their consciences.'

'There are just wars and necessary repressions,' he replied.

'You have to justify the suffering you cause to some people by the good works you accomplish for the benefit of all.'

I was silent for a moment; I could not tell him what I was really thinking: that a life, a thousand lives, weigh no more than a swarm of gnats, whereas the roads, the cities, the canals we could build, would remain on the earth for eternity; that for eternity, we would have preserved a whole continent from the dark shadows of virgin forests and foolish superstitions. He was not concerned with an earthly future that he would never see with his own eyes. But I did know the words that were capable of awakening a response in his heart.

'It will be only worldly misery that we inflict upon those poor savages,' I said. 'And ultimately we shall bring eternal truth and happiness to them, their children and to their children's children. When all those ignorant people are finally led into the Church's fold where they and their descendants will remain for ever and ever, won't you be justified in having helped Cortés?'

'But these men who are now in a state of mortal sin will die because of us,' he said hesitantly.

'They would have died anyway, in idolatry and crime,' I replied.

Charles fell into a chair. 'It's not easy to govern people.'

'Never do wrong when it serves no purpose,' I said. 'God can ask nothing more of any emperor. He knows very well that evil is sometimes necessary – after all, he, himself, created it.'

'Yes.' He looked at me anxiously. 'But I'd like to be sure,' he said.

I shrugged my shoulders. 'You'll never be sure.'

He sighed, and for a moment he fiddled with his collar in silence. 'All right,' he said. 'All right.'

He stood up suddenly and went to shut himself in his private chapel.

∾

'This city has gone mad,' I said, leaning against the window-sill.

It had begun the evening before, when the carriage with the wreathed columns and heavy leather curtains first entered the city. In their thousands, they came to meet it: peasants, artisans, merchants, some on horseback, others on mules. To the sound of fifes and drums, to the ringing of the church bells, they marched through the north gate of the city. The inn of the Knights of Saint John was overflowing with men, women, priests and town notables, who gathered in the corridors and on the steps. Young people, children, and even old men had taken up positions on the rooftops. When the monk climbed down from his carriage, the mob surged towards him, shouting wildly; women threw themselves to their knees and kissed the hem of his mud-spattered habit. All day long, through the walls of the archbishop's palace, we had heard their chants and their cries. And that night, the racket started up again. Standing upon tables, barrels and the edges of fountains, orators proclaimed the miracles Luther had accomplished. There were brass bands parading through the streets, and from the taverns could be heard both rousing canticles as well as the noise of brawls. I had seen cities on festive days before; the people of Carmona used to sing to celebrate victory, and I knew why they were singing. But what was the meaning of all this insane clamour? I slammed the window shut.

'What a carnival!'

I turned around and saw Balthus and Morel watching me in silence, and despite my friendship for them, I felt irritated.

'The man is fast becoming a martyr and a saint,' said Balthus.

'It's the natural result of persecution,' Pierre Morel remarked.

'You know, of course, that I've had nothing to do with any of this,' I said.

When Charles convoked the Diet of Worms, I had thought that we were going to settle the question of the Constitution of the Empire and establish a basis for a federation presided over by the Emperor. I had been disappointed when he pressed stubbornly for Luther's condemnation, and I was even more annoyed when the Diet, refusing to make a pronouncement without hearing the accused, obliged us to convoke him. We were losing precious time.

'How did Luther impress the Emperor?' Balthus asked.

'He considered him inoffensive,' I replied.

'And he'll remain inoffensive if we don't condemn him.'

'I know.'

At that very moment everyone throughout the palace, all over the city, was arguing passionately. Charles's councillors were divided into two opposing groups; some wanted to banish the heretic from the Empire and ruthlessly persecute his followers, while the others pleaded for tolerance. The latter thought, as I did, that these monastic disputes were dull at best, and that temporal powers had no business taking part in arguments concerning faith, works and sacraments. They also felt that Luther was less dangerous to the Empire than a Pope engaged in negotiating an alliance with France. I agreed with them, but that evening their insistence suddenly began to bother me. Were these really reasonable, disinterested men, free from superstition, who were so anxiously awaiting the Emperor's decision?

I asked sharply, 'Why do you defend him with such zeal? Has he won you over to his ideas?'

For a moment they seemed disconcerted. 'If Luther is

condemned,' said Pierre Morel, 'they'll start burning people at the stake again throughout the Netherlands, Austria and Spain.'

'You can't force a man to deny what he believes to be the truth,' said Balthus.

'But supposing he's wrong?'

'Who has the right to decide?'

I looked at them perplexedly. They were not saying everything that was on their minds. I was now certain that there was something in Luther that attracted them. What was it? They were too mistrustful to tell me, and I wanted to know. All night long, while the celebration continued unabated beneath my windows, I reread Jean Eck's reports and Luther's pamphlets. I had been sufficiently curious in the past to leaf through his writings and I found absolutely nothing reasonable in them. I considered that the fervour with which he fought Roman superstition to be no less foolish. As for Luther himself, I saw him for the first time that same afternoon; Jean Eck had interrogated him before the Diet. In a stammering voice, he declared that he needed a little more time to prepare his defence, whereupon Charles said to me cheerfully, 'It will take more than this little monk to make a heretic of me.'

Why then had these voices echoed throughout the night? Why were learned, reasonable men waiting so anxiously for dawn?

The next day, when the session opened, I watched impatiently for the door through which the monk would enter to open. Charles, wearing his black and gold Spanish clothes, was sitting impassively on his throne. A small velvet beret protected his short hair. Surrounding him, looking like statues, the dignitaries in their ermine cloaks and the princes arrayed in their golden attire stood motionless. In the corridors, cries of 'Hurrah! Hurrah!' rang out. Luther's friends were cheering him on. He entered the room, pushed back his black cowl, revealing his badly cut hair, and, walking up to the

Emperor, he greeted him confidently. No longer did he appear intimidated. He sat down at a table on which his books and pamphlets had been stacked, and he began to speak. I studied his thin, sallow face with its prominent cheekbones and dark, glittering eyes. Where did this influence he possessed come from? There seemed to be some great driving force in him, but once again he spoke only of sacraments and indulgences. I was bored. 'We're wasting time,' I thought. 'All these monks should be exterminated, the Dominicans along with the Augustinians. Churches should be replaced by schools, sermons by lessons in mathematics, astronomy and physics. At this moment we should be discussing the German constitution instead of listening to these pointless speeches.' Charles, however, listened attentively to Luther's arguments while he fidgeted with the medallion of the Golden Fleece which hung over his pleated shirt. The monk's voice rose in excitement; he was now speaking with passion, and in the tightly-packed room, stifling in the summer heat, everyone fell silent. In a frenzied outburst, he said, 'I cannot and will not retract a single word of what I have said or written, for to act against one's conscience is neither right nor honest.'

I shuddered. His words struck at me like a challenge. But it was not only the words; it was the tone in which the monk spoke them. This man dared to assert that his conscience alone was of more importance than the interests of the Empire and of the world. I wanted to gather the universe in my hands: he declared that he was a universe in himself. His arrogance fuelled a thousand stubborn wills. And this, surely, was why the people and even the wise men listened so complacently to him. He stirred up that rage of pride in people's hearts that had consumed Antonio and Beatrice. If he were allowed to continue preaching, in time he would have everyone believing that each man was sole judge of his relations with God, and judge too of his own actions. How would I then be able to make them obey?

He continued to speak, attacking the Church's established

dogma. But I began to see that it was not only dogma, grace, faith that was in question; something else was at stake: the very thing that I had dreamed of for so long. It could only be realized if men were to renounce their vanity, their whims, their follies. And it was precisely this that the Church taught. She enjoined people to obey one set of laws, to bow before one faith; if I were powerful enough, those laws could be mine. Through the mouths of priests, I could make God speak in whatever manner I wanted. On the other hand, if each individual sought God in his own conscience, I knew very well that it would not be me who he would find there. 'Who has the right to decide?' Balthus had said to me. That was why they defended Luther: they wanted to decide, each for himself. But then the world would be even more divided than it had ever been. It had to be governed by a single will: mine.

Suddenly there was a stir in the assembly. Luther declared that the council of Constance had made decisions which went against specific passages in the Scriptures. At this, Charles V slapped his gloves against his knee and abruptly stood up. There was a total silence. The Emperor walked over to a window and for a moment looked up at the sky. Then he turned around and ordered the room to be cleared.

'You're right, my Lord,' I said. 'Luther is more dangerous than the King of France. If you let him have his way, this little monk will destroy your empire.'

His eyes questioned me anxiously. Despite his abhorrence of heresy, he would have believed he were disobeying God himself if he condemned Luther against my advice.

'Do you really think so?' he said.

'Yes.' I said. 'My eyes have been opened.'

A hundred arms were raised up to carry Luther aloft in triumph. Outside they were acclaiming him, acclaiming pride and folly. Their stupid cries rang in my ears, and I could still feel on my face the feverish eyes of this monk who was challenging me. He wanted to turn people away from their true good, their true happiness, and they were so foolish that they were prepared to follow him. If they were left to their own devices, they would never discover the road to an earthly paradise. But I was there; I knew where to lead them and by which route. It was for them that I had fought against famine, against plague; and I was prepared, if necessary, to fight for them against themselves.

The next morning the Emperor stood before the Diet and declared: 'One monk, relying solely upon his own judgment, has placed himself in opposition to a faith upheld by Christianity for more than a thousand years. I have vowed to defend that holy cause, be it at the price of my domains, my body, my blood, my life, my soul.'

A few days later, Luther was banished from the Empire. An edict was published in the Netherlands, forbidding, under pain of severe punishment, the printing of any work treating of questions of faith without ecclesiastic authorization. The magistrates were ordered to prosecute Luther's followers.

At the very moment that the question of the constitution was to be discussed, we were obliged, to our great disappointment, to dissolve the Diet. François I, infuriated by the defeat he had suffered in his attempt to win the imperial crown, was preparing to declare war against us. Furthermore, disturbances were breaking out in Spain and Charles had to leave for Madrid. He confided the government of Germany to his brother Ferdinand and asked me to keep watch over him. Luther's condemnation had done nothing to quell the unrest that prevailed throughout the Empire. Monks left their monasteries and wandered about the countryside preaching heretical doctrines; armed bands of students, workers and adventurers set fire to libraries, churches and the homes of priests. New sects even more fanatical than Luther's, sprouted in the towns and cities and riots were constantly breaking out. In every village prophets arose who urged the peasants

to throw off the yokes of their princes and the former
revolutionary banner appeared in all the corners of the land:
a white flag on which was painted a golden shoe surrounded
by luminous rays and inscribed with the motto, 'Let Those
Who Want Freedom March Towards This Sun.'

'There's nothing to worry about,' said Ferdinand. 'All we
need is a handful of soldiers to restore order.'

'To restore disorder, you mean. These poor people are
right; reforms are needed.'

'What reforms?'

'That's what we have to consider.'

I had not forgotten the massacre of Carmona's weavers,
and when, two centuries before, I first wanted to control the
world, my chief aim had been to alter the economy. Never
before had the distribution of wealth been more unfair than
at this moment. Merchandise flowed into our ports, the
whole world had been opened to commerce, and our ships
brought us precious cargoes from every corner of the earth.
Yet the mass of peasants and the small shopkeepers were
poorer than ever before. A pound of saffron which was
worth two and a half florins and six kreutzers in 1515, now
cost four and a half florins and fifteen kreutzers. The price
of bread had increased by fifteen kreutzers; a quintal of sugar
sold for twenty florins instead of ten; Corinth grapes cost
nine florins instead of five. The price of every commodity
had risen while salaries had decreased.

'It's an intolerable situation,' I said angrily to the financiers
I had gathered together. They all looked at me with an
indulgent smile; it was no doubt my naivety that made them
smile. 'Speak,' I said to Muller, a banker. 'What's the reason
for this insane spiralling of prices?'

They spoke. I learned that the poverty of our time was the
direct result of the rapid development of commerce. The
gold, which the conquistadors obtained through the blood
and sweat of the Indians, flooded the old continent and
brought about increases in the prices of every commodity.

Powerful companies had been formed which chartered ships and soon monopolised commerce. Having ruined the smaller traders, within a few years they were able to sell their merchandise at twice the price and even more. This amassing of wealth led eventually to the depreciation of agricultural products; the value of money declined; wages fell at the same time as prices soared. A handful of men accumulated monstrous fortunes and dissipated them on absurd luxuries, while the mass of people wasted away from hunger.

'You will have to pass laws putting an end to monopolies, usury and speculation,' Muller advised me.

I remained silent. All of Germany's princes, including the Emperor himself, were in debt to these powerful companies which continually lent them money at usurious rates. My hands were tied. François I had attacked the kingdom of Navarre, Luxembourg and Italy; Charles had been forced to take up arms against him and was begging me to find the money to pay his troops. Our fate was in the hands of bankers and powerful merchants.

A few weeks later a revolt broke out in Forscheim in Franconia, and it spread across the whole of Germany. The peasants demanded equality, fraternity and the redistribution of land. They burned down castles, abbeys, churches; they murdered priests and landlords and divided the domains of their princes among themselves. By the end of the year, they were in control everywhere.

'There's only one solution,' Ferdinand said. 'We'll have to call upon the Swabian League.'

He paced rapidly back and forth across the large, bright stateroom, and the princes who had come to ask his help followed him with respectful looks upon their faces. There was so much fear and so much hate in their hearts that the air in the room seemed poisoned. Out there, in the countryside, the peasants had lit fires and were singing and dancing joyfully around them. They had drunk their wine and eaten their fill, and in their breasts, a new flame was burning.

I thought of the weavers' charred houses, of the women and children trampled by horses, and I murmured, 'Those poor people!'

'What did you say?' asked Ferdinand.

'I said there's only one solution.'

The princes nodded their heads approvingly. Thinking only of their own selfish interests, they crushed their peasantry with drudging work and taxes. I, on the other hand, wanted to create a world in which justice and reason would prevail, where men would find happiness. And yet I said the same thing they had said: only one solution. It was as if my thoughts, my desires, all the experience accumulated over the centuries through which I had lived, counted for nothing, were worthless. I was bound hand and foot. Some monstrous machinery had been set in motion in which each wheel inexorably turned another. In spite of myself, I was forced to the same decision as Ferdinand, the same decision as anyone else would have made in our place. Only one solution . . .

The peasants owed their fragile victory only to the surprise and isolation of their landlords. As soon as the nobles pulled themselves together and united their forces, they would soon have crushed the rebellious hordes. I then set out for the Netherlands in order to embark for Spain where I was anxious to rejoin the Emperor. I rode over the same pine forests, the same meadows and moors through which I had crossed five years earlier when I had taken Charles's proposals to the electors. At that time my heart was bursting with hope and I had thought, 'I shall hold an empire in my hands!' I had succeeded; I was at the summit of power. And what had I been able to do? I wanted to build the world anew, and yet I spent my time and energy in defending myself against anarchy, heresy, against the ambitions and obduracy of selfish men. I defended myself by destroying. I passed through ravaged lands where villages were reduced to ashes, fields left untended and cattle, half-dead, wandered aimlessly among abandoned farms. One met no one on the roads except

women and children with emaciated faces. All the rebellious
cities, villages and hamlets had been set on fire, and the
peasants tied to trees and burned alive. At Konigshoff, they
had been hunted down like a pack of wild boar; to save
themselves they climbed trees, but were slaughtered none-
theless with pikes and musket-shot. Those who fell to the
ground were trampled under horses' hoofs. In the village
of Ingolstadt, four thousand peasants were massacred; some
had sought refuge in the church: there they were burned
alive. Others had gathered in the castle, huddled together,
half-burying themselves in the earth in a vain attempt to
escape detection and pleading for God's mercy; none was
spared. Even now the nobles' wrath continued unabated.
Tortures and executions took place; the luckless peasants were
burned to death, their tongues ripped out, their fingers cut
off, their eyes gouged out.

'Is this what it is to reign?' asked Charles.

The blood had drained from his face and a corner of his
mouth was quivering. For two hours he had listened to me
without uttering a word and now he looked at me in
anguish. 'Is this what it is to reign?'

In Spain, too, much blood had to be spilled to put down
the revolts, and the repression still continued. In Valencia,
Toledo and Valladolid, every day heads fell by the thousands
under the executioner's axe.

'Have patience,' I said. 'A day will come when we shall
have rid the earth of evil. Then we shall start to build.'

'But this evil is our own doing,' he protested.

'Evil encourages evil,' I said. 'Heresy calls for the stake and
revolts for repression. It will all come to an end . . . '

'But *will* it ever come to an end?'

All day long he wandered silently through the palace.
Towards evening, during a session of the council, he fell to
the floor; overcome by nervousness, and burning with fever,
he was carried to his bed. As I did when he was a child,
I stayed at his bedside day and night, but I found no words of

hope to comfort him. The situation was very bleak. But by a stroke of good luck, we were able to enlist the services of a brilliant general, the High Constable Charles de Bourbon, who had quarreled with the king of France and had offered us his assistance. But we had to pay very dearly for his treason, for we lacked money and our exhausted troops threatened to mutiny; we were also badly in need of artillery. There was a real fear that we might be driven out of Italy.

Charles lay prostrate for a whole week. He had just got out of bed and was beginning to walk about the palace when a courier rushed in. The French army had been cut to pieces, half of France's highest nobility had perished and the King himself had been taken prisoner. Charles did not say a word. He went into his private chapel and prayed. Then he summoned all his councillors and gave the order to cease hostilities on all fronts.

Less than a year later, on 14 January 1526, the Treaty of Madrid was signed. François gave up all rights in Italy, recognized Charles's claims on Burgundy, withdrew from the league against the Emperor and promised to lend his aid in fighting the Turks. As a guarantee, he left his son with us as a hostage. Charles personally accompanied him on the road to Torrejon de Villano, a few miles from Madrid. Having embraced him for the last time, he took him aside and said to him, 'Brother, you're well aware of everything we have agreed upon. Now tell me frankly if you intend to carry them out.'

'I intend to carry them out completely,' said François. 'If you find me conducting myself otherwise, you may consider me a blackguard or a traitor.'

I had not heard him say these words which Charles reported to me on the way back, but I observed the charming way the King of France smiled at the Emperor, I saw him doff his feathered hat and bid him farewell with a sweeping gesture. Then he galloped off at full speed on the road to Bayonne.

Charles's finger crossed the Atlantic Ocean and came to rest upon a little black circle: Vera Cruz.

Geographers, for the first time, had plotted the furthest extremities of the New World: Tierra del Fuego, which was inhabited by large-footed Indians, and where Magellan had sailed past the Horn. On the yellow and green continents which emerged from the sea, they had inscribed magical names: America, Tierra Florida, Tierra de Brazil. I, too, placed my finger on the large, new map: the city of Mexico.

It was only a black dot on a sheet of parchment, but it was set among lakes which reflected its splendour, in a part of the world where the air was most transparent, and it was Cortés's capital. Upon the ruins of the ancient quarters, Mazeltan, Tecopan, Artacalco and Culpupan, stood the four districts of San Juan, San Pablo, San Sebastian, and Santa María. Churches, hospitals, monasteries and schools rose up along the city's wide avenues. And already, other new cities were being built in the wild terrain surrounding the capital. I drew my finger along a black line which represented the Cordillera de los Andes with its snow-covered peaks, and I pointed to a virgin region to the west of the chain on which 'Tierra Incognita' was written.

'El Dorado,' I said. 'Pizarro is probably crossing those mountains at this very moment.' I touched a meridian line situated three hundred and seventy leagues from the Cape Verde Islands which, ever since the Treaty of Tordesillas, separated Portuguese possessions from the Spanish domains. 'One day,' I murmured, 'we'll wipe out that frontier.'

Charles looked up at the portrait of Isabella. Beneath her light auburn hair there was a faint smile upon her beautiful, solemn face. 'Isabella will never have any claim to the Portuguese throne,' he said.

'Who knows?'

My eyes wandered over the Indian Ocean, to the spice islands, from the Moluccas to Malacca, and on to Ceylon. Isabella's nephews might die, or perhaps we would soon be strong enough to wage a war which would make Charles master of the whole peninsula as well as these lands over the seas. With the King of France defeated, we were now free to do as we wished.

'You're insatiable,' Charles remarked cheerfully. He was stroking his silky beard and his blue eyes were laughing in his florid face. He had grown into a robust man; he looked almost as old as I was.

'And why not?' I asked.

He shook his head. 'You have to know how to limit your desires.'

I raised my eyes from the yellow and green map and looked up at the panelled ceiling, the tapestries, the paintings. The palace of Granada had been draped with precious silks to receive Isabella. Fountains were playing in the garden, and streams rippled among the oleander and orange trees. I walked over to the window. The Queen, surrounded by her ladies-in-waiting, was walking slowly along the paths. She was wearing a long, russet-coloured, silk gown. Charles loved her. He loved this palace, the fountains, the flowers, the rich clothes, the tapestries, the wholesome meals, the spicy sauces. He loved to laugh. For the past year he had been happy.

'Don't you want the world to be your empire?' I asked.

'No. Let's accomplish what we've set out to do. That will be enough.'

'We'll accomplish it,' I assured him.

I smiled. I was unable to measure my desires. I could not stop at furnishing a palace, loving a woman, listening to a concert, being happy. But I was pleased that Charles was able to experience these things. I recalled the sickly child he had been, the sleepy adolescent, the hesitant young man whom I had vowed to make an emperor and I admired the calm, handsome man he had become. 'His power, his happiness,' I thought, 'these are of my making. I've built a world and I gave that man his life.'

'You once said to me: "I'll do great things." Do you remember?' I asked.

'Yes, I remember.'

'And you've already created a world,' I said, resting my hand on the map with the magical names.

'I owe it all to you. You showed me what my duty was.'

Cortés's success, the victory at Pavia, the alliance with Isabella, all seemed clear signs to him that he had obeyed God's will. So how could he now regret the deaths of a few red or black tribes? A week ago, in the port of Sanlucar, I had personally supervised the loading of plants and animals which we were sending to Cortés so that they could become acclimatised to the weather in the Indies. An armada was preparing to set sail for the new continent. On the docksides, enormous quantities of merchandise were piled high, ready to be loaded onto the galleons and even the warships. No longer was it soldiers who were embarking, but farmers and settlers. Charles was sending Dominican and Franciscan monks to Vera Cruz to establish hospitals and schools. For my part, I had put a large sum of money at the disposal of Nicolas Fernandez, a doctor from Toledo, to organize a scientific expedition. He took naturalists with him, whose job was to catalogue the American flora and fauna, and geographers to chart the unexplored areas. To the colonies of New Spain, the ships were bringing cane sugar, vine roots, mulberry trees, the larvae of silk worms, poultry, rams and ewes. Donkeys, mules and pigs were already being bred there, and orange and lemon trees were being cultivated.

Charles touched the little black dot which represented Mexico. 'If God permits,' he said, 'one day I'll go to see with my own eyes this realm he has bestowed on me.'

'If you allow me to, I'd like to accompany you,' I said.

For a moment, we stood side by side dreaming: Vera Cruz, Mexico. For Charles it was no more than a dream: the

Indies were far off, his life short. But I would see them, come what may. I stood up suddenly. Charles looked at me in surprise.

'I'm going back to Germany,' I announced.

'Are you bored already?'

'You decided to convoke a new Diet. Why wait any longer?'

'Even God rested on the seventh day,' Charles said.

'He was God.'

Charles smiled. He could not understand my impatience. In a moment, he would begin to dress carefully for the evening festivities. He would dine on some large roast or another and he would listen to music as he smiled at Isabella. But I could wait no longer: I had waited too long already. I had to hasten the arrival of the day when, looking about me, I would be able to say: 'I was able to accomplish something. This is what I have done!' When the moment came for my eyes to rest on those cities which my desires had torn from the earth, on those plains populated by my dreams, then, like Charles, would I allow myself to fall smiling into a chair. Only then would I feel my life beating calmly inside me without hurtling me towards the future. All around me, time would be like a large, calm lake in which I would rest, like God in his clouds.

A few weeks later, I crossed Germany again. It now seemed to me that I was in sight of my goal. The peasants' revolt had alarmed princes, it looked as if a solution to the Lutheran question were feasible, and there was a possibility of uniting the German States into a single confederation. Then I would turn towards the New World, whose prosperity would soon be shared with this old continent. I looked about me at the devastated countryside. New houses were already sprouting up in the ruined villages; men were toiling in the fallow fields and women were sitting on doorsteps, cradling their new-born babies. I looked disinterestedly at the traces of fires and massacres. 'After all, what does it matter?' I thought.

The dead were no longer, the living were alive; the world was just as full as ever. The same sun still shone in the same sky. There was no one to pity; there was nothing to regret.

'There'll never be an end to this!' I said angrily. 'Our hands will never be free!'

No sooner had I arrived at Augsburg than I learned that François I, his promises cast to the winds, had formed an alliance with Pope Clement VII, as well as the rulers of Venice, Milan and Florence, with the purpose of resuming wars against the Emperor. He had also made an alliance with the Turks who had just scattered an army of twenty thousand men commanded by Louis of Hungary and who now posed a dangerous threat to the whole of Christendom. Once again I had to postpone my plans and confront a thousand urgent problems.

'Where are you counting on getting money from?' I asked Ferdinand.

We needed money. In Italy the imperial troops, under the command of the Duke of Bourbon, were demanding adequate provisions and all of their back pay. They were on the verge of open mutiny.

'I was thinking of borrowing from the Fuggers again,' he replied.

I knew that that would be his answer, and I also knew how disastrous it would be to resort to this expedient. The bankers of Augsburg insisted upon guarantees, and little by little Austria's silver mines, the most fertile lands of Aragon and Andalusia, all our most important sources of revenue, were falling into their hands. The gold from the Americas belonged to them long before it entered our ports. Thus, the treasury always remained empty and we were continually forced to ask for further loans.

'And what about men?' I asked. 'Where will we get men?'

He was silent for a moment and then, avoiding my eyes,

he murmured, 'The Prince of Mindelheim has offered to help us.'

I jumped to my feet. 'Are we going to depend on a Lutheran prince?'

'What else can we do?'

I remained silent. 'Only one solution . . . What else can we do? . . . ' The machinery has been set in motion, the wheels were meshing, inexorably turning, and all for nothing. Charles had dreamed of reviving the Holy Empire; he had sworn to defend the Church at the cost of his domains, his blood, his life. And now we were about to accept the aid of his enemies to fight a Pope in whose name we had burned hundreds of people at the stake in Spain and the Netherlands.

'We have no choice,' Ferdinand insisted.

'No,' I said. 'There's never any choice.'

At the beginning of February, we marched into Italy with a reinforcement of Bavarian, Swabian and Tyrolian mercenaries, eight thousand of them, all Lutherans, and led by the Prince of Mindelheim. We went first to join forces with Bourbon who was waiting for us in the valley of the Arno. It poured with rain day and night, and the roads everywhere were transformed into bogs.

Just as we arrived in the camp, mutinous troops were marching towards the general's tent, shouting, 'Money or blood!' Their muskets were loaded, the wicks burning, ready to fire. Their britches were in tatters and some of their faces bore long scars. They resembled brigands more than soldiers.

I brought one hundred thousand ducats with me which were distributed immediately, but as the mercenaries took the money there were sarcastic comments. They demanded twice as much. To restore order, the Prince of Mindelheim shouted to them: 'We'll find gold enough in Rome!' Wasting no time, the combined armies set out on the road to Rome, vowing to make up for their privations by looting the Church's treasures. We tried in vain to dissuade them, but by now they were so inflamed that a messenger who

brought news that the Pope had made peace with Charles
had to flee to save his skin. On the way, we were joined by
bands of Italian outlaws who could scent an opportunity for
pillage. There was no way of stopping the unruly horde that
swept us along. We were prisoners of our own troops.

'Is this what it is to reign?'

We rode in silence in the teeming rain, accompanied
by their raucous yelling. I had brought these men together,
provided them with money and food, and now they were
dragging me with them towards the most absurd catastrophe
imaginable.

At the beginning of May, fourteen thousand bandits
arrived at the walls of Rome, clamouring for booty.
Bourbon, to save his throat from being slit, was forced to lead
them in an assault. He was killed at my side on the first wave.
After having been twice repulsed by the Pope's troops, the
Lutherans, the Spanish mercenaries, and the Italian brigands
invaded the city. For seven days they massacred priests and
laymen, rich and poor, cardinals and kitchen-boys. The Pope
fled, saved by his Swiss guards who laid down their lives to
the last man; later, he surrendered to the Prince of Orange
who had taken over from Bourbon.

Bodies swung from the balconies; swarms of blue flies
buzzed around the human flesh rotting in the squares;
bloated corpses drifted in the oily waters of the Tiber. There
were red pools in the streets and bloody rags among the
rubbish in the gutters. Dogs could be seen tearing greedily
at strange pink and grey entrails. The air smelled of death.
Women wept in their homes while soldiers sang in the
streets.

I did not weep; nor did I sing. 'Rome,' I said to myself.
'This is Rome.' But the word no longer moved me. Rome
had always been a more beautiful and more powerful city
than Carmona, and, years ago, if someone had said to me:
'One day you will conquer her; your soldiers will drive out
the Pope and hang her cardinals', I would have shouted for

joy. Later, I had come to revere Rome as the noblest city of Italy, and if someone had said to me: 'Spanish soldiers and German mercenaries will massacre her citizens and sack her churches,' I would have shed tears. But that day, Rome no longer meant anything to me. In her destruction I saw neither victory nor defeat, only a meaningless fact. 'What difference does it make?' I had spoken those words all too often. But if burning villages, torturing and killing were of no importance, what did new houses, bountiful crops or the smiles of babies matter? What hope was left to me? I no longer knew what it was to suffer or rejoice: a dead man. Gravediggers removed the corpses from the streets and squares, the blood stains were washed clean, the rubbish cleared away and women timidly ventured out of their houses to fetch water from the fountains. Rome was being reborn. But I was dead.

For days, I wandered deathlike through the city. And then, suddenly, one morning as I stood on the banks of the Tiber gazing at the massive silhouette of the Castle of Sant' Angelo, something beyond that lifeless scene, beyond the emptiness in my heart, began to live again. It lived both outside of me and deep within me: the pungent smell of the yew trees, a patch of white wall beneath a blue sky, my whole past. I closed my eyes and I could see Carmona's gardens. In those gardens there once walked a man who burned with desire, with anger and with joy. I had been that man; he was me. Out there, beyond the horizon, I had existed with a full heart, a living heart. That same day, I took leave of the Prince of Orange and galloped out of Rome onto the open roads.

Wars were raging throughout Italy. I, too, had fought in those valleys and on those plains; we used to burn a few crops and lay waste to a few orchards, but it only took a single season for all trace of our passage to disappear. The French and Germans, however, ruthlessly ravaged these lands which were foreign to them and took no pity on their inhabitants. Entire hamlets were burned to the ground, granaries destroyed, live-stock slaughtered, dykes pierced and fields flooded. More than once I noticed bands of children searching for edible herbs and wild roots by the side of the road. The world was growing bigger, populations were increasing, cities expanding. Forests and swamps were being turned into fertile land, new tools being invented. Yet the fighting was becoming increasingly ferocious; men were dying in battle in their thousands. They were learning to destroy as fast as they learned to build. It almost seemed as if there were a stubborn god who was determined to preserve an immutable and absurd balance between life and death, wealth and misery.

The scenery grew more familiar; I recognized the colour of the earth, the smell of the air, the songs of the birds. I spurred my horse on. A few miles from here there had lived a man who passionately loved his city, a man who smiled at the flowering almond trees, who clenched his fists, who felt the blood coursing through his veins. I was keen to rejoin that man, to merge myself with him. With a lump in my throat, I rode across the plain with its olive and almond trees. And then Carmona loomed up before me, perched on her rock, surrounded by her eight gilded towers, the same as she had always been. I gazed at her for a long while. I had pulled up my horse and I was waiting; I waited and nothing happened. I saw only a familiar scene, a place I felt I had left the day before. In a glance, Carmona had entered into my present; she stood before me now, ordinary and impervious, yet the past remained out of reach.

I rode up the hill. I thought, 'He's waiting for me behind the ramparts.' I passed through the gates. I recognized the palace, the shops, the taverns, the churches, the funnel-shaped chimneys, the pink streets and the larkspur growing against the walls. Everything was in its place, but the past was nowhere to be found. For a long while I stood motionless in the main square; I sat down on the steps of the cathedral; I wandered through the cemetery. Nothing happened.

The looms were humming, the coppersmiths were hammering on cauldrons, children were playing on the steep streets. Nothing had changed; there was no void to be filled in Carmona; no one needed me. No one had ever needed me.

I entered the cathedral and looked at the tombstones beneath which Carmona's princes lay. Under the vaulted arches, the priest had murmured, 'May they rest in peace.' They were resting in peace. And I, too, was dead, yet I was still here, a witness to my absence. 'There will never be any rest,' I thought.

&

'Germany will never be united as long as Luther has a single follower,' Charles said fiercely.

'The more ground Luther loses, the more the new sects gain; and they're even more fanatical,' I said.

'All of them must be wiped out,' exclaimed Charles, bringing his powerful hand down sharply against the table. 'It's time we did something!'

It was indeed time we did something. We had had ten years of pompous ceremonies, of petty worries, of useless wars, of massacres. Except in the New World, we had still not built anything. For a year, however, there had been some sign of hope; François I had relinquished his rights to Italy, Austria and Flanders; Germany, massed behind Ferdinand, had repulsed the Turks at the gates of Vienna; Isabella had borne Charles a healthy son, and the succession to the thrones of Spain and the Empire was thus assured; Pizarro was getting ready to conquer a new empire which promised be even richer than that of Cortés; and at the end of February 1530, Charles had been crowned Holy Roman Emperor by the Pope in Bologna Cathedral. But trouble soon began to break out in Italy and the Netherlands. The Lutheran princes joined forces and François plotted with them. Suleiman the Magnificent again threatened Christendom, and Charles, having gathered the Catholic princes around him, had begun preparations for a campaign against the Turks.

'I'm beginning to wonder if burning heretics is really the way to stamp out heresy,' I said.

'They don't listen to our preachers,' replied Charles.

'I'd like to try to understand them,' I said, 'but I don't.'

He frowned. 'The devil is in their hearts.'

He who had had no qualms about allowing the Indians to be maltreated, had nevertheless encouraged the zealousness of the Inquisition in Spain and the Netherlands. He considered it his Christian duty to fight demons.

'I'll do my best to drive out the devils,' I promised.

I could understand Charles's irritation. To have to rely on the Lutherans' support against the Pope, or on the Catholics' against the Lutheran league, was a balancing game that would lead us nowhere. We would never succeed in realizing our dream of political unity until we had stifled all eruptions of spiritual discord. I was certain that we could achieve it; it was a question of finding the right means. Persecution only tended to increase the heretics' determination, and our preachers addressed them in a false and fanatical language. But was it not possible to make them listen to the voice of reason and show them where their true interests lay?

'What do you mean by their true interests?' asked Balthus, with whom I was discussing these ideas. He looked at me quizzically. It was men of his kind whose assistance I needed, but ever since Luther's condemnation, he never spoke to me without a certain reticence.

'You're right,' I said. 'We have to find out what's at the bottom of it all.' I looked at him steadily. 'Do you know?'

'I don't associate with heretics,' he said with a prudent smile.

'Well, I'm going to associate with them. I want to know exactly what they think.'

When Charles left at the head of his army, I set out for the Netherlands where I questioned the nuncio Aleander.

Having learned that the sect with the largest number of adherents was the Anabaptists, so named because they conferred second baptisms on each other, I asked about making contact with them. I was told that it would not be difficult to introduce myself amongst them, for they made little effort to conceal their practices and they seemed to be courting martyrdom. I did in fact manage to participate at several of their meetings. Squeezed into the back room of a shop lit by a couple of oil lamps, workers, artisans and shopkeepers listened avidly to the inspired orator who was uttering his holy words. The speaker was usually a small man with soft, blue eyes who claimed to be the incarnation of the prophet Enoch. His sermons were usually insignificant; he preached the coming of a new Jerusalem where justice and brotherhood would reign. But he declaimed these visions of his in stirring tones. There were many women in the audience, as well as very young people. They listened fervently to him, their breathing became heavy and soon they began to cry out, falling to their knees, weeping hysterically, and clasping one another in their arms. Often, they even tore their clothing and dug their fingernails into their faces. Women threw themselves to the ground, their arms stretched out in the form of a cross, and men trampled over their prostrate bodies. Afterwards, they went calmly back to their homes. They seemed inoffensive enough. The president of the Inquisition, who from time to time ordered a handful of them to be burned at the stake, told me how struck he was by their gentleness and obedience. The women sang as they went to be tortured. On several occasions I tried to talk to the prophet, but he always smiled without answering.

I stayed away from the shop for several weeks. When I went there again on another evening, it seemed to me that the preacher had altered his language. He spoke much more violently than before and at the end of his sermon he cried out passionately, 'It's not enough to tear the rings off the fingers of the rich and the golden chains from their necks. Everything that is must be destroyed!'

The gathering feverishly repeated after him, 'We must destroy! We must destroy!' They shouted with such intense passion that a feeling of anxiety came over me. When the meeting broke up I grabbed the prophet's arm.

'Why do you preach destruction?' I asked. 'Tell me.'

He looked at me gently. 'We *must* destroy.'

'No,' I protested. 'We must build.'

He shook his head. 'We must destroy. Nothing else is left to man.'

'Yet you preach the coming of a new Jerusalem.'

He smiled. 'I preach it because it doesn't exist.'

'You mean you don't really hope that it will ever come about?'

'If it came about, if all men were happy, what would there be left for them to do on earth?' He seemed to be looking into the very depths of my heart and there was anguish in his eyes. 'The world weighs so heavily upon our shoulders ... There is only one way to salvation: to undo all that has been done.'

'What a strange way to salvation!' I said.

He laughed maliciously. 'They want to turn us into stones but we won't let ourselves be turned into stones!' His great prophetical voice suddenly boomed out into the night. 'We shall destroy, we shall lay waste, we shall live!'

Not long after that, the Anabaptists propagated their beliefs through all the cities of Germany, burning churches, the houses of the rich, convents, books and furniture. They destroyed cemeteries, set fire to crops, raped women and engaged in bloody orgies. They murdered any who attempted to oppose their wild fury. I learned that the prophet Enoch had become the ruler of Münster, and from time to time I heard reports of lewd, bacchanalian revelries which took place with his agreement. When the bishop finally regained possession of the city, the prophet was locked in a cage with iron bars which was suspended from one of the towers of the cathedral. I decided not to waste time wondering about this man's eccentric fate, but I could not help thinking somewhat anxiously that famine can be conquered, plague can be conquered, but can man ever be conquered?

I knew that the Lutherans, too, were appalled by the havoc the Anabaptists had wreaked. Anxious to try to exploit this mood, I asked to speak to two Augustinian monks who had just been condemned to the stake by the ecclesiastical tribunal of Brussels.

'Why do you refuse to sign this paper?' I asked, showing them a certificate of retraction. They smiled but did not answer. Both of them were heavy-featured, middle-aged men. 'I know,' I continued. 'You scorn death; you're eager to reach Heaven. You think only of your own salvation. Do you believe that God approves of such selfishness?' They looked at me in some astonishment; the words I spoke were not those they were accustomed to hearing from the Inquisitors. 'Surely you've heard of the horrors the Anabaptists have perpetrated in Münster and all over Germany?'

'Yes.'

'Well! You're the ones who are responsible for those crimes, just as you were for the rebellion ten years ago.'

'You know very well that what you say is false,' one of the monks said. 'Luther repudiated those wretches.'

'Yes, and vehemently. But only because he felt guilty. Reflect a moment,' I said. 'You demand the right to search your hearts for the truth and to preach what you find there to all the world. But what is to stop madmen and fanatics from proclaiming their truths? You've seen how many new sects have emerged, and what destruction they have wrought.'

'They preach falsehoods,' the monk replied.

'But how can you prove that, since you reject all authority?' In a pleading voice, I added, 'It may be true that the Church has often failed in her obligations. I even admit that her teachings are sometimes in error and I do not stop you condemning her in your hearts. But why must you attack her publicly?'

They listened to me with their heads bent towards the ground and their hands buried in the sleeves of their robes. I felt so sure I was right that I thought I was going to convince them.

'All men must become united,' I said. 'They must fight against poverty, injustice, war, nature's hostility. They should not waste their energies in vain disputes or sow seeds of dissension among themselves. Can't you sacrifice your own beliefs for the good of your brothers?'

They raised their heads and the monk who had until now remained silent spoke: 'There is only one good,' he said, 'and that is to act according to the dictates of one's conscience.'

The next day, flames crackled in the centre of Brussels' main square. A horrible smell of burnt flesh drifted up to the sky. Around the stakes a crowd had gathered and people were silently praying for the souls of the martyrs. From a window, I watched the black ashes swirling in the air. 'The fools!' The flames were devouring them alive, and they had chosen this fate. Like a fool, Antonio had chosen to die; like a fool, Beatrice had refused to live. The prophet Enoch starved to death in a cage suspended from the top of a tower. I stared at the stakes and I wondered whether they were really insane or whether there existed in the hearts of mortal men a secret I was unable to fathom. The flames died out. All that remained in the centre of the square was a heap of charred remains. I wished I could have questioned those ashes which the wind had begun to scatter through the city.

Nevertheless, Charles had triumphed over Suleiman; he had carried the war against the Infidels into Africa, driven the pirate Barbarossa from Tunis and put Moulay Hassan, who had agreed to recognize Spain's supremacy, on the throne. He then left for Rome to do his Easter duties. In Saint Peter's he sat on a throne beside the Pope. Together, they performed their acts of worship, and together they left the basilica. For the first time in centuries the Empire displayed a power equal to the Papacy's. But at the very moment when this triumph was revealed to the world, we learned that François I had suddenly laid claim to the Duchy of Milan for his second son and that he had just sent an army to Turin.

'No!' Charles exclaimed. 'I don't want any more wars. Always wars! What good are they? They only wear us down.' He, who was always so in control of his emotions, was now pacing back and forth, nervously stroking his beard. 'This is what I'll do,' he said. 'I'll engage François in personal combat, gambling Milan for Burgundy. And the one who loses has to take up arms on behalf of the victor in a war against the Infidels.'

'François won't take up the challenge,' I said.

I now knew for certain: never would there be an end to it, never would our hands be free. Once delivered from the French, we would have to march against the Turks, and once the Turks were defeated, we would again have to take up arms against the French. No sooner was a revolt put down in Spain than another would break out in Germany; once we had weakened the power of the Lutheran princes, we would be forced to fight the arrogance of the Catholics. We consumed ourselves in useless struggles and we no longer even knew what the stakes were. German federation, the development of the New World – we were never free to devote ourselves to those great projects.

Charles decided to attack Provence and we marched on Marseille, but failed to capture the city. We were forced to retreat to Genoa and embark for Spain. By the Treaty of Nice, we relinquished Savoy and two-thirds of Piedmont.

Charles spent the winter in Spain with Queen Isabella,

whose health was a matter of grave concern. On the first of May, after a miscarriage, she was struck down with a violent fever and she died a few hours later. The Emperor shut himself away for several weeks in a convent near Toledo. When at last he emerged from his seclusion, he had aged ten years. His back was bent, his complexion sallow and his eyes faded.

'I thought you'd never leave that convent,' I said.

'I wished I didn't have to leave.' Charles stared through the window at the harsh blue sky.

'Why didn't you stay? You're the ruler aren't you?'

He looked at me. 'It was you who once told me that my health, my happiness, counted for nothing.'

'Ah, you still remember those words.'

'Now is the time to remember them.' He passed his hand across his forehead; it was a new gesture he had acquired, the gesture of an old man. 'I want to leave Philip an empire that's still intact,' he said.

I bowed my head without answering and the great, burning silence of the Castilian summer closed in on us. How did I ever have the audacity to dictate his duty to him? How did I dare say to myself one day while listening to the fountains play in Granada, 'I gave that man his life, his happiness'? Now I would have to say, 'It was I who gave him those lacklustre eyes, that sad mouth and that unsteady heart. His unhappiness is all my doing.' His soul was cold and I felt that coldness as keenly as if I had touched a corpse with my hand.

For several weeks we were plunged in a sort of torpor. An appeal from Charles's sister Mary, who governed the Netherlands in his name, aroused us. Trouble had broken out in Ghent. For many years the ancient city had been in the shadow of Antwerp's prosperity. Her merchants saw their orders constantly diminishing, and her unemployed workers lived in poverty. When the Regent proposed that every city contribute to a national tax, Ghent refused to pay. Rebels tore up the municipal constitution, which had been accorded the people of Ghent in 1515, and they proudly wore small bits of parchment attached to their clothes as a sign of support. They had killed a magistrate and had begun to pillage the city. We asked the King of France to allow us safe passage through his territories, and on 14 February, Charles V entered Ghent with Mary, the Pope's legate, ambassadors, princes, German noblemen and Spanish grandees. Behind them followed the Imperial Cavalry and twenty thousand foot soldiers; the procession with all its baggage took five hours to pass through the gates of the city. Charles settled into the castle where he had been born forty years earlier and his troops were dispersed throughout the city. They immediately began a reign of terror, and within three days the leaders of the rebellion were forced to surrender. On 3 March the trial began. The attorney-general of Malines enumerated the city's crimes in the presence of the sovereigns, and a delegation of the people of Ghent came to plead with Mary for mercy. But she turned an angry ear to their pleas and demanded pitiless reprisals.

'Aren't you tired of punishing?' I asked Charles.

He looked at me in astonishment. 'What do my feelings have to do with it?' He appeared to have rediscovered a certain serenity. He ate and drank heartily and still took as much care as ever in his own appearance. Nothing in his behaviour led one to suspect the emptiness in his heart.

'Do you really believe that these men are criminals?'

He raised his eyebrows. 'Were the Indians in America criminals? You were the one who taught me that no one can govern without doing evil.'

'On condition that the evil committed serve some ultimate purpose,' I added.

'I need to set an example,' he explained.

I studied him for a moment and then said, 'I admire you.'

He looked away. 'I have no right to endanger Philip's inheritance.'

The next day the executions began. Sixteen of the leaders

were beheaded, while the Spanish mercenaries looted the houses of the rich and raped their wives and daughters. The Emperor had a district that contained most of the city's churches demolished and a citadel erected upon its ruins. All of Ghent's public wealth was seized; her arms, cannon, munitions and her great bell, known to the inhabitants as Roland, were removed. All her privileges were abolished and her citizens were required to make public apologies.

'Why?' I murmured. 'Why?'

Mary, who was seated beside her brother, was smiling. Thirty of the city's leading figures, dressed in black, their heads and feet bare, were kneeling at the sovereigns' feet. Behind them, in shirtsleeves and with ropes around their necks, were six delegates from each guild, fifty weavers and fifty members of the popular party. All bowed their heads and clenched their teeth. They had wanted freedom, and to punish them for this crime we forced them to crawl before us on their knees. Throughout the whole of Germany, thousands of men had been beaten, quartered, burned; thousands of noblemen and merchants had been beheaded in Spain; in the cities of the Netherlands, heretics writhed at the stake amid searing flames. Why?

That evening I said to Charles, 'I'd like to leave for America.'

'Now?' he asked.

'Now.'

It was my last hope, my only desire. The year before, we had learned that Pizarro and his army had captured the gold-bedecked Peruvian emperor and had taken possession of his domains. The first galleon returning from this new realm had arrived in the port of Seville bearing 42,486 gold pesos and 1750 silver marks. No energy was being wasted out there in the propagation of an uncertain past by means of useless wars and cruel repressions. Over there, men were planning a new future, constructing, creating.

Charles went over to the window and looked down at

the grey waters of the canal that wended its way between the stone walls. In the distance could be seen the dark mass of the belfry, stripped of its proud bells.

'I'll never see the Americas!' he said.

'You'll see them through my eyes. You know you can trust me.'

'Later,' he said. It was not an order; it was a plea. He must have been in great distress to speak to me in that supplicating tone. With greater firmness, he said, 'I need you here.'

I lowered my head. It was then that I wanted to see the Americas, but would I still want to later? It was at that moment that I should have left.

'I'll wait,' I said.

I waited ten years. Everything constantly changed and yet everything remained the same. In Germany, Lutheranism was gaining ground, the Turks were threatening Christendom once more, and the Mediterranean had again become infested with pirates from whom we failed to take Algiers. There had been another war with France which resulted in the treaty of Crépy-en-Valois, whereby the Emperor relinquished all claims to Burgundy, and François I renounced his rights to Naples, Artois and Flanders. After twenty-seven years of fighting, which had drained the strength of both France and the Empire, the two adversaries found themselves face to face with not the slightest change in their respective positions. Charles was happy to hear that Pope Paul II had convoked a Holy Council at Trent, but thereupon the Lutheran princes, immediately engaged in a civil war. Despite the gout which was torturing him, Charles personally took command, acquitted himself heroically and overcame his enemies' forces. But the Emperor's governor in Milan committed the blunder of occupying Piacenza, and the Pope, who was furious, began negotiations with Henri II, the new King of France for the Council of Trent to be moved to Bologna. At Augsburg,

Charles was forced to accept a compromise which satisfied neither Catholics nor Protestants. Both sides obstinately rejected our plans for a German constitution which we had struggled for constantly ever since Charles became emperor.

'I should never have signed that compromise,' Charles said. He was slumped in a large, deep armchair, his gouty leg resting upon a footstool; thus he passed his days when events did not oblige him to mount a horse.

'There was nothing else you could do,' I said.

He shrugged his shoulders. 'That's what they always say.'

'They say it because it happens to be true.'

The only solution . . . we have no choice . . . nothing else you could do . . . Through the years, over the centuries, the mechanism slowly unwound. Only a fool could believe that the will of a single human being was able to change its action. What did our great plans matter?

'I should have refused,' he said. 'No matter what the price.'

'It would have meant war and you would have been defeated.'

'I know.'

He drew his hand across his forehead; the gesture had become a habit. He seemed to be asking himself, 'Why not be defeated?' And perhaps he was right. In spite of everything, there were men whose desires had left their marks on earth: Luther, Cortés . . . Was it because they had accepted the idea of being defeated? For our part, we had chosen victory. And now we were asking ourselves, 'What victory?'

'Philip will never be emperor,' Charles said after a brief silence.

He had known it for a long time. Ferdinand's ambition to lay claim to an empire for his own son was too recent, too bitter. But never before had Charles openly admitted this defeat even to me.

'What does it matter?' I asked.

I looked at the faded tapestries, at the oak furniture and, through the window, at the autumn leaves being blown about by the wind. Here in Europe everything had become stagnant and outmoded: the dynasties, the frontiers, the routines, the injustices. What was the point of struggling to hold together the debris of this old, worm-eaten world?

'Make Philip a Spanish prince and Emperor of the Americas; it is only there that men can build and create . . . '

'Can they?' asked Charles.

'How can there be any doubt in your mind? You've conquered a virgin world over there, you've constructed churches, built cities, you've sown seeds and reaped harvests . . . '

He shook his head. 'Who knows what's going on over there?'

The situation was in fact confused. A war had broken out between Pizarro and one of his lieutenants, who had been defeated and condemned to death, but whose supporters had later succeeded in killing Pizarro. The viceroy, sent by the Emperor to settle these disputes, had been assassinated by Pizarro's soldiers, and they in turn had been defeated and beheaded by the Emperor's troops. All that could be said with certainty was that the new laws were not being observed and that the Indians were still being maltreated.

'There was a time when you wanted to see America for yourself,' said Charles.

'Yes.'

'Do you still want to?'

I hesitated. Something which may have been a desire still beat weakly in my heart. 'My only wish is to serve you still.'

'Well, then,' he said, slowly rubbing his gouty leg, 'go and see what we have done there. I need to know. I have to know what I'm leaving to Philip.' He lowered his voice to a whisper. 'I have to know what I've done in a reign of thirty years.'

Six months later, in the spring of 1550, I boarded a caravel in the port of Sanlucar de Barrameda and, together with three cargo vessels and two warships, we set sail for the new world. Day after day, leaning against the bulwarks, I watched the foamy path the ship left behind on the water's surface, the same path that the caravels of Columbus, Cortés, and Pizarro had followed. I had often traced it with my finger on parchment maps, but now the sea was no longer a shaded area on a scrap of paper that I could cover with my hand; it undulated and sparkled, it stretched out into the distance farther than the eye could see. 'How can anyone ever possess the sea?' I wondered. In my studies in Brussels, Augsburg and Madrid, I had dreamed of holding the world in my hands – the world, a smooth, round sphere. But now, as we slipped day after day over the blue waters, I asked myself, 'But what, after all, is the world? Where is it?'

One morning, while I was lying on the deck with my eyes closed, a sudden gust of wind brought with it an aroma that I had not smelled for five months, a warm, spicy smell, the smell of land. I opened my eyes. Before me, stretching out into the infinite distance, was a low coastline shaded by a forest of giant-leaved trees. We were nearing the archipelago of the Bahama Islands. I gazed in awe at the immense green platform which seemed to be floating upon the sea. Half a century ago a voice from the crow's nest had shouted 'Land!' and Columbus's sailors had fallen to their knees. Now, as then, we could hear the chirping of birds.

'Are we going to put into port here?' I asked the captain.

'No,' he answered. 'The islands are deserted.'

'Deserted? . . . Then it's true!'

'Didn't you know?'

'I didn't believe it.'

In 1509 King Ferdinand had authorized selling the natives of the Bahamas as slaves. Father Las Casas declared that they had been tracked down like wild game with the help of bulldogs and that fifty thousand Indians had either been wiped out or dispersed.

'Fifteen years ago, there were still a few settlers left on the islands,' the captain said. 'They lived off pearl trading. But even then a good diver could earn as much as a hundred and fifty ducats. It wasn't long before the race died out and the last of the Spaniards had to leave.'

'How many islands are there in this archipelago?' I asked.

'About thirty.'

'And all deserted?'

'All of them.'

On the map which the geographers had drawn up, the archipelago was nothing but a pattern of meaningless specks. And yet now, as we slowly sailed past them, I could see that each separate island bloomed as radiantly as the gardens of the Alhambra. They were filled with brilliant flowers, colourful birds and perfumes; between coral reefs, the trapped waters of the ocean formed calm lagoons which the sailors called 'water gardens'; polyps, medusas, algae and coral sparkled in the transparent sea, and red and blue fish swam about lazily. From time to time a solitary dune, like a stranded ship, emerged from the water's surface; occasionally, one of these sand hills would be covered with a web of creeping lianas, with palm trees growing on its banks. No longer did boats glide over the warm lakes in which the occasional fresh-water spring bubbled; no hand had ever parted the thick curtains of lianas. These lands of delight, where a naked, languorous people once lived in carefree indolence, were lost to man.

'Are there any Indians left in Cuba?' I asked as we entered the narrow channel which led to the Bay of Santiago.

'About sixty families. They used to live in the mountains and were resettled in a village at Guandora, near Havana,' the captain told me. 'There must still be a few tribes in this region here, but they keep themselves hidden.'

'I see.'

The bay of Santiago de Cuba was easily large enough to contain the entire armada of the kingdom of Spain. I looked at the pink, green and yellow cubes which rose storey upon storey over the sides of the mountain and I smiled. I liked cities. The moment I set foot on the cobblestone streets, I was happy to breathe in the smell of tar mingled with oil, the smell of Antwerp and Sanlucar. I made my way through the milling crowd on the shore. Ragged children clung to my clothes, shouting, 'Santa Lucia!' I threw a handful of coins to the ground and asked the brightest looking lad in the band to guide me through the city.

A wide, reddish-brown avenue, shaded by palm trees led up to a church of dazzling whiteness.

'Santa Lucia,' said the child. His feet were bare and his head was a black ball, completely shaven.

'I don't care for churches,' I said. 'Take me to see the shops and the market place.'

We turned the corner; all the streets were straight and laid out like a chessboard, and the houses, painted in gleaming stucco, were modelled on those in Cádiz. But Santiago did not look like a Spanish city; it was hardly a city at all. The yellow dust of unpaved streets covered my boots, and the big, open squares were no more than waste-ground in which agaves and cactuses grew freely.

'Are you from Spain?' the child asked, looking up at me with beaming eyes.

'Yes,' I answered.

'When I grow up, I'm going to work in the mines,' said the child. 'I'll make a lot of money and then I'll go to Spain.'

'Don't you like it here?'

He spat contemptuously on the ground. 'Everyone here is poor.'

We reached the market place. Women squatting on the ground were selling cactus fruits, split open and spread out on palm leaves. Others were standing behind counters laden with round loaves of bread, and baskets filled with grain, beans or chick-peas. There were also merchants selling ironware and cloth. The men, all of them barefooted, wore faded cotton clothing, and the women, who went barefoot too, were dressed in tatters.

'How much is a bushel of wheat?' I asked. I was wearing

the clothes of a nobleman and the merchant looked at me
with surprise.

'Twenty-four ducats.'

'Twenty-four ducats! That's twice as much as in Seville.'

'That's the price,' the man said sullenly.

I walked slowly around the square. A little girl in rags
darted in front of me. She stopped at every stand where bread
was sold, fingering and thoughtfully weighing the round
loaves in her hands unable to decide which one to choose.
The stallholders smiled at her. In this land where iron cost
more than silver, bread was more precious than gold. A
bushel of beans which cost two hundred and seventy-two
maravedis in Spain, cost five hundred seventy-eight here;
a horseshoe cost six ducats, and two nails, forty-six maravedis;
a ream of paper sold for four ducats, and a length of fine
Valencian scarlet cloth cost forty ducats; a pair of laced boots
was worth thirty-six ducats. The rise in prices, which was just
beginning to be felt in Spain since the discovery of the silver
mines in Potosí, had already reduced the people here
to abject poverty. I looked at the tanned faces, gaunt from
famine, and I thought, 'In five years, ten years, this is how it
will be throughout the kingdom.'

After wandering all day long through the city, plagued
by the wailing of women and old men begging for alms, by
the shrill pleading of children, I dined that evening at the
governor's palace, where I was received in great luxury. Men
and women were dressed from head to foot in silk; even
the walls of the palace were hung with silk. The table was
even more sumptuous than that of Charles V; I questioned
my host as to the natives' lot, and he confirmed what the
captain of my ship had told me. Behind Santiago and near
Havana there were still a few plantations cultivated by Negro
slaves. But on the whole, the island of Cuba, which was as
long as the distance which separated Valladolid from Rome
and which was once inhabited by twenty thousand Indians,
was deserted.

'Can't these savages be subdued without massacring them all?' I asked irritably.

'There were no massacres,' replied one of the planters. 'You don't know the Indians. They're so lazy they'd rather die than do anything the least bit tiring. They would allow themselves to be killed in order not to have to work. They would hang themselves or refuse to eat. Whole villages committed suicide.'

A few days later, on the ship that was taking me to Jamaica, I questioned one of the monks who had embarked at Cuba.

'Tell me, is it true that the Indians of these islands committed suicide out of sheer laziness?' I asked.

'The truth, my son, is that their masters literally worked them to death,' said the monk. 'The miserable wretches that survived preferred to end their lives as quickly as possible. They ate earth and stones to hasten their deaths. And they refused to let themselves be baptized because they didn't want to risk encountering the good Spaniards in Heaven.'

Father Mendonez's voice trembled with indignation and pity. He spoke to me about the Indians for a long while. Instead of the cruel, dull-witted savages that Cortés's lieutenants had described, he depicted a race of men so gentle that, being unused to weapons, they frequently wounded themselves accidentally on the sharp edges of the Spaniards' swords. They lived in huge huts built of branches and reeds where they took shelter by the hundreds. For food, they hunted, fished and grew maize, and they spent their leisure plaiting the feathers of humming birds. They did not covet worldly possessions and they were devoid of hate, envy, and cupidity. They were poor, but they led carefree and happy lives. I looked at the herd of wretched emigrants lying on the deck, crushed by the sun and by fatigue. Carrying small bundles, they had left the unyielding soil of Cuba to seek their fortunes in the mines. And I thought, 'For whom are we labouring?'

Soon, a range of jagged mountains appeared on the horizon. Beneath their azure crests, I could see deep valleys and glades of varied shades of green, from near black to very pale. Jamaica. Of the sixty thousand Indians who had lived on this island, Father Mendonez told me that there were barely two hundred left.

'So importing Africans didn't save a single Indian's life?' I asked.

'When you have wolves caring for lambs, there's no way of saving them,' said the monk. 'And how can one wipe out one crime by another?'

'But Father Las Casas himself supported that measure.'

'Father Las Casas died tormented by remorse.'

'He's not to blame,' I said sharply. 'What man can foresee the consequences of his acts?'

The monk looked at me; I averted my eyes . 'Much prayer is needed, my son,' he said.

I was aware that the law gave planters the right to burn their black slaves and torture them, or to have them drawn and quartered at the slightest provocation. In Madrid where I had listened imperviously to many such tales of horror, it was all too easy to believe that the planters never resorted to this right. It was said that certain settlers fed their dogs on the flesh of native children; it was said that Governor Nogarez had massacred more than five thousand Indians on a mere whim. But stories were also told of volcanoes which spewed forth molten gold, of Aztec cities built of solid silver. But for me, the Antilles were no longer just a land of legends; I had seen these emerald islands and their azure mountains with my own eyes. Beyond these golden sands, real men were lashing other men with real whips.

We put in at Puerto Antonio and set sail again soon after. The heat grew more stifling day by day and the sea was absolutely still; not a wrinkle ruffled the surface of the water. Sprawled out in the bows of the ship, the emigrants, their pale faces streaming with sweat, were trembling with fever.

In the morning we sighted Puerto Belo. The town nestled in a deep bay between two green promontories. The vegetation which covered the surrounding hills was so dense that not a fragment of earth was visible; it was as if two enormous plants, each four hundred feet high, had sprouted from the sea, plunging their roots deep into the water. The burning heat shimmered in the streets of the town. I was told the climate was so unhealthy that foreigners who were unable to procure mules to make the journey across the isthmus died of fever within a week. At my request, the Governor obtained mounts for all my fellow voyagers. We left behind only those who had already succumbed to the fever.

For days and days we followed a mule track which wound its way through a vast forest. Above our heads, the trees formed a thick vault and we could no longer see the sky. Enormous roots along the path hindered our progress, and we had to make frequent stops to cut away the lianas which had grown over the ground since the last convoy had passed. All around us, the shadowy air was stifling and moist. Four men died along the way, and three others lay down by the side of the track, unable to continue. Father Mendonez told me that these lands, too, were now deserted: in three months, seven thousand Indian children had died of starvation on the isthmus.

All traffic to or from Peru and Chile passed through Panama. It was a big, prosperous city and in its streets one could see merchants clothed in silks, women covered with jewels and mule trains equipped with the finest harnesses. The spacious houses of the wealthy were sumptuously furnished, but the air here was so unhealthy that the inhabitants, amid all their ephemeral riches, perished each year in their thousands.

We boarded a caravel which hugged the coast of Peru. Those emigrants who had survived the rigours of the voyage, continued on towards Potosí. As for me, I disembarked with Father Mendonez at Callao, about three leagues from the City of the King; we reached the capital without difficulty.

The city was laid out like a chessboard, with wide streets and large squares. It was so vast that its citizens proudly called it 'the city of magnificent distances'. Its adobe houses, whose outer walls were bare and windowless, were built around patios, like the houses of Andalusia. Refreshing fountains spouted water at every crossroad and the air was light and warm. Nevertheless, the climate did not suit the Spaniards, and in the streets I saw the same wretched crowds as I had seen in Santiago de Cuba. Here, too, the gold and the silver did nothing to help the people. They were building a cathedral with solid silver columns and walls of precious marble. Who was it for?

After the cathedral, the city's most beautiful building was an immense prison with bare walls. Through the window of his gold-encrusted carriage, the viceroy proudly pointed it out to me.

'In there, all the rebels of the realm are imprisoned,' he told me.

'What do you mean by rebels?' I asked. 'Those who revolt openly against the authorities, or those who refuse to obey the new laws?'

He shrugged his shoulders. 'No one obeys the new laws. We would have to reconquer Peru from her conquerors if we wanted the words "royal authority" to mean anything.'

The laws promulgated by Charles V required that the Indians be liberated, that they be given a salary and that they be compelled to work only in moderation. But everyone I questioned declared that the enforcement of these laws was impossible. Some maintained that the Indians could not be happy except as slaves; others demonstrated with figures that the magnitude of the task we had undertaken and the Indians' natural laziness made a harsh regime necessary; and still others said simply that the King's lieutenants had no way of making themselves obeyed.

'We decided to refuse absolution to settlers who treated the Indians as slaves,' Father Mendonez told me. 'But our bishops threatened us with an interdict if we persisted with this idea.'

He took me to visit a mission where old, sick Indians were cared for and orphans fed. In a courtyard shaded by palm trees, children were squatting around large bowls of rice. They were handsome children with brown skins, high cheek-bones and straight, black hair. They had large, shining dark eyes. In unison, they plunged their little brown hands into the bowls and brought them up to their mouths. They were the children of men and not little animals.

'They're beautiful,' I said.

The priest put his hand on the head of a small girl. 'Her mother was beautiful too, and her beauty cost her her life. Pizarro's soldiers hanged her, as well as two of her friends, in order to prove to the Indians that Spaniards were impervious to their women.'

'And this one?' I asked.

'He's the son of a chief who was burned alive because the tribute offered by his village was deemed insufficient.'

As we slowly made our tour of the courtyard, the history of the conquest thus unfolded itself before our eyes. As they penetrated ever deeper into these lands, Pizarro's men forced each village to surrender everything that the people had taken years to amass. Whatever food the conquerors did not eat, they wasted or burned. They killed off entire herds and destroyed the crops; wherever they set foot they left behind them a wasteland so ravaged that the Indian population died of hunger in their thousands. At the slightest pretext, a village would be burned, and if the unfortunate inhabitants tried to flee their blazing homes, they were cut down by arrows. In some cities the entire population had committed suicide at the approach of the conquistadors.

'If you still want to see this unhappy country for yourself, I'll get you a guide,' Father Mendonez offered. He pointed to a tall, brown young man who was leaning against a palm tree; he seemed to be dreaming. 'He's the son of a Spaniard and an Inca woman. His father, as often happens, abandoned his mother to marry a Castilian lady, and the child was left in our care. He's familiar with the history of his ancestors and he knows the region well for he has often accompanied me on my journeys.

A few days later, accompanied by Filipillo, the young Inca, I left the City of the King. The viceroy had placed a number of strong horses and ten Indian porters at my disposal. A thick mist hung over the coast, completely hiding the sun, and the ground was wet with dew. We set out on a road which ran along the side of a hill covered with luxuriant grasslands. It was a fine, wide road, made of slabs of stone, sturdier and better built than any in the old world.

'The Incas built it,' my guide proudly informed me. 'The whole empire was covered with roads like this. Messengers, fleeter than your horse, ran from Quito to Cuzco, carrying the emperor's orders to all the cities.'

I greatly admired this magnificent construction. The Incas had also built stone bridges across rivers, and they frequently spanned the numerous deep ravines along the way with suspended footbridges, made of woven vines held down on either side by wooden stakes.

We rode for several days. I was astonished at the strength of our Indian porters. Bearing heavy loads of provisions, blankets, and equipment, they marched almost forty miles a day without flinching. I soon learned that their strength came from constantly chewing the green leaves of a plant they called *cola*. Whenever we came to a stopping-place they would throw down their packs and sprawl out on the ground, apparently completely exhausted. Then they would start chewing a fresh leaf, rolled into a ball, and almost immediately they would become alive again.

'This is Pachacumac,' Filipillo announced.

I pulled up my horse and repeated aloud, 'Pachacumac!' The word evoked an image in my mind of a city of splendid palaces built of sculptured stone and cedar wood, of gardens

filled with aromatic plants, of great stairways leading down
to the sea, of shoals of fish and colonies of aquatic birds.
I visualised the terraces of the palaces planted with trees of
solid gold, bedecked with fruit and flowers, and golden birds.
'Pachacumac!' I opened my eyes wide.

'But I don't see anything,' I said.

'There is nothing left to see,' replied the Inca.

We rode on a little further; a terraced hill served as
a pedestal for a monument of which all that remained was a
section of wall built of enormous blocks of red-painted
stone, placed one on top of the other without any cement.
I looked at my guide. Sitting erect upon his horse, his head
held high, he was not looking at anything.

The next day, we left the coast and began to ride up into
the mountains. Gradually we rose above the mist which hung
over the ocean shore. The air became drier, the vegetation
richer. In the distance, the hills seemed to be covered in
a golden dust, but as we drew nearer, we could see immense
fields of sunflowers and daisies. There were tall, slender
grasses too, and blue cactuses. Although the road climbed
steeply, the temperature remained even. We passed through
several abandoned villages where the adobe houses were
intact but invaded by vegetation. My guide told me that at
the approach of the Spaniards, the villagers had fled across the
Andes, taking all their treasures with them. No one knew
what had become of them.

In former days, even in the smallest of these villages,
the people used to weave brightly dyed cotton, agave fibres,
and llama wool. They made pottery of red clay on which
they painted faces or geometrical designs. Now, everything
was dead.

I patiently questioned the young Inca, and bit by bit, as we
crossed the immense plateau eight thousand feet above the
sea, where blue cactuses still grew, I learned what the empire
of his fore-fathers had been like. The Incas had no concept of
private property; the land was shared by everyone and was

redistributed each year. A certain area, called 'Land of the Incas and the Sun,' was set apart for the use of officials and for supplying shops in times of scarcity. Each Indian, on appointed days, took his turn cultivating this land; he also helped to till the fields of the sick, of widows, and of orphans. He performed his tasks willingly, indeed lovingly, and friends and sometimes even the entire population of a village would be invited to cultivate a plot of ground. Those who were asked responded as eagerly as if they had been invited to a wedding reception. Every two years a general distribution of wool took place and, in the warmer parts of the realm, cotton grown on royal land was given to everybody. Each man was skilled as a builder and as a blacksmith as well as being able to cultivate his allotted field, and he did everything in his own home that needed to be done. There were no poor people among them. I listened to Filipillo and I thought: 'That, then, was the empire we destroyed, the empire I dreamed of establishing on earth and that I did not know how to build!'

'Cuzco!' the Inca cried out.

We had reached the top of a mountain pass and looking down beneath us we could see a green plateau dotted with villages: it was the delightful valley of the Vulcanida. In the distance loomed the white cone of Azuyata and the snowy peaks of the Andes. The town spread out at the foot of a hill crowned with ruins. I spurred on my horse and galloped off towards the ancient capital of the Incas.

We rode across fields of alfalfa, barley and maize, and through cola gardens. The plain was furrowed with canals dug by the Incas, and the hills had been terraced to prevent the land from slipping. These builders of roads and cities had also been better farmers than any of the peoples from the old continent.

Before entering the city, I climbed the hill; the ruins were those of a fortress where the emperor had taken refuge against the onslaughts of Pizarro's troops. It consisted of three concentric ramparts built of dark limestone blocks that fitted together perfectly. I do not now how long I stood there among those stones.

The walls of Cuzco had not been entirely destroyed; several of her towers were still standing, and a few fine stone houses still lined her streets. But in most cases, all that remained of the city's buildings were the foundations, upon which the Spaniards had hastily constructed flimsy brick dwellings. Despite its pleasant surroundings, despite the large number of Indians and settlers who lived there, the city seemed crushed beneath the weight of some dark curse. The Spaniards complained of the harsh climate and of the hatred they sensed all around them. They told me that each year, on the anniversary of the conquistadors' entry into the city, elderly Incas used to lay their ears to the ground hoping to hear the roaring waters of a subterranean river which they believed would one day carry off the Spaniards.

We spent only a few days in Cuzco and then continued on our journey. The air of the high plateaux was so dry and cold that frequently we noticed the mummified bodies of mules lying along the roadside; corpses did not decompose in these regions. From time to time, we came across the ruins of palaces, temples, and fortresses – enormous triangular or hexagonal adobe structures built without arches or vaults – of which only fragments remained. At one end of a large, dried-up lake we found the vestiges of the splendid city of Piahocanacao. Pieces of granite and porphyry lay shattered on the ground; what had once been a temple was now a mountain of rubble; rows of large, flat stones marked where the former streets had been. Gigantic, roughly carved statues lined a long stretch of the highway.

All the villages we passed through were deserted. More often than not, they had been burned to the ground. On one occasion we saw an old man standing in the doorway of a newly built hut; he had neither nose nor ears, and his eyes were hollow sockets. When Filipillo spoke to him, he seemed to hear, but he remained silent

'I suppose they must have ripped his tongue out, too,' said the Inca.

He told me that the Spaniards suspected there were seams of gold in this region and that they had therefore tortured the natives atrociously to force them to reveal their whereabouts. But the Indians fell into a stubborn, impenetrable silence.

'Why?' I asked.

'You will see the mines of Potosí,' the Inca replied, 'and you will then understand why they wanted to save themselves and their children from such a fate.'

I was soon to understand. A few days later, we passed a convoy of about four or five hundred Indians who were being led to the mines. They were attached to each other by iron collars locked around their necks and a 'G' had been branded on their cheeks. They staggered as they walked and seemed to be completely exhausted. The Spaniards supervising the Indians drove them on with whips.

'They are coming from Quito,' my guide said. 'And there may have been over five thousand of them when they left. Once, ten thousand died while marching through the hot lands. Another time, out of six thousand who began the journey, two hundred arrived alive. When they collapse from exhaustion, the Spaniards do not even take the trouble to unlock them. They simply cut off their heads.'

That evening, for the first time in a long while, we saw smoke rising from the huts of a village. Seated in the doorway of her home, a young Indian woman was cradling her child in her arms and singing. Her song had such a melancholy air that I wanted to learn the words. My guide translated them for me like this:

> *Was it in the puckey-puckey's nest*
> *That my mother gave me birth*
> *To suffer so much sorrow,*
> *To weep as I do now,*
> *Like the puckey-puckey in his nest?*

He told me that since the conquest, all the songs that mothers sang to their babies to lull them to sleep were equally sad. Only women and children were left in this village, the men having been taken away to work in the Potosí mines. And it was the same in every village through which we passed, all the way to the volcano.

Crowned in snow and spouting flames, the Potosí volcano rose twelve thousand feet above the plateau. The sides of the mountain were a labyrinth of galleries in which seams of silver, some as much as two thousand feet thick, were being mined. At its foot, a town was being built. I walked about among the wooden shacks in search of my shipboard companions. I found only about ten of them; the others had died on the way. As for those who had reached Potosí, they had great difficulty in adapting themselves to the climate of this high plateau; the women, especially, suffered from altitude sickness. All of their children were born deaf and blind and died within a few weeks. They told me that a man working on his own was barely able to mine enough silver to pay for his basic needs. They had lost all hope of making their fortunes here or even of saving enough to return some day to their own country. The only ones to grow rich were the big, influential contractors, who were able to obtain the forced labour of hordes of Indians.

'Look,' said my young guide. 'See what they have done to my people.'

For the first time, his impassive voice trembled, and in the light of our torch I could see there were tears in his eyes. In these dark galleries, an entire race toiled, a race no longer of living men but of phantoms. There was no flesh on them, no features; their brown skins were stretched taut over bones that looked as brittle as dead wood; they stared blankly and seemed to hear nothing; like robots, they swung their picks against the walls. From time to time one of these black skeletons would slump to the ground without a murmur and was beaten with whips or iron bars; if he failed to get up quickly enough, they finished him off. For more than fifteen hours each day they excavated the earth and the only food they were given was a little bread made from crushed roots. None of them survived more than three years.

From morning till night, trains of mules laden with silver journeyed down towards the coast. Every ounce of metal had been bought with an ounce of blood. And yet the Emperor's coffers remained empty and his people continued to live in poverty. We had destroyed a world, and we had destroyed it for nothing.

'Then I've failed everywhere,' said Charles V.

All night long I had spoken to him about the Americas, and the Emperor had listened to me in silence. The dawn light was filtering through the heavy curtains of his room, illuminating his face. I felt a wrench in my heart. In three years he had become an old man. His eyes were dull, his lips livid and his face was drawn; he had difficulty in breathing. He was slumped in his armchair, a cane with an ivory knob lay beside the blanket that covered legs deformed by gout.

'Why?' he asked.

During the three years I had been away, he had been betrayed by Maurice of Saxony who had appointed himself leader of the Lutheran forces. He had been forced to withdraw before this turncoat and later to accept a treaty which in one blow destroyed everything he had done during his life to achieve religious unity. He had failed in Flanders, having been unable to retake the lands left by Henri II. Further rebellion had also broken out in Italy, and the Turks continually harassed the Empire.

'Why?' he repeated. 'What was my mistake?'

'Your only mistake was to reign,' I replied.

He fingered the medal of the Golden Fleece which hung down over his velvet doublet. 'I didn't want to reign, you know.'

'Yes, I know.'

I looked at his wrinkled face, his grey beard, his lifeless eyes. For the first time, I felt older than he, older than any man had ever been, and I took pity on him, as I might a child.

'I was wrong,' I said. 'I wanted to make you ruler of the Universe. But there is no Universe.'

I got up and began pacing the room. I had not slept that night and my legs felt leaden. Now I finally understood; Carmona was too small, Italy too small, and the Universe did not exist.

'"Universe"! What a convenient word!' I said. 'What do today's sacrifices matter? The Universe lay beyond the future. What does it matter if people are burned at the stake or massacred in their thousands? The Universe is elsewhere – always somewhere else! And yet it's nowhere! There are only men, men forever divided.'

'It's sin that divides them,' said the Emperor.

'Sin?'

Was it sin, or folly, or something else? I thought of Luther, of the Augustinian monks, of the Anabaptist women who sang as they writhed in the flames, of Antonio, of Beatrice. In all of them, there was a force that eluded my carefully reasoned predictions and helped them to resist the demands of my will.

'One of the heretical monks whom we condemned to the stake said to me before dying, "There is only one good: to act according to one's conscience." If that's true, it's pointless to try to rule the world. Nothing can be done for man; his good depends only upon himself.'

'There is only one good,' said Charles, 'to seek salvation.'

'But do you believe you can ensure salvation for others or only for yourself?'

'Only for myself, with the grace of God,' he said. His hand brushed his forehead. 'I used to think it was my duty to force others to seek salvation, and that was my mistake. It was a temptation invented by the devil.'

'In my case,' I said, 'all I ever wanted was their happiness. But they're beyond my reach.'

I stopped talking. I heard their merry-making and their bloodthirsty cries; I heard the voice of the prophet Enoch: 'Everything that is must be destroyed!' It was I whom he preached against, I who wanted to make of this earth a paradise in which every grain of sand would have had its place, in which every flower would have bloomed at its proper time. But they were neither plants nor stones; they did not want to be changed into stone.

'I had a son,' I resumed, 'and he chose to die because I had left him no other choice. I had a wife, too, and because I gave her everything, she grew more dead than alive. And there are those whom we burned alive and who died thanking us. It's not happiness they want; they want to live.'

'But, what does "to live" mean?' asked Charles. 'This life is nothing,' he said, shaking his head. 'What madness to want to rule a world that is really nothing!'

'There are moments when a fire burns in their hearts; that's what they mean by living.'

Suddenly a flood of words surged to my lips. Perhaps it was to be the last time for years to come, for centuries, that it would be given to me to speak.

'I understand them,' I said. 'Now I understand them. It's never what they receive that matters to them; it's what they do. If they can't create, they must destroy. But in any case, they have to rebel against what is, otherwise they wouldn't be men. And we who aspire to building a world for them and imprison them in it, they can't help but hate us. That sense of order, that peace we dream of, would be the worst possible curse for them.'

Charles had sunk his head in his hands. He was no longer listening to these strange notions; he was praying.

'Nothing can be done either for them or against them,' I concluded. 'Nothing can be done.'

'We can pray,' said the Emperor. He was pale and the

corner of his mouth hung loose as it did when his leg was hurting him. 'The ordeal is over. If it were not, God would have left a little hope in my heart.'

A few weeks later, Charles V retired to a small house in Brussels, situated in the middle of an estate near the gate of Louvain. It was a single-storey lodge filled with scientific instruments and clocks. The Emperor's room was small and bare, like a monk's cell. When the death of Maurice of Saxony delivered him of his most powerful enemy, he refused to take advantage of it. He had decided not to concern himself any longer with Germany's problems, and at the same time he stopped pursuing his attempts to acquire the Empire for his son. For two years he occupied his time putting his affairs in order, and during that period all his undertakings were crowned with success. He drove the French from Flanders, signed the Treaty of Vaucelles and brought about the marriage of Philip to Mary Tudor, Queen of England. But his decision to abandon the Empire remained unshaken.

On 25 October 1555, in the great hall of his palace in Brussels, he summoned a solemn gathering at which he appeared leaning on the arm of William of Orange and dressed in mourning clothes. After Councillor Philibert of Brussels had finished reading an official declaration of the imperial will, Charles rose to speak. He recalled how forty years ago, in this same hall, his emancipation had been proclaimed; how he had succeeded to the Imperial Crown through his maternal grandfather, Ferdinand. He described how he had found Christianity torn asunder and his domains surrounded by hostile enemies against whom he had to defend himself all his life. Now, his strength was abandoning him, he explained, and he wanted to bequeath the Netherlands to Philip and the rest of the Empire to Ferdinand. He exhorted his son to respect the faith of his ancestors, to respect the peace and justice. As for himself, he said he had never knowingly wronged anyone.

'If ever I did anybody an injustice,' he said, 'I beg that person's forgiveness.'

As he spoke these final words, he had grown very pale, and when he sat down again there were tears streaming down his cheeks. No one who was there could restrain from weeping. Philip threw himself at the feet of his father, who then embraced him tenderly. Only I knew why he was weeping.

On 16 January 1556, he signed a document in his room whereby he renounced Castile, Aragon, Sicily and Spanish America in favour of Philip. That day, for the first time in years, I saw him laugh and joke. In the evening he ate a sardine omelette and a large portion of eel paté; then, after his meal, he listened to a concert of viols for an hour.

He had a house built in the heart of Spain, close to the monastery of Yuste, and one day he asked me, 'Will you come there with me?'

'No,' I answered.

'What can I do for you?'

'Didn't we agree that no one can do anything for anyone?'

He looked at me gravely. 'I shall pray God that one day he grant you rest.'

I went with him as far as Flushing and stood there on the shore, watching the ship that carried him away.

And then the sails disappeared beyond the horizon.

'I'm tired,' Regina said.

'We can sit down, if you like,' suggested Fosca.

They had been walking for a very long time and they were deep in the forest. The night was warm beneath the cover of the trees. Regina felt like stretching out among the bracken and sleeping forever. She sat down.

'Don't go on,' she said. 'There's no point. It will be the same story right to the very end. I know it.'

'The same story, and every day different,' said Fosca. 'You have to hear it all.'

'A little while ago you didn't want to tell it to me.'

Fosca lay down on the ground beside Regina. For a moment he silently contemplated the dark leaves of the chestnut trees. 'Can you picture that sail disappearing over the horizon and me standing on the shore, watching it disappear?'

'Yes, I can,' she said. And it was true; now, she could.

'When I've finished my story, I shall watch you disappear down the road. You know very well that you will have to disappear.'

She buried her face in her hands. 'I don't know. I don't know anything any more.'

'But I know. And as long as I can still go on talking, I'll talk.'

'And after?' she asked.

'Let's not think about after. I'll speak and you listen. For the time being, we have no questions to ask each other.'

'Very well. Go on,' she said.

BOOK III

I continued walking straight across the marsh which extended as far as the eye could see. The spongy ground gave way under my feet and water squirted from the rushes with a faint sigh. The sun was setting over the horizon; Far across the plains and seas and beyond the mountains, there was always a horizon, and every evening the sun would set. Many years had passed since that day I threw away my compass and began my solitary wanderings over these monotonous lands, not knowing what day or month it was and unaware of the time. I had forgotten my past, and as for my future, it was this endless plain which stretched out to the sky. I was testing the ground with my foot, trying to find a piece of solid earth where I might lie down for the night, when I noticed a large pink expanse of water in the distance. I walked towards it and discovered that it was actually a bend in a river wending its way among rushes and tall grass.

A hundred years, or even fifty years earlier, my heart would have pumped wildly. I would have thought, 'I've discovered a great river and the secret is mine alone!' But now, the river reflecting the pink sky, meant nothing to me. My only thought was that I would be unable to cross it at night. As soon as I found a patch of solid ground hardened by the first frost, I threw down my pack and took out my fur rug. Then, with my axe, I chopped a tree stump and gathered up enough kindling to make a fire. Every evening I lit a fire so that even when I was not actually there, there would be this crackling sound, this smell, this red, burning, living flame rising from the earth towards the sky. The river was so calm that not even the slightest murmur of its waters could be heard.

'Hello! Hello!'

I gave a start. It was a human voice, the voice of a white man.

'Hello! Hello!' I shouted back.

I threw an armful of wood into the leaping flames. Still shouting, I ran towards the river and noticed a faint light on the other side; he too had lit a fire. He shouted something I was unable to understand, but he seemed to be speaking French. Our voices crossed in the humid air, but the stranger could probably no more understand me than I him. Finally, he stopped trying and I cried out three times at the top of my voice, 'Until tomorrow!'

A man! A white man! As I lay rolled up in my rug, I could feel the warmth of the fire on my face and I began to think back. Ever since I had left Mexico, I had not set eyes upon a single white face. Four years! (I had already started counting the time.) I had seen a flame flicker on the other side of the river and here was I saying to myself: 'Four years since I've seen a white man!' Between us, through the night, a dialogue had begun. 'Who is he? Where has he come from? What does he want?' I wondered. And he was asking the same questions, and I was answering him. I was answering. Suddenly, on the bank of that river, I found myself once more with a past, a future, a destiny.

A hundred years earlier, I had embarked at Flushing to sail round the world. I had hoped to manage without human company. I wanted to be no more than an anonymous face, a look. I crossed oceans and deserts, I sailed on Chinese junks. At Canton, I was shown a massive block of solid gold valued at over two hundred million. I visited Kathung and, dressed as a priest, I scaled Tibet's high plateaux. I saw Malacca, Calcutta, and Samarkand, and in Cambodia, in the heart of a dense forest, I gazed in awe at a temple as vast as a city, with almost a hundred towers. I dined at the tables of the Great Mogul and of Abalana, the Shah of Persia. I made my way across the islands of the Pacific by a hitherto unknown route. I fought against Patagonians. Finally, having reached Vera Cruz and, later, Mexico, I set out alone on foot to explore the heart of this unknown continent. For four years I trod the prairies and the forests, not going anywhere in particular, without a compass, and lost beneath the sky and in eternity. And even a little while ago, I was still lost. But now I was lying at a precise point on the planet, a point whose latitude and longitude could be determined by an astrolabe. It was situated in the north of Mexico. But how many thousands of miles from anywhere? To the east or west? The man who was sleeping on the other bank knew where I was.

As soon as dawn broke, I stripped off my clothes and packed them away with my rug in a bag made of buffalo hide. I strapped it to my back and plunged into the river. The icy water took my breath away, but the current was weak and I soon reached the opposite shore. After drying myself, I put my clothes back on. The stranger was asleep beside a small pile of ashes. He was a man aged about thirty, with light brown hair and a short, bushy beard that hid the lower part of his face. I sat down next to him, and I waited.

He opened his eyes and looked at me in surprise. 'How did you get here?' he asked.

'I crossed the river.'

His face lit up. 'You have a canoe?'

'No, I swam across.'

He threw off his blanket and jumped to his feet. 'Are you alone?'

'Yes.'

'Are you lost, too?'

'I can't get lost,' I replied. 'I'm not going anywhere.'

He ran his fingers through his tousled hair. He seemed perplexed. 'Well, I'm lost,' he said bitterly. 'My companions either lost me or abandoned me. We had reached the source of a river we had been following ever since we left Lake Erie. An Indian had told me that when we got to the source, we'd find a trail leading to another river, a very big river. I set out with the two other men to look for it. We discovered it and started following it down. But on the third day I woke up and found myself alone. I thought my companions must have gone on ahead, but I've come as far as this and I still haven't found any trace of them.' He grimaced. 'They were carrying all the provisions.'

'You should retrace your steps,' I suggested.

'Yes, but will the others still be waiting for me? I'm afraid they may have planned it all.' He smiled. 'What a wonderful feeling it was when I saw your fire last night. Do you know this river?'

'This is the first time I've ever seen it.'

'Oh,' he said disappointedly. He glanced at the muddy waters as they slowly meandered through the swamp. 'It runs from north-east to south-west. There can be no doubt that it flows out into the Pacific, can there?'

'I have no idea,' I replied. I was also gazing at the river; suddenly it was no longer just a mass of rippling water, it was a road; it led somewhere. 'Where were you going?' I asked.

'I'm trying to discover a route to China. And if this river really leads from the lakes to the ocean, I've found it.' Again, he looked at me and smiled. It seemed strange that anyone could still smile at me. 'And you?' he asked. 'Where did you set out from?'

'Mexico.'

'On foot? And alone?' he asked in astonishment.

'Yes.'

There was an eager expression on his face. 'What do you do for food?'

I hesitated a moment. 'From time to time I kill a buffalo, and the Indians give me a little maize.'

'I haven't eaten for three days now,' he said cheerfully. There was a brief silence. He was waiting for me to say something.

'I'm sorry,' I said, 'but I haven't any food. I can sometimes go for a week or two without eating. It's a secret I learned in Tibet.'

'Ah!' He pursed his lips and his face became drawn. But suddenly he forced himself to smile again. 'Teach me the secret, now,' he said.

'It takes years,' I replied brusquely.

He looked all around and then silently started to fold up his blanket.

'Isn't there any game around here?' I asked.

'None. The prairie begins about a day's walk from here, but it's been burned.' He spread out a sheet of buffalo hide on the ground and began to cut a new pair of moccasins. 'I'm going to try to find the others,' he said.

'And if you don't find them?'

'Then I'm at the mercy of God.'

He hadn't believed me. He thought I did not want to share my provisions with him. Yet I would gladly have given him something in return for his smile.

'I know an Indian village about five days walk from here,' I said. 'They'll surely give you some maize.'

'Five days!'

'It will set you back ten days. But between the two of us, we could carry enough food to live on for several weeks.'

'Are you coming back to Montreal with me?'

'Why not?'

'Well, let's get started then,' he said.

We swam back across the river – the water was less cold than it had been in the early morning – and all day we trudged through the swamp. My companion seemed very tired. He said very little. I learned, however, that his name was Pierre Carlier, that he was born in Saint-Malo and ever since he was a child he had sworn to himself that he would become a great explorer. He had sold everything he owned to raise enough money to reach Montreal and organize an expedition. He had spent five years exploring the Great Lakes, linked to the Atlantic by the Saint Lawrence River, from where he hoped to find a route leading to the Pacific. His money was almost gone and his government refused to help him. They wanted the French settlers to make their homes in Canada and not go wandering about in unexplored lands.

We reached the prairie on the second day. The Indians had set fire to it here as well. It was the hunting season. From time to time, we came across the bones of buffalo and saw their tracks in the ground. But we knew that for miles around not a single living animal would be found. Carlier stopped speaking altogether. He was completely exhausted. During the night, I discovered him gnawing on the buffalo hide from which he cut a new pair of moccasins every day.

'Can you really not give me anything to eat?' he asked me the next morning.

'You can search my pack,' I said. 'I have nothing.'

'Then I can't continue with you.' He lay down on the ground, folded his hands behind his neck and closed his eyes.

'Wait for me,' I said. 'I'll be back in four days.'

I left a gourd filled with water within reach of his hand and set off at a rapid pace. I had no trouble finding the way. My footprints were still visible in the marsh, and the trodden grass showed me the way I had come. I continued walking until nightfall and set out again the next day at dawn. I reached the village in two days. It was empty. All the

Indians had left to go hunting. But I found corn and meat stored away in a hiding place.

'Gently, Carlier,' I said, 'gently'. He bit greedily into the hunk of meat. His eyes glittered.

'Aren't you eating?' he asked.

'I'm not hungry.'

He smiled. 'It's wonderful to eat.'

I returned his smile. Suddenly, I had a strong desire to be this man who was hungry and who ate, this man who was searching so desperately for a route to China.

'And now what are you going to do?' I asked.

'I'll go back to Montreal and try to raise enough money to organize a new expedition.'

'I have some money.' In the bottom of my pack there were jewels and gold ingots.

'Are you the devil by any chance?' he asked cheerfully.

'Supposing I were the devil?'

'I'd gladly sell you my soul in exchange for the route to China. I'm not concerned about the next life. This one is enough for me!'

There was such ardour in his voice that the desire to be like him again seized me. 'Can I ever become a living man again?' I thought.

'Well, I'm not the devil,' I said.

'Who are you?'

A word formed on my lips: 'nobody.' But he was looking at me, questioning me. I had saved his life. For him, I existed. And I felt a long forgotten burning in my heart. My own life was beginning to take shape again.

'I'll tell you who I am,' I said.

The oars struck the water with a steady rhythm, and the canoes glided slowly down the winding, lazy river. Carlier was sitting beside me. Resting on his knees was the log-book in which he entered the daily events of our journey and he was now busy writing these down. I was smoking. It was a custom I had learned from the Indians. From time to time Carlier looked up. He gazed at the fields of wild rice and the savannas where clumps of trees rose up here and there. Occasionally a bird would dart up from the river bank with a shrill screech. The air was warm. The sun was beginning to sink in the sky.

'I like this time of day,' he said.

'You say that at any time of day.'

He smiled. 'Well, I like this season . . . and this country.'

He started to write again. He noted down the trees, the birds, the colour of the sky, the varieties of fish. All these things were important to him. In his notebook, each day had something distinctive about it, and he looked forward with curiosity to the adventures that still awaited him before reaching the river's estuary. As far as I was concerned, the river simply had an estuary like any other river, and beyond that estuary stretched the sea, and beyond the sea lay other lands and other seas, and the world was round. There was a time when I thought it extended forever. Upon leaving Flushing, I still hoped that I might spend eternity discovering it. Standing on a mountain top, above a blanket of clouds, I had been thrilled to glimpse a patch of golden plain through a crevice. I had known the sense of joy one experiences looking down upon an unknown valley from the heights of a pass, or wandering through a gap hemmed in by gigantic walls, or landing on an undiscovered island. But now I knew that behind each mountain there was a valley, that every gorge had an exit, every cavern walls. The world was round and monotonous: four seasons, seven colours, a single sky, water, plants, flat or hilly land. Everywhere, the same boredom.

'North-east to south-west,' said Carlier. 'It doesn't alter its direction.' He closed his notebook. 'This is like a stroll through a park.'

In Montreal we had carefully chosen trustworthy men and

we filled six canoes with provisions, clothing, and instruments. Over a month ago we had passed the place where we had first met and the expedition had encountered no serious obstacles. The savannas provided us with buffalo, deer, wild turkey and quail in abundance.

'After we've reached the estuary, I'm going to return to the source,' he said. 'There must be a waterway linking the river to the lakes.' He looked at me somewhat anxiously. 'Don't you believe there is one?' Every night he spoke these same words, and every night he repeated them with the same fervour.

'Why not?' I replied.

'Then we'll charter a ship, won't we? and we'll go to China.' He frowned. 'I don't want anyone to reach China by that route before me.'

I drew on my pipe and exhaled a cloud of smoke through my nostrils. I tried to share in his life and to make his future mine, but it was useless; I could not be him. His hopes, his constant anxieties, were no less strange to me than the particular tranquillity of that time of day.

He put his hand on my shoulder. 'What are you thinking of?' he asked tenderly.

For all of three centuries no man had ever put his hand on my shoulder, and since Caterina's death, no one had ever asked me, 'What are you thinking of?' But he spoke to me as if I were someone just like him, and it was for that reason that I'd come to like him so much.

'I'd like to be in your place,' I said.

'You? In my place?' With a smile, he held out his hand to me. 'Let's change places.'

'Alas! It's not possible.'

'Ah!' he said fervently. 'If only I were immortal!'

'There was a time when I used to wish I was too.'

'Then I'd be certain of finding the route to China. I'd sail down every river on earth. I'd plot maps of every continent.'

'No,' I said. 'You'd soon lose all interest in China, you'd lose interest in everything, because you'd be alone in the world.'

'Are you alone in the world?' he asked me reproachfully. His face and movements were virile, but there was a feminine gentleness in his voice and his eyes.

'No,' I answered, 'not now.' Far off in the savanna an animal gave a raucous cry. 'I never had any friends,' I said. 'People always looked upon me as a stranger – or as a dead man.'

'I'm your friend,' he said.

For a long while we listened in silence to the soft murmur of the oars feathering the water. The river meandered so much that we could not have made much headway since the morning. Suddenly Carlier stood up.

'A village!' he shouted.

Puffs of smoke rose in the air, and then, hidden behind a clump of trees, we noticed some cone-shaped huts made of matted rushes. Some Indians were standing on the bank and they were yelling loudly and waving their bows.

'Silence,' ordered Carlier.

The men continued to row without saying a word. Carlier opened a sack that contained the merchandise we brought with us for trading with the natives – lengths of material, mother-of-pearl necklaces, needles, and scissors. The Indians' dugouts were now barring our way. Holding a multicoloured shawl in his hands, Carlier began to speak to them in a gentle, voice, and in their own tongue. I understood nothing of what they were saying; for many years now, anything requiring effort seemed pointless to me and I had not bothered to learn the savages' language. Soon, the Indians stopped their yelling and indicated that we should come ashore, and they approached us without any display of hostility. They were dressed in brightly coloured deer skins, trimmed with porcupine bristles. While we were stepping ashore and making fast our boats, the Indians were conferring among themselves. Eventually, one of them walked up to Carlier and spoke noisily to him.

'They want to take us to their chief,' Carlier said. 'Let's

follow them. But don't part with your guns under any pretext.'

The chief was seated on a mat of rushes in the middle of the village grounds. He wore sixteen fine pearls on each of his ears and others adorned his nose. In front of him were two hollow stones filled with tobacco and he was smoking a peace pipe decorated with feathers. Removing the pipe from his mouth, he indicated that we should sit down. Carlier laid out the gifts he had brought in front of the chief and the chief smiled benevolently. They began to talk. In a low voice, one of the members of the crew translated their conversation for me. Carlier explained that he wanted to continue down the river to the sea but the chief appeared very displeased with this project. He told Carlier we would soon come to another river that was impossible to navigate since the way was blocked by scattered rocks, treacherous rapids and precipitous falls, as well as trunks of trees which would be sent crashing against our canoes by the turbulent waters. Along its shores lived savage tribes who would attack us with axes. Carlier resolutely replied that nothing could stop him from continuing his journey. The chief resumed lengthy discussions, but Carlier displayed the same firmness. Finally, a faint smile appeared on the chief's lips.

'We will talk about it again tomorrow,' he said. 'The night will bring wise counsel.'

He clapped his hands. Servants brought forth bowls of rice, boiled meat, and maize which they placed before us on the ground. We ate in silence from glazed earthenware bowls. Gourds filled with an alcoholic drink were passed around by the servants, but I noticed that the chief did not offer us his peace pipe.

Towards the end of the feast, several of the Indians began beating on drums or violently shaking a type of gourd filled with pebbles. Soon the whole tribe started to dance, brandishing their tomahawks. The chief shouted an order and two men emerged from a hut carrying on their shoulders a live crocodile bound from head to tail with thin twine. The rhythm and the dancing then began to redouble in violence. I watched in astonishment as the Indians attached the creature to a tall, red-painted stake which stood at one end of the grounds. The chief stood up, solemnly walked up to the crocodile, took a knife from his belt and cut out its eyes. He then returned to his seat. With terrifying howls, the warriors proceeded to cut long gashes in the hide of the living beast. Then they riddled it with arrows. Carlier and the crew members had grown pale. The Indian chief continued to smoke his pipe impassively.

I took a gourd which a servant held out to me, raised it to my lips and drank thirstily. I heard Carlier's voice: 'Don't drink!' he commanded. But the men all continued to drink nevertheless. As for him, he hardly wet his lips. The chief said something to him in an imperious tone of voice and Carlier merely smiled back. When the gourd was again passed to me, I took several long gulps. The beating of the drums, the Indians' howls, their frenetic dancing, the eeriness of the spectacle I had just witnessed, and this fire water running down my throat, all combined to make my blood beat feverishly in my veins. I felt as if I were changing into an Indian. They were dancing; from time to time one of them would swing his tomahawk at the red stake to which the crocodile was bound and then sing noisily in praise of the heroic deeds he had accomplished during his life. I drank another mouthful. My head was a gourd full of pebbles, my blood was on fire. I was an Indian. Ever since birth I had gazed on the banks of this river; in my heaven, horrible tattooed gods reigned; the rhythm of the drums and the cries of my brothers gladdened my heart; one day I would be borne away to a paradise of dances, feasts and bloody victories . . .

When I opened my eyes, I found myself rolled in my rug, upstream from the village, at the place where we had moored our canoes. My head was throbbing painfully. I looked at the yellow waters of the river; the air around me had a flat, familiar taste. 'I'll never be an Indian,' I thought. 'My opinions will never change. Always the same past, the same feelings, the same rational thoughts, the same sense of boredom. A thousand years. Ten thousand years. I'll never escape from myself.' I looked at the yellow waters and suddenly I jumped to my feet. The boats were no longer there!

I ran over to Carlier. He was still asleep. The whole crew was asleep with their guns lying beside them. The Indians had probably been reluctant to murder them for fear of setting off a war with the white men. But during the night they had set our canoes adrift. I put my hand on my friend's shoulder. When he opened his eyes, I pointed to the river's empty waters.

To the dismay of the crew, we spent the whole of that day discussing the possibilities that lay open to us. To attack the Indians and take their boats and provisions was out of the question; they greatly outnumbered us. To hollow out tree trunks with our axes and continue down the river was too hazardous; the villages would probably be hostile and we no longer had merchandise to exchange for food. Furthermore, if we were to encounter rapids, we would have to have solid canoes.

'There's only one solution,' I said. 'We'll have to build a fort to protect ourselves against Indian raids. Then we can store up game and smoked fish to see us through the winter. In the meantime, I'll go by foot to Montreal and as soon as the ice melts on the rivers, I'll come back with canoes, food, arms and men.'

'But Montreal is two thousand miles away,' said Carlier.

'I can cover them in three or four months.'

'Winter will overtake you on the way.'

'I can walk through snow.'

Carlier lowered his head and pondered for a long while. When he raised it again, his expression was sombre. 'I'll go to Montreal myself,' he said.

'No.'

'Why not? I can walk fast, too, and I can walk through snow.'

'You can also die along the way,' I said. 'What will become of these men?'

He stood up and plunged his hands in his pockets. Something quivered in his throat. Once, in the past, a man had stood before me with that same expression on his face, that same lump bobbing in his throat.

'You're right,' was all he said.

He turned around and took a few steps, kicking a stone along with his foot. I remembered; it was Antonio who had looked at me in the same way.

'Look!' I cried out to my companions. 'Fort Carlier!'

Their oars stopped dead in the water. The fort was located just past the second bend in the river; as the crow flies it was only a few hundred feet away. It was a sturdy structure made of large, dark logs surrounded by a triple stockade. No one seemed to be there. I stood up at the bows of the canoe and shouted, 'Hello! Hello!' and I continued shouting until we drew alongside the fort. I jumped to the bank, grown over with young, tender grass and spring flowers and ran towards the outer stockade. Carlier was leaning on his gun, waiting for me in front of the gate of the first enclosure. I shook him by the shoulders. 'How glad I am to see you again!' I exclaimed.

'So am I,' he said. He was not smiling. His face was pale and puffy; he had aged a great deal.

I pointed to the eight big canoes loaded down with food, arms and merchandise for trading. 'Look!'

'So I see,' he said. 'Thanks.'

He pushed the gate open and I followed him into the fort. The building consisted of a single large room with a low ceiling and a floor of hard, trampled earth. A man was lying in a corner on a bed of straw and furs.

'Where are the others?'

'The two others are in the attic. They're keeping watch over the savanna.'

'The *two* others?'

'Yes,' he said.

'What happened?' I asked.

'Scurvy. Thirteen men died. This one here may recover: it's spring and I'm making him drink an extract made from the leaves of white spruce. That's what cured me. I almost died myself.' He looked at me and finally seemed to realize who I was. 'It was about time you turned up!'

'I've brought fresh fruit and maize.' I said. 'Come and see.'

He went over to the man. 'Do you need anything?'

'No,' he answered.

'I'm going to bring you some fruit,' Carlier said. He turned and followed me to the canoes.

'Did the Indians attack you?'

'Three or four times the first month. But we fought them off. There were a lot of us then.'

'And after that?'

'After? Well, we hid our losses from them. We buried the dead at night: had to make do covering them with snow, for the ground was too hard to dig graves.' His eyes wandered. 'When spring came, we had to bury them again. There were just five of us left then, and my knee had begun to swell.'

My men had moored the canoes and were plodding their way towards the fort, bent double beneath the weight of cases and sacks.

'Do you think the Indians will try to stop us from going on?' I asked.

'No,' Carlier replied. 'It's now two weeks since the men left the village. I think there's a war going on in the prairie.'

'We'll start out again as soon as my crew has had a chance to rest a little. It won't be more than three or four days.'

I pointed to the canoes. 'They're good, sturdy boats. We'll be able to negotiate the rapids.'

He nodded his head. 'That's good.'

We spent the following days preparing for our departure. I noticed that Carlier hardly questioned me at all about my journey; he told me about the hard winter they had had at the fort. In order to cover up their losses from the Indians, he made every able-bodied man act a part in a continuous comedy by making them leave the fort while he pretended to chase after them as if they had disobeyed his orders. He recounted these events in a cheerful tone of voice, but he never smiled. It was as if he no longer knew how to smile.

On a fine May morning we set out again on our expedition. The man who had been suffering from scurvy was beginning to feel better and we lay him carefully in the bottom of one of the canoes. There were only women and old men left in the Indian village, and we rowed past without incident. The days passed slowly and monotonously, marked by the rhythm of the oars.

'The river is still flowing from north-east to south-west,' I said to Carlier.

His face brightened. 'Yes, I know.'

'One day there'll be forts and trading posts all along this river,' I said. 'And where Fort Carlier now stands, there'll be a city bearing your name.'

'One day,' he said. 'But I won't be here to see it.'

'What's the difference? You'll have done what you wanted to do.'

He looked at the yellow waters and the flowering savanna, at the branches of the firs from which tender, green needles were growing. 'That's what I used to think, too,' he said.

'And now?'

'Now I can't bear the thought that you'll see all those things and that I won't,' he replied bitterly.

My heart sank and I thought, 'It's happened, then. With him too, it's happened.'

'Other men will see them, too,' I said.

'But they won't have seen what I see. And one day they'll die, each in his turn. I don't envy them in the least.'

'And you shouldn't envy me, either.'

I looked at the muddy river, at the flat savanna. At times it seemed as if the world belonged to me alone, as if none of its transitory visitors could ever dispute it with me. But there were other times when, seeing the love which they bore it, I had the feeling that I was the only one for whom it was deaf and faceless. I was riveted to it, and yet I was excluded.

The days grew warmer, the river wider. Within a week, it had assumed the proportions of a lake, and shortly afterwards we saw that it emptied into another river whose wild waters flowed from our right to our left.

'There it is!' I cried out. 'The great river!'

'Yes,' Carlier said quietly. There was a look of deep anguish on his face. 'It flows from north to south.'

'It may change course a little further on.'

'Not a chance. We're scarcely six hundred feet above sea level.'

'We must wait,' I said. 'It's still too soon to tell.'

We continued on our way. For three days the yellow and blue waters flowed side by side without mingling; then ours finally vanished in that great limpid mass which was winding its path through the plains. There was no longer any possible doubt: we had found the great river. It had neither rapids nor cataracts, but it did flow from north to south.

Throughout one morning, Carlier sat on the river's edge, his eyes fixed on the horizon towards which the current carried its cargo of branches and tree trunks. I put my hand on his shoulder.

'It's not the route to China,' I said, 'but it's certainly an important river, and no one knew of its existence before. Columbus believed he had reached India, whereas he had actually chanced upon a new world.'

'I don't care a damn about this river,' Carlier said in a dull voice. 'I wanted to find the route. We might just as well go back to Montreal.'

'That would be madness! Let's go on to the estuary. You can look for the route again later.'

'But it doesn't exist,' Carlier said in despair. 'The northern part of the lakes has been explored and nothing was found. The great river was the last chance.'

'If it doesn't exist, why are you so upset about not having found it?'

He shrugged his shoulders. 'You don't understand. Ever since I was fifteen, I've promised myself I'd discover it. I even bought myself a Chinese robe at Saint-Malo; it's with the rest of my things in Montreal. I would have taken it with me when I left for China.'

I remained silent for a moment. I did not, in fact, understand him. Finally, I said, 'If, as I believe, you've just discovered the river that will enable man to cross this continent from north to south, you'll be as famous as if you had found the route to China.'

'I don't care about being famous,' he said angrily.

'You'll have rendered just as great a service to mankind. As for China, they can always travel by the old route; they'll manage well enough.'

'And they'd have managed just as well without this river, too,' said Carlier.

He sat on the river bank all day long without eating any food. Patiently, I attempted to encourage him and the next morning he agreed to continue the expedition.

The days passed. We came across the mouth of another, very silted river, out of which floated enormous tree trunks. Our rowers had great difficulty in avoiding them, for as the waters of the two rivers met, whirlpools were created which sucked in our canoes. We succeeded, however, in escaping them. A few miles from there, we sighted a village; our guns were already in our hands when the man in charge of the lead canoe shouted, 'Everything is burnt!'

We drew alongside the village. Nothing but piles of cinders remained of most of the huts. In the centre of the village, headless, mutilated bodies were tied to stakes; still more bodies were piled up in one of the huts that had not been burned. By the side of the river we found embalmed heads, the size of fists, from which the skulls had been removed. All the villages we encountered during the following days had been similarly ravaged.

The river widened. The climate grew warmer and the vegetation was now semi-tropical. The men shot alligators to keep them away from the boats. The marshy banks were covered with reeds, among which clumps of aspen trees rose up here and there. One day we found a crab buried in the mud; I leaned over, cupped my hand and tasted the water. It was briny.

A short distance further on, the river divided into three branches. After some hesitation, we chose the middle channel. For two hours we slowly made our way through a labyrinth of low islands, sand banks and reeds. Then suddenly the crew leapt to their feet and shouted for joy. We had emerged at the sea.

'Aren't you happy?' I asked Carlier.

The men pitched camp for the night. During the day they had killed several wild turkeys which they were now roasting, and they laughed and sang merrily.

'There's something wrong with my astrolabe,' Carlier said. 'I can't get the longitude.'

'What does it matter?' I replied. 'We'll come back. We'll come back by sea, with a real ship. This is a great discovery!'

Carlier's face remained grave. 'Your discovery,' he said.

'Why?'

'It was you who saved my life on the prairie. It was you who went to Montreal for help. It was you who persuaded me to continue the expedition. Without you I wouldn't be here.'

'And neither would I be here without you,' I said gently.

I lit my pipe and sat down beside him. I looked out at the sea: always the same sea, the same sounds, the same smells. I glanced over his shoulder; he was writing down some figures in his log-book.

'Why haven't you written anything in there for so many days?' I asked.

Carlier shrugged his shoulders.

'Why?' I repeated.

'You were always making fun of me!'

'I was making fun of you?'

'Oh, you never said anything, but I saw it on your face.' He let himself fall back, put his hands under his head and stared up at the sky. 'It's a terrible thing to have to live under that gaze of yours. You're looking at me from such a distance; you're already beyond my death. For you, I'm a dead body: a corpse who was aged thirty in the year 1651, who searched for a route to China and failed, who discovered a great river that others would have discovered by themselves a little later.' Without a trace of bitterness, he added, 'If you had wanted, you wouldn't have needed me to make this discovery.'

'But I was incapable of wanting to do that,' I said.

'And what about me? Why should something that is of no interest to you be of interest to me? Why should I be happy? I'm not a child.'

A thick fog crept into my heart. 'Would you prefer that we part?' I asked.

He did not answer, and in my distress I thought, 'If I leave him, where shall I go?

'It's too late,' he said at last.

We returned upriver to Montreal and the following spring we chartered a ship which we sailed down the Atlantic coast of the American continent. After rounding Florida, we skirted along a coastline that was at the same latitude Carlier had measured at the mouth of the great river. Unfortunately,

we did not know the longitude of the estuary and a dense
fog hung over the entire littoral, obscuring our view. We
sailed slowly and very cautiously, for we had to stay as close
to the shore as possible and were afraid of running aground
on sandbanks or reefs.

'Look!' cried a sailor. He was one of the men who had taken
part in the earlier expedition. He pointed in the direction
of the coast, which was barely visible through the white fog.
'Don't you see anything?' he asked.

With both hands resting against the bulwark, Carlier
peered into the mist. 'All I see is a sandbank,' he said.

I, too, saw only reeds and strips of land covered with
gravel.

'Water!' Carlier suddenly exclaimed. 'I can see water!' He
spun around and called out, 'Lower a canoe!'

A few moments later we were rowing towards the shore.
Winding its way among a labyrinth of flat islands and sand
banks, a vast, muddy river emptied itself into the sea along
an estuary that was several miles wide. We went back to the
ship, certain of having found the estuary for which we were
searching.

Our plan was to sail up the river and its subsidiary as far
as the track where I had first met Carlier. There, we would
build a fort where we would lay fruit and vegetables in store
for the winter; we would leave a few men behind to guard
the ship, and the rest of us would return by canoe to
Montreal where we would proclaim our discovery. We had
no doubt that aid would then be granted for us to establish
trading posts, to explore the sources of the great river, to
search for a waterway connecting it to the Saint Lawrence
by way of the lakes, and perhaps even to construct canals.
Soon, villages would spring up. The new continent would
henceforth be opened up to the world.

The ship put about. Slowly, it sailed towards the widest
channel, preceded by a canoe which led the way. As we drew
nearer, the impact of the turbulent waters issuing from the

river caused the ship to pitch heavily. Just as we were about to enter the channel, there was a dull thud. The ship had struck a reef.

'Cut down the masts!' Carlier cried out.

The crew did not move. The stricken ship continued to pitch dangerously; its heavy, menacing masts creaked and swayed. I grabbed an axe and started to chop away at one of them. Carlier set to work on the other. The two masts came down with a great crash. But the ship continued to sink deeper into the water. We lowered the canoes and rowed them to shore. We were able to salvage only a few small bundles of merchandise and a little food. Two hours later, the ship had completely disappeared.

'We'll go up the river by canoe,' I said cheerfully to Carlier. 'What's one boat? Your discovery is worth a fortune! You'll have twenty boats just for the asking.'

'I know.' He looked out at the sea, separated by a blue line from the torrent of yellow water and the alluvial deposits. 'We can't turn back now,' he said.

'Why should there be any question of turning back?'

'You're right,' he replied.

He took my arm and we started out in search of dry ground where we could pitch camp.

We spent the next morning hunting buffalo and fishing for trout. Then, having allocated the crew members to each of the four canoes, we began our voyage upstream. On either side of the river, monotonous plains stretched out into the distance. Carlier seemed preoccupied.

'Does this landscape look familiar to you?' he asked me.

'I think it does.'

The same tall reeds capped by pale green tufts lined the banks of the river. Beyond them were the same flowers, creeping vines and clumps of aspens. Alligators dozed in the warm mud.

We continued rowing for four days; on the afternoon of the fifth, we sighted a village. Its windowless huts were made of mud and had large, square doors. I did not recognize the place. Standing on the river's edge were Indians, waving their arms in what appeared to be a friendly way. They were wearing white loincloths tied around their waists with a rope from which two large tassels hung.

'There were no villages less than two weeks' journey from the estuary,' Carlier said.

We moored our canoes. The chief of the tribe, a benevolent-looking man, welcomed us into his hut which was decorated with leather shields. Since there were no windows, the room was lit up by torches made of dried, plaited reeds. Carlier asked the chief what was the name of the river and he replied that it was called simply the 'red' river. Carlier also asked whether he knew of another large river in the region, and the chief said that far to the east there was a river that was wider and longer than any other that was known. We offered him a few gifts, and in exchange for a package of needles, an awl, a pair of scissors and a few yards of fabric, he gave us a plentiful supply of maize, dried fruits, salt, turkeys, and chickens.

'And now what shall we do?' Carlier asked when, having smoked the peace pipe, we took our leave of the chief.

'We must find the great river,' I replied.

Carlier bowed his head.

I reflected a moment. 'I'll go in search of the river,' I said. 'When I've found it, I'll come back and lead you there. The land here is rich and these Indians received us as friends; you'll be able to wait here for me as long as necessary.'

'I'm going with you,' Carlier said.

'No. It's a long way to the river and we don't know the country or its peoples. What I can do alone, I can't do if you're with me.'

'I'll go with or without you,' he said stubbornly. 'I'm going, whatever you decide.'

I looked at him. A word I had uttered centuries ago came to my lips. 'What pride you have!' I said.

He began to laugh; I did not like the way he laughed.

'Why are you laughing?'

'Do you think anyone can live with you and retain an ounce of pride?' he enquired.

'Let me go on my own.'

'You don't understand! You don't understand anything! I can't stay here. If I could stay in one place, I would have stayed in Montreal, I would have stayed in Saint-Malo. I would have settled down in a quiet little house with a wife and children.' He pursed his lips. 'I've got to feel that I'm alive,' he said 'even if I die in the attempt.'

Over the following days, I tried in vain to persuade him. He refused even to answer me. He filled a pack with provisions, adjusted his instruments and it was he who said to me one morning, 'Let's go.'

We each carried a heavy load. We brought along buffalo hides from which we made moccasins every morning, for we wore out a pair in a single day. We took a gun, cartridges, axes, fur rugs, a canoe made of buffalo skins and two months' supply of food. Heeding the advice the Indians gave us, we set out along a buffalo trail; following the tracks of wild animals was the surest means of not missing any running water. We proceeded in silence. I was happy to be walking towards a goal. Ever since I joined Carlier, there had always been a goal before me, a goal that gave me a future and at the same time masked the future. The harder it was to attain, the greater the confidence I felt in the present. The great river seemed very difficult to reach and every minute mattered.

After a week it began to rain. We crossed a prairie where the tall, rough grass scratched our hands and arms as we pushed our way through it. The sodden ground made it difficult to walk and at night the dripping trees provided scant shelter. Next, we came upon a forest where we had to cut our way laboriously through an old, unused buffalo trail. We crossed several rivers. Beneath the grey mist which uniformly covered it, the country seemed deserted. No bird or wild animal fled at our approach. And our supply of food was dwindling.

We silently approached the first village we came across. Ferocious cries and the beating of drums filled the air. I darted from tree to tree; on the village grounds I saw a circle of Indians dancing around other Indians who were bound hand and foot; the war was still raging on the plains. Henceforth, we took care to avoid villages. On another occasion, we spotted a column of painted Indians on the warpath, who were letting out wild roars. We hid in the foliage of a high tree and luckily they did not see us.

It rained for thirty-five days, and during that period we encountered no less than twenty streams. Finally, a strong wind blew up and cleared the sky. Our journey became easier. But we had only two weeks' supply of food left.

'We'll have to turn back,' I said to Carlier.

'No,' he protested. His face had regained its former aspect: tanned and youthful, hardened by a beard, softened by long, supple hair. But he had never regained his precise, carefree eyes: there was always an absent-minded look about him. 'Now that the rains have stopped, we'll be able to kill some buffalo,' he added casually.

'But we won't kill a buffalo every day,' I said. In this dank climate it was impossible to preserve a piece of meat for more than twenty-four hours.

'Then we'll come across villages where they'll sell us maize.'

'There's a war on,' I reminded him.

'They're not fighting everywhere.'

I gave him an angry look. 'Aren't you in a hurry to die?'

'Death is unimportant to me,' he said.

'If you die, your discoveries will be buried with you. Don't imagine that any of your men will bother to search for the great river. They'll settle down where we left them and mingle with the Indians.' After a brief silence, I added, 'And I won't look for it either.'

'What does it matter to me?' Carlier put his hand on my

shoulder; it was a long time since he had made this friendly gesture. 'You convinced me that the route to China wasn't so important. Well, neither is the great river important.'

'Let's retrace our steps,' I said. 'We'll organize a new expedition.'

He shook his head. 'I've run out of patience.'

We continued on our way. I killed a small deer, a few wild hens and some quail, but our provisions were running out. When we at last came upon a vast blue river, we had only a three days' supply of food left.

'You see! I made it!' Carlier exclaimed. He stared bitterly at the river; there was an ugly expression on his face.

'Yes, and now we must go back.'

'I made it!' he repeated. There was a stubborn smile on his lips, as if he had played a good trick on someone.

I urged him to leave and he followed me indifferently. He did not speak, he did not look at anything. The second day, I killed a turkey, four days later, a doe, but after that, we went a whole week without encountering any game. Our provisions were now completely gone. I killed a buffalo and roasted a huge chunk of loin which we took along with us; two days later it had to be thrown away.

We decided to try our luck in the next village we should come upon. One morning we saw some huts; as we approached them, we noticed there was no smoke rising from the village and no sound could be heard. But I recognized the smell: the foul smell of the meat we had thrown away. Hundreds of bodies were piled up on the village grounds; the huts were empty, the storage places where corn and meat were kept were empty.

We continued to walk for another two days and on the third morning, as I was about to lift my pack, Carlier said to me, 'I'm staying here. Good-bye.'

'I'll stay with you.'

'No, leave me alone.'

'I'm staying,' I insisted.

All day long I scoured the prairie; a small deer darted from the brush in the distance; I shot at it and missed.

'Why did you come back,' asked Carlier.

'I'm not going to leave you.'

'Go,' he pleaded. 'I don't want to die with you looking at me.'

I hesitated. 'All right, I'll leave.'

He looked at me suspiciously. 'Are you really telling me the truth?'

'Yes, that's the truth. Good-bye.'

I turned around and walked until I was out of his sight. Then I lay down by a tree. 'And now, what's to become of me?' I thought. If I had never met him, I might have continued to wander aimlessly over the continent for a hundred years, a thousand years. But I had met him, I had stopped, and now I could no longer take up my solitary journey again. I watched the moon climbing in the sky and suddenly, in the silence, I heard a single gunshot. I did not move. 'For him, it's over,' I thought. 'But for me will it never be possible to relinquish this body of mine and leave behind only a few bare, naked bones?' The moon was shining just as it had shone one night when I had dragged myself, happy and shivering, out of a dark canal, just as it had on another night, shining down on burnt-out houses. That night a dog was howling at death, and now, inside me, I heard that long plaintive cry rising up towards the sphere of suspended light. Never would the light of that dead star be extinguished, and neither would that bitter taste of solitude and eternity that it was my destiny to endure ever fade away.

'Yes, I suppose it had to end that way,' said Regina. She stood up and brushed off the twigs that clung to her skirt. 'Let's walk a little.'

'It could have ended differently,' Fosca said. 'He made the choice.'

'It had to end that way,' she repeated.

The road led to a clearing, beyond which the roofs of a village could be seen. They walked on in silence.

'I won't have the courage,' Regina said at last.

'Do you need courage? In just a few more years . . . '

'You don't know what you're talking about.'

'It must be so comforting to know that you can stop living whenever you want,' said Fosca. 'Nothing then is irreparable.'

'I wanted to live,' Regina said.

'I tried. I went back to Carlier, took his gun and shot myself in the chest and then in the mouth. It stunned me for a while. And then I found myself alive again.'

'What did you do after that?' She did not really care what he did, but he was right: as long as he spoke, as long as she listened to him, there were no questions to ask. She wished his story would never end.

'I walked towards the sea until I came upon a village on the coast. The chief agreed to let me live there and I built myself a hut. I wanted to become like those men who lived naked under the sun. I wanted to lose myself.'

'And did you succeed?'

'Many years passed, but the day finally came when I had to confront myself again, and I still had just as many years to live.'

They continued to walk until they reached the village. All the doors were locked, the shutters closed; not a sound, not a light. In front of the *Soleil d'Or* was a green wooden bench. They sat down. Through the shutters, they could hear the rhythmic sound of someone snoring.

'And then?' asked Regina.

BOOK IV

I began to run. My heart was pounding wildly. The yellow waters had burst from the river bed with a thunderous roar and were rushing towards me and I knew that if the foam touched me, my body would be covered with black spots and that all of a sudden I would be reduced to ashes by the boiling water. I ran, my feet barely touching the ground. At the top of the mountain a woman was waving at me. Caterina! She was waiting for me. I had only to touch her hand and I would be saved. But the ground was sinking under my feet; I was in a swamp. I could no longer run. Suddenly the ground gave way. I barely had time to raise my hand and cry out 'Caterina!' before I was swallowed up by the molten earth. 'This time I am not dreaming,' I thought, 'This time I am finally dead for good.'

'Sir!'

In a flash, the dream shattered into a thousand pieces. I opened my eyes. I saw the canopy of the bed, the window, and through the window, the tall chestnut tree with its branches swaying in the wind; the everyday world, with its distinct colours, its precise configurations and all its dreary customs.

'The carriage is waiting, sir.'

'Very well.'

I closed my eyes and stretched out my arm over them. I wanted to go back to sleep, to flee somewhere else, not to another world – any world would have been the same for me – but to the strange realms of my dreams, which I loved because they took place elsewhere. In dreams, I escaped along a mysterious thread to the other side of the sky, to the other side of time itself. There, no matter what happened, I would no longer be myself. I pressed my arm against my face; golden spots shimmered in the green darkness. But I could not fall asleep again. I heard the sound of the wind in the garden, of footsteps in the corridor; each step rang sharply in my ears. I was awake, and once again the world lay soberly beneath the sky, and I was lying in the middle of the world with that bitter taste of my life forever on my lips. 'Why did he wake me up? Why did they wake me up?' I thought angrily.

It had happened twenty years ago. I had spent a good many years in the Indian village. The sun had burned my skin. Like a snake, I had sloughed it off, and a witch doctor tattooed sacred symbols on my new body. I ate what they ate and sang their war chants. Several of their women lived successively under my roof; their bodies were warm, brown and soft. Lying on a straw mat one day, I watched the shadow of a palm tree reach out along the sand. It was slowly creeping towards a large rock sparkling in the sun. The shadow would soon touch the rock; I knew that in just a few moments it would touch the rock, and yet I could not see it lengthen. Day after day I watched it and never was I able to catch it moving. I watched intently, and although I could see it was not where it had been an hour earlier, it did not appear to be moving. And I might have spent years, centuries, watching the shadow of that palm tree initially huddle up at the foot of the tree and then extend itself insidiously. I might even have succeeded in losing myself completely; there would have been only the sky, the sea, the shadow of that palm tree in the sun and I might have ceased to exist. But one day, at the precise moment that the rock was beginning to darken, they appeared and said, 'Come with us.' They took me by the arm and pushed me towards their boat; they dressed me in their clothes and then deposited me on the shores of the old continent. And now, here was Bompard, standing in the doorway, saying, 'Shall I unharness the horses?'

I raised myself on one elbow. 'Can't you let me sleep in peace?'

'You asked for the carriage at seven o'clock.'

I got out of bed. I knew that it was useless to try to go back to sleep. They had woken me and now a series of questions raced one after the other through my head. What shall we do? Where shall we go? And whatever I did, wherever I went, I could never escape from myself.

I straightened my wig and asked, 'Where shall we go?'

'You had planned on visiting Madame de Montesson.'

'Haven't you anything more amusing to suggest?'

'Count de Marsenac has been complaining about not seeing you lately at his suppers.'

'And he'll never see me at them again,' I said.

How could a man who had heard the screams of children being strangled and women being raped in the streets of Rivella, in the streets of Rome and Ghent, amuse himself at their timid orgies . . .

'Think of something else.'

'But everything bores you,' he said.

'Ah! One can't breathe in this city!'

Paris had seemed immense to me when I first arrived there with a sack full of diamonds and gold ingots slung over my shoulder. But now that I had done the rounds of all her cabarets, her theatres, her salons, her squares and gardens, I knew that with a little patience it would eventually be possible to know each of her inhabitants by name. And nothing happened there that was not predictable; even the murders, the brawls, the knifings, were all accounted for in the police statistics.

'There's no reason why you have to stay in Paris,' said Bompard.

'One can't breathe on this earth. Anywhere.'

The earth, too, had seemed immense to me at one time. I remembered once standing on top of a hill and thinking to myself, 'Out there is the sea, and beyond the sea other continents, without end.' But now I knew not only that the world was round, but that its circumference had even been measured, and that its precise curvature at the equator and between the poles was presently being determined. And they were doing their best to make it still smaller by drawing up minutely detailed inventories of the most obscure places. They had just compiled such a precise map of France that not a single village or stream went unmarked. What was the point of going away? Every voyage was over before one even began. They had catalogued the plants and animals on the planet. There were only a very small number of them, and a very small number of landscapes, colours, tastes, smells, faces; they were always the same, vainly repeating themselves by the thousand.

'Well, go to the moon then,' Bompard said.

'That's my only hope,' I said. 'We must pierce open the sky.'

We walked down the steps in front of the house and I said to the coachman, 'Madame de Montesson's.'

Before entering the salon, I stopped for a moment in the hall and looked at myself derisively in a mirror. I was wearing a plum-coloured velvet suit embroidered in gold; after twenty years, I was still not used to these masquerade costumes. Beneath my white wig my face seemed to belong to a stranger. Yet the others appeared to feel perfectly at ease in these absurd clothes. They were small and puny, and they would have cut a sad figure in Carmona or at the court of

Charles V. The women looked ugly, with their white-powdered hair and red splotches that flushed their cheeks. The faces of the men annoyed me; they were constantly in motion: they smiled, their eyelids creased, their noses twitched, and they never stopped talking or laughing. From the hall, I could hear them laughing. In my time it was the job of buffoons to divert us; we enjoyed great fits of laughter, but not more than four or five times in an evening, not even happy, carefree Malatesta. I opened the door and noticed with satisfaction that their faces froze and their laughter died down. No one except Bompard knew my secret, but I frightened them. I had amused myself by bringing about the ruin of several of these men and humiliating many of the women. In each of my duels, I had killed my opponent and a legend had grown up around me.

I walked over to the chair in which the mistress of the house was sitting; a circle of guests surrounded her. She was a gay, malicious old woman whose remarks sometimes succeeded in amusing me. And I knew she liked me, for she said I was the most malevolent man she had ever known. But for the moment, talking to her was out of the question. Old Damien was discussing something with little Richet. They were arguing about the role of prejudice in human life. Richet was defending rationalism. I hated old men because they were aware of their whole lives behind them, round and full like a huge cake. And I hated young people because they could sense their whole future ahead of them. I loathed that look of enthusiasm and intelligence that animated everyone's face. Madame de Montesson alone listened dispassionately to the argument, as she dug her needle back and forth through the tapestry she was sewing.

'You're both wrong,' I said abruptly. 'Neither reason nor prejudice is beneficial to man. Nothing is beneficial to man because men are incapable of doing anything for themselves.'

'It's just like you to say something like that,' said Marianne de Sinclair disdainfully. She was a tall, rather pretty young

woman who filled the function of reader to Madame
de Montesson.

'Men must create their own happiness and that of others,'
said Richet.

I shrugged my shoulders. 'They'll never be happy.'

'They will be the day they become rational,' he said.

'They don't even want to be happy,' I retorted. 'They're
only too happy to kill time while waiting for time to kill them.
All of you are simply killing time by dazzling yourselves with
your long words.'

'What should you know about men?' said Marianne
de Sinclair. 'You hate them.'

Madame de Montesson looked up; she held her needle
in suspension above her tapestry.

'Oh! Enough of that!' she exclaimed.

'Yes,' I agreed, 'enough words.'

Words; that was all they had to offer me: freedom,
happiness, progress. It was on such tasteless food as this
that people were fed at this period. I turned around and
walked towards the door; I felt as if I were suffocating in
their tiny rooms, stuffed with furniture and knick-nacks.
There were rugs, ottomans and tapestries everywhere, and
the air was heavy with perfumes that gave me a headache. I
glanced around the salon; they had begun their prattling
again. I was able to freeze their enthusiasm for a brief
moment, but it did not take long for them to become
animated again. Marianne de Sinclair had withdrawn to a
corner with Richet, where they were engaged in earnest
conversation. Their eyes gleamed; they agreed with each
other and both agreed with themselves. I felt like cracking
open their heads with a solid blow of my heel. I reached the
door. In the adjacent hall, men were seated around gaming
tables; unlike the others, they did not speak, did not laugh;
their lips were compressed, their expressions were blank.
Winning or losing money was apparently their principal
diversion in life. In my time, horses galloped across plains,

we held lances in our hands. In my time . . . Suddenly I thought, 'But isn't this also my time?'

I looked at my ornate shoes with their buckles, at my lace cuffs. For twenty years it seemed to me that I had been taking part in a game, and that one day, at the stroke of midnight, I would return to the land of shadows. I glanced up at the clock. Above its gilt face, a porcelain shepherdess was smiling at a shepherd. In a little while, the hands would be pointing to midnight; they would point to midnight tomorrow and the next day, and I would still be there. There was no other land for me but this planet where I felt I no longer belonged. I had been at home in Carmona and in the court of Charles V, but that was long before. Henceforth, the years that would stretch out endlessly before me would be years of exile. All my clothes would be costumes and my life a perpetual play.

The Comte de Saint-Ange walked past me; he was very pale. I stopped him. 'Aren't you playing any more?' I asked.

'I've already played too much,' he answered. 'I lost everything.'

There were beads of sweat on his forehead. He was weak and stupid, but he was a man of his times, at home in the world in which he lived, and I envied him. I took a purse from my pocket. 'Here, see if you can win back some money.'

He grew even paler. 'And if I lose?'

'You'll win. In the end one always wins.'

With a brusque gesture he took the purse and sat down at a table. His hands were trembling. I leaned over his chair; that particular game amused me. If he lost, what would he do? Kill himself? Throw himself at my feet? Would he sell me his wife like the Marquis de Vintenon? Sweat gathered on his upper lip. He was losing. He was losing and he felt his life beating in his chest, burning in his temples. He was risking his life. He was alive. 'What about me?' I thought. 'Will I never feel what even the most wretched among them feel?' I stood up and walked over to another table. 'At least I can lose my fortune.' I sat down and threw a fistful of gold Louis on the felt-covered table.

A stir swept through the room. Baron de Sarcelles came over and sat down opposite me. He was one of the richest financiers in Paris.

'Well, now,' he said. 'Here's a game that promises to be interesting.'

He too threw a handful of gold Louis on the table and we played out our cards in silence. After half an hour, not a single Louis was left to me and my pockets were empty.

'I'll bet fifty thousand crowns on my word,' I said.

'Very well.'

A crowd of people was now pressing around our chairs, holding their breath, staring at the bare green baize. When Sarcelles laid down his hand and I threw my cards into the pack, sighs and gasps escaped from their mouths.

'Double or quits,' I said.

'Double or quits.'

He dealt the cards. I looked at their shiny backs and felt my heart beginning to beat a little faster. If I could lose, lose everything, perhaps the flavour of my life would change . . .

'Beat that,' said Sarcelles.

'Two cards,' I responded. I looked at the cards. Four kings. I knew I had Sarcelles beaten.

'I'll raise you ten thousand,' he said.

I hesitated for a second. I could have thrown in my cards and said, 'You win.' But something – perhaps it was anger – stuck in my throat. Was I reduced to that? Was I going to cheat myself out of winning? Was it forbidden to me now to live without cheating?

'I'll see you,' I said, laying down my cards.

'The money will be at your home before noon tomorrow,' Sarcelles promised.

I bowed, crossed the room and returned to the salon. The

Comte de Saint-Ange was leaning against a wall; he looked as if he were about to collapse.

'I lost all the money you lent me,' he said.

'He who doesn't want to lose, doesn't lose,' I answered. 'When would you like to be paid?'

'Within twenty-four hours. Isn't that the convention?'

'I can't,' he said. 'I haven't got that much money.'

'Then you shouldn't have borrowed it.'

I turned my back on him and met the gaze of Mademoiselle de Sinclair. Her blue eyes were sparkling with anger.

'There are crimes unpunished by law which are even more heinous than straightforward murder,' she said.

'I don't condemn murder.'

We stared at each other in silence. This woman was not afraid of me. She turned away abruptly; I put my hand on her arm.

'You have a great aversion for me, haven't you?'

'What other feeling can you expect to inspire?'

I smiled. 'You don't know me very well. You ought to invite me to your little Saturday gatherings. I'll unburden my heart to you . . .'

My words seemed to strike a soft spot; her cheeks flushed slightly. Madame de Montesson was unaware that some of the salon's habitués had been visiting her reader's home. And she wasn't the sort of woman to forgive her easily.

'I only invite my friends,' she said.

'It's better to have me for a friend than an enemy.'

'Are you trying to bargain with me?'

'Take it as you wish.'

'My friendship cannot be bought,' she said.

'We'll talk about it again another time. Think it over.'

'I've already thought it over.'

I pointed to Bompard who was dozing in a large, deep armchair. 'Do you see that fat, bald man over there?'

'Yes.'

'When I first came to Paris some years ago, he was a gifted

and ambitious young man. At that time I was nothing but an ignorant savage and he tried to make a fool of me. Well, look what I've made of him.'

'Nothing you do could ever surprise me.'

'I didn't tell you that to surprise you, but only to make you think.'

At that moment I saw the Comte de Saint-Ange leaving the salon. He was walking unsteadily, like a drunken man.

'Bompard!' I called out.

Bompard started. I liked to watch him waking up. He would suddenly find himself back among the realities of his life, with me there waiting for him, and then he would remember that right up until the moment of his death he would find me there every time he awoke.

'Let's follow him,' I said.

'What's it all about?' Bompard asked.

'He has to pay me twenty thousand crowns tomorrow morning. And he doesn't have them. I wonder if he'll be stupid enough to take his own life.'

'Of course,' said Bompard. 'There's nothing else he can do.'

We followed Saint-Ange across the courtyard of the residence.

'How can that possibly still amuse you?' Bompard asked. 'Haven't you seen enough corpses in five hundred years?'

'He might board a ship for the West Indies, go begging in the streets; he might even try to kill me. Then again he might continue to live a peaceful, if dishonoured, life in Paris.'

'He won't do any of those things,' said Bompard.

I shrugged my shoulders. 'You're probably right. They all do the same thing.'

Saint-Ange entered the gardens of the Palais-Royal and walked slowly along the colonnades. I hid behind a pillar; I enjoyed observing flies, spiders, the convulsions of frogs, beetles fighting mercilessly to the death. But what I liked most was witnessing a man struggling with himself. Nothing was forcing him to kill himself. If he did not want to die, he had only to decide: 'I will not kill myself.'

A shot rang out, a soft thud. I walked over to the body and experienced the usual disappointment. While they were alive, their deaths were events I awaited with great curiosity, but when I looked down upon their corpses, it was as if they had never existed. Their deaths meant nothing.

We left the gardens. 'Do you know the worst trick that you could play on me? I asked Bompard.

'No.'

'To shoot yourself in the head. Doesn't the prospect tempt you?'

'It would make you too happy,' he replied.

'On the contrary. I'd be extremely disappointed.' I slapped him amiably on the shoulder. 'Fortunately, you're too much of a coward. You'll be with me a long time: until you die in your bed.'

Something stirred in his eyes. 'Are you quite sure you'll never die?'

'Poor Bompard! No I shall never die. Nor shall I ever burn those papers you worry so much about. You'll never be rid of me.' The light in his eyes faded. 'Never,' I repeated. 'No one knows the meaning of that word, not even you.'

He did not answer.

'Let's go home,. We're going to do some work,' I said.

'Are you going to stay up all night again?' he asked.

'Probably.'

'But I want to sleep.'

I smiled. 'Very well! You shall sleep.' I said.

Tormenting him hardly ever entertained me any more. I had ruined his life, but he had grown to accept it, and, now that he slept soundly through the nights, he forgot. The worst disasters never prevented him from going to bed every evening and sleeping. Saint-Ange had shuddered in anguish, but now he was dead, he had escaped me. For them, there was always a means of escape. But for me, on this earth to which I was eternally bound, happiness meant no more or less than unhappiness, hate was as insipid as love. There was nothing they could do for me.

The carriage brought us back to the house and I went directly to my laboratory; I should never have left it. Only there, far from human life, was I sometimes able to forget myself.

One had to admit that many astonishing discoveries had been made during my long absence from Europe. After I had sailed home to the old continent, I learned to my amazement that the earth, which I had always believed stood motionless in the middle of the heavens, actually turned both on its own axis and around the sun. Some of the most mysterious phenomena – lightning, rainbows, the tides – had been fully explained. It had been proved that air had weight and the method of weighing it was now established. The earth had shrunk, but the universe had grown larger; the skies were now filled with new stars that astronomers had brought within reach of the human eye, thanks to the telescope. Due to the microscope, an invisible world had been revealed. Hitherto unknown forces in nature had been brought to light and were gradually being tamed and harnessed. Yet the men who had made these discoveries were very foolish to be so proud of them, for they would never know history's verdict; they would all be dead before that time. But I would profit from their efforts, I would know. The day that science finally reached its ultimate conclusions, I would be there. Their labours were for my benefit. I looked at the flasks, the beakers, at all the idle apparatus. I picked up a glass slide; it lay there, perfectly still in my fingers, a piece of glass no different to any of the other pieces of glass I had seen and touched during the five hundred years of my life. All the objects around me were silent, inert, as they had always been, and yet I had only to rub this piece of matter to make unknown forces rise to its surface. Beneath this apparently quiet surface, obscure powers were waiting to be unleashed. Deep in the very air I breathed, the earth on which I trod, a mysterious life was flickering. An entire invisible world, stranger and more unpredictable than the images of my dreams, was hidden within this old universe of which I had grown so weary. Within the four walls that surrounded me, I felt freer than in the dreary streets, than on the infinite plains of America. One day, all these forms, all these worn-out colours would burst apart; one day I would pierce through this immutable sky in which the four seasons were inexorably reflected; one day I would gaze upon the other side of this illusory decor which had always masked men's eyes. I could not even imagine what I would see then, but it was enough for me to know that it would be something else, something totally different. Perhaps it would be something inaccessible to the eyes, the ears, the hands; perhaps I would then be able to forget that I was forever cleaved to these eyes, ears and hands; perhaps I would at last become someone other than myself.

A dark deposit remained in the bottom of the retort. 'It failed,' said Bompard in a mocking tone.

'That proves there are still impurities in this carbon,' I said. 'We'll have to start all over again.'

'But we've already tried it a hundred times,' he protested.

'But that's because we've never had really pure carbon.'

I tilted the retort and spread out the ashes on a slide. Were those ashes merely the residue of foreign matter? Or did carbon possess some sort of indestructible mineral tissue? The evidence was unrevealing.

'We'll have to perform the experiment with a diamond,' I said.

Bompard shrugged his shoulders. 'How do you burn a diamond?

At the back of the laboratory, a fire was burning quietly. Outside, dusk was falling. I walked over to a glass door. The first stars were beginning to appear in the dark blue of the sky; one could still count them. Lurking in the twilight were millions upon millions of others waiting to make their appearance. And beyond these, there were still others that remained invisible to our feeble eyes. But it was always the same stars that appeared first. For thousands of years the celestial vault had remained unchanged; for centuries there had been the same icy twinkling above my head.

I went back to the table where Bompard had set the microscope. In the salons, the regular visitors were beginning to arrive, women were preening themselves for the ball, and laughter would soon ring out in the cabarets. For them, the evening that had just begun was different to all other evenings, unique. I put my eye to the eye-piece and looked at the greyish powder. Then I suddenly felt within me the first flutter of that storm-force wind I knew so well. It rushed through the quiet laboratory, swept away the flasks, ripped the roof from above my head, and my life shot heavenwards like a flame, like a scream. I felt it in my heart; it burned, it leapt from my chest. I could feel it at my fingertips: a desire to break, to destroy, to strangle. My hands tightened on the microscope.

'Let's get out of here!' I said.

'You want to leave now?'

'Yes. Come with me.'

'I'd much rather go to sleep.'

'You sleep too much,' I said. 'You're getting fat.' I shook my head. 'How sad it is to grow old!'

'Oh, I'd just as soon be in my skin as yours,' he said.

'It's good to know how to face up to misfortune so cheerfully,' I said. 'But you were ambitious in your youth, weren't you?'

'What fortifies my soul,' he said with a smile, 'is the knowledge that I could never possibly be as unhappy as you.'

I threw my coat over my shoulders, took my hat and said, 'I'm thirsty. Give me something to drink.'

Was I really thirsty? There was a painful yearning raging through my body that was neither a need for food, nor for drink, nor for a woman. I took the glass that Bompard held out to me and swallowed its contents in one gulp. With a grimace, I set it down on a table.

'I can understand your predilection for the experimental method,' I said. 'If a man told me he was immortal, I would certainly attempt to determine the truth for myself. But I beg you, stop spoiling my wine with your poison.'

'The fact is you should have died a hundred times over,' he said bitterly.

'You'd better get used to it,' I said. 'I'll never die.' I smiled at him. I knew perfectly how to imitate their smiles. 'Besides, it would be a great loss for you. You haven't a better friend in the whole world than me.'

'Nor you than me,' he said.

I set off towards Madame de Montesson's town house. Why did I feel like seeing their faces again? I knew there was nothing I could expect from them. And yet I could not bear the thought that they were alive under the sky while I was alone in my tomb.

Madame de Montesson was sitting by the fireplace doing her tapestry; her friends formed a circle around her chair. Nothing had changed. Marianne de Sinclair was serving coffee and Richet was looking at her with an expression of half-witted satisfaction. They were laughing and talking. No one, during all these weeks, had noticed my absence. Angrily, I thought, 'But I'll make them notice my presence.'

I went up to Marianne de Sinclair. 'Coffee?' she asked gently.

'No, thank you. I don't need your drugs.'

'As you wish.'

They were laughing, they were talking; they were pleased to be together, they had convinced themselves that they were alive, that they were happy. There was no way of persuading them otherwise.

'Have you thought about our last conversation?' I asked.

'No,' she replied, smiling. 'I think of you as little as possible.'

'I see that you're determined to hate me.'

'I'm a very determined person.'

'And I'm no less so,' I said. 'I've heard that your gatherings are extremely interesting. It seems that the most advanced ideas are bandied about and that the best minds of the age scorn this venerable salon to group themselves around you . . . '

'Excuse me,' she said, 'but I have to serve coffee.'

'Then I'll go and talk to Madame de Montesson.'

'Just as you wish.'

I walked over to the mistress of the house and leaned against her chair. She always greeted me warmly; my maliciousness amused her. While we were discussing the latest court and city gossip, I caught Marianne de Sinclair looking at me. She immediately averted her eyes, but even though she feigned indifference, I knew very well she was anxious. I bore no grudge against her, for although she hated me, it was never really I who was hated – or loved. It was a borrowed self for whom I felt only indifference. As for my true self, what feelings was I able to inspire? Beatrice had told me one day: neither miserly nor generous, neither courageous nor cowardly, neither evil nor good. In truth, I was no one. I followed Marianne de Sinclair with my eyes as she walked to and fro across the room. There was something noble and nonchalant in her bearing that I liked. Beneath the soft swathe of tulle that covered her head, a rolling mass of light brown hair could be discerned; blue eyes shone in her eager face. No, I wished her no harm. But I was curious to know what would happen to her calm dignity when faced with misfortune.

'There are not many people here this evening,' I said.

Madame de Montesson looked up and glanced quickly around the room. 'The weather is bad.'

'And I believe the taste for disinterested conversation is waning. People are becoming increasingly bound up in politics . . . '

'Politics will never be discussed under my roof,' she said authoritatively.

'You're right,' I said. 'A salon is a salon and not a club. It seems that Mademoiselle de Sinclair's Saturdays are degenerating into public meetings . . . '

'What Saturdays? What are you talking about?' asked Madame de Montesson.

'Don't you know about them?'

She glared at me with her small, piercing eyes. 'You know very well that I know nothing about them. Marianne receives on Saturdays? Since when?'

'For about six months now she has been holding brilliant little gatherings at which her guests do their best to demolish and reconstruct the social order.'

'Ah! the sly little thing!' she said with a slight laugh. 'Demolish and reconstruct the social order . . . it must be fascinating!'

She leaned over her tapestry again and I took my leave of her. Little Richet, who was speaking animatedly to Marianne de Sinclair, walked over towards me.

'You've just done a vile thing,' he said.

I smiled. He had a large mouth and bulging eyes, and despite the obvious sincerity of his anger, his effort to appear dignified only accentuated his naivety. It was laughable.

'You will answer to me for that,' he said.

I continued to smile. He was trying to provoke me. He did not know I had no honour to defend, no anger to satisfy. And neither was there anything to stop me from striking him, beating him and throwing him to the ground. I was not subject to any of their conventions. If they knew to what degree I was free of them, they would truly have been frightened of me.

'Don't laugh,' he snarled.

He was disconcerted; he had not foreseen that it would turn out this way. All his courage and pride was not enough to tolerate my smile.

'Are you in such a hurry to die?' I asked.

'I'm in a hurry to rid the world of your presence,' he replied.

In the heat of his passion, he had still failed to realize that the death of which he was so defiant might strike him rather than me. And yet I had only to speak a word . . .

'Would you care to meet me at five o'clock at the Passy gate? Bring two seconds along.' I looked at him steadily and added, 'I don't think a doctor will be necessary. I never wound my opponents. I kill them outright.'

'At five o'clock, at the Passy gate.'

He crossed the room, said a few words to Marianne de Sinclair and walked towards the door. As he left, he turned around and looked at her, thinking perhaps that it was the last time he would ever see her. A moment earlier, he had thirty or forty years of life ahead of him. And then suddenly, only one night. He departed and I went over to Marianne de Sinclair.

'You take considerable interest in Richet, don't you?' I asked her.

She paused a moment. She wanted to crush me with scorn, but she also wanted to know what I was going to say.

'I take an interest in all my friends,' she said. Her voice was icy, but under that mask of indifference I could feel her curiosity throbbing.

'Did he tell you we were going to fight a duel?'

'No.'

'I've fought eleven duels in my life, and on each occasion I killed my opponent.'

The blood rushed to her cheeks. She could control her handsome body and her facial expressions, her voice and the movement of her lips, but she was unable to prevent herself blushing, and she now seemed very young and very vulnerable.

'You're not going to kill a child?' she said. 'He's a mere child!'

'Do you love him?' I asked her abruptly.

'What difference does it make to you?'

'If you love him, I'll take care not to harm him.'

She looked at me in anguish; she was searching for the word that would save Richet, trying to avoid the one that might condemn him. In a trembling voice, she said, 'I don't love him, but I have the most tender affection for him. I beg you to spare him.'

'If I spare him, would you consider me as friend?'

'I would be immensely grateful to you.'

'And how would you prove it to me?'

'By treating you as a friend. My door would be open to you every Saturday.'

I laughed. 'I'm afraid your door will no longer be open to anyone on Saturdays. Madame de Montesson doesn't seem to appreciate your little gatherings very much.'

Again she blushed and looked at me in a sort of stupor. 'I'm sorry for you,' she said. 'I'm very sorry for you.'

The sadness in her voice was so sincere that I made no attempt to answer her. I stood there without moving, as if nailed to the floor. Was there someone who still existed behind the phantom I had become, someone with a living heart? It seemed to me that it was I, my actual self, who was the object of these words. Her eyes had pierced through me. Under the costumes, the masks, under that steely armour the centuries had forged around me, I was there; it was me: a pitiable creature who took pleasure in petty acts of malice. I really was the person she felt sorry for, this person she did not know, this person I was.

'Listen to me . . . '

She had walked away. Yet what, in any event, would I have been able to say to her? What true words could have passed from me to her? One thing was certain: I had caused her to be driven from that house and she felt sorry for me.

But all my excuses, like all my challenges, would have never been anything other than lies.

I opened the front door. Outside, it was a beautiful, cool, moonlit night. The streets were deserted; people were shut away cosily in their salons, their garrets: their homes. Nowhere was I at home; the house in which I lived had never been a home to me: it was an encampment. This century was not my century, and this life of mine which was so relentlessly prolonged was not my life. I turned a corner and found myself on the embankment. I saw the apse of the cathedral with its white flying buttresses and its statues which formed a solemn procession descending from the rooftop. The river was flowing cold and black between ivy-covered walls. Sunk in the depths of its waters was the round moon. I walked, and as I walked, it followed me; there it was in the depths of the water, in the depths of the sky, the loathsome moon which had accompanied me for five hundred years, chilling everything with its icy glare. I leaned against a stone parapet. The church loomed up before me, rigid in the deathly light, and like myself, lonely and inhuman. All these men who surrounded us would die, and we would still be standing. 'One day it too will collapse,' I thought, 'and there will be nothing in its place but a mass of ruins; one day no trace at all will be left of it, and the moon will be shining in the sky, and I will still be here.'

I continued to walk along the river. Perhaps Richet, at that very moment, was looking at the moon; he was gazing at the moon and the stars and thinking, 'This is the last time I shall ever see them.' Perhaps he was thinking of Marianne de Sinclair, remembering each of her smiles and asking himself, 'Have I seen her for the last time?' In fear, in hope, he was feverishly awaiting the dawn. Had it been mortal, my heart would also have been beating, this night would have been unique; the pale glimmer in the sky would have been death beckoning to me, waiting for me at the end of the gloomy street. But no, nothing ever happened to me; the duel was a pretence. It was the same adventureless, joyless, painless nights. A single night, a single day, repeating themselves endlessly throughout eternity.

The sky was beginning to grow light when I arrived at the Passy gate. I sat down at the edge of the river bank. Within me I heard a voice: 'I'm sorry for you.' She was right. It was a pitiful creature who was sitting on that river bank, waiting to commit an absurd murder. Cities had been burned to the ground, armies had slaughtered each other, an empire had been born and collapsed in my hands. And there I was, empty and foolish; I was about to kill another man without risk and without joy, just to occupy my time. Was there anyone to pity more than me?

The last star had just faded when I saw Richet coming towards me. He was walking slowly, looking down at his shoes which were wet with dew. And suddenly, out of the distant past, a brief moment of my life flashed through my memory, a moment that I believed had vanished forever. I was sixteen. It was a hazy morning and I was sitting astride my horse, a lance in my hand. The armour of the Genoese gleamed in the dawn light, and I was afraid. And because I was afraid, the light was softer, the dew fresher than on any other morning. An inner voice spoke to me: 'Be brave,' it said. No one had ever spoken to me with such fervent affection. And then the voice was still, the dawn lost its freshness. I no longer experienced either fear or courage. I stood up. Richet held out a sword to me. Around him the dawn was breaking for the last time and the fresh smell of earth was rising in the air. He was ready to die and he held his whole life against his heart.

'No,' I said.

He held out the sword to me, but I stood motionless, my hand did not move from my side. No, I was not going to fight. I looked at the two men behind Richet.

'I refuse to fight. Bear witness to it.'

'Why?' asked Richet. He had a troubled, disappointed look on his face.

'I don't feel like fighting. I prefer to apologize to you.'

'Yet I know you're not afraid of me,' he said in astonishment.

'I repeat, I offer you my full apology.'

He stood planted there before me, disconcerted, his heart overflowing with all his useless courage, which was as useless as my hate, my anger and my envy. For a fleeting moment he, like me, was lost beneath the sky, cut off from his life, then thrown back into that life, not knowing what to do with himself. I turned my back on him and strode rapidly towards the road. In the distance a cock was crowing.

I dug my cane into the ant hill and shook it from side to side. They came streaming out, all of them black, all alike, thousands of ants, thousands of replicas of the same ant. In a remote corner of the grounds that surrounded my country house, they had spent twenty long years constructing this huge mound, which was so teeming with life that the grass itself seemed alive. They ran in every direction, even more haphazardly than the bubbles that danced above the flames in my retorts. And yet they stubbornly pursue their plans. Were some of them industrious and others lazy, some thoughtless, other serious? Or did they all work with the same foolish eagerness. I wished I could have followed them one by one with my eyes, but no sooner did I pick one out than it became lost in that monstrous ballet. The only way of distinguishing them would have been to tie ribbons around their bodies – red, green, yellow . . .

'Well! Do you hope to learn their language?' asked Bompard.

I looked up. It was a fine June day. A scent of lime blossom filled the warm air. Bompard was holding a rose in his hand. He was smiling.

'It's my own creation,' he said proudly.

'It looks like any other rose to me,' I said.

He shrugged his shoulders. 'That's because you haven't got eyes to see with.'

He walked away. Ever since we had withdrawn to Crécy he spent his leisure in grafting rose-bushes. I again looked down at the busy ants, but they no longer held my interest. In the special furnace I had had built, a diamond was being heated in the bottom of a golden crucible. Neither did that interest me any longer. I knew that in a few years every schoolboy would know the secrets of the elements and compounds; I had all the time I needed . . . I lay down on my back and looked up at the sky. For me too, it was as blue as the skies above Carmona on a fine day. I, too, could smell the sweet scent of roses and lime blossom. And yet I would again allow this springtime to go by without living it. Here, a new rose had just been born; over there, the fields were strewn with snowy petals of almond blossom. And I, a stranger both here and there, would pass through this season of flowers like a dead man.

'Sir!' Once again Bompard stood before me. 'There's a lady asking to speak to you. She's come from Paris by coach and wants to see you personally.'

'A lady?' I said in surprise.

I got to my feet, brushed the earth off my clothes and walked towards the house. 'It might while away an hour,' I thought. Seated in a wicker chair, in the shade of a tall linden tree, I saw Marianne de Sinclair. She was wearing a linen dress with lilac-coloured stripes, and her unpowdered hair fell in curls over her shoulders. I bowed to her.

'What a surprise!' I said.

'Am I disturbing you?'

'Not at all.'

I had not forgotten the sound of her voice. 'I'm sorry for you.' She had uttered those words, and the phantom I had become had been transformed into a man of flesh and bones. And it was that malicious, guilty man who now stood before her. Was it hate, scorn, or pity that I saw in her eyes? The gnawing shame which gripped my heart once again testified that it really was me she was looking at. She turned her head away.

'How pretty these grounds are,' she said. 'Do you like the country?'

'Above all, I like being away from Paris.' A brief silence followed, and then she resumed somewhat haltingly, 'I've been wanting to see you for a long time. I wanted to thank you for having spared Richet's life.'

'Don't thank me,' I said brusquely, 'I didn't do it because of you.'

'That doesn't matter,' she said. 'What matters is that you acted generously.'

'It wasn't through generosity,' I said impatiently.

It irritated me that she too could have been deceived by that strange figure who, as a result of my actions, happened to have moulded himself around me.

She smiled. 'I suppose that whenever you do a good deed, you always find evil motives for it.'

'Did you think my motives were good when I told Madame de Montesson about you?' I asked.

'Oh, I don't say that you're not capable of base acts, too,' she said in a quiet voice.

Perplexed, I studied her carefully. She looked much younger than when I had last seen her at Madame de Montesson's salon, and she seemed more beautiful, too. What had she come for?

'You don't bear any grudge against me?' I asked.

'No. In fact, you did me a favour,' she said gaily. 'I didn't want to spend the rest of my life being a slave to a selfish old woman.'

'So much the better,' I replied. 'And to think that I almost felt remorse for what I did.'

'You'd have been wrong. My life is much more interesting now.' There was a hint of defiance in her voice.

'Did you come here to offer me absolution?' I asked curtly.

She shook her head. 'I came to talk to you about a project . . . '

'A project?'

'For quite a long time now my friends and I have wanted to found an independent university which would compensate for the insufficiencies of official teaching. We believe that the development of the scientific spirit will have a great influence on social and political progress . . . ' She stopped speaking and handed me a notebook which had been in her hand. Then, in the same timid manner as she had begun, she said, 'All our ideas are explained in this booklet.'

I took the notebook and opened it. It began with a rather long dissertation on the advantages of the experimental method and the moral and political consequences which could be expected to result from its diffusion; next, a curriculum was proposed for the future university; in conclusion, a few pages written in a firm and impassioned tone, announced the advent of a better world. I laid the tract on my lap.

'Did you draft it?'

She gave a slightly embarrassed smile. 'Yes,' she answered.

'I admire your faith,' I said.

'Faith alone isn't enough. We need partners and money. A great deal of money.'

I laughed. 'You came here to ask me for money?'

'Yes. We've opened a subscription list. I hope you'll be the first to make a donation. And we'd be even happier if you would consider accepting a chair in chemistry.'

There was a moment of silence, then I said, 'Why did you think of approaching me?'

'You're very rich,' she replied. 'And you're a great scientist. Everyone is talking about the work you've done with carbon.'

'But you know what I'm like. You've often reproached me for hating mankind. What made you think I'd agree to help you?'

Her face grew animated, her eyes more brilliant. 'On the

contrary. I *don't* know you. You might refuse, but you might accept, too. I decided to take a chance.'

'And why should I accept? To make up for the wrong I did you?'

She stiffened. 'I told you that you did me no wrong.'

'For the pleasure of doing you a favour, then?'

'In the interests of science and humanity.'

'I'm not interested in science except insofar as it is inhuman.'

'It amazes me how you dare to hate people,' she said in a sudden flash of anger. 'You're rich, learned, free; you do everything you like, while most of mankind lives in misery and ignorance, enslaved to joyless jobs. And you have never tried to help them. They are the ones who should hate *you*.'

Her voice was so full of passion that I felt the need to defend myself. But how could I tell her the truth?

'At bottom, I think I envy them,' I said.

'You?'

'They're alive. For years now, I haven't been able to feel alive.'

'Ah!' she said compassionately. 'I knew you were very unhappy.'

Suddenly, I stood up. 'Come for a walk around the grounds, since you find them so pretty.'

'I'd love to.'

She took my arm and we strolled beside the stream where goldfish were swimming.

'Even on such a beautiful day as this, don't you feel alive?'

With her fingertips she touched one of the roses Bompard had created. 'Isn't there anything here you like?' she asked.

I plucked the rose and gave it to her. 'I'd like this rose, if you were wearing it.'

She smiled, took the flower and deeply breathed in its fragrance.

'It says something to you, doesn't it?' I said. 'What does it tell you?'

'That it's good to be alive,' she said gaily.

'It tells me nothing. For me things have no voice.'

I looked hard at the saffron-coloured rose, but there had been too many roses in my life, too many springtimes.

'That's only because you don't know how to listen to them.'

We walked for a while in silence. She looked at the trees and flowers. No sooner did she turn her eyes from me than I felt life flowing out of me.

'I'm curious to know what you think of me,' I said.

'I used to think very ill of you.'

'What made you change your opinion?'

'Your attitude to Richet made me see you in a new light.'

I shrugged my shoulders. 'It was a simple caprice.'

'I wouldn't have thought you capable of that kind of caprice.'

I felt as if I were deceiving her. I was ashamed. But it was impossible to explain.

'It would be wrong to take me for a kind-hearted soul,' I said.

She smiled. 'I'm not stupid, you know.'

'And yet you hope to interest me in the happiness of humanity.'

She prodded a pebble along the path with her foot and did not answer.

'Come now,' I said. 'Do you reckon I'll give you that money or not? Which way would you bet, yes or no?'

She looked at me gravely. 'I don't know,' she said. 'You're free to do as you please.'

For the second time she touched my heart. It was true; I was free. All the centuries through which I had lived seemed to perish and die in that very moment which burst from beneath that blue sky, as new, as unexpected as if the past had never existed. In that instant I would give Marianne an answer that did not derive from any of the forgotten moments of my life. And it was I, yes, it was I who had to decide. It was up to me whether I disappointed Marianne or gratified her.

'Must I decide at once?'

'As you like,' she said a little coldly.

I looked at her. Disappointed or gratified, she would walk back through the gates and all I need do would be to go back and lie down on the grass near the ant hill.

'When will you give me your answer?' she asked.

I paused. I felt like saying 'Tomorrow' to be sure of seeing her again. But I did not say it. In her presence, it was I who spoke, who acted – the real I. It would have shamed me to exploit the situation for the sake of a mere whim.

'Straight away,' I said. 'Would you mind waiting for a moment?'

I returned a few minutes later with a bill of exchange in my hand. When I gave it to Marianne, the blood rushed to her cheeks.

'But it's a fortune!' she exclaimed.

'It's not my whole fortune.'

'But it must be a large part . . . '

'Didn't you tell me you needed a great deal of money?'

She looked at the paper, then at my face. 'I don't understand,' she said.

'You can't understand everything.'

She stood before me, looking bemused.

'It's late,' I said. 'You ought to leave. There's nothing more we need to talk about.'

'I have one more favour to ask of you,' she said slowly.

'But you're insatiable!'

'Neither my friends nor I know much about business. Apparently you're a skilled financier. Help me get our university started.'

'Is it in your interest or mine that you ask me that?'

She seemed disconcerted. 'Both,' she said.

'More one, or more the other?'

She hesitated; but she loved life so much that she always relied on the truth.

'I believe that the day you allow yourself to come out of yourself, a lot of things will change for you . . . '

'Why do you take such an interest in me?' I asked.

'Can't you understand that it's quite possible for someone to take an interest in you?'

For a moment we stood silently facing each other.

'I'll think it over,' I said. 'And I'll bring you my answer.'

'Twelve, rue des Ciseaux. That's where I live now.' She held out her hand. 'Thank you.'

'Twelve, rue des Ciseaux,' I repeated. 'I should be thanking you.'

She climbed into the carriage and I listened to the noise of the wheels as they rolled along the road. Then, with both arms I hugged the trunk of the tall linden tree, I pressed my cheek against its rough bark and thought with desire, with anguish, 'Will I become a living man again?'

There was a knock at my door. Marianne entered and came over to my desk.

'Still at work?' she said.

I smiled. 'As you see.'

'I'm sure you haven't moved from this room all day.'

'That's true.'

'Did you at least eat something?' she asked. I hesitated for a moment and she said half-angrily, 'Naturally you didn't eat. You're going to ruin your health.'

She gave me a worried look and I felt ashamed. Not to eat, not to sleep; to give up one's money, one's time, did not have the same meaning for her as it did for me. I was lying to her.

'If I hadn't come in, you would have stayed here all night . . . ' she said.

'I get bored when I'm not working.'

She began to laugh. 'Don't make excuses for yourself.' With a firm hand, she pushed away the papers scattered in front of me. 'That's enough. You must have dinner now.'

I glanced regretfully at the desk piled high with papers and folders, at the heavy curtains drawn over the windows, at the opaque walls. My Paris residence had become the planning centre for the future university and, with precise tasks before me to accomplish, I felt at ease in this study. As long as I was here, I had no desire to go elsewhere. It was out of the question . . . '

'Where shall I have dinner?' I asked.

'There are lots of places . . . '

Abruptly, I said, 'Come and eat with me.'

She hesitated. 'But Sophie is waiting for me.'

'Let her wait.'

She looked at me. There was a hint of a smile on her lips and she asked coquettishly, 'Would that really make you happy?'

I shrugged my shoulders. How could I explain that I sought her company simply to kill time, that I needed her to live. Words would betray me; I would say either too much or too little. I wanted to be sincere with her, but sincerity was not something I could afford.

'Of course,' I said briefly.

She seemed somewhat disconcerted and then said decisively, 'All right, take me to that new cabaret everyone is talking about. I've been told they have wonderful food.'

'Dagorneau's?'

'That's it.'

Her eyes sparkled. She always knew where to go, what to do; she always had desires or curiosities to satisfy. Had I been able to follow her through life, I would no longer have been a burden to myself.

We went down the stairs and I asked, 'Shall we walk?'

'Of course,' she replied. 'It's such a beautiful, moonlit night.'

'Ah! So you like the moonlight!' I said bitterly.

'Don't you?'

'I hate the moon.'

She laughed. 'Your feelings are always excessive.'

'When all of us are dead, it will still be there, sneering in the heavens.'

'I don't envy it,' Marianne said. 'I'm not afraid of death.'

'Really? If you were told that you were going to die in a little while, wouldn't you be afraid?'

'Ah! But I want to die when my time is up.'

She was walking at a quick pace, avidly absorbing the sweetness of the night through her eyes, her ears, through every pore of her body.

'How much you love life,' I said.

'Yes, I do love it.'

'Were there ever times when you were unhappy?'

'Occasionally. But that too is part of being alive.'

'I'd like to ask you a question,' I said.

'Ask it.'

'Were you ever in love?'

'No,' she answered immediately.

'And yet you have a passionate nature.'

'That's just it,' she said. 'Other people always seem indifferent, luke-warm. They're not alive . . . '

I felt a small wrench in my heart. 'And neither am I alive.'

'You've already told me that once,' she said. 'But it's not true, not true at all. You're excessive both in what's good and what's evil; you can't stand mediocrity. That's being alive.' She looked at me steadily. 'Basically, your unkindness was simply a form of revolt.'

'You don't know me,' I said drily.

She blushed and we walked the rest of the way to the cabaret in silence. A stairway led down to a large vaulted room with smoke-blackened beams. Waiters wearing brightly coloured caps were scurrying about among the tables around which noisy groups were congregated. We sat down at a small table at the back of the room and I ordered supper.

After the waiter had placed the hors d'œuvre and a jug of

rosé wine in front of us, Marianne asked me, 'Why do you always get so angry whenever I appear to think well of you?'

'I feel as if I'm an impostor.'

'Isn't it true that you give unsparingly of your time, your money and your efforts to our enterprise?'

'But it doesn't cost me anything,' I answered.

'Precisely. That's true generosity. You give everything and yet you always feel as if it costs you nothing.'

I filled our glasses with wine. 'Have you already forgotten what I used to be like?'

'No,' she replied. 'But you've changed.'

'One never changes.'

'Ah! I don't believe that. If people never changed, all our work would be worthless,' she said spiritedly. She gazed at me. 'I'm certain that you would not now be able to amuse yourself by driving a man to suicide.'

'That's true . . . ' I said.

'You see.'

oeShe took a mouthful of pâté. When she ate she had a serious, animal look about her. Despite her shy and graceful movements, she gave the appearance of a wolf transformed into a woman. Her teeth shone with a cruel sparkle. How could I explain it to her? Doing evil no longer amused me; but I had not become any better for that: 'neither good nor bad, neither miserly nor generous.'

She smiled at me. 'I like this place very much. Do you?'

At the other end of the room, a young woman was singing, accompanying herself with a hurdy-gurdy; the audience took up the refrains in chorus. Ordinarily, I hated such loud, human boisterousness, the peals of laughter, the voices. But Marianne was smiling and I could not bring myself to hate anything that brought such a smile to her lips.

'Yes, I like it too,' I replied.

'But you're not eating,' she said reproachfully. 'You worked too hard; it's ruined your appetite.'

'Not in the least.'

I pushed a slice of pâté around my plate. All about me, men were eating and drinking, and at their sides were women who were smiling at them. And I too was eating and drinking, and a woman was smiling at me. A sudden feeling of warmth rose up from my heart. 'It's almost as if I were one of them,' I thought.

'She has a pretty voice,' Marianne remarked.

The hurdy-gurdy woman had come over to our table and was looking gaily at Marianne as she sang. She gave a signal with her hand and everyone began to sing with her. Marianne's clear voice mingled with the others. She leaned towards me.

'You must sing too.'

Something akin to shame caused a lump to form in my throat. Never before had I sung with them. I looked at them. They were singing and smiling at the women next to them; a flame was burning in their hearts. And a flame had begun to burn in *my* heart; when that flame burned, neither the past nor the future were of any importance. Whether one died tomorrow, in a hundred years time, or never, made no difference. It was the same flame, the same flame that burned in all of them. 'I'm living! I'm one of them!' I thought.

I began to sing along with them.

'It's not true,' I thought. 'I'm not one of them . . .' Half-hidden behind a column, I watched them dancing. Verdier's hand was touching Marianne's and at times their bodies brushed against each other; he was breathing in the fragrant scent of her hair. She was wearing a full, blue dress, decolleté and off the shoulders. I wanted to press that fragile body against mine, but I felt paralyzed. 'Your flesh is of another kind.' My hands and my lips were granite; I was unable to touch her, I was unable to laugh as they were laughing, with that lustful ease of manner. They were her kind, and I had nothing in common with them. I walked towards the door, but as I was about to leave, Marianne's voice stopped me.

'Where are you going?'

'I'm returning to Crécy,' I answered.

'Without saying good-bye to me?'

'I didn't want to disturb you.'

She looked at me in surprise. 'What happened?' she asked. 'Why are you leaving so early?'

'You know I'm not very sociable.'

'But I wanted to speak to you for a few minutes.'

'Very well.'

We crossed the tiled hall and she pushed open the door to the library. The large room was empty. The muted sounds of the violins penetrated through the book-lined walls.

'I wanted to tell you that we would all be very sorry if you really refused to take part in our charity committee. Why don't you want to?' she asked.

'I wouldn't be capable,' I replied.

'But why?'

'I'd make mistakes,' I said. 'I'd burn old people instead of building homes for them. I'd set lunatics free and imprison your philosophers in cages.'

She shook her head. 'I don't understand. It is only thanks to you that we were able to found the university. Your inaugural address was magnificent. And yet there are times when you appear convinced that our efforts are useless.' I remained silent and she said somewhat impatiently, 'What do you really believe?'

'To be truthful,' I said, 'I don't believe in progress.'

'Yet it's quite evident that we're closer now to truth and even to justice than ever before.'

'Are you so sure that your truth and your justice are worth more than the truths and justices of past centuries?'

'Well, you must agree that science is preferable to ignorance, tolerance to fanaticism, freedom to slavery.'

The naive ardour with which she spoke irritated me. It was their language she was speaking.

'A man,' I said, 'once told me that there is only one good, and that is to act according to one's conscience. I think he was right and that all we pretend to do for others is worthless.'

'Ah!' she said in a triumphant voice. 'And supposing my conscience commands me to fight for tolerance, reason, and freedom?'

I shrugged my shoulders. 'Then do it,' I said. 'My own conscience never orders me to do anything.'

'If that's the case, why did you help us?'

She looked at me with such sincere anxiety that once again I felt an almost uncontrollable desire to confide in her totally. Only then would I become truly alive again; only then would I become myself. We would be able to talk without lying. But then I remembered Carlier's tortured face.

'To kill time,' I replied.

'That's not true!' she exclaimed.

In her eyes there was gratitude, tenderness, faith. I longed to be the person she saw. But my whole being was a lie; every word, every silence, every gesture, even my face lied to her. I could not tell her the truth and I hated deceiving her. The only thing left for me was to leave.

'It *is* true. And now I'm going back to my retorts.'

She forced herself to smile. 'It's a very sudden departure.' She put her hand on the doorknob and asked, 'When will we see each other again?'

There was a long silence. She was leaning against the door, very close to me, and her bare shoulders shone in the half-light and I could smell the sweet scent of her hair. Her eyes were beckoning to me: just a word, just a gesture. But it would all be a lie. Her happiness, her life, our love would be nothing but lies. My every kiss would betray her.

'I don't believe you need me any more,' I said.

Her face suddenly relaxed. 'What is it that bothers you, Fosca? Are we not friends?'

'You have so many friends.'

She made no attempt to restrain her laughter. 'You wouldn't be jealous, by any chance?'

'Why not?' Again I lied; it was not a human jealousy I had in mind.

'That's foolish,' she said.

'I'm not made to live in society,' I said light-heartedly.

'You're not made to live alone.'

Alone. I could smell the scents of the garden around the mound teeming with ants, and once again I felt the taste of death in my mouth. The sky was bare, the plain deserted; suddenly, my heart was empty. And the words I did not want to speak formed on my lips.

'Come with me.'

'Come with you?' she said. 'For how long?'

I held out my arms. Everything would be a lie, even the desire that was swelling my heart and my arms that embraced her mortal body. But I no longer had the strength to fight; I held her to me as if I were any other man holding a woman in his arms.

'For a lifetime,' I answered. 'Could you spend a lifetime beside me?'

'I could spend eternity beside you.'

When I returned to Crécy the next morning, I knocked at Bompard's door. He was dunking a piece of buttered bread in a large cup of coffee. He had already taken on the mannerisms of an old man. I sat down in front of him.

'Bompard, I'm going to astound you,' I said.

'Come, come now,' he said indifferently.

'I've decided to do something for you.'

He did not even look up. 'Really?'

'Yes. I feel guilty about having kept you with me for so long and not letting you take your opportunities in the world. I've heard that the Duke de Frétigny is leaving on a mission to the Russian imperial court and is looking for a secretary. A crafty schemer could go far there. I'm going to recommend you warmly and give you a decent sum of money so that you can cut a good figure in Saint Petersburg.'

'Ah!' said Bompard. 'So you want to get rid of me?' He smiled unpleasantly.

'Yes,' I said. 'I'm going to marry Marianne de Sinclair. I don't want you around when she's here.'

Bompard dunked another piece of bread in his cup. 'I'm getting old,' he said. 'I don't feel like travelling any more.'

A lump formed in my throat and I realized that I had become vulnerable. 'Be careful,' I warned. 'If you turn down my offer, I'll tell Marianne the truth and send you off without further ado. It won't be easy for you to find another job.'

He could not guess the price I would have paid to keep my secret. Besides, he was old and tired.

'It will be very hard for me to leave you,' he said. 'But I count on your generosity to soften the rigours of exile.'

'I hope you'll be happy in Russia and that you'll spend the rest of your days there.'

'Oh, I wouldn't want to die without seeing you again.'

There was a note of menace in his voice and I thought, 'I have something to fear now, something to defend. I'm in love and I can suffer. I'm a man again, at last.'

❧

'I can hear your heart beating,' I said to Marianne.

Day was dawning. My head was lying on her bosom which rose and fell with an even rhythm, and I could hear the muffled throb of her heart. Every beat pumped a stream of blood into her arteries, and then that same pulsating blood flowed back to her heart again. Far away, on a silvery beach, waves, driven by the moon, were rising and falling as they beat against the shore. In the heavens, the earth was hurtling towards the sun, the moon towards the earth, in one immense, fixed and frozen fall.

'Of course it's beating,' she said.

It seemed perfectly natural to her that blood should stream through her veins, that the earth should move beneath her feet. But I was still not used to these strange notions. I listened carefully: I could hear her heart-beats. Could not the earth's pulse be heard as well?

She gently pushed me away. 'Let me get up,' she said.

'You have plenty of time. I'm so comfortable . . .'

A ray of light filtered through the curtains. In the half-light I could see the silk-padded walls, the dressing-table covered with ornaments, frilly petticoats thrown higgledy-piggledy over a chair. There were flowers in a vase. All these things were real; they were not like things one sees in dreams. And yet these flowers, these porcelain figures, that scent of iris, did not really belong to my life either. It seemed to me as if in an immense leap through eternity, I had landed in a moment of time which had been prepared for someone else.

'But it's late,' said Marianne.

'Are you bored with me?'

'I'm bored with doing nothing,' she answered. 'I have so much to do.'

I let her go. She was eager to start her day. It was normal; time did not have the same value for her as it did for me.

'What are these many things you have to do?' I asked. 'Firstly, the decorators are coming to do the small drawing-room.' She drew the curtains. 'You haven't told me what colour you prefer.'

'I don't know.'

'But you must have a preference. Almond green or lime green?'

'Almond green.'

'You just say anything,' she said reproachfully.

She had set about redecorating the house from top to bottom, and it amazed me to see her taking so long considering a wall-paper design or the shade of a piece of silk. 'Is it worth it, going to all that trouble for a mere thirty or forty years?' I thought. It was as if she were preparing to settle down for eternity. For a moment I watched her silently bustling about around the room. She always dressed with great care; she liked clothes and jewellery as much as she liked flowers, paintings, books, music, the theatre and politics. I admired the way she could devote herself to everything with the same passion. She stopped abruptly in front of the window.

'Where shall we have the aviary?' she asked. 'By the big oak or under the linden tree?'

'It might be nice if the brook ran through it,' I suggested.

'You're right! We'll put it over the brook near the blue cedar.' She smiled. 'You see? You're becoming an excellent adviser.'

Almond green or lime green? She was right; if you looked carefully there were hundreds of shades of green and as many of blue; there were more than a thousand varieties of flowers in the meadows, more than a thousand species of butterflies. Every time the sun set behind the hills, the clouds were of different colours. And Marianne herself had so many different faces that I thought I would never know them all.

'Aren't you getting up?' she asked.

'I'm quite happy just looking at you.'

'How lazy you are! You told me you were going to begin your experiments with diamonds again today.'

'Yes, you're right,' I said, standing up.

She looked at me anxiously. 'It seems to me that if I didn't push you, you'd never set foot in your laboratory. Aren't you curious to know whether or not carbon is a pure element any more?'

'Yes, I am curious. But there's no hurry.'

'You always say that. It's funny. I always have the feeling of having so little time.'

She was brushing her beautiful chestnut-brown hair, hair that would turn white, would fall from her head; and then the skin of her scalp would shrivel and turn to dust. So little time . . . We would love each other for thirty years, forty years, and then her coffin would be lowered into a grave just like those in which Caterina and Beatrice lay. And once again I would become a shadow. I suddenly took hold of her and pressed her to me.

'You're right,' I said. 'Time is too short. A love like ours should never end.'

She looked at me tenderly, slightly surprised at this sudden burst of passion. 'It will only end with us, won't it?' She ran her fingers through my hair and added cheerfully, 'If you die before me, I'll kill myself, you know.'

I hugged her tighter. 'So would I,' I said. 'I won't outlive you.'

I let go of her. Suddenly every minute seemed precious to me. I dressed quickly and hurried down to the laboratory. A hand was turning on the face of the clock; for the first time in centuries, I wanted to stop it. So little time . . . Before allowing thirty years to go by, before allowing a year to go by, before tomorrow, her questions had to be answered, for what she did not know today, she would never know. I placed a diamond in a crucible. Would I finally succeed in making it burn? It sparkled, limpid and obstinate, concealing its stubborn secret somewhere within its transparency. Would I ever discover that secret? Would I discover the secrets of the air, of water, of all those familiar yet mysterious things before it was too late? I remembered the old loft with its smell of herbs. The secret was there, hidden in the plants and powders, and I had thought angrily, 'Why can't it be discovered today?' Petrucchio had spent his life bent over his retorts and he died without knowing. Blood flowed in our veins, the earth was turning, and he did not know it; he would never know it. I wished I could have turned back the clock and brought him armfuls of those scientific discoveries of which he dreamed so much. But it was impossible; the door had closed. And one day another door would close. Marianne too would sink into the past, and I was powerless to leap ahead into future centuries to find and bring back to her the knowledge for which she yearned. There was nothing to do but wait for time to pass, to endure each minute of its fastidious unfolding. I stopped staring at the diamond whose false transparency fascinated me. I shouldn't waste my time dreaming. Thirty years, a year, a day, a mere mortal lifetime. Her hours were numbered. My hours were numbered.

Seated by the fireside, Sophie was reading *Pygmalion*, and the others, assembled at the far end of the small drawing-room, lined with almond-green silk, were discussing the best system for governing mankind. As if there were any way to govern man! I pushed open the doors to the terrace. Why hadn't Marianne returned yet? Dusk had already fallen. All that could be seen were the black trees in the white snow. The garden smelt cold: a pure mineral smell which I seemed to be breathing in for the first time. 'Do you like the snow?' When I was with her, I liked the snow; she should have been there, beside me. I went back into the drawing-room and glanced moodily at Sophie who was reading quietly. I disliked her calm face, her sudden effusions of gaiety and the down-to-earth good sense she always displayed. I did not care for Marianne's friends. But I felt a need to talk to someone.

'Marianne should have been home long ago,' I said.

Sophie looked up. 'She must have been detained in Paris,' she said as if it were patently obvious.

'Unless she has had an accident . . .'

She laughed, revealing her large, white teeth. 'What a worrier you are!'

She returned to her book. They never looked as if they had the slightest suspicion that their species was mortal. And yet a blow, a fall – a horse's hoof, a carriage wheel flying off – was enough to break their brittle bones to pieces, to make their hearts stop beating, to silence them forever. In my heart, I could feel that biting feeling I knew so well. Sooner or later, it would happen; I would see her dead. *They* could think, 'I shall die first. We shall die together,' and for them, loneliness would be finite . . . All of a sudden, I rushed to the door and ran down the steps. Muffled by the snow, I had recognized the sound of her carriage.

'You gave me such a fright! What happened?'

She smiled at me and took my arm. Her waist was hardly swollen at all, but her face was drawn, her complexion sallow.

'Why are you so late?' I asked.

'It's nothing,' she said. 'I felt slightly sick and I just waited until I felt better.'

'Sick!'

I looked angrily at her tired eyes. Why had I given in to her? She had wanted a child, and now strange and dangerous alchemies were taking place inside her. I sat her down by the fire.

'That's the last time you're going to Paris.'

'What nonsense! I'm feeling wonderful!'

Sophie gave us an inquisitive, knowing look.

'She felt sick,' I said.

'That's only normal,' Sophie remarked.

'Yes, and dying is normal, too,' I replied.

She smiled in a knowing, competent way. 'Pregnancy isn't a mortal illness, you know.'

'The doctor said I don't need to rest until April,' Marianne observed. Two men from the other group walked over to join us and, looking at them cheerfully, she said, 'What will become of the Museum if I stop giving my time to it?'

'They'll have to do without you soon whether you like it or not.'

'Between now and April, Verdier will have completely recovered,' Marianne said.

Verdier looked at me and said cheerfully, 'If Marianne is tired, I'll go back to Paris immediately. These four days in the country have already done me a world of good.'

'Don't be insane!' Marianne exclaimed. 'You need a good, long rest.'

He did not look well in fact. His complexion was pale and there were dark patches under his eyes.

'Well, then, why don't you both take a rest?' I said impatiently.

'In that case, we might just as well close down the University,' Verdier replied.

His ironical tone annoyed me. 'Why not?' I said. Marianne looked at me reproachfully and I added, 'Nothing is so important that you risk ruining your health.'

'Yes, but if you have to look after it so carefully, good health is no longer a boon,' Verdier stated.

I looked at them irritably. They formed a solid block against me. Grouped together as they were, they refused to measure their strength, to count their days; each one refused on his own account as well as for each other; in their common obstinacy they felt united as one. And yet my concern carried no weight with Marianne. Despite all my love for her, I was not of her kind; any mortal man was closer to her than I was.

'What's new in Paris?' asked Sophie in a conciliatory tone.

'There was confirmation that chairs in experimental physics are going to be created throughout France,' Marianne replied.

Prouvost's face lit up. 'That's the most important thing we've yet achieved,' he said.

'Yes, it's a great step forward,' Marianne agreed. 'Who knows? Things may move faster than we ever dared hope.'

Her eyes were beaming brightly; I walked quietly towards the door. I could not bear to hear her speaking so fervently of those days when even the memory of her would be blotted from the face of the earth. It was perhaps that, more than anything else, that separated me from them so irremediably; their lives stretched out towards a future in which their present efforts would reach fruition. While for me, the future was a loathsome, unknown time, a time when Marianne would be dead, when our life together would be buried beneath the centuries, useless, lost. And *that* time, in turn, was also destined to be buried, lost and useless.

Outside, it was a fine night, cold and dry. Thousands of stars were twinkling in the sky: the same stars. I looked up at those motionless bodies pulling at each other with opposing forces. The moon was being pulled towards the earth, the earth towards the sun. Was the sun being pulled? By what unknown stars? And could it not be possible that its flight compensated somehow for the earth's and that in reality our planet was fixed in the middle of the heavens? How could one know? Would it ever be known? And would they ever know why masses attract each other? Attraction: it was a handy word that was used to explain everything. But was it any more than a word? Were we really any wiser than the alchemists of Carmona? We had brought to light certain facts which they did not know, and we had classified them in an orderly manner. But were we a single step closer to the mysterious heart of things? Was the word Force any clearer than the word Virtue? Or Attraction clearer than Soul? And when it was said that Electricity was the cause of those phenomena which resulted from rubbing amber or glass, were we any better informed than when God was considered to be the cause of the world?

I lowered my eyes to the ground. The light from the windows of the drawing-room shone over the white lawn, and on the other side of those windows, by the fireplace, they were talking, talking of that future time when nothing would be left of them but dust. All around them stretched the infinite sky, endless eternity, but one day there would be an end for them; that was why it was so easy for them to live. In their tightly sealed arks they drifted fearlessly from night to night; they drifted together. I walked slowly towards the house; for me there was no shelter, no future, no present. Despite Marianne's love, I was forever excluded.

❧

'Snail, show me your horns,' chanted Henriette. She had filled her pail with snails and was taking them one by one and sticking their suction-cup bellies against a tree trunk. Jacques was circling around the linden tree, trying to repeat the simple refrain; Marianne followed him apprehensively.

'Don't you think Sophie is right? It seems to me that his left leg is a little twisted,' she said.

'Take him to a doctor.'

'I did, but he didn't notice anything.'

She examined his chubby little legs anxiously. Both children were pictures of health, but she could never stop worrying about them. Would they be handsome enough, healthy enough, intelligent, happy? I felt guilty about not being able to share her worries. I liked the children because Marianne had carried them inside her womb, but they were not really my children. I once had a son, a son of my own: he died at the age of twenty; not a trace of his bones remained in the earth.

'Will you buy a snail from me?'

I stroked Henriette's cheek. She had my high forehead, my nose, a hard, precise little air about her. She bore no resemblance to her mother.

'This one is certainly sturdy enough,' said Marianne. She studied the little face, as if trying to decipher the child's future. 'Do you think she'll be pretty?'

'Yes, of course.'

No doubt she would be a pretty young woman one day. And then she would grow old, become ugly and toothless, and one day I would learn of her death.

'Which one do you prefer?' Marianne asked.

'I don't know. I like both of them equally.'

I smiled at her and she slipped her hand in mine. It was a beautiful day. The birds were singing in the aviary and wasps were buzzing among the wisteria. I was holding

Marianne's hand in mine, but I was lying to her. I loved her, but I did not share her joys, her troubles, her anguish; I did not love what she loved. Next to me, she was alone, and she was unaware of it.

'Well now!' she said, 'I wonder who could be calling on us today.'

Bells were tinkling along the avenue, a carriage passed through the gate and a man stepped out. He was an old man, rather portly and well dressed, who appeared to have difficulty in walking. He came towards us with a smile on his large face. It was Bompard.

'What are you doing here?' I asked in a surprised voice which barely concealed my anger.

'I returned from Russia last week,' he answered, still smiling. 'Introduce me.'

'This is Bompard,' I said to Marianne. 'You must have noticed him at Madame de Montesson's some years ago.'

'Yes, I remember.' She studied him with curiosity, and once he had sat down, she said, 'So you've just returned from Russia. Is it a beautiful country?'

'It's cold,' he replied bitterly.

They began to speak of St. Petersburg, but I stopped listening. The blood had risen from my heart to my throat, from my throat to my head. I was suffocating. I recognized that black sensation of dizziness: it was fear.

'What's the matter?' Marianne asked.

'The sun's given me a headache.'

She gave me a surprised, worried look. 'Would you like to go and rest?' she asked.

'No, it'll go away.' I stood up. 'Come,' I said to Bompard, 'I'll show you around the grounds. Excuse us for a moment, Marianne.'

She nodded. But she followed us with puzzled eyes. I had never kept any secrets from her.

'Your wife is charming,' Bompard said. 'I'd like to know her better and speak to her of you.'

'Be careful, Bompard,' I said menacingly. 'I can still take revenge on you. Remember?'

'It seems to me that you would now stand to lose a great deal if you resorted to any misplaced violence.'

'I take it you want money. How much?'

'You're really very happy, aren't you?' Bompard said.

'Don't worry yourself about my happiness. How much do you want?'

'Happiness is never too expensive. I want fifty thousand pounds a year.'

'Thirty thousand,' I said.

'Fifty thousand. Take it or leave it.'

My heart was pounding violently. This time I was not playing to lose, but to win; I was not cheating. My love was real, and a real menace was hanging over me. I had to prevent Bompard from suspecting the true extent of his power, otherwise he would have soon ruined me with his demands. I did not want Marianne to be reduced to a life of poverty.

'I'll leave it,' I said. 'Go and speak to Marianne. She will eventually forgive me for deceiving her, and you'll have gained nothing.'

He hesitated. 'Forty thousand.'

'Thirty thousand. Take it or leave it.'

'I'll take it,' he said.

'You'll have the money tomorrow. And now get out of here.'

Wiping my sweaty hands, I watched him walk away. I felt as if I had just gambled with my life.

'What did he want?' Marianne asked.

'Money.'

'Why weren't you more welcoming?'

'He brings back bad memories.'

'Is that why you seemed so upset when you saw him?'

'Yes.'

She examined me suspiciously. 'It's funny,' she said, 'but it is almost as if he frightened you.'

'You're imagining things. Why should I be frightened of him?'

'Perhaps there's something between you two that I don't know about.'

'I've already told you that he's someone to whom I once did great harm. I felt very guilty about it.'

'Is that all?' she said.

'Of course.' I drew her close to me. 'What are you worrying about? Did I ever keep any secrets from you?'

She stroked my forehead. 'Ah! If only I could read your thoughts,' she said. 'I'm jealous of anything that goes on in your head that doesn't concern me, as well as of your whole past which I scarcely known anything about.'

'I've told you everything.'

'You told me, but I don't *know* it.' She pressed herself to me.

'I was unhappy,' I said. 'I was no longer alive. You gave me happiness, you gave me life . . . '

I suddenly broke off. Words were forming on my lips. I had an overwhelming longing to stop lying to her, to lay bare the whole truth before her. It seemed to me that then, if she still loved me as an immortal man, I really would be saved, together with my whole past and my hopeless future.

'Yes?' she said.

Her eyes were questioning me. She sensed that I had something else to tell her. But I remembered other eyes: Carlier's, Beatrice's, Antonio's, and I was frightened of seeing the change in her expression.

'I love you,' I said. 'Isn't that enough?'

I smiled and her worried face relaxed. She smiled back confidently at me.

'Yes, that's enough for me,' she said.

I pressed my lips gently against her mouth, those lips she believed to be perishable, like her own. And I prayed: 'May Heaven prevent her from ever discovering my treachery!'

Fifteen years went by. Bompard had asked me several times for rather large sums of money, which I gave him, but for some time I had heard nothing further from him. We were living happily. That evening, Marianne had put on a black taffeta dress with red stripes. Standing in front of her mirror, she studied herself carefully. I still found her very beautiful. Abruptly, she turned around.

'How young you look!' she exclaimed.

Little by little, I had whitened my hair; I wore glasses, I did everything possible to create the illusion of an elderly man, but I could not disguise my face.

'You look young, too,' I said with a smile. 'You don't notice it when people you love grow old.'

'That's true,' she said. She leaned over a bouquet of chrysanthemums and began plucking the faded petals. 'I'm so sorry about having to go to that ball with Henriette. It's an evening lost. I like our evenings together so much . . . '

'There'll be others,' I said.

'But this one will be lost,' she said with a sigh. She opened one of the drawers of her dressing-table and took out a few rings which she slipped on her fingers. 'Jacques liked this one so much. Do you remember?' she asked, showing me a heavy silver ring in which a blue stone was set.

'Yes, I remember,' I answered. But in truth, I did not remember; I remembered almost nothing about him.

'He was always so sad whenever we went to Paris without him. He was so sensitive, much more so than Henriette.'

She remained silent for a moment; her face was turned towards the window. Outside it was raining, a fine autumn rain. Above the half-bare trees, the sky looked like cotton. Marianne walked cheerfully up to me and put her hands on my shoulders.

'Tell me what you're going to do, so that when I think of you I'll have a clear picture in my mind.'

'I'm going down to the laboratory and I shall work until I feel sleepy. And you?'

'We'll go back to the house to have a snack and then I'll be bored stiff at the ball until one o'clock in the morning.'

'Are you ready, Mother?' Henriette asked as she entered the room.

She was slender and shapely like her mother, and she had inherited her blue eyes. But her forehead was a little too high, her nose too severe – the Fosca nose. She was wearing a dress covered with little sprays of flowers which did not suit the strong features of her face. She proffered her forehead to me.

'Good-bye, Father. Are you going to be bored without us?'

'I'm afraid so,' I replied.

She laughed as she kissed me. 'I'll have fun enough for two.'

'Till tomorrow morning,' said Marianne. She gently stroked my face and murmured, 'Think of me.'

I leaned against the window and watched them climb into their carriage which I followed with my eyes until it reached the first turning in the avenue. I felt at a loss. No matter what I did, I remained a stranger in this house. I felt as if I had moved in only yesterday and would be leaving tomorrow. I could never feel at home anywhere. I opened one of the drawers of the dressing-table. Inside it, there was a little chest which contained a lock of Jacques' hair, a miniature picture of his face, some dried flowers. In another box, Marianne had stored some souvenirs of Henriette's childhood: a first tooth, a page of writing, a piece of embroidery. I closed the drawer. I envied Marianne possessing so many treasures.

I went down to the laboratory; it was empty. The sound of my steps on the white tiles echoed dolefully in the room. Around me, the flasks, test tubes and retorts had a stubborn, hostile aspect. I went over to the microscope. Marianne had sprinkled a fine golden powder over one of the slides. I knew it would make her happy if I were able to give her an exact description of my experiment. But as far as I was concerned, I no longer had any illusions: I would never break through the crusty surface of the exterior world. Even with the aid of microscopes and telescopes, it was still only with my eyes that I saw things; objects existed for us only when they were visible and tangible, situated sensibly in space and time amid other objects. Even if we were to fly to the moon, or go down to the ocean depths, we would still remain men in the heart of a human world. As for those mysterious realities which revealed themselves to our senses – forces, planets, molecules, waves – they were nothing more than the yawning gulf of our ignorance which we disguised with words. Nature would never yield up her secret to us; she had no secrets. We were the ones who invented questions and then formulated the answers to them; in the depths of our retorts we would never discover anything but our own thoughts, thoughts that might in the course of centuries multiply, become more complex, be formed into ever more vast and subtle systems. But never would these thoughts be capable of tearing me from myself. I put my eye to the microscope; everything would always pass through my eyes, through my thoughts. Never would anything be *other*, never would I be anyone other.

It was close to midnight when, to my surprise, I heard the jingling of bells, the sound of an approaching carriage. The wet earth splashed beneath the horses' hoofs. With a torch in my hand, I went to the front door. Marianne jumped down from the carriage; she was alone.

'Why are you back so early?' I asked.

She walked past me without kissing me, without even looking at me. I followed her into the library. She went over to the fire and she seemed to me to be shivering.

'Are you cold?' I asked, touching her hand.

She recoiled quickly. 'No.'

'What's wrong?'

She turned her face towards me. Beneath her black hood, she was very pale. She looked at me as if she were seeing me for the first time. I had seen that expression in other eyes. It was one of horror.

'What's wrong?' I repeated. But I knew.

'Is it true?' she asked.

'What are you talking about?'

'What Bompard told me, is it true?'

'You saw Bompard? Where?'

'A messenger brought a letter to the house. I went to his home. I found him there sitting in an armchair, paralyzed. He told me he wanted to take his revenge on you before dying.' She spoke haltingly. Her eyes glared. She came towards me. 'He's right,' she said. 'Not a wrinkle on your face.' She held out her hand and touched my hair. 'It's been dyed, hasn't it?'

'What did he tell you?'

'Everything. Carmona, Charles V . . . It seems incredible. Is it true?'

'It's true,' I said.

'True!' She stepped backwards and stared at me with a wild expression on her face.

'Don't look at me like that, Marianne. I'm not a ghost.'

'A ghost would be less of a stranger to me than you,' she said slowly.

'Marianne! We love each other,' I said. 'Nothing can spoil a love like ours. What does the past matter? Or the future? What Bompard told you changes nothing between us.'

'Everything is changed, forever.' She fell into an armchair and hid her face in her hands. 'Ah! I'd rather you were dead!'

I kneeled down in front of her and pulled her hands apart. 'Look at me,' I said. 'Don't you know me? It's me, it really is me. I haven't become someone else.'

'Why did you hide the truth from me?' she said vehemently.

'If I hadn't, would you have loved me?'

'Never!'

'Why not?' I asked. 'Do you believe I'm accursed? Is there a demon inside me?'

'I gave myself to you completely,' she said. 'And I believed you had given yourself to me for life, for death. And you were only lending yourself to me for a few scant years.' A sob choked her voice. 'Just another woman among millions. One day you won't even remember my name. And it will still be you. It will be you and no one else.' She stood up. 'No! No! It's not possible!' she cried out.

'My love, listen to me. You know very well I belong to you. I've never belonged like this to anyone else, and I never will again.'

I took her in my arms and she abandoned herself to me with a sort of indifference. She looked deathly tired.

'Listen,' I said. 'Listen to me!' She nodded her head. 'You know very well that before I met you I was dead. It was you who brought me to life. And when you leave me, I'll become a ghost again.'

'You weren't dead,' she said, tearing herself away from me. 'And you'll never be a real ghost. Never for a moment were you like me. Everything was false.'

'You could never make a mortal man suffer more than I'm suffering at this moment,' I said. 'None of them could ever have loved you as I love you.'

'Everything was false,' she repeated. 'Your suffering is not like mine, and you love me from the depths of another world. You're lost to me.'

'No,' I said. 'We've just found each other, because now we'll live with the truth.'

'There can be no truth between you and me.'

'My love is true.'

'What is your love?' she said scornfully. 'When two mortal beings love each other, that love moulds them together body and soul; it's their very substance. But for you, it's . . . it's an accident.' She put her hand to her forehead. 'How alone I am!'

'I'm alone, too,' I said.

For a long while we sat side by side without speaking. Tears were trickling down her cheeks.

'Have you tried to understand what my fate is?' I asked.

'Yes,' she answered. She looked at me and her face twisted and fell. 'It's horrible.'

'Don't you want to help me?'

'Help you?' She shrugged her shoulders. 'I can help you for ten or twenty years. But what's that?'

'You can give me strength for centuries.'

'And after that? Another woman will come to your aid.' Passionately, she added, 'All I want is to stop loving you.'

'Forgive me,' I said. 'I had no right to impose such a fate on you.'

Tears welled in my eyes. She threw herself into my arms and began to sob desperately.

'And I can't even hope for another fate,' she said.

I pushed open the gate to the meadow and went to sit down in the shade of a red beech tree. Cattle were grazing on the sun-drenched grass; it was very hot. With my fingers, I cracked the empty shell of a beechnut. I had spent several hours bent over a microscope and it was a pleasure simply to be looking at the ground with my own eyes. Marianne was waiting for me by the linden tree, or in the cool drawing-room with its lowered blinds, but I felt better away from her. As long as we were apart, we could imagine ourselves being together again.

A cow had stopped beside a tree and was rubbing its head against the trunk. I imagined for a moment that I was that cow; I felt a rough caress against my cheek, and inside my belly it was dark, green and warm; the world was a huge meadow which I consumed with my mouth, with my eyes. It felt as if the illusion could last for ever. Why wasn't I able to remain eternally beneath that beech tree without moving, without a single desire?

The cow now stood directly in front of me. It was staring at me with its huge eyes with their red lashes. Its stomach

swollen with fresh grass, it calmly contemplated the mysterious creature which was there in front of it and which
seemed to serve no purpose. It stared at me and yet it did
not see me; it was imprisoned in its ruminant universe. And
I in turn looked at the cow, at the smooth sky, the poplar
trees, the golden grass. And what did I see? I was imprisoned
in my own human universe, imprisoned forever.

I lay on my back and gazed at the sky. Never would I pass
through to the other side of that sky. Prisoner of my own
being, I was forever condemned to see nothing around me but
the walls of a dungeon. I looked again at the meadow. The
cow was lying down and chewing the cud; a cuckoo sang out
twice and its calm call, which called to nothing, was swallowed
up by the silence. I stood up and walked towards the house.

Marianne was in her boudoir, seated by the open window.
She smiled at me – a mechanical smile from which life had
withdrawn.

'Did your work go well?'

'I began another experiment today. You should have come
to help me. You're getting lazy.'

'We're no longer in such a hurry, are we?' she said. 'You
have all the time in the world.' Her mouth twisted slightly.
'I'm tired.'

'Don't you feel any better?'

'Still the same.'

She had been complaining of pains in her stomach. She
had grown very thin and her skin had become yellow. Ten
years, twenty years . . . Now I was counting the years, and
sometimes I caught myself thinking, 'Quickly! Let it happen
quickly!' From the day she had discovered my secret, death
had set in upon her.

'What am I going to tell Henriette?' she said after a while.

'Haven't you decided yet?'

'No. I think about it day and night. It's such a serious
matter.'

'Does she love this man?'

'If she loved him, she wouldn't ask my advice. But she might be happier with him than with Louis . . . '

'Perhaps,' I said.

'If she had another kind of life, she'd certainly be very different, don't you think?'

'Certainly.'

We had already had the same conversation more than twenty times, and for the sake of my love for Marianne I wanted to take an interest in the affair. But what difference could it make. Whether Henriette stayed with her husband or went off with her lover, she would still be Henriette.

'Except that if she leaves him, Louis will keep the child. What kind of life would that child have?' Marianne looked at me. Lately, she wore an obsessive, anxious expression on her face. 'Will you look after her?' she asked.

'We'll look after her together,' I replied.

She shrugged her shoulders. 'You know very well I won't be here much longer.' She reached out of the window and picked a cluster of mauve flowers from the wisteria. 'It should give me a sense of security to know that you'll still be here, that you'll always be here. Did it make the others feel secure?'

'Which others?'

'Caterina, Beatrice.'

'Beatrice didn't love me,' I said. 'And Caterina no doubt hoped that God would allow me to join her in heaven one day.'

'Did she tell you that?'

'I don't know. But I'm sure she must have thought it.'

'You don't know? You don't remember?'

'No,' I answered.

'Do you remember anything she ever said?'

'Yes, a few things.'

'And her voice? Can you recall her voice?'

'No,' I admitted. I touched Marianne's hand. 'I never loved her the way I love you.'

'Oh, I know you'll forget me. And it's probably better that way. They must weigh heavily upon you, all those memories.' She placed the flowers in her lap and twisted the petals in her thin fingers.

'You'll live in my heart longer than you'd have lived in the heart of any mortal man,' I said.

'No,' she said bitterly. 'If you were mortal, I'd go on living in you until the end of the world, because for me your death would be the end of the world. Instead, I'm going to die in a world that will never end.'

I said nothing. There was nothing I could say.

'What will you do afterwards?' she asked.

'I'll try to want what you would have wanted, to do as you would have done.'

'Try to remain a man among men,' she said. 'There's no other salvation for you.'

'I'll try,' I promised. 'I care for people now, because they belong to the same species as you.'

'Help them. Put your experience at their service.'

'I will.'

She often spoke to me about my unhappy future, but she could not prevent herself picturing it with her mortal heart.

'Promise me,' she said. A little of her old spirit shone in her eyes.

'I promise.'

A wasp buzzed around the cluster of mauve flowers; in the distance, a cow mooed softly.

'This may be my last summer,' Marianne said.

'Don't speak like that.'

'There will eventually be a summer that will be my last.' She shook her head. 'I don't envy you. But don't envy me either.'

We remained seated by the window for a long while, unable to help one another, more apart than if one of us had been dead, no longer capable of acting in consort or, scarcely, of speaking to each other. And yet we loved each other desperately.

'Carry me over to the window,' Marianne said. 'I'd like to see the sun set one last time.'

'That will tire you.'

'Please. For the last time.'

I pulled back the covers and lifted her in my arms. She had grown so thin that she weighed no more than a child. She drew the curtains apart.

'Yes,' she said. 'I remember. It was so beautiful.' She let the curtains fall back into place. 'For you, everything will continue to exist,' she said with a sob.

I laid her down again in her bed. Her face was yellow and shrivelled; her hair was cut short because its weight tired her, and her head had become so small that it reminded me of those shrunken heads strewn over the grounds of the Indian village.

'So many things will happen,' she said. 'Great things. And I won't be here to see them.'

'You can still hold out for a very long time. The doctor said your heart was very strong.'

'Don't lie,' she said in a sudden fit of anger. 'You've lied enough to me! I know it's over. I'm going, and I'm going alone. And you, you'll stay here without me, forever.' She began to weep uncontrollably. 'All alone! You're letting me leave the world on my own!'

I took her hand and squeezed it tightly. How I longed to be able to say to her: 'I'll die with you. They'll bury us in the same grave. We've lived out our lives and now nothing more exists.'

'Tomorrow the sun will set and I'll be nowhere,' she said. 'There'll be only my body. And one day, when my coffin is opened, there will be nothing left but a handful of dust. Even the bones will have been turned to ashes. Even the bones . . . And for you, everything will go on as if I'd never existed.'

'I'll live with you, through you . . . '

'You'll live without me,' she said. 'And one day, you'll have forgotten me. Oh!', she sobbed, 'It's so unfair!'

'I wish I could die with you.'

'But you can't.'

Sweat was pouring down her face; her hands were cold and moist. 'If only I were able to say to myself: "He'll join me again in ten years, twenty years," it wouldn't be so hard to die. But no. Never! You're leaving me forever.'

'I'll think of you constantly,' I said.

But she seemed not to hear me. Worn out, she fell back on her pillow and murmured, 'I loathe you.'

'Marianne, don't you know how much I love you?'

She shook her head. 'I know everything. I loathe you.'

She closed her eyes; after a moment she seemed to have fallen asleep, but she was weeping as she slept. Henriette came in and sat down beside me; she was a tall woman with hard features.

'Her breathing is slowing down,' she remarked.

'Yes, it's the end.'

Marianne's fingers stiffened, the corners of her mouth dropped in a grimace of suffering, disgust, and reproachfulness. Then she gave one last sigh and her whole body grew slack.

'How peacefully she died,' Henriette said.

Marianne was buried two days later. Her tomb stood in the middle of the cemetery, a stone among stones, taking up no more space under the infinite sky than the precise dimensions of a grave. When the ceremony was over, they went away, leaving Marianne, her tomb and her death behind them. Alone, I sat down on the gravestone. I knew that it was not Marianne who was there in the tomb; it was the body of an old woman with a heart full of bitterness. Marianne, with her smiles, her hopes, her kisses, her tenderness, still stood there

at the edge of the past. I could still see her, I could still speak
to her, smile at her, and I could still feel her eyes upon me,
those eyes that had made me a man among men. In a
moment the door would close forever. I desperately wanted
to prevent it from closing; I had to remain perfectly still,
to see nothing, hear nothing, renounce the actual world. I
lay flat on the ground, closed my eyes, and by exerting all
the strength at my command, I kept the door open, stopped
the present from being born so that the past could continue
to exist.

It lasted a day, a night, and a few hours of the following day.
And then, suddenly, my body gave a start. Nothing actually
happened, but I could distinctly hear the buzzing of bees
among the cemetery's flowers; in the distance, a cow mooed.
I heard it. In the depths of my being, I felt a dull thud. It was
done; the door had closed. No one would ever pass through
it again. I stretched out my numb legs and raised myself
on one elbow. What was I going to do now? Would I get to
my feet and continue to live? Caterina was dead, and Antonio,
Beatrice, Carlier – all those I had loved – were dead, and
I went on living. I was there, the same as I had been for
centuries. My heart might beat a moment in pity, in revolt, in
distress, but I soon forgot. I dug my fingers into the ground
and said aloud in despair, 'I don't want to go on.' A mortal
man could have refused to continue on his way, could have
made his rebellion eternal: he could have killed himself. But
I was a slave to a life which dragged me inexorably towards
indifference and oblivion. It was useless to resist. I got up and
walked slowly back to the house.

When I reached the garden, I looked up and saw that half
the sky was covered with heavy, black clouds, while the other
half was a calm blue. One side of the house seemed grey, while
the frontage was a hard, glaring white. The grass looked
yellow. From time to time the trees and bushes sagged in
the storm-force wind; then everything was still again.
Marianne liked storms. Could I not make her live through

me? I sat down beneath the linden tree, where she used to sit. I watched the violently changing shadows, the white glare of the house; I breathed in the scent of magnolias. But the light and the shadows and the smells did not speak to me. That day was not mine; it remained in suspension, demanding to be lived by Marianne. But she was not there to live it and I could not substitute myself for her. With Marianne's death, an entire world had foundered, a world that would never again emerge into the light. Now, all the flowers began to look alike, the sky's varied shades grew indistinguishable, and the days ahead would have but a single colour: the colour of indifference.

A maid had opened the front door of the inn and, looking at Regina and Fosca suspiciously, had thrown a bucketful of water over the pavement. There was a sound of Venetian blinds being opened on the floor above.

'Perhaps they'll give us some coffee,' Regina said.

They went inside. On hands and knees, a woman was washing the dining-room floor with a large cloth. Regina and Fosca sat down at one of the oilcloth-covered tables.

'Could you give us something to drink?' asked Regina.

The woman looked up, squeezed the wet cloth over a bucket of dirty water and suddenly began to smile.

'I can bring you some coffee with milk.'

'Make it good and hot,' said Regina. She turned to look at Fosca. 'So, only two centuries ago you were still capable of loving.'

'Yes, only two centuries ago.'

'And of course you forgot her immediately, didn't you?'

'Not immediately,' said Fosca. 'I lived beneath her gaze for a long period. I looked after Henriette's daughter, watched her grow up, get married, die. She left a little boy, Armand, and I looked after him, too. Henriette died when the boy was fifteen. She was a hard, selfish old woman and she hated me because she knew my secret.

'But did you think often of Marianne?'

'The world in which I lived was her world, the people were her kind. In working for them, I was working for her. That helped me while away almost fifty years. I did a good deal of research in physics and chemistry.'

'But all that didn't prevent her dying,' Regina said.

'Was there any way to prevent her dying?'

'No, there was surely no way.'

The maid placed a coffee pot, a jug of milk and two large bowls on the table – pink bowls decorated with blue butterflies. 'They're just like the bowls we had when I was a child,' Regina thought. It was a mechanical thought; the words had already lost their meaning. She no longer had a childhood, nor a future; for her, too, there was no more light; no longer any colours or smells. What she could still feel was the sharp, burning sensation in her mouth, her throat. She drank avidly.

'The story is almost over,' Fosca said.

'Finish it,' she said. 'Let's get it finished.'

BOOK V

Somewhere at the far end of the corridors, a drum was beating and everyone turned towards the door. There were tears in Brennand's eyes; Spinelle pursed his lips and his Adam's apple bobbed convulsively up and down in his thin neck. Armand plunged his hand into his coat pocket; his face was deathly pale beneath his short beard. The windows were closed, but the cries rising from the square below could be plainly heard. They were shouting, 'No more Bourbons! Long live the Republic! Long live La Fayette!' It was very hot. Beads of sweat formed on Armand's forehead, but I knew that an icy shiver was running down his spine. Now, after all the hundreds of years, I could read their thoughts. I could feel the cold of the metal in his damp hand, the cold of the iron railing of the balcony against my own hand. They were shouting, 'Long live Antonio Fosca! Long live Carmona!' A church was burning in the night; victory blazed up to the sky and the black ashes of defeat fell as rain on my heart. There was an atmosphere of falsehood in the air. I gripped the balustrade and I thought, 'Is there nothing a man can do?' And *his* hand tightened around the butt of

a revolver and he was thinking, 'I can do something.' He was
ready to die to convince himself of it.

Suddenly the drum stopped beating. There was a sound
of footsteps and a man appeared in the doorway. He
was smiling, but he was pale, as pale as Armand. Beneath
the tricolour sash across his chest, his heart was beating
heavily; his mouth was dry. La Fayette was walking beside
him. Armand slowly withdrew his hand from his pocket.
I grabbed his wrist.

'It's useless,' I said. 'I took out the bullets.'

A thunderous roar filled the hall – the roar of the sea, the
wind, of volcanos. The man walked past us. I held Armand's
wrist tightly and it grew limp in my hand. I took away his
revolver. He looked at me and his cheeks became slightly
flushed.

'You've betrayed us,' he said.

He walked to the door and ran down the stairs. I ran after
him. In the square they were waving tricolour flags and some
were still shouting, 'Long live the Republic!' But most of
them were now silent; hesitant, they were staring fixedly the
windows of the City Hall. Armand took a few steps and
grabbed hold of a lamppost, like a drunken man. His legs
were trembling. He was crying. He was crying because he
had been defeated and because his life had been saved. He
was lying on a bed with a hole in his belly; he was the victor
and he was dead. He was smiling. Suddenly a great clamour
arose from the crowd. 'Long live La Fayette! Long live the
Duke of Orléans!' Armand lifted his head and saw the general
and the Duke embracing each other on the balcony of the
City Hall, draped in the folds of a tricolour flag.

'They won,' Armand said. In his voice there was no anger,
only a great weariness. 'You had no right to do that. It was
our only chance.'

'It would have been a pointless suicide,' I said drily. 'What
does the Duke matter? Nothing. His death wouldn't change
anything. The bourgeoisie has made up its mind to snatch

this Revolution from us, and it will succeed because the country isn't yet ripe for the Republic.'

'Listen to them!' Armand said. 'They allow themselves to be manoeuvered like children. Won't someone ever open their eyes?'

'You're a child yourself,' I said, putting my hand on his shoulder. 'Do you think three days of violence are enough to educate a whole people?'

'They wanted freedom,' said Armand. 'They gave their blood for it.'

'They gave their blood, but do they know why? They themselves don't know what they really want.'

We had reached the banks of the Seine. Armand was walking beside me, his head bowed, wearily dragging his feet.

'Just yesterday, victory was within our reach,' he said.

'No. You would never have been victorious because you weren't capable of exploiting your success. You weren't ready.'

A white surplice, ballooning up in the water, was drifting down the river. Tied up alongside the quay was a boat flying a black flag. Men were carrying stretchers which they set down on the river bank and the stench rose up towards the silent crowd leaning over the parapet of the bridge. It was the smell of Rivella, of the Roman squares, of the battlefields, the smell of victories and defeats, so insipid after the red burst of blood. They piled up the bodies on the boat and they covered them with straw.

'So they died for nothing,' said Armand.

I looked at the sun-coloured straw beneath which human flesh, crawling with maggots, was fermenting. They had died for humanity, liberty, progress, happiness; they had died for Carmona, for the Empire, for a future that wasn't theirs; they had died because they always die eventually, die for nothing. But I did not utter the words that came to my lips; I had learned to speak *their* language.

'They died for the Revolution of tomorrow,' I said. 'During these three days, the people have discovered their power. They still don't know how to use it, but tomorrow they will know. They'll know if only you devote yourself to preparing for the future instead of seeking a pointless martyrdom.'

'You're right,' he said. 'It's not martyrs the Republic needs.' He leaned against the parapet for a moment longer, his eyes fixed on the funeral boat, and then he turned around. 'I think I'll go over to the newspaper.'

'I'll go with you,' I said.

We walked away from the river. At the corner of the street a man was sticking a poster on a wall. Printed in large, black letters it read, 'The Duke of Orléans is not a Bourbon, he is a Valois.' Further on, posted on a fence, we saw the shredded Republican manifesto.

'And there's nothing we can do!' Armand exclaimed. 'Yet yesterday we could have done anything!'

'Patience,' I said. 'You have your whole life before you.'

'Yes, thanks to you.' He gave me a forced smile. 'How did you guess?'

'I saw you loading your revolver. It's not very difficult to read your thoughts.'

As we crossed the street, Armand studied me with a perplexed expression on his face. 'I often wonder why you look after me with such concern,' he said.

'I've already told you. I loved your mother very much, and you've become dear to me because of her.'

He said nothing, but as we passed in front of a shop window covered with bullet-holes, he stopped me. 'Have you ever noticed how alike we look?' he asked.

I looked at the two reflections: this immutable countenance that had been mine for centuries and his inexperienced, young face with its long, black hair, its short beard, its ardent eyes. We had the same nose, the Fosca nose.

'What's on your mind?' I asked.

He paused. 'I'll tell you some other time.'

We arrived in front of the building in which the *Progrès* was published. On the pavement was a mob of men dressed in tatters who were taking turns at barging down the closed door with their shoulders. They were shouting: 'Shoot the Republicans!'

'The idiots!' Armand exclaimed.

'Let's go in by the back door,' I said.

We circled the block of houses and knocked at the rear door. A small window opened, then the door.

'Come in quickly,' said Voiron. His shirt was open and his chest was damp with sweat. He was holding a rifle in his hand. 'Try to make Garnier leave. They'll kill him.'

Armand bounded up the stairs. Garnier, surrounded by a group of young people, was sitting on the edge of a table in the editorial room. They were unarmed. From the ground floor, bloodthirsty yells and a dull pounding could be heard.

'What are you waiting for?' Armand said. 'Get out by the back door.'

'No,' Garnier said firmly. 'I want to be here to greet them.'

He was afraid. I could see it in the corners of his mouth and in his clenched fingers.

'The Republic doesn't need martyrs,' Armand said. 'Don't let yourself be murdered.'

'I don't want them to smash my presses and burn my papers. I'll wait for them.'

His voice was firm, his eyes cold. But I could sense the fear in him. Were he not afraid, he would no doubt have agreed to leave.

'I'm not stopping anyone else from leaving,' he added haughtily.

'That's not true,' I said. 'You know very well that these young people here won't desert you.'

He looked around him and seemed to be wavering. But at that very moment, there was a loud crash, followed by the sound of a wild rush on the staircase. 'Death to the

Republicans!' they shouted. The glass door flew open and they stormed into the room with their bayonets thrust forward. They looked half drunk.

'What do you want?' Garnier asked in a calm, dry tone of voice.

They hesitated and then one of them cried out, 'We want your dirty Republican hide!'

As the man thrust forward, I threw myself in front of Garnier. The bayonet struck me full in the chest.

'Are you murderers?' Garnier cried out.

His voice came to me from very far away. I could feel the blood soaking my shirt and there seemed to be a mist surrounding me. 'Perhaps this time I'll die,' I thought, 'Perhaps it will finally be over!' And then I found myself lying on a table with a white cloth wrapped around my chest. Garnier was still speaking and the men were retreating towards the door.

'Don't move,' Armand said to me. 'I'll go and find a doctor.'

'It won't be necessary,' I said. 'The bayonet hit a bone and stopped dead. There's nothing wrong with me.'

Outside in the street below, they were still shouting, 'Shoot the Republicans!' But the men who had burst into the room now turned on their heels and disappeared down the stairs. I got up, buttoned my shirt and put on my coat.

'You saved my life,' Garnier said.

'Don't thank me before you know what life has in store for you.'

'Now you'll have to go on living in fear for years,' I thought.

'I'm going home to rest,' I said.

Armand came with me. For a few moments we walked along in silence, and then he said, 'You should be dead.'

'The bayonet struck a bone . . .'

'No normal man,' he interrupted, 'could get up and walk away after being wounded like that.' He seized my wrist. 'Tell me the truth.'

'What truth?'

'Why do you watch over me? Why do we look alike? Why didn't you die when the bayonet went right through you?' He spoke in a feverish voice and his fingers tightened around my arm. 'I've suspected it for a long time . . . '

'I don't know what you're talking about.'

'Ever since I was a child, I've known that among my ancestors there is a man who will never die. And ever since childhood I've wanted to meet him . . . '

'Your mother spoke to me of that legend,' I said. 'Does it really seem credible to you?'

'I've always believed it,' he said. 'And I always thought that we'd be able to do great things together if he was at all fond of me.'

His eyes gleamed and he looked at me fervently. Charles had turned his head away; his lower lip had sagged loosely, his eyes had seemed dead beneath his drooping eye-lids. And I had promised, 'We'll do great things!'

I remained silent and Armand said impatiently, 'Is it a secret? Why all the mystery?'

'You believe me immortal and you can still look at me without feeling horrified?'

'Why should I be horrified?'

A smile lit up his face. He suddenly seemed very young, and something stirred in my heart: something sickly, something very ancient and a little musty. Fountains were playing in a garden.

'It's you, isn't it?' he said.

'Yes.'

'Then the future is ours!' he said. 'Thank you for having saved my life!'

'Don't be so happy about it. Being with me is dangerous for mortal men. Their lives suddenly seem too short, their undertakings pointless.'

'I realize I have only a normal man's life before me,' he said. 'Your presence doesn't change that at all.' He looked at me as if he were seeing me for the first time, and already he was desperately seeking to take advantage of the extraordinary opportunity that had just been given to him. 'What things you must have seen! Did you take part in the great Revolution?'

'Yes.'

'Will you tell me about it?' he said.

'I wasn't very involved in it.'

'Oh,' he said, looking at me disappointedly.

'Well, here I am,' I said abruptly as we arrived at the door to my house.

'Would you mind if I came in with you for a moment?'

'I never mind anything.'

I opened the door to the library. From out of an oval frame, Marianne was smiling, her blue dress revealing her young shoulders.

'That's your mother's grandmother,' I said. 'She was my wife.'

'She was beautiful,' Armand said politely. His eyes circled the room. 'Have you read all those books?'

'Most of them.'

'You must be a great scientist.'

'I'm no longer interested in science.'

I looked at Marianne and I felt a strong desire to speak to her. She had been dead many years, but for Armand she only began to exist from that day. If only she could come to life again – young, ardent and beautiful – in his heart.

'She had faith in science,' I said. 'Like you, she believed in progress, reason, freedom. She was passionately devoted to the happiness of mankind.'

'Don't you believe in that?' he asked.

'Of course. But for her, it was more than that. She was so alive; everything she touched came to life: flowers, ideas . . . '

'Women are often more wholehearted than us,' said Armand.

I drew the curtains and lit a lamp. What was Marianne to him? One dead person among millions of others. She was smiling, but her smile was frozen in the middle of an oval portrait. She would never be born again.

'Why aren't you interested in science any more?' asked Armand. He was swaying from fatigue and his eyelids were twitching, but he was determined not to leave before discovering how to make the most of me.

'It doesn't allow man to escape from himself,' I said.

'But is it necessary for man to escape from himself?'

'For you, I'm sure it's not necessary.' I looked at him and added sharply, 'You ought to get some rest. You look completely worn out.'

'I haven't slept much for three days,' he said with an apologetic smile.

'It's a trying experience dying and coming to life again all in the same day,' I said. 'Lie down on the couch and go to sleep.'

He threw himself on the divan. 'I'll take a little nap,' he said.

I stood beside the couch. Evening was falling. Outside, the clamour of festivities was drifting through the dusk, but in my study, with the curtains drawn, no other sound could be heard but Armand's light breathing. He was asleep already. For the first time in four days, he was set free from fear, from hope. He was sleeping, and it was I who was watching, feeling in my heart the weight of that long day that was slowly dying on the other side of the windows. Pergola's deserted squares, Florence's glittering, inaccessible domes, the flat taste of wine on a balcony in Carmona . . . But there had also been the triumphant rapture, Malatesta's hearty laughter, Antonio's smile as he lay dying, Carlier looking at the yellow river and snarling, 'I made it.' And there was I, ripping open my shirt with both hands, choking with life. And in my breast there had also been hope, the red sun in a cloudy sky, the blue line of hills far away on the plain, sails disappearing over the horizon, snatched up by the earth's invisible curvature. I leaned over Armand and looked at his young face with its black stubble of a beard. What was he dreaming of? He was sleeping, as Tancredi, Antonio, Charles, and Carlier had slept. They all looked alike, and yet for each of them life had a unique flavour, a taste that none of the others had ever known. Their lives would never begin again; in each of them it was complete, wholly new. He wasn't dreaming of Pergola's squares, nor of the great yellow river. He had his own dreams and I could not rob him of even the smallest particle of them. Never would I be able to escape from myself, to slip inside one of them and live his life. I could try to serve him, but I would never see through his eyes, feel with his heart. I would forever drag behind me the red sun, the tumultuous, muddy river, the hateful solitude of Pergola. My past! I walked away from Armand; I could hope for no more from him than from any of the others.

The smoke formed a bluish ring in the yellow air, then the ring stretched, became deformed and finally broke. Somewhere, on a silvery beach, the shadow of a palm tree was creeping towards a white rock. I wished I were lying on that beach. Every time I forced myself to speak their language I felt empty and tired.

'Regarding the printing and publication of written matter, *flagrante delicto* exists only when a summons to revolt is actually in the process of being printed in a place known in advance to the authorities. Not a single one of the writers arrested on a warrant within the past month was actually caught in *flagrante delicto*.'

In the next room, Armand was reading my article aloud and the others were listening attentively. From time to time they applauded in approval. They applauded, but if I had pushed open the door, their faces would have frozen. Even though I worked with them every night and wrote what they wanted me to write, I still remained a stranger to them.

'I say that when an innocent man is taken from his home, when he is held for weeks in a dungeon under an illegal accusation, when you dare to condemn him on a pretext, because his despair and anger made him speak bitterly against your magistrates, then you are trampling upon the sacred rights the French people have bought so dearly with their blood.'

As I listened to those words I had written, I thought, 'Marianne would be pleased with me.' But already, I no longer recognized them. There was nothing in me but silence.

'Now there's an article that will create a stir!' Garnier said. He had walked into my study and he was looking at me expectantly. His mouth twisted nervously; he wanted to say a few friendly words. Of all of them, he was the only one who wasn't afraid of me, but somehow, we had never been able to talk to each other.

'There'll be a trial,' he said finally. 'But we shall win it.'

The door flew open and Spinelle burst into the room. His cheeks were flushed and you could sense the cold night air in his curly hair. He threw his scarf on a chair.

'There was a riot at Ivry,' he said. 'The workers smashed the weaving looms and troops were called in. They made a bayonet charge.'

He spoke so rapidly that he stuttered. He was not concerned with the workers, or the smashed looms, or the spilled blood; he was happy because he was bringing news for his newspaper.

'Was anyone killed?' asked Garnier.

'Three deaths and several wounded.'

'Three deaths . . . '

Garnier's face was tense. He, too, was far from Ivry, far from the shouting and the stabbings. He was imagining the headline in heavy, black characters: TROOPS CHARGE WORKERS WITH BAYONETS. He was already pondering the first words of the article.

'Smashed the looms!' Armand exclaimed. 'We'll have to explain to them that that's idiotic . . . '

'What does it matter?' said Garnier. 'The important thing is that there was a riot.' He turned toward Spinelle. 'I'm going down to the composing room. Come with me.'

They left and Armand sat down in a chair facing me. He thought for a while and then finally said, 'Garnier is wrong. These riots serve no purpose at all. You were right when you explained to me that the people have to be educated first.' He shrugged his shoulders. 'To think that they've gone as far as breaking up looms!'

I did not answer. He did not expect any answer. He gave me a perplexed look and I had no idea what thoughts he was reading on my face.

'What makes things difficult is that they're suspicious of us,' he said. 'Evening courses, public meetings, pamphlets! That's not the way we'll reach them. Our words just go in one ear and out the other.' There was a note of urgency in his voice.

I smiled. 'What do you expect me to do about it?'

'To be able to control them, you have to live among them, work with them, fight at their sides. You have to be one of them.'

'You want me to become a worker?'

'Yes,' he replied. 'You could do an immense amount.'

He gazed at me avidly and I felt a certain sense of security in his gaze: a force to be exploited, nothing more. I inspired neither horror nor friendship in him; he made use of me, that was all.

'It would be a great sacrifice to ask of a mortal man. But for you, I don't imagine ten or fifteen years matter very much.'

'Indeed,' I said, 'it matters very little.'

His face lit up. 'So you agree?'

'I can try,' I said.

'Oh, it won't be difficult. If you try, you'll succeed.

'I'll try,' I repeated.

I was lying on the ground near the ant hill, and she had come, and I had stood up, and she had said to me, 'Be a man among men.' I could still hear her voice as I looked around at them. 'These are men,' I said to myself. But in the studio, where it was growing darker as night fell, as I brushed red, yellow, and blue paint onto the damp rolls of paper, I could not silence that other voice which was saying to me, 'But what *are* men? What can they do for me?' Beneath our feet the whirring of machines made the floor shake; it was the vibration of time itself, restless and sluggish.

'Is there much more to go?' asked the child.

Standing on his step-ladder, he was wearily grinding colours in a mortar. I could sense how numb his legs must feel, his bent back, his head, so empty, so heavy, drawing him towards the floor.

'Are you tired?'

He did not even answer.

'Rest for a moment,' I said.

He sat down on the topmost step of the ladder and closed his eyes. Since early morning we had been swabbing rolls of paper with brushes dripping with liquid colours; since early morning we had been standing there in the same dim light, with the same smell of paint, and the even, rhythmic whirring of the machines. Always and always ... Since morning, since the very beginning of the world, always this boredom, this weariness, the vibration of time. The looms were humming: always and always ... through the streets of Carmona, through the streets of Ghent where the weavers' shuttles wove in and out, in and out. Houses were ablaze, voices were raised up in song amid crackling flames, blood mingled with the violet water in the gutters, and the machines rumbled on obstinately: always and always. Hands were dipping brushes in the red paint, stroking the brushes against paper. The child's head was bent over his chest; he was sleeping. For them, living merely meant not dying. What was the point of struggling for them? Not dying for forty or fifty years and, eventually, dying. They would soon be released in any case; they would die, each in his turn. Far off, in another world, the shadow of a palm tree was creeping towards a stone, the sea was beating against the shore. I felt like walking out of that door and trying to become a stone among stones.

The child opened his eyes. 'Didn't the bell ring?'

'It will ring in five minutes.'

He smiled and, eagerly, I shut that smile away in my heart. And because of that light in his face, the whirring of the machines, the smell of the paint, everything seemed to have changed. Time was no longer a slack, sluggish expanse; there were new hopes and sorrows on earth, hatred and love. In the end, there was always death, but, before that, they lived. Neither ants nor stones, they were men. Through that smile, Marianne again seemed to motion to me: 'Believe in them, stay with them, remain a man.' I put my hand on the child's head. How much longer would I still be able to hear her voice? And when their smiles and their tears found no further echo within me, what would become of me?

'It's all over,' I said.

The man remained seated on the edge of his chair. With a dumbfounded look on his face, he stared at the blue mask lying on the pillow. A woman had died and another on the sixth floor had been saved. It might just as easily have been the other way around. As for me, it made no difference; but for the man it was *this* woman, his wife, who was dead.

I left the room. At the beginning of the epidemic I had offered my services as a nurse and since then I spent my nights applying vesicatories and leeches to infected bodies. They wanted to be cured and I was trying to cure them. I was trying to help them and not ask myself questions.

The street was deserted, but to the right a noisy, metallic rattling could be heard. It was one of those artillery wagons that were being put to use to cart away coffins. People said that the jolting often ripped the wooden boards apart, and the bodies burst out onto the cobblestones, splattering the street with their entrails. Through the narrow, pink side-streets, on mattresses and planks, men were carrying white bodies covered with black spots which they threw pell-mell into hastily dug pits. All those who were able to flee, had fled; on foot, on the backs of horses and mules, they rode through the posterns; in coaches, carts and cabs, they galloped through the gates of Paris. The peers of France, the rich bourgeois, the clerks, the deputies, all the wealthy were fleeing, and those who were sentenced to die danced away the nights in abandoned mansions. Each morning they listened to the voice of the tall, dark monk who was preaching in the square. The poor had been unable to flee; they remained in the infested city, sprawled on their beds, frozen stiff or burning with fever, blue masks on some faces, black masks on others, their bodies covered with dark blotches. In the morning, the bodies were lined up along the walls and the smell of death rose up heavily towards the blue sky. Beneath a grey sky, the dying were carried to hospitals, the doors closed quietly on their death pangs. In vain did their relatives and friends stand watch at the gates to receive their last sighs.

I pushed open the door. Armand was sitting on the edge of the bed and Garnier was standing beside a table on which a candle was burning.

'Why did you come?' I asked. 'It's folly! Don't you trust me?'

'We weren't going to let him die alone,' said Armand.

Garnier said nothing. He stood there with both hands in his pockets, staring at the body lying on the bed. I leaned over Spinelle. His shrunken skin was stretched taut over his bones. The outlines of a death's head could be seen forming beneath the blue parchment of his face. His mouth was white and beads of cold sweat covered his forehead. I took hold of his wrist; it was cold and clammy; his pulse was scarcely beating.

'Can't anything be done?' Armand asked.

'I tried everything.'

'He looks like a corpse already.'

'Twenty years old,' Garnier said. 'And he loved life so much . . .'

In despair, both of them looked at the shrivelled face. For them, this life which was about to be snuffed out was unique, the life of Spinelle who was twenty years old and who was their friend; he was unique, like each of the golden dots that danced in the air among the rows of cypresses. I had looked at Beatrice and had asked myself, 'Is she no different from those ephemeral insects?' I loved her then, and she did seem different; but now I no longer loved her, and her death was of no more importance to me than an insect's.

'If he can just hold out until morning, he may still save himself,' I said.

I slipped my hands beneath the sheets and began slowly, then vigorously, rubbing his icy body. I had laid him out on my overcoat and my hands kneaded his young muscles. For the second time, I had brought him into the world and he had left the world with a hole in his belly. I had brought him maize and smoked meat and he shot himself in the head because he was dying of hunger. I rubbed him for a long while and gradually a little heat began to warm his heart.

'He might hold out,' I said.

Outside, people were running past the window. They were probably seeking help at the emergency station whose red lantern shone out at the street corner. Then there was silence again.

'You ought to get out of here,' I said. 'You can't do anything for him.'

'We must stay,' said Armand. 'I'd like to have my friends around me when *I* die.'

He looked tenderly at Spinelle and I knew he did not fear death. I turned towards Garnier. The man intrigued me. There was no tenderness in his eyes, only fear.

'Just think about it. The risk of infection is enormous.'

His mouth twisted slightly and once again it seemed to me that he wanted to speak to me. But he was walled in upon himself; he was almost never seen to smile and no one knew what he was thinking. Suddenly, he walked to the window and opened it.

'What's going on?'

A great clamour arose from the street. Every night fires were lit at all the main crossroads in the hope that they would purify the atmosphere. By the light of the flames, we saw a mob of men and women dressed in rags pulling a cart through the square. They were shouting, 'Death to the oppressors!'

'They're the ragpickers,' said Garnier.

A statutory order had been put into effect making it obligatory for refuse to be removed during the night, before the ragpickers had a chance to gather their pitiable harvest. Reduced to misery, they cried out with hatred, 'Death to the oppressors!' Then, 'Sons of the devil!' they cried, and they spat on the ground.

Garnier closed the window.

'If only we had leaders,' said Armand. 'The people are ripe for a revolution.'

'For a riot, at best,' Garnier said.

'We could easily transform a riot into a full-scale revolution.'

'No, we're too divided.'

With their foreheads pressed against the windows they were dreaming of riots, of murders. I looked at them incomprehendingly. At times it seemed to me that men attached a ridiculous price to a life that death would ultimately destroy: why had they looked so despondently at Spinelle? And at other times they seemed all too willing to run the risk of obliterating themselves forever: what was the point of staying in that infested room? Why were they planning bloody riots?

'Armand,' a voice murmured. Spinelle had opened his eyes; it was as if his eyeballs, lost in the depths of their hollow sockets, had melted. But they were living eyes, they could see.

'Am I going to die?'

'No,' Armand said. 'Try to sleep. You're going to be all right.' Spinelle's eyelids closed and Armand turned towards me. 'Is it true? Will he be all right?'

I took Spinelle's hand. It was no longer cold. His pulse was beating.

'If he gets through the night,' I said, 'perhaps he'll survive.'

Dawn was already breaking. A large black horse-drawn wagon passed by under the windows. From house to house, coffins were being collected and piled in the van behind funeral curtains. Along the hilly street with its pink cobble-stones, carts stopped from house to house, and bodies were piled up under tarpaulins. Armand was sitting in a chair; he had closed his eyes and was sleeping. Garnier was leaning against a wall, a closed expression on his face. At the cross-road the fire was dying out and the ragpickers had dispersed. For several minutes the square remained empty, and then a janitor appeared at his doorway. He inspected the cobble-stones suspiciously. It was said that chunks of meat and strange, sugared pills or tablets, deposited by mysterious hands, were sometimes found at porchways in the morning. There were people, it was rumoured, who poisoned the fountains and the meat in butcher shops; a vast conspiracy was supposed to threaten the population. The rumour circulated that I had made a pact with the devil and they spat in disgust as I passed by.

'He survived the night,' Garnier murmured.

'Yes.'

A little colour had appeared in Spinelle's cheeks; his hand was warm and his pulse was beating steadily.

'He's all right,' I said.

Armand opened his eyes. 'All right?'

'Almost certainly.'

Armand and Garnier looked at each other. I averted my eyes. With that look, they mutually shared the joy that had just burst into their hearts. It was in those triumphant exchanges that they found both the strength to confront death and a reason for living. Why did I feel compelled to turn my eyes away? I recalled Spinelle's face: he was twenty, he loved life; I remembered his shining eyes, his young, stuttering voice. I had saved him, had swum through the icy lake, I had brought him back to shore and carried him in my arms. I had gone in search of an Indian village and, laughing with joy, he had devoured the corn and meat I had brought back. A hole in his belly, a hole in his temple. How would this one die? There was not a spark of joy in my heart.

'Well?' said Garnier.

In the editorial room of the *Progrès*, the members of the Central Committee and the departmental heads of the Society for the Rights of Man had gathered around old Broussaud. They were all looking at me anxiously.

'Well, I didn't succeed in joining the Society of Gauls or its organizing committee,' I said. 'The only one I was able to get anywhere with was the Friends of the People. They were in favour of an insurrection, but they haven't reached any firm decision yet.'

'How can they possibly decide anything without knowing what we decide?' Armand said. 'And how can we make any decisions without them?'

There was a brief silence, then Garnier said, '*We* have to make the decision.'

'Since we're not having much success in coordinating our efforts,' old Broussaud said slowly, 'it would be better to abstain from making any decisions. In the present situation, it would be impossible to launch a full-scale revolution.'

'Who knows?' Armand said.

'Even if the insurrection were only a riot, it would still be worthwhile,' said Garnier. 'Every time there's a revolt, the people become more and more aware of their strength, and the chasm that separates them from the ruling class becomes deeper and deeper.'

A murmur spread through the room. 'There's a danger of much blood being spilled,' said a voice. 'Much blood spilled, and all in vain,' said someone else.

For a moment they argued noisily. In a low voice, Armand asked me, 'What do you think?'

'I have no opinion.'

'But you don't lack experience,' he said. 'You must have some opinion.'

I shook my head. How could I have given them advice? Did I know what value they placed on life and death? It was for them to decide. Why live, if living is merely not dying? But to die in order to save one's life, is not that the greatest delusion of all? In any event, it wasn't for me to choose for them.

'There's no doubt that there will be incidents,' Armand said. 'If you don't want to incite an insurrection, then let us at least take precautions in case one breaks out.'

'That's right,' said Garnier. 'Let us not give the order ourselves, but let us be ready, and if the people begin to march, we shall march with them.'

'I'm afraid they won't begin to march without first calculating their chances of success,' said Broussaud.

'In any case, the Republican party has to stand behind them.'

'On the contrary . . . '

Once again voices were raised. They were speaking loudly and their eyes were shining, their voices quavering. On the other side of those walls there were, at this very moment, millions of men who were speaking with the same quavering voices, the same gleaming eyes. And while they were speaking, the insurrection, the Republic, France, the future of the whole world were there, in their hands. So they believed, at least. They held the destiny of mankind closely to their breasts. Half the city was seething around the catafalque in which lay the remains of General Lamarque, to whom no one was giving a thought.

None of us slept that night. We were at work establishing communications between the various groups along the lengths of the boulevards. If the insurrection succeeded, we would have to try our best to persuade La Fayette to accept leadership, for he alone, thanks to the prestige of his name, was capable of rallying the masses. Garnier entrusted Armand, in the event that they were successful, with the task of negotiating with the principal Republican leaders. For his part, having assembled a group of men at the Austerlitz bridge, he intended to incite the citizens of the Saint-Marceau district to revolt.

'But you should be the one to negotiate,' said Armand. 'Your voice carries more weight than mine. And Fosca, who's a lot closer than we are to the workers, can hold the Austerlitz bridge.'

'No,' Garnier said. 'I've done enough talking in my life. This time I want to fight.'

'And if you got yourself killed, that would be clever, wouldn't it?' Spinelle said. 'What will happen to the paper?'

'You'd get along very well without me.'

'Armand is right,' I said. 'I know the workers of Saint-Marceau. Let me go and organize the uprising.'

A dry smile appeared on Garnier's face. 'You saved my life once,' he said. 'That's enough.'

I looked at his nervous mouth, at the creases on either side of it, at that tormented face with its hard, somewhat shifty eyes. He was gazing at the horizon beyond which the turbulent river was hidden; green tufts on tall reeds were waving in the breeze, and alligators were sleeping in the warm mud. 'I've got to feel that I'm alive, even if I have to die in the process,' he said.

At ten o'clock the next morning, all the members of the Society for the Rights of Man and the Friends of the People, as well as the medical and law students, were gathered in the Place Louis XV. The students of the Ecole Polytechnique were missing; the rumour was that they had been confined to their quarters. Green branches, banners and tricolours fluttered above their heads; everyone was holding some kind of insignia in his hand, and some were carrying arms. The sky was cloudy. It was drizzling. But the bloody fires of hope were burning in their hearts. Something was going to happen, they were going to make it happen. They believed it. They believed that they were capable of doing something, and with their hands gripping the butts of revolvers, they were ready to die to prove it, ready to give their lives to prove that each one of them had a purpose on earth.

Six young men were pulling the hearse and La Fayette was holding the cords of the canopy. Two battalions of ten thousand municipal guards were following behind. The government had stationed guards all along the route, but this huge show of force, far from setting the people's minds at ease, only made them more aware of the threat of disturbance. Crowds of people thronged the pavements, the windows, the trees, and the rooftops. Italian, German and Polish flags, reminders of the tyrannies the French government had been unwilling to combat, hung from balconies. As the procession moved along, the people sang revolutionary hymns. Armand was singing, and so was Spinelle whom I had saved from cholera. The sight of the dragoons filled their hearts with anger and people ripped branches from trees and picked up stones to serve as arms. We crossed the Place Vendôme and the young men pulling the hearse broke off from the planned route and processed round the monument. Someone behind me cried out, 'Where are they leading us?' and a voice answered, 'To the Republic!' I thought: 'They're being led to a riot, to their deaths.' What, after all, did the Republic mean to them? Not one of them knew what cause it was for which they were prepared to fight. Yet they were certain that the cause was dear to them for they were going to pay for it with their blood. 'What's Rivella?' I had said. But it was not really Rivella that Antonio had coveted; he had wanted victory. He died for that victory and he had died contented. They gave their lives to prove that they were living men: 'not ants, or flies, or blocks of stone; we won't let ourselves be turned into stones.' And the stakes blazed, and they were singing. And Marianne was saying: 'Be a man among men.' But what was the use? I could march beside them, but I couldn't risk my life with theirs.

When we reached the Place de la Bastille, we saw the Polytechnique students, heads bare and their clothes in disarray, running toward us. They had escaped despite their detention. The crowd started to shout, 'Long live the engineering students! Long live the Republic!' and the band in front of the catafalque struck up the 'Marseillaise'. A rumour was circulating that an officer of the 12th Regiment had just told some of the students that he was a Republican, and the word spread from mouth to mouth among the marchers. 'The troops are with us.'

The procession drew to a halt at the Austerlitz bridge. A platform had been erected, and La Fayette climbed up on it to give his speech. He spoke of General Lamarque who we were about to bury. Others spoke after him; but no one was concerned with these speeches, nor with the dead general.

'Garnier should be over there, at the other end of the bridge,' Armand said. He was looking hard, but it was impossible to pick out a face in the milling crowd.

'Something's going to happen now,' said Spinelle.

Everyone was waiting for something, without knowing what it was. Suddenly, a man on horseback appeared, dressed in black and carrying a red flag on top of which was a Phrygian cap. There was an immediate outcry; people looked at each other and voices shouted, 'No red flags!'

'It's a trick, a betrayal,' said Spinelle, stammering in anger. 'They want to intimidate the people.'

'Do you think so?'

'Yes,' Armand said. 'The troops and the municipal guards are afraid of the red flag. And the crowd can sense it.'

We waited a moment longer, and then Armand said abruptly, 'Nothing's going to happen here. Go and find Garnier and tell him to give the signal himself. Meet me at the *National*. I'm going to try to get the Republican leaders together.'

I made my way through the crowd and found Garnier at the place we had marked on the map during the night. A rifle was slung over his shoulder. The streets behind him were filled with sombre-faced men, many of whom were carrying rifles.

'Everything's ready,' I said. 'The people are ready for the riot. But Armand asks that you give the signal.'

'Very well.'

I watched him in silence. He was frightened, I knew – as he was every day, and every night – afraid of the death that would swoop down upon him in spite of himself and would reduce him to dust.

'The dragoons!'

Their shining helmets and bayonets could be seen above the dark mass of the crowd; they were streaming out onto the Quai Morland and riding in columns towards the bridge. 'They're charging us!' Garnier cried out. He grabbed his rifle and fired. No sooner had he done so than shooting burst out all around him and a loud clamour arose: 'To the barricades! To arms!'

Barricades were hastily erected. Men with guns rushed forth from every neighbouring street. Followed by a veritable army, Garnier headed for the barracks on Rue Popincourt. We stormed the building, and the soldiers gave way after offering only token resistance. We took twelve hundred rifles and handed them out to the insurgents. Garnier then led them to the cloister of Saint-Merri which they then set about fortifying.

'Tell Armand that we're holding the whole district,' Garnier said. 'And that we'll hold it as long as we have to.'

Everywhere, people were erecting barricades. Men were cutting down trees and laying them across streets; others were dragging iron beds, tables and chairs from houses. Women and children were carrying cobblestones which they had dug out of the ground. Everyone was singing. Around fires of celebration, the peasants of Ingolstadt were singing.

I found Armand in the offices of the *National*. His eyes were beaming with joy. The insurgents were holding half the city and they had captured most of the barracks and munition stores. The government had decided to bring the troops out against them, but they weren't at all sure that the troops were loyal. The Republican leaders were about to name a provisional government with La Fayette at its head, and the national guard was expected to rally to its former chief.

'Tomorrow the Republic will be proclaimed,' Armand said.

I was given fresh supplies of food and ammunition which I was to take to the cloister of Saint-Merri for Garnier and his men. Bullets were whistling through the streets. People tried to stop me at every crossroads: 'Don't go that way! There's a barricade!' they shouted. I ran on. A bullet tore through my hat, another struck me in the shoulder. I continued to run. The sky sped by above my head and the earth leaped beneath my horse's hoofs. I was running; I was free of the past and the future, free of myself and that bitter taste of boredom in my mouth. Something existed that had never existed before: that frenzied city, swollen with blood and hope, and its heart was beating in my breast. In a flash, I thought, 'I'm alive!' and then immediately afterwards, 'It may be the last time.'

Garnier was sitting among his men behind a pile of bricks, tree trunks, furniture, cobblestones and sacks of cement. On top of that hastily constructed wall they had stuck green branches. They were busy making cartridges, using shreds from their shirts and bits of posters they had ripped from the walls as wadding. They were all naked from the waist up.

'I've brought some cartridges,' I said.

With shouts of joy, they pounced on the boxes. Garnier looked at me in surprise.

'How did you get through?' he asked.

'I got through.'

He pursed his lips. He envied me. I wanted to say to him, 'No, you're wrong to envy me. I'm not allowed to be either brave or cowardly.' But it wasn't the moment to speak of myself, or of him.

'The provisional government will be proclaimed some time tonight,' I said. 'They're asking you to hold out till morning. If we want the whole of Paris to rise up, the insurrection must not falter.'

'We'll hold out.'

'Will that be difficult?'

'The troops attacked twice. We repulsed them on both occasions.'

'Were there many dead?'

'I haven't counted.'

I remained sitting beside him for a moment. He was tearing up pieces of white cloth with his teeth and stuffing them, with an absorbed look on his face, into cardboard cartridge cases. He wasn't very adroit with his hands and it was obvious that he did not like sitting there making cartridges. I knew he wanted to speak to me. But when I stood up to go, we still hadn't exchanged a word.

'Tell them we'll hold out through the night.'

'I'll tell them.'

Once again I kept close to the walls, hid in porches and ran through barrages of bullets. When I got to the offices of the *National*, I was dripping with sweat and my shirt was soaked with blood. I thought of Armand's smile; his eyes would light up with joy when I told him that Garnier was holding the district securely.

'I saw Garnier. They'll hold out.'

But no smile appeared on Armand's face. He was standing in front of the door to the office. Standing in front of the fortress, Carlier stared vacantly into space. He was sitting in the canoe, staring at the yellow river which flowed from north to south. I knew that look.

'What happened?' I asked.

'They don't want the Republic.'

'Who?'

'The Republican leaders don't want the Republic.'

His face was so full of despair that for a moment I tried to re-awaken an echo in myself, a memory. But I remained empty and dry.

'Why?'

'They're afraid.'

'Carrel doesn't dare risk it,' said Spinelle. 'He claims the people can't do anything against a loyal regiment.' His voice was choked. 'And yet the troops would come over to our side if only Carrel had spoken out.

'They're not afraid of a defeat,' Armand said. 'They're afraid of a victory, afraid of the people. They call themselves Republicans, but the republic they want would be no different to this putrid monarchy. They even prefer Louis-Philippe to the kind of regime we want to establish.'

'Is it really hopeless?' I asked.

'We talked for over two hours. Everything's lost. With La Fayette, with the municipal troops, we could have won. But we can't fight against the armies that are marching on Paris.'

'So what are you going to do?'

After a brief silence, Spinelle said, 'We still hold half of Paris.'

'We don't hold anything,' said Armand. 'Our cause hasn't even got any leaders, it disowns itself. All those people who are getting themselves killed, are getting killed for nothing. There's nothing for it but to stop this slaughter.'

'Then I'll go and tell Garnier to lay down his arms immediately,' said Spinelle.

'Fosca will go. He knows his way around better than you.'

It was six o'clock in the evening; night was falling. At every crossroads there were municipal guards and soldiers. Fresh regiments had just arrived and they were fiercely attacking the barricades. Bodies were sprawled out on street-corners, and men could be seen carrying the wounded on stretchers. There were red puddles on the streets. The insurrection was beginning to weaken; the people had not heard a word of hope for hours and they no longer really knew why they were fighting. Many of the streets which the insurgents had held only a short while ago were now teeming with red uniforms. I saw from afar that the barricade defended by Garnier was still standing; I ran towards it through a hail of bullets which whistled past my ears from every direction. Garnier was leaning against the sacks of cement; bloody bandages were wrapped around his bare shoulder and his face was black with gunpowder.

'What news?'

'They couldn't reach an agreement,' I said.

'I knew it,' he said indifferently.

The calmness with which he took the news astonished me; he was almost smiling.

'The troops aren't going to come over to our side. There's no longer any hope of winning. Armand asks that you stop fighting.'

'Stop fighting?' This time he laughed openly. 'Look at us.'

I looked. There were only a handful of men left around Garnier. Their faces were black and bloody; all of them were wounded. Bare-chested bodies were laid out against the walls; their eyes had been closed and their hands folded over their chests.

'Would you happen to have a clean handkerchief?'

I pulled a handkerchief from my pocket. Garnier wiped his blackened hands and face.

'Thanks.' His eyes fell upon me and he suddenly seemed surprised to see me there. 'But you're wounded!'

'Just a few scratches.'

There was a moment's silence and then I said, 'You're going to get yourself killed for nothing.'

He shrugged his shoulders. 'Does anyone ever get killed for *something?* Is there anything that's worth a life?'

'Ah! So that's the way you think,' I said.

'Don't you?'

I paused. I had developed the habit of never saying what I really thought. 'It seems to me that useful results can sometimes be achieved.'

'Do you think so?' Garnier asked. He was silent for a moment, and then it was as if something were suddenly released in him. 'Suppose the negotiations had been successful. Do you believe our victory would have been worthwhile? Have you ever thought of the tasks the Republic would have had to accomplish? Having to rebuild society, moderate the party, satisfy the people, bring the rich to heel, and having to conquer the whole of Europe because all the other nations would immediately rise up against us. Added to that, we're only a small minority and we lack political experience. It may well be a stroke of luck for the Republic that it didn't triumph today.'

I looked at him in surprise. I had often said these very same things to myself, but I never imagined that any of them had ever entertained such ideas.

'In that case, why this insurrection?' I asked.

'We don't have to depend on the future to provide meaning for our actions. If that were the case, all action would be impossible. We have to conduct our fight the way we have decided to conduct it, that's all.'

I had kept the gates of Carmona closed and I did not expect anything.

'I've given a lot of thought to the subject,' he said with a dry smile.

'Have you chosen to die out of a sense of despair, then?'

'I've never despaired because I've never hoped for anything.'

'Can one live without hope?'

'Yes, if you believe in something with absolute certainty.'

'For me, nothing is certain,' I said.

'As for me, just being a man is a great thing.'

'A man among men.'

'Yes, that's enough. That's well worth living for; and dying for too.'

'Are you sure your comrades think as you do?' I asked.

'Try asking them to surrender!' he said. 'Too much blood has been spilled. Now we have to fight to the end.'

'But they don't know that nothing came of the negotiations.'

'Tell them if you like,' he said angrily. 'What do they care? What do I care about their deliberations, their decisions and counter-decisions? We swore to defend the district and we shall defend it, that's all.'

'The battle is not fought purely on these barricades. To carry it through, you have to go on living.'

He stood up, leaning against the fragile rampart and looked down the empty street. 'Perhaps I lack patience,' he said.

'You lack patience,' I responded quickly, 'because you're afraid of death.'

'That's true,' he admitted.

Suddenly, he seemed far away from me. His eyes were fixed on the street out of which death would soon loom, a death he had chosen. The stakes were blazing, the wind was scattering the ashes of the two Augustinian monks. 'There is only one good: to act according to one's conscience.' Lying on his bed, Antonio was smiling. They were neither insane nor arrogant; I understood this now. They were men who wanted to fulfil their human destinies by choosing their own lives and their own deaths; they were free men.

Garnier fell at the first salvo. By morning, the insurrection had been crushed.

Armand was sitting at the edge of my bed and I felt the weight of his hand on my shoulder. He was leaning towards me. His face had grown thin.

'Tell me about it,' he said. His upper lip was swollen and there was a blue bruise on his temple.

'Is it true they dragged you to the tribunal by force?' I asked.

'Yes, but I'll tell you about that later. First tell me what happened to you.'

A yellow lamp was hanging from the ceiling; I watched it swing back and forth. The dormitory was empty, but the sounds of clinking glasses, laughter and cheerful voices could be heard coming from another room; the guards were holding a banquet for the workers. Soon the prisoners would straggle back to the dormitory, half-drunk with food, drink, friendship and laughter. They would barricade themselves behind their beds, engage in a mock revolutionary battle and, for their evening prayer, they would kneel down and sing the 'Marseillaise'. I had grown used to these rituals, and I felt quite contented lying on my bed, watching the yellow lamp swinging back and forth on the ceiling. Why stir up the past?

'It's always the same,' I said.

'What do you mean?'

I closed my eyes. With much effort I plunged into that long, confused night which stretched out endlessly behind me. Blood, fire, tears, songs. They had ridden into the city at a gallop, they had thrown flaming torches into the houses. Their horses had shattered children's skulls, crushed women's breasts. Blood was on their hoofs and a dog was howling at death.

'They slit open women's throats, smash children's heads against stone walls. The cobblestones turn red, and where there were once living creatures, there are only dead bodies.'

'But what happened on the 13th of April at Rue Transnonain?' asked Armand. 'That's what I want to know.'

Rue Transnonain, the 13th of April. Why that memory rather than another? Was the past less dead after three months than after four hundred years?

'We went out into the street,' I said. 'We were told that Thiers himself had announced on the rostrum that the insurrection at Lyons had been triumphant. We raised barricades. Everyone was singing.'

They had assembled on the square. They raced through the streets shouting, 'Death to the son of the devil!' They were singing.

'And then?' Armand asked.

'The troops attacked in the morning. They swept right through the barricades and went into the building. They killed everyone they could lay their hands on.' I shrugged my shoulders. 'I told you. It's always the same.'

We were both silent for a moment and then Armand said, 'How did you not realize it was a trap? Thiers knew on the evening of the 12th that the insurrection had been put down in Lyons. And when he incited the riot, all the leaders had been arrested. I had already been arrested . . . '

'We didn't know that until afterwards.'

'But you have lots of experience. You should have sensed the danger and stopped the uprising.'

'They wanted to go down to the street; I went down with them.'

Armand shrugged his shoulders impatiently. 'You should be enlightening them rather than obeying them.'

'But I can't do it for them,' I said. He looked at me irritably and I continued, 'I can do whatever they ask me to do. But how can I decide for them? How can I possibly know what they believe to be good or bad for themselves?'

Antonio had died with a smile on his face at the age of twenty; Garnier was lying in wait for death as it approached around the corner of the street; and Beatrice's podgy, mournful face was pouring over her manuscripts. They alone were the judges.

'Do you believe they wanted that massacre?' Armand asked harshly.

'Is it so great an evil?' I said.

The dead were dead, the living alive. The prisoners did not hate their prison; they were released from their exhausting work; they could finally laugh, rest, converse. Before dying, they had sung . . .

'I'm afraid these months in prison have tired you out,' Armand said.

I looked at his pale face. 'Aren't you tired?' I asked.

'On the contrary.'

There was such passion in his voice that it pierced through the calm haze behind which I had taken shelter. Suddenly, I got out of bed and paced back and forth for a few moments.

'The organization lost all its leaders, didn't it? That's like beheading someone.'

'Yes. It's our own fault. You don't engage in conspiracies out in the open. It was a lesson that will be useful to us one day.'

'When?' I asked. 'They're going to sentence you to ten or twenty years.'

'In twenty years, I'll only be forty-four years old.'

I looked at him silently for a moment and then said, 'I envy you.'

'Why?'

'Because one day you'll die. You'll never be like me.'

'Ah! If only I didn't have to die!' he said.

'Yes, that's what I used to say.'

I squeezed the greenish bottle in my hand and I thought, 'The things I'll be able to do!' With rapid little steps, Marianne scurried about the room. 'I've so little time left,' she said. I looked down at Armand and for the first time it occurred to me that he was our child.

'I'll get you out of here,' I said.

'How?'

'There are only two guards in the courtyard at night. They're armed, but someone who's not afraid of bullets can attract their attention and give an agile man enough time to scale the wall.'

Armand shook his head. 'I don't want to escape at the moment. We're depending a great deal on the repercussions our trial will have.'

'But they might separate us from one day to the next,' I said. 'It's an extraordinary stroke of luck that we should have met like this. You should seize the opportunity.'

'No, I must stay,' he insisted.

I shrugged my shoulders. 'You too!'

'Me too? What do you mean?'

'Like Garnier, you've decided to become a martyr.'

'Garnier chose a pointless death and I blame him for that. But I reckon there's nowhere I can do as much useful work as I can here.'

Armand looked around at the large, empty dormitory. In another room, seated around a table laden with food and drink, they were laughing heartily and singing drinking-songs.

'People say that here at Sainte-Pélagie the discipline is not too strict. Is that so?'

'Yes, it's true. The bourgeois even have their own private rooms. This dormitory is only for the workers . . .'

'Well then!' he said. 'Don't you see what a wonderful opportunity this is for making contacts, for discussions? Before I leave here, a united front *must* be formed.'

'But doesn't the prospect of ten or twenty years of imprisonment frighten you?'

He gave a short laugh, but did not look amused. 'That's another question.'

Across the plain, the Genoese could be seen scurrying about their red tents. The dusty road was deserted. I turned my eyes away; it was not for me to ask myself questions.

I had kept Carmona's gates closed . . . I had been that man and yet I no longer understood him.

'What makes you think that a man must prefer the cause he happens to be serving to his own destiny?' I asked.

'I make no distinction between the two.'

'Yes,' I said.

I had kept the gates closed and I had said to myself: 'Carmona will be the equal of Florence.' I had no other future.

'I remember.'

'You remember?' he asked, perplexed.

'I was once your age . . . it was a very long time ago. I believed then that the cause I was serving and my own destiny were one.'

A glimmer of curiosity flickered across his calm eyes. 'And you don't any more?'

'Not entirely.'

'And yet your fate should be completely bound up in humanity's destiny because you'll last as long as humanity.'

'And perhaps even longer,' I said. I shrugged my shoulders. 'You're right. This prison life has wearied me. It will pass.'

'I'm sure it will pass,' he said. 'And then you'll see how much good we'll accomplish.'

There were two opposing tendencies in the Republican party. One group was in favour of maintaining the privileges of the bourgeoisie: they demanded liberty, but they demanded it only for themselves. They only desired political reforms and rejected the notion of any social reforms, seeing them as nothing more than new forms of repression. Armand and his friends, on the other hand, maintained that liberty could not be the prerogative of a single class, and that only the advent of socialism would allow the workers to become free. Nothing compromised the success of the revolution more seriously than this division, and it did not surprise me therefore that Armand sought a united front so passionately. Yet I admired his perseverance. In just a few days he had transformed the prison into a political club. From morning till evening and through a large part of the night, discussions took place in the rooms and dormitories. Although they never led anywhere, Armand never became discouraged. In the meantime, the guards would seize hold of him and his comrades several times a week and drag them by force through the corridors of the prison to the tribunal; their heads would sometimes strike the stone floor or the steps of a stairway. But each time they would come back smiling. 'We didn't talk,' they would say. One evening, however, when he returned to his room where I had been waiting for him, I saw that same expression on his face that I had seen in front of the offices of the *National*. He sat down and for a long time he was silent. Finally, he said: 'The men from Lyons talked.'

'Is that so serious?'

'They destroyed everything our silence achieved.' He buried his head in his hands. When he looked up at me again, his face had hardened, but his voice quavered. 'We mustn't delude ourselves. The trial is going to drag on and on, and it won't have the effect we had hoped for.'

'Do you remember what I once suggested?' I asked.

'Yes.' He stood up and paced nervously back and forth. 'I don't want to leave on my own.'

'You can't all escape.'

'Why not?'

Before three days had elapsed, Armand had found a way of escaping from Sainte-Pélagie with his comrades. Opposite the door which gave onto the courtyard was another door leading to a small cellar. Workers who were making repairs in the prison told Armand that this cellar extended beneath a neighbouring garden. It was decided that we would try to dig our way out into the garden. There was a guard stationed in front of the door; some of the prisoners were to distract his attention by playing ball in the courtyard while the others were digging. The noise of the repair work would disguise the sounds of our hammering and shovelling. In six days the tunnel was virtually completed; only a light covering of earth separated us from daylight. Spinelle, who had escaped the April 13th arrests, was to come during the night, with some weapons, bringing ladders to help us get over the garden walls. Twenty-four of the prisoners were planning to escape and seek refuge in England. But one of us, renouncing all hope of freedom, had to detain the guard while he was making his rounds.

'I'll do it,' I said.

'No, we'll draw lots,' Armand said.

'What's twenty years of prison to me?'

'That's not the question.'

'I know,' I said. 'You think I can be of greater help to you than any of the others. Well, you're wrong.'

'You've already been of great help to us.'

'But there's no guarantee that I'll continue to be. Leave me here. I'm quite happy staying here.'

We were sitting in his room facing each other, and he looked at me more attentively than at any time during the past four years. That day, he believed it worthwhile trying to understand me.

'What's the reason for all this apathy?'

I laughed. 'It came upon me gradually. Six hundred years . . . Do you know how many days that makes?'

He was not amused. 'Even if I'd live for six hundred years, I'd still go on fighting. Do you think there's less to do on earth today than in former times?'

'*Is* there something to do on earth?'

This time he laughed. 'It seems there is to me, at least.'

'Basically, what makes you want freedom so much?' I asked.

'I like to see the sun shining,' he said in a fiery voice. 'I like rivers and the sea. How can anyone allow those magnificent forces that are in man to be suppressed?'

'And what would he do with them?'

'It doesn't matter. He'll do whatever he likes with them. But first he has to be released.' He leaned towards me. 'Men want to be free. Don't you hear their voices?'

I could hear her voice: 'Stay a man.' They had the same faith in their eyes. I put my hand on Armand's shoulder.

'This evening, I can hear you,' I said. 'That's why I say: accept my offer. This may be the last evening. Every evening may be the last. Tonight, I want to help you, but tomorrow, perhaps, I might not have anything to offer you any more.'

Armand looked at me intensely and there was a worried expression on his face. He suddenly seemed to have discovered something which he had never before suspected and which frightened him a little.

'I accept,' he said.

Lying on my back, lying on the frozen mud, on the wooden deck, on the beach of silvery sand, I stared at the stone ceiling, I could feel the grey walls surrounding me, the sea all about me, the plain, and the horizon's grey walls. Years had gone by: after centuries, and years as long as centuries, as short as hours, I was staring at the ceiling and I was calling out, 'Marianne'. She had said, 'You'll forget me,' but I fought against the hours and centuries to keep her alive in me. I stared at the ceiling and occasionally, for a brief instant, an image of her formed in the depths of my eyes; it was always the same image: the blue dress, the bare shoulders, that portrait which did not look like her. I tried again. Something stirred in me that was almost a smile and it lasted as long as a flash of lightning, but then it faded as quickly. What was the point? Embalmed in my heart, in the depths of that freezing cellar, she was as dead as she was in her tomb. I closed my eyes, but even in my dreams I could no longer escape. The mists, the ghosts, the adventures, the metamorphoses, they all had that stale, stagnant taste: the taste of my saliva, the taste of my thoughts.

Behind me the door creaked. A hand touched my shoulder and their voices came to me from very far away. 'It had to happen,' I thought. They touched my bare shoulder and they said: 'Come with us,' and the shadow of the palm tree vanished. After fifty years, or one day, or a single hour, it always ended by happening. 'The carriage is waiting, sir.' I had to open my eyes. There were several men around me who were saying that I was free.

I followed them along the corridors and I did everything they ordered to me to do. I signed papers, I took a package which they placed authoritatively in my hands. And then they led me to a door which closed behind me. It was drizzling. The tide was low; as far as the eye could see, there was nothing but grey sand all around the island. I was free.

I put one foot forward, then the other. To go where? In the swamp, the rushes spat drops of water with a raucous, murmuring sound, and I moved forward, step after step, towards the horizon which receded with each step. With my eyes fixed on the horizon, I set foot on an embankment. And then, a few feet away, I saw him, holding out his hands and smiling. He was no longer a young man. With his broad shoulders and heavy beard, he looked as old as me. 'I came to find you,' he said.

His warm, hard hands gripped mine. On the far side of the river a fire was burning, a fire was burning in Marianne's eyes. Armand had taken my arm. He was speaking, and his voice blazed. I followed him, setting one foot forward and then the other, thinking, 'Will it begin again then? Will it always go on? Always go on beginning again, day after day, forever and ever?'

I followed him along a road; there were always roads, roads which led nowhere. And then we climbed into a coach. Armand continued speaking. Ten years had passed, a large chunk of his life. He was telling me his story and I was listening. The words still had meaning: always the same meaning, the same words. Horses were galloping; outside it was snowing; it was winter. Four seasons, seven colours. The stuffy air smelled of old leather. I even recognized the smells. People were getting out of the carriage, others were climbing in. It had been a long time since I had seen so many faces, so many noses, mouths, so many pairs of eyes. Armand was speaking. He was telling me about England, the amnesty, the return to France, his efforts to obtain a pardon for me and his joy when at last it was granted.

'I had been hoping for a long time that you would escape,' he said. 'It wouldn't have been difficult for you.'

'I didn't try,' I said.

'Oh!'

He looked at me and then he turned his eyes away. He began to speak to me again without asking me questions. He was living in Paris in a small apartment with Spinelle and a woman he had met in England. He was expecting me to live with them, too. I acquiesced.

'Is she your wife?' I asked.

'No, just a friend,' he replied curtly.

We arrived in Paris after travelling all night. It was early morning, the streets were covered with snow. That was a familiar old setting too. Marianne had liked the snow. Suddenly, she seemed both closer and more lost than in the cellar at the back of my mind. There was a place for her on this winter morning, and that place was empty.

We walked up a staircase. Nothing had changed in ten years, in five centuries; there were always ceilings above their heads, and around them, beds, tables, chairs, paper on the walls, olive green or almond green. And between those walls, they lived while they waited to die, intent on achieving their mortal dreams. In the byres, there were cows with their warm green stomachs, their large, soft eyes in which dreams of hay and green meadows were reflected into infinity.

'Fosca!'

Spinelle gripped my hand in his and grinned broadly at me. He was the same as ever; his features had hardened only slightly. What is more, after that long night, I found Armand's face the same as I had always known it. It seemed to me that I had only just left them the previous day.

'This is Laura,' Armand said.

She looked at me with a serious expression on her face and, without smiling, held out a small, hard, nervous hand. She was not very young. She had a slender waist, large, dark eyes and an olive complexion. Her hair fell in black curls to her shoulders which were covered by a shawl with long fringes.

'You must be hungry,' she said.

She had placed large bowls of coffee and a plate of buttered toast on the table. They ate, and Armand and Spinelle spoke animatedly. They both seemed very happy to be with me again. I took only a few gulps of coffee: I had lost the habit of eating in prison. I tried to answer their questions and to smile, but it seemed to me as if my heart were buried under cold lava.

'In a few days there's going to be a banquet in your honour,' Armand said.

'A banquet?'

'The leaders of the principal workers' organizations are going to be there. You're one of our heroes . . . The April 13th uprising, ten years' imprisonment . . . You can't imagine the weight your name carries today.'

'No, I hadn't the slightest notion,' I said.

'You must be surprised at this idea of a banquet,' said Spinelle. I shook my head but he continued imperiously, 'I'll explain.'

He still spoke in the same voluble, stuttering manner. He explained that the tactic of fomenting insurrection had been abandoned. Violence was to be reserved for the day when the revolution would really be unleashed. In the meantime, what they were trying to do was to unite all the workers in one vast union. The exiles who had been in London had learnt the importance of a united workers' front. The banquets were occasions to manifest this solidarity; they would take place all over France. He spoke for a long while. From time to time, he turned towards Laura as if to ask her approbation, and she nodded her head in approval.

'I see,' I said when he had finished.

There was a brief silence. I felt I wasn't saying the words or making the gestures that were expected of me. But I was incapable of inventing them.

Laura stood up. 'Don't you want to have a rest?' she asked. 'I'm sure the journey must have been very tiring.'

'Yes, I'd like to get some sleep. I used to sleep a lot there.'

'I'll show you to your room.'

I followed her. She pushed open a door and said, 'It's not a very beautiful room, but if you like it here, it would make us very happy.'

'I'm sure I'll like it.'

She closed the door and I stretched out on the bed. There were clean clothes on a chair. Shelves were filled with books. Outside, voices and the sound of footsteps could be heard. Occasionally, a cart passed by. It was Paris, it was the world. I was free, free between the earth and the sky and the grey walls of the horizon. In the Faubourg Saint-Antoine machines were humming always, always. Children were being born in hospitals, old people were dying. Behind the snow-laden clouds, the sun was red. Somewhere a young man was looking at that sun and something was bursting in his heart. I held my hand against my heart. It was beating, always, always, and the sea was beating against the shore, always, always. It was beginning again, it was going on, and it would go on beginning again, always, always.

Night had long since fallen when someone knocked at my door. It was Laura. She was holding a lamp in her hand.

'Would you like me to bring you your dinner here?'

'No, don't bother. I'm not hungry.'

She put down the lamp and came over to the bed. 'Perhaps you didn't want to leave prison,' she said.

She had a soft, rather husky voice. I raised myself up on one elbow. A woman. Just like the seasons, the hours, the colours, they were the same as they always were; their hearts beating beneath warm flesh, their white teeth, their eyes constantly in quest of life, the smell of their tears.

'We thought we were doing the right thing,' she said.

'But you did do the right thing . . .'

'One never knows.' She looked at my face, at my hands, and she murmured, 'Armand told me . . .'

I got out of bed, glanced in the mirror and walked over to the window. I pressed my forehead against the glass pane. The street-lamps were lit. In their homes, families were gathered around tables. For centuries and centuries, eating, sleeping . . .

'I imagine it's tiring to begin living again,' she said.

I turned towards her and said something I had said once before, 'Don't worry about me.'

'I worry about everything and everyone,' she said. 'That's how I'm made.' She walked over to the door. 'You mustn't hold it against us.'

'I don't hold it against you. I hope I'll still be able to be useful to you.'

'But can't anyone be useful to *you*?' she asked.

'Whatever you do, don't try it,' I answered.

'It's going to be a terrific manifestation!' exclaimed Spinelle.

His foot was propped on a chair and he was energetically brushing an already sparkling shoe. Laura was leaning over a table, ironing a shirt.

'I know of nothing more depressing than those banquets,' she murmured.

'They serve a purpose,' said Armand.

'I'd like to think so,' she said.

Armand was going through a pile of papers stacked on the marble mantelpiece beneath which a thin fire was burning.

'You know more or less what you have to say, don't you?' he asked.

'More or less,' I answered unenthusiastically.

'It's a shame I can't speak in your place,' said Spinelle. 'I feel inspired tonight.'

Laura smiled. 'You're always inspired.'

He spun round to face her: 'Wasn't my last speech good?'

'That's what I mean. Your speeches are always marvellous.'

A log broke in the fireplace Spinelle had begun violently brushing his other shoe, Laura was sliding the iron back and forth over the white shirt, Armand was reading, and the pendulum of the big clock was swinging peacefully to and fro: tick-tock, tick-tock. I heard it, I breathed in the smell of the hot material, I saw the flowers that Laura had arranged in vases; Marianne had once told me what they were called. I saw each piece of furniture in the room and the yellow stripes of the wallpaper. I noticed every expression in their faces, every inflection in their voices. I even heard the words they did not speak. They chatted gaily to each other, they worked together, and each of them would have given his life for the other. And yet a drama was unfolding among them. They always managed to create dramas in their lives: Spinelle loved Laura, but she didn't love him; she loved Armand, or at least she regretted no longer loving him; and Armand dreamed of a woman who was far away or who did not love him. I turned my back on Eliana and looked at Beatrice, thinking, 'Why must it be Antonio whom she looks at in that way?' Laura's hand moved back and forth over the smooth cloth; her tiny hand was the colour of dull ivory. Why didn't Armand love her? She loved him, she was there: a woman, a real woman. And the other one was nothing more than a woman herself. And why did Laura refuse to love Spinelle? Was there such a difference between Armand and him? One had dark brown hair, the other chestnut, one was serious and the other gay. But they each had those eyes that saw, those lips that moved, those hands that gestured . . .

They all had those eyes, those lips, those hands. There
were at least a hundred of them in the hall where the table
was laden with bottles and food. And their eyes were looking
at me. Some of them knew me. They slapped my back, shook
my hand and laughingly remarked, 'You haven't changed a
bit.' At Spinelle's bedside they had looked at each other and
their hearts burst with joy. I had envied them. Today it was
me they were looking at, but their gaze slipped over me: in
my heart, there was not a spark. Buried beneath the cold lava,
beneath the ashes, the old volcano was more dead than the
craters of the moon.

I sat down beside them. They ate and drank, and I ate and
drank with them. Marianne was smiling at them. A woman
was singing and everyone took up the refrain. 'You have to
sing, too.' And I had sung. One after the other they stood
and drank toasts to my health. They recalled incidents from
the past: Garnier's death, Rue Transnonain, Sainte-Pélagie,
and those ten years I had lived in the underground dungeons
of Mont Saint-Michel. With those words that fell from
mortal lips, they created a radiant legend which stirred them
even more than songs. Their voices trembled with emotion
and there were tears in the women's eyes. The dead were
dead, and from that dead past the living created a burning
present. The living were alive.

They also spoke of the future, of progress, of humanity.
Armand stood up and spoke. He said that if only the workers
could learn to unite, if only they wanted it strongly enough,
they would become the masters of these machines to
which they were enslaved. One day, those very machines
would become the instruments of their deliverance, of their
happiness. He conjured up images of a time when swift trains
speeding along steel rails would break down the barriers raised
by the selfish protectionism of nations. The world would then
become an immense market-place which would provide the
whole of mankind with all its needs. His voice filled the hall.
They had stopped eating, stopped drinking. They were

listening. Wide-eyed, they looked beyond the walls of the hall and saw golden fruits, streams of milk and honey. Through the frost-rimmed windows, Marianne was looking. In her womb she felt the warm, heavy weight of the future, and she was smiling. Screaming women threw themselves on their knees, they tore their clothes, and men trampled upon them. On the squares, in the back rooms of shops, in the open countryside, prophets were preaching: a time would come when justice would prevail, a time of happiness. When her turn came, Laura stood up. In her ardent, husky voice, she too spoke of the future. Blood was flowing, houses burning, shouts and songs ripped through the air, and in the green fields of the future white sheep were grazing. The time would come . . . I listened to their heavy breathing. Well, here it was! The time had come, the future was now; the future of the charred martyrs, of the peasants with their throats slit, of the orators with their zealous voices, the future that Marianne had longed to see. The future was these joyless days punctuated by the droning of machines, the physical exhaustion of children, the prisons, the hovels, the weariness, the hunger, the boredom . . .

'It's your turn,' Armand whispered to me.

I got to my feet, I wanted to obey him. 'Stay a man . . . ' I leaned my hands on the table and I began: 'I'm happy to be among you again . . . '

And my voice dried up in my throat. I was not among them. That future which for them was pure and smooth, and as inaccessible as the azure blue of the sky, would for me become a present through which I would have to live day after day, in boredom and weariness. 1944: I would read that date on a calendar while other men would gaze ahead in wonder at the year 2044, the year 2144 . . . Stay a man. But she had also said to me: 'We don't live in the same world. You look at me from the depths of another age.'

Two hours later, when I was alone with Armand, I said to him, 'I'm sorry.'

He put his hand on my shoulder. 'There's nothing to be sorry about. Your silence was much more effective than a long speech.'

I shook my head. 'I'm sorry because I've realized that I can no longer work with you.'

'Why not?'

'Let's just say I'm tired.'

'That doesn't mean anything to me,' he said impatiently. 'What are the real reasons?'

'What good would it do you if I told you?'

Somewhat irritably, he shrugged his shoulders. 'Are you afraid of convincing me of something? That's being a little too scrupulous.'

'Oh, I know only too well that you're capable of resisting both the devil and God,' I said.

'Then explain yourself.' He smiled. 'Perhaps *I'll* convince *you*.'

I looked at the flowers in the vases, at the yellow stripes on the wall, at the pendulum swinging back and forth with the same even rhythm.

'I don't believe in the future,' I said.

'There will be a future, that at least is certain.'

'But you all speak of it as if it were going to be a paradise. There won't be any paradises.'

'Of course not.' He studied me. He seemed to be searching my face to find the words he should say to me. 'Paradise for us is simply the moment when the dreams we dream today are finally realized. We're well aware that after that other men will have other, new requirements.'

'How can you have any desires at all, knowing that man will never be satisfied?'

He smiled at me coldly. 'Don't you know what it's like to have desires?'

'Yes, I've had desires,' I said. 'I know.' I paused for a moment, 'But it's not simply a question of desires. You're fighting for others. You want *their* happiness.'

'We're fighting together, for ourselves,' he said. He continued studying me attentively. 'You always use the term "man" and you look at people through the eyes of an outsider. If I were God, then it might very well be that I would find no reason to do this or that for them. But I'm one of them. With them, on their behalf, I want certain things rather than others. And I want them today . . .'

'I once wanted Carmona to be free,' I said. 'And because I saved her from being subjugated by Florence and Genoa, she was lost along with Florence and Genoa. You want a republic, freedom. Who is to say whether your success won't ultimately lead to worse tyrannies? If one lives long enough, one sees that, sooner or later, every victory turns to defeat.'

My tone no doubt irritated him, for he said sharply, 'I've learned a little history. You're not teaching me anything. Everything one does is eventually undone, I realize that. And from the moment one is born one begins to die. But between birth and death there's life.' His voice grew more gentle. 'I believe that the main difference between us is that one human destiny – for you, an ephemeral, human destiny – isn't very important in your eyes.'

'That's true,' I said.

'You're already far off in the future,' he said. 'And you look upon these moments as if they belonged to the past. All past enterprises appear derisory when they're seen only as dead, embalmed and buried. That Carmona should have been great and free for two hundred years doesn't matter to you much today. But you know very well what Carmona meant to those who loved her. I don't believe you were wrong in defending her against Genoa.'

The fountains were playing, a white doublet shone against the dark yew trees and Antonio was saying, 'Carmona is my country . . .'

'Then why was Garnier wrong, according to you, to defend the cloister of Saint-Merri to the bitter end?'

'It was an act that led nowhere,' said Armand. He thought

for a moment. 'In my opinion, we should concern ourselves
only with that part of the future on which we have a hold.
But we should do our best to extend our hold on it as much
as possible.'

'You're doing exactly what you reproached me for doing,'
I said. 'You're looking down on Garnier's action without
participating in it.'

'Perhaps,' Armand said. 'Perhaps I have no right to pass
judgement on him.'

'You admit,' I said after a brief moment, 'that you're only
working for a limited future.'

'A limited future, a limited life: that's our lot as men. And
it's enough,' he said. 'If I knew that in fifty years it would be
against the law to employ children in factories, against the
law for men to work more than ten hours a day, if I knew
that the people would choose their own representatives, that
the press would be free, I would be completely satisfied.'
Once again his gaze fell upon me. 'You find the workers'
conditions abominable. Well, think of those workers you
have known personally, only of them. Don't you want to
help change their lot in life?'

'One day I saw a child smile,' I said. 'It seemed very
important to me then that that child should be able to smile
sometimes. Yes, there are moments when I'm moved.' I
looked at him. 'But there are also moments when everything
is obliterated.'

He stood up and put his hand on my shoulder. 'And if
everything were obliterated for good, what would become
of you?'

'I don't know,' I answered.

The flowers, the pendulum, the wallpaper with its yellow
stripes . . . if I left those things, where would I go? If
I stopped obeying them submissively, what would I do?

'You have to live in the present, Fosca,' he said in an
urgent tone of voice. 'With us, for us. And it will also be for
you. The present must become important to you.'

'But words dry up in my throat,' I said. 'Desires dry up in my heart and gestures at my finger-tips.'

In his eyes, I again noticed that precise, practical look I knew so well.

'At least allow us to make use of you. There's so much prestige attached to your name, to your person. Attend the banquets, come to the meetings, go with Laura on a tour of the provinces.'

I remained silent.

'Will you do it?'

'What reason could I have for refusing?' I said to him.

'For just two francs a month,' Laura was saying, 'all the mill workers would be protected against illness, unemployment and the miseries of old age. You could even stop work for several days whenever you think it necessary to go on strike.'

They looked sullen and weary as they listened to her speaking; barely a handful of men were present. It was the same in every city. They were too worn out by their daily work to find the strength to wish for any other future but their evening meal and sleep. And their wives were afraid.

'Who would make use of all that money?' one of them asked.

'You'll elect a committee which will provide you with monthly accounts.'

'That committee would be very powerful.'

'You'll control what it spends.'

'Who'll oversee it?'

'Everyone who comes to the meetings.'

'It would be a lot of money,' the man repeated.

They would willingly have sacrificed two francs every month, but they were wary of the obscure power the relief fund would represent in the hands of one of their own colleagues. They were afraid of creating new masters. In her hoarse, ardent voice, Laura pleaded with them, but their faces remained closed.

'They mistrust us,' she said to me with a sigh as we left the meeting room.

'They mistrust themselves.'

'Yes,' she said. 'It's hardly surprising: they've never known anything but their own weakness.'

She pulled her shawl around her shoulders. The air was mild but it was drizzling. From the time we had arrived in Rouen, it had not stopped raining or drizzling.

'I've caught a cold,' she said.

'Come and have a hot grog before you go back to your room.'

Her shawl was very threadbare, her shoes let in water. When she sat down in the leather chair, I noticed her red nose and the heavy bags under her eyes. She could have been sitting peacefully by a fireside, sleeping through long nights, she could have been beautiful, elegant and no doubt well-loved. But she toiled on from place to place, eating badly, scarcely sleeping, neglecting her appearance, wearing out her shoes and her strength. To what ends?

'You tire yourself out too much,' I said.

She shrugged her shoulders.

'You ought to pay more attention to yourself.'

'One can't pay attention to one's self,' she replied.

There was a note of regret in her voice. Armand paid very little attention to her and Spinelle paid her the wrong kind of attention. He irritated her. And I followed her through the towns and cities of France, hardly ever speaking to her.

'I admire Armand,' she said. 'He has so much inner strength; he never has any doubts.'

'Do you have doubts?'

She put down her glass. The fuming alcohol had brought a little colour to her sallow cheeks.

'They don't want to hear what we've just been telling

them. Sometimes I wonder if it wouldn't be better to let them live and die in peace.'

'And what would you do then?'

A smile crossed her face. 'I'd go back and live in the warm countries. That's where I was born. I'd stretch myself out in a hammock and forget everything.'

'Well, why not do it?' I said.

'I can't,' she replied. 'Because I wouldn't really be able to forget. There's too much misery, too much suffering in the world. I'll never be able to just sit back and accept it.'

'Even if you were happy?'

'I wouldn't be happy.'

In a faded, yellowing mirror opposite us, I could see her face, her damp locks of hair beneath her black hat, her velvety eyes in her tired face.

'Nevertheless, we're doing useful work, aren't we?' she asked.

'Of course.'

She looked at me and shrugged her shoulders. 'Why don't you ever say what you're thinking?'

'Because I never think anything,' I answered.

'That's not true.'

'I assure you, I'm incapable of thinking of anything.'

'Why?'

'Let's not talk about me,' I said.

'On the contrary.'

'Words don't have the same meaning for you as they do for me.'

'I know. One day I heard you say to Armand that you didn't belong to this world.' She looked down at my hands and then up to my face. 'But it isn't true,' she said. 'Here you are, sitting beside me. We're talking. You're a man, a man with a strange destiny, but a man of this world.'

Her voice had an urgent tone: both a caress and a cry for help. Far away, in the darkest depths, beneath the cold ashes and the hardened lava, something stirred. The rough bark of a tree against my cheek, a lilac-coloured dress disappearing down a path.

'If you want,' she said, 'I could be your friend.'

'You don't understand,' I said. 'No one can understand who I am, what I am.'

'Explain it to me.'

I shook my head. 'You should go to be sleep.'

'I don't feel like sleeping.'

Like a well-behaved child, she kept her hands on the table, but her nails were scratching the marble. Alone beside me, alone among her comrades, alone in the world, with all that weight of suffering she carried upon her shoulders.

'You're not happy,' she said.

'No.'

'Well!' she exclaimed with a sudden burst of enthusiasm. 'You see! It's quite clear that you too belong to the world of men; people can feel sorry for you, people can love you . . . '

She laughed as she breathed in the fragrant scent of the roses and lime-blossom. 'I knew you were unhappy.' And I hugged the tree trunk in my arms. Would I come alive again? Beneath the cold lava, a warm steam was coming to the boil. She had loved me for a long time, I knew.

'One day you'll be dead and I'll forget you,' I said. 'Doesn't that make friendship impossible?'

'No,' she replied. 'Even if you forget me, our friendship will have existed. The future could never affect it.' She looked up; a new expression came over her face. 'That whole future in which you'll forget me, that past in which I didn't exist, I accept them: they're a part of you. It's you, the real you, that is sitting here with that future and that past. I've often thought about it and I'd say to myself that time could never separate us if only . . . ' Her voice choked and she hurried to finish her sentence, ' . . . if only you were my friend.'

I held out my hand. Because of the strength of her love, despite the past, despite the future, here I was feeling fully present, fully alive for the first time in centuries. I was there: a man loved by a woman, a man with a strange destiny, but a man of this world. I touched her fingers. Just one word, and that dead crust would have cracked, the febrile lava of life would be unleashed again, the world would once more have a face. There would be expectations, joys, tears.

'Let me love you,' she said very softly.

A few more days, a few more years, and then she would be lying on a bed with that shrivelled face. All the colours would merge together, the sky would fade, all fragrances would freeze. 'You'll forget me.' Her image is forever in the middle of the oval frame. There are no longer any words with which to say: 'She's not here.' *Where* is she not? I see no emptiness around me.

'No,' I said. 'There's no point. Everything is pointless.'

'Is it because I mean nothing to you?'

I looked at her. She knew I was immortal, she had weighed the meaning of that word, and yet she loved me. She was capable of such love. Had I still known how to use human words, I would have said, 'Of all the women I've ever known, you're the most generous, the most passionate, the noblest and the purest.' But those words no longer meant anything to me. Laura was already dead. I withdrew my hand from hers.

'Nothing. You couldn't understand.'

She sank back into the leather chair and stared at her reflection in the mirror. She was alone, she was weary. She would grow old, alone and weary, without receiving anything in return for the gifts she had given so generously and which were not even asked of her; struggling on their behalf, fighting without them, against them, doubting them and doubting herself. In my heart, something still trembled: it was pity. I could have torn her away from her present life; enough of my former wealth still remained to be able to take her to the warm countries. She would stretch herself out in a hammock in the shade of a palm tree and I would tell her I loved her.

'Laura.'

She smiled timidly. There was still a little hope in her eyes. And Beatrice's podgy face was bending over the red and gold manuscript. 'I want to make you happy,' I had said. And I had lost her more surely than I had lost Antonio. She was smiling. But why should I prefer her smiles to her tears? There was nothing I could give them. Because I wanted nothing for myself *with* them, there was nothing I could want *for* them. I would have had to love her. I did not love her. I wanted nothing.

'Go back and sleep,' I said. 'It's late.'

Among the rows of cypresses, golden dots rose and fell as if they were being pulled by invisible strings, rose, fell, rose again. Drops of water burst forth and fell back to earth. The foam was always the same and always different. And the ants came and went, thousands of ants, thousands of times the same ant. They came and went at the offices of the *Réforme*. They walked over to the window, they walked away, slapped each other on the shoulder, sat down, got up, and they prattled ceaselessly. The rain was beating against the windows, seven colours, four seasons; and they were all speaking at once: 'Is it the Revolution? . . . The success of the Revolution demands that we must . . . ' The good of Italy, the good of Carmona, the security of the Empire. They were droning on, their hands gripped around the hilts of their swords, on the butts of their revolvers, ready to die in order to convince themselves.

'I'd like to see what's happening,' Laura said. 'Would you care to come with me Fosca?'

'Certainly.'

The street was teeming with people. A slanting rain was pounding the roofs and the pavement. A few umbrellas were held over their heads, but for the most part they walked unconcerned through the wet night. '*Le jour de gloire est arrivé.*' They were singing and waving flags and torches. Every house was lit up, lamps and paper lanterns had been hung from the walls, at the crossroads blazing fires were waging a battle against the wind and rain. '*Aux armes, citoyens!*' They were singing. Cries of feasting, clamours of death, hymns and chants rose from the taverns along with the sounds of brawls. The day of justice had arrived. '*Aux armes!*' They streamed out onto the streets, they danced around joyous fires, waved flaming torches. The foam was always the same foam and always different. 'Down with Guizot!' they were shouting. There was a strange smile on Laura's lips. She was looking at something in the distance that I could not see. Sitting in the canoe in the middle of the calm waters, he was gazing into the distance at the invisible mouth of the river which may or may not have flowed out into the Pacific.

'Don't go that way!'

A woman hidden in a doorway motioned us to turn back. In front of us, the street was deserted. A shot rang out. People stopped dead in their tracks. Laura grabbed my arm and led me through the hesitant crowd.

'Is this prudent?' I asked.

'I want to know what's going on.'

The first person we saw was a man in shirtsleeves. His face was flat against the ground and his arms were outstretched as if he were trying to grip the cobblestones to prevent himself from slipping to his death. The second was looking up at the sky with eyes wide open. There were some who were still writhing and moaning in the last pangs of death. From the adjoining streets came men bearing stretchers, their torches lighting up the red cobblestones on which the dead and wounded were sprawled, cobblestones strewn with umbrellas, canes, hats, crushed lanterns and tattered flags. The squares of Rome were red. In the gutters, dogs were fighting over nauseating pink and white objects, and another dog was howling into the night at death, women and children turned faces mutilated by horses' hoofs towards the moon, flies were buzzing around bodies lain out on the hard ground between the bamboo huts, and a low moaning arose from the dust trampled upon by the soldiers. Not to die for twenty years or sixty years; and then finally, inexorably, to die.

'To the Bastille!'

There was now a crowd on the square. They had stopped a wagon into which they were piling the dead bodies. 'To the Bastille!' they shouted. 'Vengeance! They're killing innocent people!' Laura's face was completely white. Her fingers tightened around my arm. 'This is it,' she murmured. 'It's the Revolution.' The tocsin was ringing; the wagon was under way. 'To the Bastille! Vengeance!' The dead were still warm, the blood on the cobblestones still wet. A few moments before, they were alive and now they were dead, dead forever. And the living continued to live as if they should never have to die; they would be carrying these submissive corpses throughout their lives. The tocsin was ringing, and from every street streamed bands of people waving flags and carrying torches which cast a red glow on the wet cobblestones. The procession grew from minute to minute, the boulevard was submerged under a black sea, this immense human sea, erect, intact, the same as ever, the same as always. There had been plagues, cholera, famine, executions, massacres, wars, revolutions, and still it was there, this indestructible, human sea. The dead were in the earth, the living upon the earth, the same foam . . . They were marching: marching towards the Bastille, towards the Revolution, towards the Future. Tyranny was about to be vanquished, and soon there would be no more poverty, no more classes, no more frontiers, no more wars, no more murders. There would be justice, fraternity, liberty and reason – *my* reason – would soon govern the world. A white sail was vanishing over the horizon, men were going to conquer leisure and prosperity, they would root out the earth's riches, they would construct huge, bright cities. I swept away forests, cleared brushlands, roads streaked across the green, yellow and blue globe which I held in my hands, the sun flooded the new Jerusalem where men in white robes exchanged the kiss of peace. They danced around joyous fires, trampled upon screeching women in dark back rooms. They spoke as they sat in perfumed boudoirs, they spoke from the tops of their rostrums in measured voices, low voices, high voices. 'Vengeance!' they cried. There, beyond the dark boulevards, a red and gold paradise opened to them, a paradise in which happiness was tinged with anger. It was towards that paradise that they were marching. Each step brought them closer. As for me, I walked over the flat plain where rushes spat drops of water as I trod upon them. I advanced step by step towards the horizon which receded with each step, and on which the same sun set every evening.

'Long live the *Réforme!*'

They had stopped under the windows of the newspaper. Armand appeared on the balcony; he gripped the iron balustrade in his hands, his words rang out. In the distance a church was burning, flares cast a blood-red glow on the statues in the main square. 'Long live Antonio Fosca!' Perched on rooftops and in trees, they shouted, 'Long live Luther!' And glasses clinked together. Carlo Malatesta was laughing and life was burning; it was burning in Carmona, in Worms, in Ghent, in Münster, in Paris, right here, at this very minute, in the hearts of living men, mortal men. And I tramped over the flat plain, testing the frozen ground with my foot, blind, an outsider, dead as the cypress trees that knew no winter and bore no blossom.

They started to march again, and I heard myself call out: 'Marianne!' She would have had eyes to see and ears to hear, her heart would have beaten faster. For her, too, the future would have burned brightly beyond the dark streets: liberty, fraternity. I closed my eyes and she appeared to me as she once had been, as the person I thought I had lost, in a dress with the red and black stripes, with her hair carefully arranged, with her calm smile. 'Marianne.' I saw her. Horrified, she drew close to me and held me tightly. She hated disorder, violence, shouting. She would have avoided these dishevelled women, she would have blocked her ears to shut out this wild uproar; she had dreamed of a reasonable revolution. 'Marianne.' I tried to think: had she been living now, she would be different, she would know these people, she would love them, she would be used to the smell of gunpowder and death. I looked at Laura. Her hair was wet and in disarray, she was holding her shawl tightly around her shoulders and her eyes shone. She was Laura; she was not Marianne. To have remained here at my side, Marianne would have had to stop being herself. She was frozen in the depths of the past, in her own times, and I was no longer able to call her to me, not even her image.

I looked up; I saw the moonless sky, the illuminated façades, the trees, and around me this crowd of people, her fellow creatures. And I realized that the last bond which tied me to the world had just been broken. It was no longer Marianne's world and I could no longer contemplate it through her eyes. The image of her face was now snuffed out completely; and her heart had stopped beating, even in my own heart. 'You'll forget me.' It was not I who had forgotten her. She had slipped out of the world, and she had slipped out of me who would never leave this world. There was no trace under the sky, neither on the waters nor on the earth, no trace in any heart; there was no void, no absence, everything was full. It was the same foam and always different, forever the same, forever different.

They were marching. They were nearing the Bastille and the procession was an immense turbulent river. They came out of every street, from beyond the boulevards, out of the depths of time; through the streets of Carmona, the streets of Ghent, of Valladolid, of Münster, on the roads of Germany, Flanders, Italy, France, by foot, on horses, in tunics, in shirt-sleeves, in flowing white robes, or protected by coats of mail; they came, the peasants, the workers, the bourgeoisie, the vagabonds, in hope, in anger, in hate, in joy, their eyes fixed on the paradise of the future; they came, leaving behind them a wake of sweat and blood, their feet torn by the rocks on the roads, they came step by step and with each step the horizon receded a step, the horizon on which the same sun set every evening; tomorrow, in a hundred years' time, in twenty centuries, they would still be marching, the same foam and always different, and the horizon would continue to recede before them, day after day, always, always, trampling over the black plain for centuries and centuries as they had trampled over them for centuries and centuries.

That evening, however, I threw my pack on the frozen ground, lit a fire and lay down; I lay down only to set off again the next day. And so, sometimes, they did stop marching. In the square in front of the City Hall, they stopped, they shouted, they fired their guns in the air; a woman standing on the mounting of a cannon was singing the 'Marseillaise'. 'Long live the Republic!' The King had just abdicated, they believed they had victory within their grasp, they were holding goblets filled with wine in their hands, they were laughing, Caterina was smiling, Malatesta was laughing, Pergola's walls were crumbling amidst shouts of joy, the domes of Florence sparkled in the sun, the cathedral bells were ringing out, proclaiming the victory. Carmona was saved, peace had been achieved. Armand came out on the balcony; on a huge banner they had painted in big letters: LONG LIVE THE REPUBLIC! They hung it up over the windows and threw down fistfuls of leaflets on which were written words of faith and hope. 'Long live the Republic!' shouted the crowd. 'Long live Carmona!' and Carmona was lost, it was war, we were turning our backs on Florence which we had been unable to enter; with sunken hearts, we were leaving deserted Pergola; the peasants of Ingolstadt were writhing in agony in those fires they had lit . . . I felt Armand's hand on my shoulder.

'I know what you're thinking,' he said.

For a moment we stood side by side, motionless, watching the delirious mob. With their tomahawks they struck at the tall, red pole and they let out wild cries; they danced, they smashed the heads of new-born babies against walls, fireworks lit up the night sky, they hurled flares into the palace, the cobblestones were blood-red, embroidered banners fluttered at windows, hung from balconies, from lampposts, dead bodies were swinging slowly to and fro, cries of horror, cries of joy, funeral dirges, hymns of peace, the sound of clinking glasses, the noise of weapons, the tears and laughter rising up to the skies. And then silence closed in again; on the well-scrubbed squares, women came to fetch their daily water, they cradled babies in their arms, the spinning machines began to hum again and the weavers' shuttles wove in and out, in and out, the dead were dead, the living alive, Carmona was stagnating on her rock, motionless, like a giant mushroom, boredom hung in the air and crushed the earth until such time as a new fire would begin to roar. A new voice, always the same voice and always different, burst out into the night: 'Long live the Republic!' Standing on the mounting of a cannon a woman was singing.

'Tomorrow we'll have to fight again,' Armand said. 'But today we're victorious. Whatever may happen, this is a real victory.'

'Yes.'

I looked at him. I looked at Spinelle and Laura. Today. The word had a meaning for them. For them, there was a past, a future: there was a present. In the middle of the river that was flowing – from north to south? or east to west? – he was smiling. 'I like this time of day.' Isabella was walking slowly in the garden, the sun was playing on the beautiful, polished furniture, and he was smiling as he stroked his silky beard; in the centre of the square stood the gallows around which a crowd had gathered, and as they moved forward, they were singing; they were clutching their entire pasts to their breasts. The people had shouted, 'Down with the Republic!' and he had wept; and because he had wept, because he was smiling now, his victory was a real victory.

The future could do nothing to destroy it. He knew that the next day he would have to begin wanting again, refusing again, fighting again. Tomorrow, he would begin again, but on this day he was the victor. They looked at each other, laughed together, spoke to each other. They were the victors. And because they looked at each other and spoke to each other, they knew they were neither flies, nor ants, but men. And they knew too that it was important to be alive and to be victorious. They had risked and given their lives to convince themselves of it, and they were convinced. There was no other truth for them.

I walked towards the door. I could not risk my life, I could not smile at them; there was never a flame in my heart nor tears in my eyes. A man from nowhere, without a past, without a future, without a present. I wanted nothing; I was no one. I advanced step by step towards the horizon which receded with every step; drops of water sprang forth and fell to earth again, each instant destroying the last. My hands were forever empty: an outsider, a dead man. They were men, they were alive. I was not one of them. I had nothing to hope for. I went out the door.

EPILOGUE

For the first time since Fosca had begun telling his story, his voice quavered. He lowered his head. His hands were spread out on the oilcloth either side of the blue bowl. He looked at them as if he did not recognize them. He moved his right index finger, then the left, and then his hands were still again. Regina looked away. It was broad daylight; there were peasants seated around tables, eating soup and drinking white wine. In the world of men, a new day had begun. On the other side of the window, the sky was blue.

'And on the other side of the door, was there still something?' asked Regina.

'Yes. The square opposite the City Hall, Paris. And then a road which led off into the country, some woods, a thicket; sleep. I slept for sixty years. When they awakened me, the world was just the same as ever. I told them: "I slept for sixty years." And they put me in an asylum. I wasn't unhappy there.'

'Don't go so fast,' said Regina.

She stared at the door, thinking, 'When he's finished, I'll

have to walk through that door, and on the other side of it there will be something else. I won't be able to go to sleep, and I won't have the courage to die.'

'There's nothing more to tell,' Fosca said. 'Every day the sun rose, then set. I went to the asylum, I came out. There were wars: after each war, peace, and after the peace, another war. Men are born every day, and others die.'

'Stop it,' she said. 'Stop it!'

She held her hands to her mouth. A feeling of anguish moved from her throat down into her heart, to her stomach. She wanted to scream.

A moment later, she asked, 'What are you going to do now?'

Fosca looked around him, and suddenly his face seemed to slump. 'I don't know,' he said.

'Sleep?'

'No, I can't sleep any more.' He lowered his voice. 'I have nightmares.'

'You? Nightmares?'

'I dream that there are no more men,' he said. 'They're all dead. The earth is white. The moon is still in the sky and it lights up an earth that's completely white. I'm alone with the mouse.' He was speaking very softly and his expression was that of a very old man.

'What mouse?'

'That accursed little mouse. There will be no more men and the mouse will go on turning around in circles throughout eternity. It was I who condemned it. That was my greatest crime.'

'It doesn't know,' Regina said.

'Precisely. It doesn't know, and it goes on spinning in circles. And then one day there will be nothing but that mouse and me on the surface of the earth.'

'And I'll be under the earth,' said Regina.

She pursed her lips. A scream rose from her stomach to her heart, from her heart to her throat. In her head, a great, burning light was vibrating, more blinding than the night. She had to stop herself from screaming. And yet if she screamed, it seemed to her that something would happen. Perhaps that painful trembling would cease, perhaps the light would go out.

'I'm going to leave now,' said Fosca.

'Where are you going?'

'Anywhere. It doesn't matter.'

'Then why go?'

'There's a need to move in my legs,' he said. 'I have to take advantage of those needs.'

He walked towards the door and she followed him.

'What about me?' she asked.

'Oh, you.' He shrugged his shoulders. 'It will come to an end.'

He went down the two steps in front of the door, and with long strides walked along the road which led out of the village. He was walking very rapidly, as if in the distance, beyond the horizon, something was waiting for him: a world entombed beneath a glass dome, without men, without life, white and bare. She walked down the two steps. 'Let him go!' she said to herself. 'Let him disappear forever!' She watched him striding away, and for a moment it was as if that sorcery with which he had stripped her of her being had left with him. He disappeared round the corner. She took a step and stopped, nailed to the spot. He had disappeared, but she remained as he had made her: a blade of grass, a midge, an ant, a fleck of foam. She looked around her; perhaps there was a way out. Furtive as the fluttering of an eyelid, something rose up in her heart; it was not even a hope and it had already vanished. She was too tired. She held her hands tightly to her mouth, her head slumped forward. She was defeated. In horror, in terror, she accepted the metamorphosis: midge, foam, ant, until death. 'And it's only the beginning,' she thought. She stood motionless, as if it were possible to play tricks with time, prevent it from following its course. But her hands grew taut against her quivering lips.

It was when the bells began to chime the hour that she let out the first scream.

Books by post

Virago Books are available through mail order or from your local bookshop. Other books which might be of interest include:~

☐ That Kind of Woman   Bronte Adams
         and Trudi Tate (eds.)   £6.99

☐ Women of the Left Bank, Paris
     1900–1940   Shari Benstock   £11.99

☐ The Other Woman   Colette   £5.99

☐ Simone de Beauvoir   Judith Oakley   £5.99

☐ Fernhurst, Q.E.D. and Other Early
     Stories   Gertrude Stein   £8.99

☐ Virginia Woolf: Introductions to the
☐   Major Works   Julia Briggs (ed.)   £9.99

☐ Orlando   Virginia Woolf   £4.99

Please send Cheque/Eurocheque/Postal Order (sterling only), Access, Visa or Mastercard:

☐☐☐☐☐☐☐☐☐☐☐☐☐☐☐☐

Expiry Date: _____   *Signature:* _____

Please allow 75 pence per book for post and packing in U.K.
Overseas customers please allow £1.00 per copy for post and packing.

All orders to:
Virago Press, Book Service by Post, P.O. Box 29, Douglas,
Isle of Man, IM99 1BQ.   Tel: 01624 675137.   Fax: 01624 670923.

Name: _____

Address: _____

_____

Please allow 20 days for delivery.
Please tick box if you would like to receive a free stock list ☐
Please tick box if you do not wish to receive any additional information ☐

Prices and availability subject to change without notice.